all these beautiful strangers

all these beautiful strangers

A NOVEL

ELIZABETH KLEHFOTH

wm
WILLIAM MORROW
An Imprint of HarperCollinsPublishers

ALL THESE BEAUTIFUL STRANGERS. Copyright © 2018 by Elizabeth Klehfoth. All rights reserved. Printed in the United States of America. No part of this book may be used or reproduced in any manner whatsoever without written permission except in the case of brief quotations embodied in critical articles and reviews. For information, address HarperCollins Publishers, 195 Broadway, New York, NY 10007.

HarperCollins books may be purchased for educational, business, or sales promotional use. For information, please email the Special Markets Department at SPsales@harpercollins.com.

FIRST EDITION

Designed by Bonni Leon-Berman

Library of Congress Cataloging-in-Publication Data has been applied for.

ISBN 978-0-06-279670-7

18 19 20 21 22   LSC   10 9 8 7 6 5 4 3 2 1

To Mom, Dad, Mark & Annie

prologue

My father built the house on Langely Lake for my mother, in the town she grew up in. It was a hundred miles from the glassy skyscrapers my father built in the city, and a world away from the Calloway family name and money and penthouse on the Upper East Side.

The house on Langely Lake looked unlike any of the other houses in town, with their graying vinyl siding and slouching carports. No, the house on Langely Lake wasn't a house at all. It was a fortress three stories tall, built of stone, with a thick fence and impenetrable hedges all the way around.

When I was a little girl, we spent our summers in that fortress. I remember slumber parties in a tent on the back lawn and afternoons spent sunning on the raft just offshore. I remember tall glasses of lemonade sweating on the patio and the sundresses my mother wore and her wide-brimmed hats.

Once I thought my father had built that house to keep everyone else out, but then my uncle Hank found the photographs. They were in a shoebox, hidden under a loose floorboard in my parents' bedroom. They were taken that summer, 2007, a few weeks before my mother disappeared. I saw the photographs and I realized I had been wrong about everything.

Because my father hadn't built the house on Langely Lake to keep everyone else out. He'd built it to keep us in.

part one

one

CHARLIE CALLOWAY

2017

It all started that morning with a note, printed on thick card stock, no bigger than a business card.

> *Good morning, good day, some say, "Salut."*
> *Herein lies a formal invitation, just for you.*
> *Forgive the anonymity of the sender, but you know who we are.*
> *And we're big admirers of yours, from afar.*
> *We're the opposite of the Omega, the furthest from the end,*
> *Follow this clue to find us; we're eager to begin.*

The note was balanced on top of Knollwood Augustus Prep's "Welcome Back!" flyer, printed in the school's royal blue and gold colors, which announced that Club Day would be held in Healy Quad on Friday afternoon and encouraged every student to attend. This was followed by a list of all of Knollwood Prep's student clubs and organizations. At the bottom, in delicate gold lettering, was the school's mission statement to "foster students whose exacting inquiry and independence of thought drive them to excellence both inside and outside of the classroom."

I might have missed the card stock note altogether if it hadn't fluttered to the ground as I removed the flyer from my mailbox in the entrance to Rosewood Hall, the girls' dormitory for upperclass-men. My heart stopped when I saw the note, for the first part—the sender—wasn't difficult to figure out. *You know who we are . . . We're the opposite of the Omega, the furthest from the end.* It was the A's—the only club not listed on Knollwood Prep's flyer and, in my mind, the only club worth joining.

It was the second part of the note I puzzled over as I sat in Mr. Andrews's Introduction to Photography class. Normally, I couldn't have gotten away with zoning out in class like that. Every class at Knollwood Prep was supposed to follow the Harkness method, meaning we all sat around a table facing each other, and we were expected to participate in the discussion with minimal interven-tion from our instructor. Some instructors even kept a notebook with every student's name, and they would put a little tally mark next to our names as we talked. If, at the end of class, your name didn't have a satisfactory number of tally marks next to it, they would send you a little note saying something like, *We missed your voice in class today.* Or, *When not everyone speaks up, we all lose.* Or, my personal favorite, *You miss one hundred percent of the discussions in which you don't participate.*

But Mr. Andrews was new, just out of college, and he was much more lax than the other teachers. His Introduction to Photogra-phy class had been the most sought-after arts elective this semes-ter, not because of the subject matter, but because Mr. Andrews was, well, hot. He had that dark, rugged hipster thing going for him—flannel button-downs that he didn't tuck in; beanies to hide dark, unwashed hair; liquid brown eyes rimmed with baby-doll lashes longer than my own. Also, he had a distinct edge over most Knollwood Prep boys—he could grow facial hair. He always had a perfect five o'clock shadow cloaking his well-defined cheek-bones.

Today, Mr. Andrews hadn't come in with thick packets of photography theory for us to parse; instead, he came in with a nice-looking camera with a very long lens, which he passed around to all of us.

"This is called a telephoto lens," Mr. Andrews said. "It produces a unique optical effect, which can create the illusion that two subjects separated by a great distance are actually very close. It's a powerful tool for capturing candid moments when you can't get physically close to your subject."

He clicked a button on his laptop and a photo of a lion lounging on an African savanna displayed on the projector screen in front of the class.

"One of the most obvious examples of this is in wildlife photography or sports photography," Mr. Andrews went on. "The photographer would physically be in danger if he or she were close to, say, a lion, or a professional baseball player up to bat. However, another, less obvious use is street photography, where an artist needs distance not for safety but to preserve the candidness of the shot."

He clicked another button on his laptop and this time a photograph of a young woman and her child on a busy New York street filled the screen.

As he spoke, I stared down at the camera in my lap and fiddled with the zoom. I puzzled over the second half of the A's riddle.

> I have a head but never weep.
> I have a bed but never sleep.
> I can run but never walk.
> Come meet me after dark.

The "when" was obvious enough—tonight after curfew. But the "where" was a giant question mark. What place had a head? Could it be a play on the headmaster's office? Was the next line—*I have a bed but never sleep*—some riff on Headmaster Collins's vigilance? Maybe, but I couldn't make the next line fit with that. Okay, so what place had a bed? Like, bedrock? Could it be talking about the quarries?

Something hard nudged my shin underneath the table and I looked up to see Royce Dalton, the most popular boy in the senior class, giving me a look from across the table. I was slow to catch on, but then he cleared his throat and glanced at Mr. Andrews, and I realized the whole class was quietly and expectantly looking at me. I sat up in my seat and set down the camera.

"That's an excellent question," I said slowly and deliberately as I racked my brain for what Mr. Andrews could have possibly asked me, or a tangent I could lead him on to distract him from the fact that I hadn't been paying attention.

My eye caught on the screen in front of the class, on the picture of the woman and her child. The child was upset, and the woman had stopped; she was bending down so that she was eye level with the little boy. She was reaching out, about to tuck a strand of the child's hair behind his ear, to comfort him. I hadn't noticed at first, but the woman appeared distraught as well. It made me wonder what had happened just before the picture had been snapped, and what had happened after. It was jarring to me that the photographer had captured this private, painful moment and put it on display for everyone to see. There was an illusion of being close, when the photographer was actually far away—not just physically, but emotionally as well. The photographer remained safe and protected, while displaying this vulnerable moment to the world for observation, for art.

"This may be a little off topic," I said, "but your discussion of street photography got me thinking. I guess I understand the necessity of distance to capture the truth of a moment. But it seems ironic that in order to capture truth, you have to be duplicitous.

Distance allows the subject to act naturally precisely because the subject doesn't know they're being watched. I guess, in the end, that raises an ethical question for me. Is that art—or an invasion of privacy? I'm curious to hear your take on that. I apologize if I'm jumping ahead."

This was a defense mechanism I had learned a long time ago: 1) String enough buzzwords together to make it seem like you were paying attention. 2) Admit that your comment might be tangential to cover your bases. 3) Deflect with another question. With some teachers, the more tangential, the better, actually, because it made it seem like you were really considering the topic at hand. 4) End with a backhanded apology that hinted that your intellectual curiosity was leaps and bounds ahead of the pace of instruction. Suddenly, you weren't the slacker zoning out in class; you were the deep thinker ahead of the game.

Mr. Andrews looked a little surprised by my deflection.

"Hmm . . . interesting question, Miss . . . ?" he said.

It was almost endearing that he hadn't bothered to memorize our names from the course roster over the summer.

"Calloway," I said. "Charlie Calloway."

A flicker of recognition lit up his eyes at my name and there was a slight pause, just a hair longer than was appropriate. That was a common response when I met people. I could see the gears clicking in their brains. *Not one of* those *Calloways, surely? She's not the girl whose mother . . . well . . . Poor thing.* I could tell they always wanted to ask, but they rarely did.

"Miss Calloway," Mr. Andrews said, his hand stroking his bearded chin as he considered my question. "Ethics and art. That's always an interesting discussion."

As Mr. Andrews started off again, I looked across the table at Dalton, who subtly lifted his finger to his lips like a cocked gun and blew at the imaginary smoky tip of the barrel. *Killed it.*

Thanks, I mouthed silently to him, and he gave me a conspiratorial wink.

The sky outside the dining hall was beginning to darken. There were only three hours left until curfew and I still hadn't figured out the A's riddle for the meeting place. The closest I had come were the old quarries about half an hour from campus. They were abandoned and had flooded with rainwater years ago, and sometimes in the late spring or early fall, Knollwood Prep students would go up there on weekends. The brave ones would jump off the rocks and the lazy ones would drape themselves along the sides and sunbathe. I could easily imagine the quarry as a meeting place for the A's, could even see some kind of initiation ritual that involved catapulting oneself off the highest rock in a pitch-black night when the lake was all but invisible below, but I couldn't make all of the lines of the riddle fit.

As I turned the riddle over and over in my mind, I picked at the smoked salmon Alfredo on my plate and pretended that my mouth was full every time Stevie Sorantos asked me what her campaign slogan should be. She was running for treasurer of the student council—*again*—and she was harassing all of us into contributing a pithy line that would catapult her to the top of the polls.

"How about 'Vote for me, or whatever,'" Drew offered, tossing her thick mane of dirty-blond corkscrew curls over her shoulder. "DGAF is today's YOLO."

"I like it," Yael said. "Commanding yet disaffected. Playing hard to get."

"It certainly works with the menfolk," Drew said, wiggling her thick eyebrows at all of us.

"But I don't want people to think I don't care," Stevie said, a hint of exasperation in her voice.

I rolled my eyes at Drew, who took a giant bite of her dinner roll to keep from laughing. As if anyone would ever think that Stevie Sorantos didn't care.

Sometimes—okay, often—Stevie grated on my nerves because she just tried too damn hard. Treasurer of the student council. President of the Student Ethics Board. Always the first to shoot her hand into the air when an instructor asked a question. Once I caught her in the bathroom, eyes raw and puffy and wailing like her dog had just died because she had gotten a B+ on a lab report. More than once I had considered grinding Ambien into her water bottle just so she would be forced to chill the fuck out.

I knew why she was like that, of course. We all did. Stevie was a scholarship student, not that she ever told us this, and not that we ever talked about it. Knollwood Prep tried hard to eliminate socioeconomic distinctions with uniforms, and free tuition, Mac-Books, and iPads for students who needed aid. But try as they might, Knollwood Prep couldn't erase where we came from. Stevie didn't wear the Cartier bracelets that we did; she didn't have a YSL backpack or, well, brand-name anything. Her family never went on vacation. She didn't have a car. But none of these things gave Stevie away quite so much as her blatant eagerness to prove that she belonged. It was exhausting, and it missed the mark altogether. Because the only thing that mattered to the people who mattered was acting like nothing really mattered. As paradoxical as that was.

"Come on, Charlie," Stevie said as I took another bite that I pretended was too big to talk over. "You always have the best ideas."

"Hey now," Drew said, pointing the asparagus-loaded prongs of her fork at Stevie. "What about my idea? That shit is gold."

Freshman year I had talked Stevie into doing a *Sopranos*-themed campaign. Yael took these great black-and-white photos of Stevie, one of her dressed up in a suit and sunglasses, another with Stevie in an upholstered armchair, a cigar hanging out of the side of her mouth and a cloud of smoke ballooning in the air. Drew and I blew the pictures up to poster-board size and put Tony Soprano quotes across the front:

"A wrong decision is better than indecision."

"Well, seeing as you called me up here, I might as well tell you . . . I'm in charge now."

"All due respect, you got no f***** idea what it's like to be number one."

In the bottom right-hand corner, in bold red letters that mimicked the title card of the show, we wrote: **Vote Sorantos.**

All of the other candidates had gone the serious route with posters spewing platitudes, or worse—making some pun off their name. Stevie won by a landslide.

"Fine," I said, because I saw I had no other choice. "How about, 'I've been doing this job for two years now. If you don't think I'm qualified, go fuck yourself.'"

Yael pretended to consider it. "So much subtlety and finesse," she said. "But is it *too* sophisticated?"

Stevie set her glass of milk down so hard on her tray that it sloshed over the sides of the glass. I looked down and saw white pearls of milk dotting my sleeve.

"I see even *pretending* to take this seriously is too much to ask," Stevie said, slinging her cheap Target bag over her shoulder and standing up.

"Stevie—" Yael started.

"I'm going to the library," Stevie said, and headed off toward the far end of the dining hall, her bag bouncing against her back with every purposeful stride she took.

Yael sighed and gathered her things, giving Drew and me an exasperated smile.

"DEFCON Three," she said. "I'll run damage control."

"Now I feel bad," Drew said when Yael was gone. "But I was serious about my DGAF idea."

I shrugged and grabbed a napkin to dry my sleeve.

Stevie and Yael were my friends by default only—mainly because they were always around Drew, and Drew and I were always together. We ate our meals together, we sat next to one another in class, we spent long hours hanging out in the common room before curfew, and we shared a room. So, I made an effort with them—I went sailing with Yael's family over the summer when our families were on Martha's Vineyard at the same time. I invited Stevie to spend Thanksgiving with my family in Greenwich, since I knew the plane ticket to spend the holiday with her own family in Ohio was too expensive and she would have been stuck on an empty campus alone. I got along with them all right (most of the time, anyway), and I liked them okay, but we didn't click the way Drew and I clicked. She and I just got each other.

Drew and I had been serendipitously placed together in the same dorm room freshman year with another girl we loathed named River, who never shaved and didn't believe in deodorant, table salt, or listening to her folk music at a courteous volume. Apparently, she didn't believe in studying either, because she was gone by the next semester. Living with River was like being hazed, and Drew and I had gone through it together. It had created an unbreakable bond.

Now I eyed Drew as she chewed animatedly and talked about the upcoming volleyball meet against our rival, Xavier. I tried to ask her without asking her: Did you get one too? Did the A's pick you? Because I couldn't, well, just ask.

"What?" she said, and I realized too late that my attempts at telepathy had resulted in creepy hard-core staring. "Do I have something on my face?"

"Yeah, some sauce, just here," I lied, pointing to a spot on my own chin for reference.

"Thanks," Drew said, dabbing the corresponding spot on her chin with her napkin.

It was hopeless. Drew had an impenetrable poker face. So, I scanned the dining hall for my cousin Leo instead. Leo was two months my junior, but you'd never have guessed it by the way he loomed over me at six foot two. You also wouldn't know we were cousins based solely off appearance. Leo had the traditional Calloway good looks; he was all bright turquoise eyes, golden-blond hair, and distinguished cheekbones. I, on the other hand, looked like my mother. I got her dark brown hair and wide gray eyes and pale, translucent skin, her short stature. This was a ring of hell that Dante had not imagined: looking in the mirror every day and seeing the one person you wanted most desperately to forget.

I spotted Leo two tables away, sitting next to Dalton and a mix of other popular junior and senior boys. His hair was still wet from his post-football-practice shower and it hung down into his eyes slightly as he leaned forward to say something to his friends. I knew just by looking at him that he had been tapped by the A's—I didn't even have to ask. I saw it in the way he smiled that cocky, lopsided smile of his, the one that made the dimples peek out of his left cheek. Leo and I had always had an uncanny ability to read one another, a result of his seeing me through the hellfire that was my childhood. Leo had been the one to save me in the end, or at least, he had been the one to show me how to save myself.

"Shit," Drew said. She had knocked over her water glass. The water spilled everywhere, running off the side of the table. I picked up my napkin and started to dab at the mess as Drew righted her glass.

"Your bag," Drew said, and I pulled it off the table just before the spill reached it.

And then, it clicked. That was it. I knew where the A's were meeting that night.

"I'm sorry," Drew said. "I'm such a klutz."

"No, thank you," I said, without really thinking.

"What?"

"Uh, nothing," I said. "I meant, it's no big deal."

Curfew at Knollwood Prep was nine o'clock on weeknights. Normally Drew and I hung out in the common room until as late as possible, and then we'd sit up for hours at our desks finishing our readings or assignments and talking. But tonight, we both turned in early. I lay in bed and stared at the ceiling in the dark, trying to tell from Drew's breathing if she had fallen asleep across the room and wondering how I would sneak out our window without waking her.

I couldn't stop thinking about the A's.

Knollwood Prep had four types of clubs: the athletic, the academic, the special interest, and the, well, ridiculous (see the Cheese Club, where they sat around and, you guessed it, ate cheese). Being in these clubs meant silly rituals, or sweaty practices in the gymnasium doing suicides across the court in some primitive drive to prove your physical prowess, or meetings where you sat around a buzzer and answered questions while an elected secretary kept inanely detailed minutes. These clubs had meets with other schools and held events like bake sales or car washes to raise money for the local women's shelter. At Knollwood Prep, you were expected to collect these clubs like trinkets on a charm bracelet so that on your college application, you could say that not only did you get a rigorous academic education at one of the top preparatory schools in the country, but you were also a contributing member of your community, and were—that buzzword college admissions officers salivated over—"well-rounded."

But being in the A's wasn't something you could put on your college application. It wasn't even something you could, well, *tell* anyone about. The A's didn't do bake sales or car washes; they didn't involve cleats or sweating; and they most certainly didn't have a secretary keeping minutes.

Last year, when the new dean of arts tried to make a Saturday morning cultural enrichment class mandatory, the A's unleashed a smear campaign so vicious that the dean was gone by the end of fall semester. In the end, no one "knew" how the dean's scandalous emails with a fifteen-year-old girl with daddy issues from Maine had leaked to every student, administrator, and faculty member on Knollwood Prep's LISTSERV, but everyone "knew" that the A's were somehow behind it. While the headmaster had launched an investigation into this breach of school security, in the end, he could do little but applaud that this indecent man was exposed and send him packing, effectively putting an end to those dreaded classes and preserving our precious Saturday mornings for the sacred act of sleeping in.

The A's were the reason we had No-Uniform Fridays, single-room dorms for seniors, and a prom so decadent it was sometimes mentioned on Page Six. No one knew what dark form of blackmail, bribery, or manipulation went into acquiring these beloved rights and traditions, but everyone knew the A's were behind them. The A's could also get you out of some sticky situations. My freshman year, Celeste Lee, a supposed A, got in a fight with Stephanie Matthews in the girls' restroom on the second floor of the science building and gave her a bloody nose. Celeste would have gotten suspended if Stephanie reported her to the administration. No one knows for sure what sort of arm twisting the A's did behind closed doors, but when the headmaster called Stephanie into his office later that afternoon, she kept her mouth shut.

The A's reach went beyond Knollwood Prep. It was rumored they had key players on the admissions boards of all the Ivy Leagues and Seven Sisters, and that their influence could get you in the door at the Fortune 500 company of your choosing after college graduation.

The A's were something everyone knew about without *really* knowing anything about them. There was no way of even knowing who the A's were, really, unless you were one of them. Because unlike all of the other clubs at Knollwood Prep, you didn't choose to be in the A's. The A's chose you.

Drew called out my name softly in the dark, just loud enough for me to hear if I was awake but not loud enough to wake me if I was asleep.

I debated answering but eventually said, "Yeah?"

She sat up and flicked on the light. "Just say it already," she said.

"Say what?"

"Do you have somewhere to be tonight?"

"Maybe," I said.

"Thank god," Drew said. She climbed out of bed and crossed the room to her closet. "I've been watching you all day to see if you had gotten one too, because I couldn't just ask," she said as she pulled on a pair of thick black leggings and boots.

"Who else do you think got in?" I asked as I dragged myself out of bed and started to rummage through my own closet. What did one wear to a late-night rendezvous with the most notorious secret society on campus? I decided on a pair of dark skinny jeans, my Keds, a black tank with oversized armholes, and a hoodie.

"I'll throw myself off the Ledge if Marissa Wentworth got in," Drew said.

So she had figured out the riddle. What has a head but never weeps? What has a bed but never sleeps? What runs but never walks? A river, of course. The A's were meeting at the Ledge above Spalding River. People called it the Ledge because that's what it was—a clearing in the woods off the county road that looked over a steep ravine and the river below.

"Marissa Wentworth is not A material," I said. "They want someone with an edge. Someone who isn't afraid to get their hands dirty."

"Do you think Leo got in?" Drew asked.

"Of course Leo got in."

"He told you?"

"Not in so many words," I said. "But come on, what world do we live in that Leo wouldn't get in?"

"True," Drew said, rolling her eyes.

Drew and Leo had dated for two seconds during our freshman year, which was about twice as long as Leo had been with anyone. It had ended how all of Leo's trysts ended: badly. Still, even though Drew wasn't Leo's biggest fan, she had to admit that Leo was an obvious choice for the A's.

Leo put an unconscionable amount of thought into everything he did, so it wouldn't be right to say he was "effortlessly" cool—though something about the way he carried himself did evoke that word. Leo wore his hair slicked back from his forehead. He always dressed nicely—tailored jeans and V-neck tees that were fashionably distressed and sleek leather jackets. Leo exuded a confidence that made whatever he did seem cool. It would have been pointless to tease him about anything, because Leo thought more of himself than anyone I'd ever met, besides perhaps my grandfather.

One after the other, Drew and I slipped out our second-floor dormitory window into the thick arms of the elm that towered over Rosewood Hall dormitory. We lowered ourselves into the deep V of its trunk. Neither of us were strangers to forbidden late-night excursions.

In the Rosewood Hall parking lot, Drew turned her headlights off and shifted her BMW into neutral. Together we pushed the car to the road, only jumping in when we were sure we weren't in danger of waking Ms. Stanfeld, our housemother, who lived in an apartment on the ground floor of the dormitories.

When we were far enough down the road, Drew opened her sunroof and howled at the moon. I laughed and put my arm out the window, fanning my fingers to catch the damp night air as it slid past.

We didn't talk about what was happening or what was to come. We didn't speculate about what the A's would make us do to become one of them, even though we both knew that whatever it was, it would not be easy. Instead, we exuded an attitude of cool nonchalance and pretended we were neither excited nor terrified, when we were both.

CHARLIE CALLOWAY

2017

There was a story on campus about a student who had died many years ago—so long ago that no one remembered anymore what his name was or how he had died exactly, but there were reports every now and again of a sighting of his ghost. Some said he'd hanged himself in the showers of the senior boys' dormitory over a broken heart; others said he'd overdosed on pills and fallen into an eternal slumber in his dorm bed over a failing exam grade. It was bad luck if you saw him, a harbinger of terrible things to come. Bryce Langston had reported seeing the ghost on his way home from the library one night. The next morning, he got a rejection letter from Harvard. Everyone had thought he would be a shoo-in, and he hadn't even gotten on the waiting list. The next year, Amanda King supposedly saw the ghost right before she got in a fatal car accident. I always thought about the ghost when I was walking around campus at night by myself. I imagined seeing a white smear in the corner of my vision, but every time I turned my head, there was nothing there.

I couldn't help but think about the ghost now as I stood in the clearing above the Ledge. The A's had lit a small bonfire, and we all stood close enough to be visible in its glow, but Dalton held a flashlight anyway. The way it hit the underside of his jaw as he talked, throwing his features into shadows, unsettled me. I crossed my ankles and leaned back against the cool metal hood of Drew's BMW.

There was no need for introductions; everyone who was any-one at Knollwood Prep already knew one another. But we were all glancing around regardless, looking one another up and down like we'd never met. And, in a way, we hadn't. Before, we were just kids who went to Knollwood. Some of us belonged to things—the soc-cer team, the student council. Some of us had reputations. Some of us were preceded by our family name. But here, now, there was one thing that united us: we were all A's.

As I looked at the seniors spread around the campfire, some of the A's seemed fairly predictable. There were Royce Dalton, an all-American, captain of the soccer and lacrosse teams; Crosby Pierce, the son of an A-list movie star and lead singer in a band called the Lady Killers, who performed at the coffee shop downtown some-times and were actually kind of good; Wes Aldrich, whose mother was a senator and whose grandfather had been a majority whip for the House of Representatives; Ren Montgomery, a professional model who had worked for Calvin Klein and walked in New York Fashion Week; and Harper Cartwright, the features editor of the *Knollwood Chronicle*.

Darcy Flemming, however, was a bit of a surprise. She was pres-ident of the senior class, the daughter of a French diplomat, and an accomplished equestrian who spoke French and Portuguese flu-ently. She seemed like too much of a Goody Two-shoes to be an A. It was hard to imagine she had had a hand in the dean of arts's smear campaign.

I glanced around the circle at the new junior recruits and found a similar mixture of naturals and oddballs. I had been right about Leo, of course. He stood across the circle from me, next to Dalton, who was one of his best friends. Then there was Meryl York. She was the daughter of one of my father's friends, and our families had vacationed together when we were younger, but she had always struck me as kind of a wet blanket. Regardless, her family was practically an institution at Knollwood Prep. The observatory had been donated by her father and was named after her grandfather. Brighton Maverick seemed like another obvious choice with his floppy blond hair and eternal tan even in the harsh New Hampshire winters. He played on the soccer team and had grown up in Santa Barbara, where he surfed on soft white-sand beaches.

But the others I wouldn't have immediately pegged as A's: Imogen Reeves, who was a theater geek and had had a small part last summer in an off-Broadway play; Jude Bane, who was practically glued to his laptop and always had humongous headphones clamped over his ears; and Auden Stein, who, yes, was some kind of math prodigy, but was too pompous to really tolerate. I couldn't help but wonder what the A's would want with them.

Of course, I knew why I was there. Leo may have made it into the A's just as he was, but I was there for no other reason than that I was Charlie Calloway, the oldest child of Alistair Calloway and the heir to the Calloway Group, one of the largest real estate dynasties in New York City. I'd grown up in a penthouse on the Upper East Side, and I summered on an estate on Martha's Vineyard (the summer home my father bought when he could no longer bear to return to the house on Langely Lake). My family owned half the Upper East Side, and one day, it would all be **mine**. All of the laws of nepotism said so.

"You're all here because we saw something in you," Dalton was saying. "But if you want to stay, to be one of us, you'll have to play the Game.

"In the coming months, you'll find three tickets in your school mailbox. Each ticket will have an item. You must procure that item by any means necessary and bring it to the A's meeting by the specified time and date. If you fail to procure the item in time, don't bother showing up. You're out.

"You may beg, borrow, lie, steal, or cheat to procure your item. In fact, we only have one rule to the Game: don't get caught."

Ren Montgomery stepped forward and took the flashlight from Dalton. She held it in her hands like a microphone. Ren was tall and rail thin, with a deceptively deep and husky voice that I'm sure guys found thrilling.

"To that end," Ren said, "if you get caught, you've never heard of us. We don't exist. Loyalty is the most prized trait of an A. Without it, we're nothing. We chose you because we think you have this quality. But we've been wrong before and we need . . . *assurances* in case that happens."

Ren stopped and picked a camera out of the purse that hung at her hip. She flashed a smile at us.

"Rest assured we're not asking you to do anything we haven't already done ourselves," Ren said.

I understood what she was saying: they wanted us to provide the bullets and load the gun they could place to our own heads if we screwed up.

"Auden, you're up first," Ren said. She turned and headed off into the woods, the darkness quickly swallowing her up as she stepped out of the warm glow of the bonfire. And Auden followed her, his hands buried deep in his pockets.

When they were gone, Dalton fished a cooler out of his trunk, and Crosby turned on the stereo system in his car and propped open his doors so that I could feel the hum of the bass in the ground, coming up through the soles of my sneakers. Drew grabbed two IPAs and I uncapped them with the bottle opener on my key chain.

"Don't worry about Ren," Dalton said, and he gave me a smile as if to soften everything. "Her bark is worse than her bite."

"I don't know about that, man," Crosby said, rubbing his chin. "As someone who's been there—I can safely say her bite is nothing to sneeze at."

Crosby and Ren were the most notorious on-again-off-again couple on campus.

"Tsk, tsk," Drew clucked her tongue in mock disapproval. "A gentleman never kisses and tells."

"Well, I never claimed to be a gentleman," Crosby said.

"So, any hints about the types of things we'll be asked to re-trieve?" Drew asked, twirling her hair. The way the corner of her lips twitched up at the end, I could tell she was into him.

"Yes, actually," Crosby said. "First on the list is Dalton's vir-ginity."

"And will you be providing the time machine?" I asked.

Crosby laughed and clinked his beer bottle against mine. "Nice. Cheers."

Next to me, Dalton groaned. "Harsh, man," he said. "Isn't any-one going to defend my honor?"

Dalton was sort of the "It" boy at Knollwood Prep. He was as old money as they come—his grandfather came from a family of British banking royalty. His father worked on Wall Street and his mother was an American, some big-time surgeon whom people flew from all over the world to see. So, he had a good pedigree. He was also very good-looking: tall, dark hair, dreamy eyes, that sort of thing. It wasn't that surprising then that Dalton was always dating someone.

"Sorry, Dalton. You're kind of what we girls refer to as a man whore," I said.

"Speaking of which," Crosby said, and he nodded across the clearing toward Harper Cartwright, who was talking with Darcy Flemming. "Dalton's latest victim keeps giving us the stink eye. Has anyone noticed?"

I glanced over at Harper and saw her glaring at us.

"That's just the way her face looks," Dalton said. "What is it they call it? Resting Bitch Face? I assure you we had an amicable breakup."

"Sure, because what high school breakup isn't amicable?" Crosby asked.

"Yeah, Harper looks like she wants to amicably murder you right now," I said. "Or me."

We drank our beers and laughed and talked about things that didn't matter. No one talked about what was happening as Ren returned with one junior recruit and wandered off with another into the darkness. No one spoke about what they had done when they returned.

When Ren came back with a sullen-looking Meryl, she called my name. Only, she didn't call *just* my name.

"Leo," she said. "You too."

Leo handed his beer to Brighton Maverick and laughed at whatever Brighton had just said, as if this whole thing were no big deal, as if this were just another Monday night. Leo had always been like that. Arrogantly fearless.

We followed Ren close at her heels as we made our way through the pitch-black woods until we reached a clearing that led out to the empty county road. There was a car parked along the side of the road—an Audi A8. Ren pressed a button on her remote and then held the back door open for us.

"Step into my office," she said, gesturing toward the backseat.

I slid in first and Leo followed, closing the door behind him. Ren climbed in the front seat and turned on the ceiling light. I blinked and threw up a hand to shield my eyes. After the dark woods, it was blindingly bright.

Ren took out her camera and looked through the lens at Leo and then me.

"You two are close, aren't you?" Ren asked, putting down the camera.

"Thick as thieves," I said, glancing sideways at Leo.

"I thought so," Ren said. "How nice to actually like somebody in your family. Everybody in my family is an asshole. I mean, I'm kind of an asshole too, but I'm a likeable asshole. At least, I like to think so."

She brought the camera to her face again and adjusted the lens.

"Charlie, scoot to your right a little, you're not in the frame."

I did as she said, until my bare arm was flush against Leo's.

"Great. Leo, put your arm around her. Uh-huh. Perfect. Now, Charlie, tilt your head a little. Good. Now lean in, closer, closer . . ."

"Uh," I said, "lean in to what exactly?"

"Why, those lush Calloway lips," Ren said with a smirk.

I could feel my heart hammering in my chest. I glanced at Leo, who narrowed his eyes at Ren and gave her a wry smile.

"I always knew you had a dark side, Montgomery," he said.

Ren smiled back at him. "Oh, you don't know the half of it, Calloway." She raised the camera to her eye again. "Now, you just told me you liked each other. Show me how much."

Something sour slid into the pit of my stomach.

I was many things. I was a Calloway. I was *the girl whose mother . . . well . . . Poor thing.* Those things meant something to most people, but none of those were things I'd earned. I'd inherited them or they had been thrust upon me. But this—being part of the A's— this was something I was determined to do on my own. I may have gotten a bid based on my name, but I would earn being there. I would become someone who wasn't afraid of anything, some- one powerful, who could bend others to her will. I would become someone who made the dean of arts flee the state when he so much as made me wake up early on a Saturday morning. Maybe no one else outside the A's would ever know about the things I did, but I would know, and that was all that mattered.

I turned to Leo and for one cold, emotionless minute, pressed my lips to his. Then I pulled back and leveled a stare at Ren.

"Satisfied?" I asked.

"Cute," Ren said. "But cute isn't exactly what we're going for here."

Leo and I both looked at her and she put the camera down and gave an exasperated sigh. "Listen, maybe this isn't the best fit," Ren said, her hand already on the door handle. "Not everyone is cut out for this."

"Wait," Leo and I both said at the same time.

Leo looked at me, and he didn't say it but I could tell he was asking me all the same, whether it was okay, whether I was okay, and I gave him the slightest, almost imperceptible nod. He slid his hand gently along the side of my face, until he was cupping my chin, and he leaned in and kissed me so softly, his lips were just barely grazing mine.

When we were five, he had kissed me once behind our grandmother's rosebushes. It had been Easter and my mother had made me wear this bright floral dress with ridiculously puffy sleeves that I hated and kept pulling at. We were at my grandparents' house in Greenwich, and Leo had chased me through my grandmother's garden and pinned me down beneath the roses when he caught me. His kiss had been light and quick on my lips, like a feather.

This kiss started like that one but shifted quickly. There was something underneath it that was different, darker, more danger-ous. Leo's tongue parted my lips; his arm slid around my waist, pulling me closer. I could feel his warm fingertips against the bare skin at the small of my back, under my shirt.

Leo had a reputation with the girls at Knollwood Prep for being somewhat of a player. More than a few times I had witnessed groups of girls, chatting animatedly to one another, fall silent when he passed in the hall, followed by blushes, hands cupped to shield whispers. That reputation was well earned, and not half as bad as what he deserved. Leo had even invented a secret game around his promiscuity that he played with the guys in his inner circle. He called it the Board of Conquests.

He had shown me the gridlike game board once with the bases along the top and a bunch of girls' names in the boxes below. It looked sort of like a bingo board, but for oversexed teenage boys instead of senior citizens. Every semester, the guys made a new board with new names, and every semester, they raced each other to be the first to round the bases and get "four in a row." Leo was always creative in the names he put on the board and in the way he arranged them. He included not just the pretty or easy girls, but the prudes, the freshmen, the awkward drama geeks. You couldn't get four in a row without hooking up with someone you wouldn't have been caught dead with, or coaxing some prudish sophomore across a line she'd never crossed before. Getting four in a row was a rare accomplishment. Leo himself had only done it once, in the spring semester of his sophomore year. The game was a huge hit among Leo's friends. Crosby had even broken up with Ren one semester just so he could play. Basically, teenage boys were all pigs, which is why I had never had a boyfriend.

The peak of my experience was making out with Cedric Roth the previous summer at my father's house on Martha's Vineyard. Cedric was an older boy, a college boy, and he had taught me to drive his father's Ferrari down quiet, abandoned streets at night. We had a habit of kissing—just kissing—in the library in my father's summerhouse on a dusty couch surrounded by old and forgotten books. I knew I would rarely see him again when the summer was over. I knew I didn't, could never, have real feelings for him. He had this gap between his front teeth that emitted a little whistling sound when he breathed with his mouth open, and he had a habit of saying "literally" all the time, which literally drove me crazy. But I relished these minor flaws, collected these annoyances like armor, and played them over and over in my mind until my skin crawled.

I wouldn't have kissed Cedric if I had real feelings for him. It seemed dangerous—reckless even—to let someone get so close to you. To care that much. I had seen my own father's heart broken by my mother. His love had blinded him, made him weak and vulnerable, when Alistair Calloway was a man who was anything but weak and vulnerable. I knew what my mother had done to him, to all of us, because we had been weak enough, stupid enough, to love her. It was a mistake I wouldn't make again.

When Leo kissed me now, there was an urgency to it, a feeling that almost made me forget for a moment where we were. A feeling that almost—almost—silenced the quiet clicking of Ren's camera.

Normally, I was not one to get drunk, mostly because I didn't like letting my guard down, the feeling of not being fully in control of my actions. But when I got back to the clearing, I let Dalton uncap beer after beer for me, until I felt dizzy and gloriously numb. I felt empty and hollow and nauseous, and I wanted desperately to feel nothing at all.

"I have to pee," Drew said after a while, pulling on my arm.

"All right, all right," I said, trying not to slur my words. "I'll go with you."

"Here, take my flashlight," Dalton said, handing it to me.

I took it and let Drew pull me behind her into the woods. I held Dalton's flashlight and tried to illuminate a path for us as we went, but I was far from steady on my feet and kept slipping, pulling Drew down on top of me.

"Easy there, Calloway," Drew said.

When we were far enough away from the clearing, Drew squatted and I turned my back to her. I aimed the flashlight blindly into the woods, turning it this way and that, and then I saw it—a white and translucent figure, in between the thick trees. I dropped the flashlight and the light went out.

"Shit," I said.

"I can't see anything," Drew complained. "I don't want to piss on myself."

"All right, all right, hold on," I said as I stumbled along the ground, searching for the flashlight. My hand caught along the cold, circular metal handle and I picked it up and turned it on, flashing the light back toward the spot in the trees where I had last seen the figure.

There was nothing there.

"I think I saw someone," I said. "Someone moved over there. Did you see it?"

"We're not the only ones out here," Drew said.

"What?" I took a step away from her, toward the spot where I had seen the figure in the distance, scanning with my flashlight.

"Um, yeah," Drew said. "It's, like, nature . . . It was probably a squirrel or something."

"Right," I said.

I was just being paranoid, I told myself. I hadn't seen the ghost—I hadn't seen anything. I was just unsettled from everything that had happened earlier with Leo and Ren in the back of Ren's car. The way Ren had winked at us when it was all over. "Secrets bind us to each other," she had said. And even though I had felt sick to my stomach, I told myself that there was also something strangely comforting about the whole thing. Because, in a way, Ren was right: we all belonged to each other now. We held each other's secrets. It was a bond that could make us, just as surely as it was a bond that could destroy us all.

CHARLIE CALLOWAY

2017

In second grade Miss Wilkes asked us to write about a superpower we wished we had. In my story there was a girl my age and she met a genie near the Bethesda Fountain in Central Park who offered to grant her one wish. The girl wished to be invisible and that wish came true.

The girl went wherever she pleased and did whatever she wanted. She walked right into the Central Park Zoo without paying. She rode the carousel and climbed the turrets of Belvedere Castle and for a while everything was wonderful. But then the girl grew tired of this and she returned home and tried to get back into her old routine, but nothing was the same. Her parents didn't come to tuck her in at night because they didn't know she was there. Her teacher never called on her in class. She sat with her friends at lunch but their conversation and games never included her. The girl grew lonely and sad.

She returned to the genie at the fountain, who was the only one who could still see her. She asked if she could make another wish. The genie solemnly shook his head and told her that that was impossible. Most kids never even got to make one wish; it was unthinkable for one girl to get to make two. The girl started to cry because she realized too late that being seen was more powerful than being invisible.

If I had been any other seven-year-old in the class, I'm sure Miss Wilkes would have thought I was precocious and given me a check-plus for creativity, but this was after the summer that my mother disappeared. My father had hired a private investigator to find her, and the private investigator had told us what had happened to my mother, or, at least, all that he could know. So, the long and short of it was that Miss Wilkes was not amused or pleased by my story, but concerned. She told my father, and my father made me see a therapist.

Her name was Dr. Malby, and she specialized in adolescents with especially traumatic pasts. One of the boys she treated was about my age, and he had seen his father, a stockbroker, kill himself with a handgun to the mouth over an investment that went south. He told me this in the waiting room while he played with a G.I. Joe action figure and I fiddled reluctantly with a puzzle at the kids' table. Another, older girl who was sometimes there before me had bandages up and down her forearms. She never talked to me or played at the kids' table. She always slouched in her chair and thumbed through magazines.

The walls of the inside of Dr. Malby's office were cotton-candy pink. We sat on the floor around a large coffee table on a fluffy rug and played Jenga as she probed my inner psyche.

"You can say anything you want in here," Dr. Malby said.

"Are you going to tell my father?" I asked.

She gingerly removed a wooden log from the bottom of the block structure and set it on top.

"We're all here so you can start to feel better," Dr. Malby said, which didn't answer my question. "Is there something you want to say?" she asked. "Something that maybe you feel you can't say out there?" She motioned to the cotton-candy-colored walls.

"Fuck," I said. "Fuck, fuck, fuck."

It was what my uncle Teddy had said on the boat that summer when he had dropped his beer overboard while adjusting the jib, and I knew it wasn't something I should repeat because Aunt Grier immediately said his name in that way that meant a lot more than just his name. It always amazed me how much Aunt Grier could say with just one word, or even just a look if she was feeling particularly economical. A stern glance could get Leo to wear his gray scratchy blazer to dinner; a raised eyebrow could silence my cousin Piper's whine that I—and not she—had gotten to steer the boat. This time, Aunt Grier said, "Teddy," but she meant, "Teddy-not-in-front-of-the-children."

I didn't know what the word "fuck" meant, exactly. At least, I didn't know the literal meaning. I just knew how it made me feel when I said it. Like it encapsulated this anger and shame and loneliness that there was no other way to give voice to. Those things never sounded the way they felt inside. But "fuck" somehow captured it. It was teeth against lip, bone against flesh to start. It was round and whole in the middle. And it was harsh and clawing at the end.

"Does that make you feel better?" Dr. Malby asked.

I nodded because yes, actually, it did. And so Dr. Malby sat there patiently and let me say it again and again to the cotton-candy-colored walls of her office. Fuck, fuck, fuck, fuck, fuck. I savored the word each time, the way my mouth felt when I formed it, how the hollows of my chest felt when I released it. It was like taking a breath of air when you've been holding your breath so long that your lungs are about to burst.

In my mailbox the morning after the night in the woods with the A's was a note, hastily written on a scrap of paper:

Charlotte,
    MUST *see you. Meet me at 9 p.m. at Rosie's Diner. Very important.*
    Hank

My heart sank a little when I realized it was not my first ticket from the A's.

Hank? Who the hell was Hank? And why did he want to meet me in the local greasy spoon in Falls Church, the closest town to campus? My first thought was that it was some lovesick under-classman who had gotten up the nerve to arrange a face-to-face meeting and maybe was too embarrassed to do it on campus. There was something in the sloppiness of the handwriting that I couldn't help but read as desperation.

Then, all at once, my confusion morphed into white-hot anger and panic. Shit. I knew who Hank was—and it wasn't some dopey freshman. It was Uncle Hank, my mother's oldest brother.

Which meant that he had been there, on campus, sometime in the last several hours. Was he still there—lingering, watching? I turned and glanced quickly over my shoulder at the rest of the mailroom, half expecting to see him standing there.

I hadn't seen Uncle Hank in years—since I was ten, and my father issued the restraining order.

It had happened like this: Uncle Hank had picked me up from my elementary school one afternoon. I had been a bit surprised to see his rusted truck idling there in front of the sidewalk at the parent pickup spot in front of the school, but he had explained everything—how the nanny had gone home sick, and my sister was at a friend's house, and my father would be late at work (my father was always late at work—he was president of the Calloway Group, which kept him very busy). Uncle Hank said he had come by to look after me and take me out for a bite to eat. So I said okay, and he held the passenger-side door of his truck open, and I slid in.

He took me to a cheap pizza parlor across the city that smelled like burned cheese, and he ordered me a giant plastic cup of soda. As I sat across the booth from him, sucking dumbly on my straw, he started to ask me about my mother.

No one besides Dr. Malby ever talked to me about my mother. But he wanted to know. What had that last month been like with her? Had she seemed different in any way? Who came and went at the house? How had things been between her and my father? And that night that she disappeared—what had I heard? What had I seen?

That was it. We talked. It felt good, actually, to talk about it, to talk about my mother with someone who had known her, too. To not keep it all inside like it was some dark, forbidden thing. For someone in my own family to want to know, to listen.

It was dark out when he drove me home and the truth was, I wasn't scared or even aware that anything was wrong until we pulled up to the curb in front of my building, and I saw the police car parked there, its lights flashing red and blue moons that were orbiting the sidewalk. And that's when I started to cry, panic welling up in my chest.

As soon as my uncle Hank stopped the truck, I unbuckled my seat belt and started pulling at the door handle, trying to open it, but it wouldn't open because it was old and finicky and got stuck if you didn't do it just right, and so I started to scream. And that's what the police officers and my father saw when they came running out to the curb—me, in the front passenger seat of Uncle Hank's truck, screaming and pounding the glass with my palms like some caged animal. Uncle Hank hurriedly got out and went around to try to open the door from the outside.

He didn't get to open the door though, because my father caught him just as he was rounding the hood of his truck, and my father took Uncle Hank by the lapels of his jacket and pushed him up against the hood. I couldn't hear what he was saying through the glass and my screams.

Later, when Uncle Hank and the police officers were gone, my father asked me where Uncle Hank had taken me, what we had done, was there anything we'd talked about? And I recounted the trip in the rusted truck, and the soda at the pizza parlor, and the questions Uncle Hank had asked about my mother. About him.

Later that week, during math lessons, when our teacher left us to quietly work out equations at our desks while she took the attendance forms down to the office, I heard it mounting in the room behind me, like it was a real, physical thing filling the room, pressing up against me, stealing the breath from my lungs—the whispers, the snickering. I got that old familiar feeling in my chest—the one that had suffocated me the year after my mother disappeared—the feeling of being looked at, talked about, held up for speculation. It hollowed me out inside, made me want to hold my breath and close my eyes and disappear.

"Ask her," someone whispered loud enough for me to hear, and finally Tommy Hartman leaned forward in his desk and poked me hard in between my shoulder blades with his pencil.

"Hey, Charlotte," he said, his voice loud and unkind.

I debated whether I should answer him, but finally I half-turned in my desk to face him. Whatever was coming, it was best to just rip it off quick, like a Band-Aid.

"What?" I asked. I could feel heat rushing into my cheeks, the hot panic in my chest. And I hated that they could see it on my face, hear it in my voice—that I was afraid.

"How'd he do it?" he asked.

"How'd who do what?" I asked.

"You know," he said, irritated, as if I were playing games with him, as if I knew exactly what he was talking about.

Everyone had abandoned the work in front of them; I could feel all my classmates' eyes on me.

"I *don't* know," I said. My palms were sweaty and I wiped them on the thighs of my pants, hoping nobody could see.

And then he said it.

"How'd your dad kill your mom?" Tommy Hartman asked.

The hairs on the back of my neck stood up, and I couldn't breathe. I opened my mouth to say something, but nothing came out. My mouth hung open stupidly and I just gaped at him like a fish caught on dry land, gasping for air.

"I bet he strangled her," Monica Petrosky, the prettiest and cruelest girl in the class, said.

They all started in then, as if this were some sanctioned event.

"Where'd he put her body?"

"Aren't you scared your dad is gonna murder you?"

"Shut up," I said. "Shut up!"

It came out louder than I expected, that silent rage inside me. They were quiet, shocked, but only for a second.

"Ooooohhhh," somebody in the back of the class crowed. "Watch out, or Charlotte Calloway is gonna murder *you*."

Tommy Hartman howled with laughter; Monica Petrosky laughed so hard she snorted.

I bit my lip and tried with everything that was in me to stop it, but I couldn't. I could feel them coming, the hot tears filling my eyes. I looked up and saw our teacher, Mrs. Holiday, standing in the doorway.

She put her hands on her hips and glared at all of us. "And just what is going on here?" she asked.

Everyone got really quiet really quickly and once again, everyone's eyes fell on me. I wanted desperately for everyone to Just. Stop. Looking. At. Me. I couldn't cry in front of them—I wouldn't.

"Charlotte?" Mrs. Holiday asked. And her voice was not kind or comforting, but demanding, as if I were responsible for stirring up the class in her absence. And a part of me was thankful for her cruelty, because I knew one gesture of kindness would have undone me.

"My stomach hurts," I said. "Can I go to the nurse?"

I hid in the nurse's office until recess, and it was Heather Frank, a quiet girl who wore thick-lensed glasses, who finally showed me what had started the whole thing. Sitting on the empty bleachers, she pulled the thin tabloid from her bag.

REAL ESTATE BILLIONAIRE MURDERS WIFE, WIFE'S BROTHER TELLS ALL, the title said in large, blood-red letters. Below it was a picture of my father, dressed sharply in a suit, ducking into a limo, his arm around the back of some faceless blonde in a halter dress. He looked handsome and haughty in that picture, but he had a wrathful sneer on his face. It made him look dangerous. Predatory.

Next to the picture of my father was a picture of my mother with a halolike glow around the edges. I recognized it. I had seen it hundreds of times at my Grandma Fairchild's house hanging in the stairwell with the pictures of Uncle Hank and Uncle Lonnie and Uncle Will, my mother's brothers. My mother couldn't have been more than eighteen. She was wearing a soft, cream-colored dress, her hair loose around her shoulders, smiling at the camera. She looked so young and sweet and innocent in the picture next to my father. Doe-eyed and fragile. Something in my heart seized, and I started to read.

> No one could have predicted that what started as a fairy tale
> would end so tragically. Grace Fairchild, daughter of mill
> worker Frank Fairchild and preschool teacher Alice Fairchild,
> had a humble upbringing in Hillsborough, Connecticut. When
> she caught the eye of billionaire Alistair Calloway, heir to the
> Calloway Group, she was introduced to a whole new world:
> a penthouse apartment on the Upper East Side, luxurious
> weekend trips on private jets, lavish gifts. Grace thought she had
> found her Prince Charming. Little did she know that beneath the
> surface lurked a killer.
> "She was blinded by his charm, his money," Grace's older

brother Hank says. "She didn't see him clearly. And then when she saw what he really was, it was too late. That month before she went missing, Alistair and Grace fought constantly. She was going to ask him for a divorce. The night she disappeared, she told him to leave. They got into an argument. She screamed at him not to touch her anymore. She said, 'Get your hands off me.'"

I stopped reading. I had told Uncle Hank about that. Sitting across from him in that cheap pizza parlor, sucking on that soda he had bought me as he plied me with questions, I had told him my mother's last words to my father. Like a traitor. Like a worthless, pathetic traitor. But I hadn't known he would do this—sell it to the highest bidder, for the whole world to see.

I had told him other things, too. Happy things. Why hadn't he told them any of that?

I handed the tabloid back to Heather. The glossy pages felt slick and slimy under my fingers.

"It wasn't like that," I said. "How they make it sound. How *he* makes it sound. They weren't getting a divorce."

I couldn't believe this was happening. *Again.*

When my mother had first gone missing, it had been big news— splashed across the cover of every gossip magazine, a topic on every news outlet. The police took my father away for questioning; there were search parties formed to comb the woods near the house and divers who searched the dark depths of Langely Lake. Everyone was looking for a body. Nobody ever found one.

It didn't matter that my father had an alibi. It didn't matter that he hadn't even been at the house that night when she went missing; he was at our apartment in the city, a hundred miles away. It didn't matter that my father had loved her, that he would never have hurt her. It was a dark and juicy story, and so people ate it up. *Murderer,* they whispered. *Wife-killer,* they said.

After my mother went missing, my father hired a private investigator to find her, and that's when the investigator found the bank tapes. There was security footage at the local branch of Connecticut Mutual. Days before she disappeared, my mother withdrew hundreds of thousands of dollars from the safety-deposit boxes she shared with my father. She'd taken that money and walked out of our lives forever. I was seven; my sister, Seraphina, was barely five. The national news channels played those bank tapes for weeks—the humiliating evidence that proved my mother had robbed and abandoned us.

My father searched for her for a year and could never find so much as a trace of her. On the anniversary of her leaving, he let the private investigator go. He said if my mother was that determined not to be found, then he didn't want to find her.

I had endured the stares, the pitying glances, the whispers, for a year after my mother left us—we had all endured it. And now, just when things were starting to return to normal, this happened.

I hate him, I thought. I would never forgive Uncle Hank for doing this to my father, for making *me* do this to my father. For this dark cloud that he had dragged over us when the storm had finally seemed as if it were starting to clear.

"It sure sounds like he did it," Heather said, as if she hadn't heard me. And I knocked those stupid glasses off her face, the metal stand under our feet leaving a permanent scratch on the left lens.

Later, my father sat me and my sister down in his study and told us we were not to speak to our uncle Hank again, that he wasn't to come near us, unless my father was present. He couldn't bring himself to look at me as he spoke, and I tried not to hold that against him.

"Your uncle Hank is not well," my father said. And then he told us how we were going to live with our uncle Teddy and aunt Grier for a little bit, until things blew over. And I tried not to hold that against him, either.

Now I crumpled up the note Uncle Hank had left in my mailbox and threw it in the trash. I willed myself not to think about it.

I looked up and saw through the window to the mailroom Leo walking across the quad with Dalton and Crosby. Good, a distraction. I adjusted the strap of my bag over my shoulder and ran after them.

"It's a fifty-dollar buy-in," Crosby was saying when I caught up to them.

"Big plans for tonight?" I asked, slightly out of breath.

"Just a couple of guys playing a friendly game of five-card draw," Leo said.

"Is this a 'boys only' thing because you're scared to lose to a girl?" I asked.

Crosby put his arm around my shoulder. "Charlie, my boy Dalton here is the biggest feminist I know."

"Yeah, male, female, I like to beat them all equally," Dalton said. "I'm not afraid to take your money, Calloway."

"All right, then," I said. "What time are we talking?"

For the second night in a row, I snuck out of my window after curfew. Only this time, instead of heading to the Rosewood Hall parking lot, I headed north toward the edge of campus. The quickest way to the upperclassman boys' dormitory was through a well-lit campus patrolled by Old Man Riley, Knollwood Prep's security guard. Instead, I skirted the edge of campus, cutting through an undeveloped field, with grass that came up to my knees in places. There was just a sliver of moon in the sky to light my way.

Dalton's room was on the ground floor of Acacia Hall, the upper-

classman boys' dorm. Because he was a senior, he had the entire
room to himself. The boys had left a candle in the window in front
of a closed curtain so I would know which room to go to. I knocked
on the windowpane three times before Dalton swept back the curtain, blew out the candle, and let me in.

"We were beginning to wonder if you'd show," Crosby said as
Dalton shut his window behind me and drew the curtain tight so
there was no chance of Old Man Riley's catching a glimpse of our
late-night game on his rounds. "You know, pregame jitters."

Dalton had an old card table set up next to his single bed. On
the other side was his swivel desk chair and on the third side of
the table was a trunk. I was the last to arrive and so there was only
one seat left: a spot on Dalton's bed next to Crosby.

"I did have some reservations about coming," I said as I sat on
Dalton's bed and folded my legs underneath me to get comfortable.
"Number one: will they still like me when I beat them to kingdom
come and take all their money? Number two: what if they cry? I've
never seen a whole room of boys cry before."

"She certainly talks a big game," Crosby said, shuffling the cards.

"Pride cometh before a fall, Calloway," Dalton said, taking a seat
on his trunk.

Auden pulled out a large pencil case and started divvying up the
"chips." We couldn't play with real poker chips, for the same reason
none of us had brought any money to the game. Gambling was an
automatic suspension at Knollwood. Instead, we played with Post-it
notes ($10), pencils ($5), erasers ($2), and Skittles ($1), so that we
had plausible deniability in the event we were caught around a card
table. The money was real enough, and the losers would square
away with the winners by the end of the week.

Dalton dealt first and I picked up my hand with an almost giddy
glee. It was a strong hand: a pair of queens and an ace. But I was
less focused on my cards than on watching the other players, not-

ing when they limped or raised, how many cards they exchanged, whether they folded early or called the hand.

I'd always loved poker because it was a game of reading people. Everyone had a tell—a quickening of the breath, a facial tic, a knot of muscles tensing in the neck. It almost wasn't fair to Leo that I was playing, because I knew him so well. His tell for a good hand was the same as when he was talking to a pretty girl: a practically imperceptible twitch of the right corner of his mouth that gave him an almost arrogant smirk. You had to really know him to catch it.

Sometimes a person's tell wasn't so much a physiological response as a behavior. I quickly learned that Auden was a cautious player; he almost always limped from round to round and folded early, so you knew if he raised the bet or stayed in after the second round he had a winning hand. Crosby played like he lived: with a practiced nonchalance, raising when he should fold, rarely bowing out until the last draw. Dalton was the most difficult to read; the whole game, I couldn't get a handle on him.

It was nearly two in the morning, and we were down to our last hand. It was the final round of betting. We had all gone big this round; there was nearly $65 in the pot. Leo was out and Auden had just folded. Dalton was up. He could put another $20 in to limp, or raise, or fold. We all knew why he was hesitating: at this point, he was up $100, the most of all of us. But if he put in another $20 to stay in and lost and I took the pot, I would best him at $95 to $80. If he folded right now, he'd still be in first, regardless of whether I won the pot or not.

I put my cards facedown and pushed them forward, like I thought it was my turn and I had decided to fold.

"It's not your turn," Auden whispered.

"Oh, sorry," I said. I made a show of scooping my cards up and acting all embarrassed. If I could have blushed on command I would have.

"I'm in for twenty dollars," Dalton said, putting two Post-its from his large stack into the middle of the table.

As soon as he laid his Post-its down, I scooped my cards back up and moved two Post-it notes of my own into the middle of the card table.

"I'll see your twenty dollars," I said, "and raise you another ten dollars."

I pushed two pencils into the middle of the card table.

"You angler," Dalton said. He had a smile on his face but there was a hardness to his eyes. He was trying to play it cool but I could tell I had upset him.

"That's cheating," Auden said.

"Morally ambiguous," I corrected him. "If I did it on purpose. Maybe I didn't mean to go out of turn."

"Did you?" Auden asked.

"Would you believe me if I said no?" I asked.

"I like her," Crosby said to the room. "I like you," he said to me, clapping his hand on my back. "I hope you did do it on purpose."

Auden looked to Leo for support, but that was useless. Leo laughed and leaned back in his swivel chair. He shook his head. "I told you guys not to let her play," he said.

"I'll see your ten dollars," Crosby said, moving two of the pencils from his stack into the middle of the table. Dalton reluctantly did the same.

Then, all together, we turned over our hands. Dalton had three jacks. Crosby had two pairs. I had a flush.

Crosby did a doleful slow clap. Dalton let out a heavy sigh. Auden cursed under his breath.

"Well done, cousin," Leo said.

"Lovely playing you all," I said as I leaned forward and scooped all of the pencils, Post-its, erasers, and Skittles to my end of the table. "And I wasn't kidding earlier. I really will freak out if you start to cry."

The campus felt eerily quiet that early in the morning as I made my way back from the boys' dormitory to Rosewood Hall. I shrugged deeper into my jacket and quickened my pace. Out there alone at night in the dark, I couldn't help but think of the ghost—that dead boy wandering around campus, looking for someone to curse.

When I reached the abandoned field, which was all that separated me now from the dormitories, I got the distinct feeling in the pit of my stomach that I was being watched.

Don't be stupid, Charlie, I told myself. *There's no ghost. No one is watching you.*

Still, I started to walk faster. I heard the faint sound of something moving behind me. *Ghosts don't have bodies. Ghosts don't have footsteps,* I told myself.

I stopped abruptly and I both heard and felt something very real and solid stop in the distance behind me. Someone, a very real someone, was following me. I started to run.

The field was mostly barren besides two old oak trees on the far end, and through them, in the distance, I could see Rosewood Hall, with the lights in the kitchen on the ground floor still on. Sometimes Mrs. Wilson, the cook, stayed up late whipping up the batter for the next morning's biscuits. If I could make it there—to the light that spilled onto the front lawn—then I was sure I would be safe.

But the thing was, I didn't know if I would make it. I could feel the blood hammering in my ears, the stitch piercing my side as I ran. And whoever was behind me—I could hear their breath, their footsteps, drawing closer. I ripped my keys from the pocket of my hoodie and laced them between my fingers like claws. I stopped and turned around to face the person behind me, my fist ready at my side. I was winded, but I choked out the words nonetheless.

"St-stay where you are," I said. "Or I'll scream."

It was too dark to make out the figure completely, even though he was barely five feet away from me. I could tell that he was male, with a thick beard and big burly shoulders.

He held up his arms in mock surrender. "Don't scream," he said, and the gruff voice sounded vaguely familiar. "I didn't mean to scare you. I just—I waited, and you never showed up."

My first thought was that this was all some big misunderstanding. This big burly man stalking me in the darkness had mistaken me for someone else. But then I remembered the note I had found in my mailbox that morning.

"Uncle Hank?" I asked.

He took a step toward me and I took a step backward, my heart still in my throat. I raised my fist of keys. He stopped when he saw that he had startled me. His shoulders sank as if I had offended him.

"Charlotte," he said, and the way he said my name, with so much tenderness and familiarity, almost disarmed me. "Charlotte, it's me. It's okay. I'm not—I would never—hurt you. You have to know that."

I lowered my fist, unsure.

"What are you doing here?" I asked.

"I had to see you," he said, a little breathless. "It's about your mom."

"I don't want to hear," I said.

"You have to," Uncle Hank said. "You have to listen. I have something you need to see."

"I'm not interested," I said, and turned to go. I didn't want to hear any more of his theories, didn't want to answer any more of his questions, didn't want to be sucked back into that tangled web he had woven all those years ago. I couldn't go back there; I wouldn't.

"Charlotte," Uncle Hank said, grabbing my arm to stop me, to hold me there. He was close enough I could smell the whiskey thick on his breath.

I tried not to panic, not to show him how angry I was.

"She's not dead," I said firmly. "She left us. She's gone, and she's not coming back. You have to accept that and move on. The rest of us have."

I tried to shrug off his grasp, but his fingers only gripped my forearm more tightly. I winced.

"Listen," Uncle Hank started up again. "I know what you must think of your mom, considering the story you've been told—"

"Story?" I said. "I've seen the bank tapes, Uncle Hank. The whole damn world has seen the bank tapes."

I couldn't help but think that every moment of that last month with her had been a lie. Every time she tucked me in at night or drew my bath or sliced up the strawberries to put on my morning oatmeal, she must have known she was going to leave me.

"That's not—that's not what you think," Uncle Hank said. "Grace would never do that—leave you and Seraphina like that. She loved you more than anything in the world. It's not what it looks like. It's not what you've been told."

"Let go of me," I said. "You're hurting me."

Uncle Hank looked down at his hand on my arm and seemed almost shocked to find it there. He let go of me.

"You need to see this," Uncle Hank said. As he grabbed for the bag that he had slung over his shoulder, I contemplated making a run for it. Now that I had caught my breath, maybe I could make it to the safety of the dormitory. But what if I didn't make it, and my running away provoked him further? He'd said he wouldn't hurt me, and maybe he wouldn't mean to, but he was so much bigger than me, and so desperate, and, frankly, kind of crazy. Who knew what he was capable of?

While I was still debating what to do, Uncle Hank handed me a manila envelope.

"What is that?" I asked.

"See for yourself," he said.

I took the envelope. It was old and yellowing. There was a postage stamp in the top right corner, and my mother's name and the address to the lake house were written in a hasty scrawl on the front. The seal was broken. Inside was a stack of photographs and a piece of paper. I took out the piece of paper first. Someone had written in all capital letters, *I KNOW*.

I took out the photographs next and thumbed through them slowly, using the flashlight from my phone to illuminate them in the darkness. There must have been over a hundred pictures. The first dozen were snapshots taken in quick succession from a distance. They were of my mother. She was sitting at a booth next to the window in some diner. Her face was clearly visible in the shot. She looked upset. Across from her in the booth was a man. In this shot, I couldn't see his face, just his hand reaching across the table to console my mother. In the next shot, his hand was on top of hers.

I glanced up at my uncle Hank. He was watching me intently.

"Do you recognize him?" he asked. "The man in the pictures with her—have you seen him before?"

I looked back down at the pictures. I turned to the next one. This one was taken at a different angle. I could see the man's face in this one. He had a dark beard and a wide nose. The skin under his eyes looked sunken and gray. He was slightly balding and looked to be in his thirties. He was wearing a suit.

"No," I said. "I've never seen him before."

I flipped through the rest of the shots, but the man didn't appear in any of the ones taken outside of the diner. They were all pictures of my mother with me and Seraphina. There we were in the front driveway of the lake house. My mother had Seraphina in her arms in one and she was unloading us from her SUV. There were pictures of us coming out of the supermarket in Hillsborough with Grandma Fairchild; the three of us in my uncle Hank's truck; me and Seraphina swimming in the lake while my mother watched from the shoreline. I thought of the long-lensed camera Mr. Andrews had shown us in class—the telephoto lens he had told us about.

I came to the last photo, which stopped my heart. Because there was no illusion of closeness in this shot. The photographer was right there, one hand outstretched so that you could see it in the frame of the shot, and there I was by myself in the backyard of my grandparents' house in Hillsborough, Connecticut, looking up into the lens of the camera, within reach. When I flipped it over, I saw something had been written on the back. Just one word: *STOP*.

Stop what?

"What are these?" I asked.

"I found them in the lake house. Under a loose floorboard in your parents' old room."

"What were you doing in the lake house?"

My father would flip once he found out Uncle Hank had broken into our house, gone through our things.

"I had questions," Uncle Hank said. "I went looking for answers myself. And I think I found something. I don't know what these are yet or what they mean, but I'm sure they mean something."

As much as I wanted to argue with him, I couldn't. Because these photos had left me cold and hollow and breathless. Had someone been following us? Had these photos been some kind of threat? And if so, why? What had my mother done to make someone want to threaten us?

"Do you remember who took this photo?" Uncle Hank asked.

I stared at the photo in my hand and shook my head. It unnerved me to the core, but I had no memory of its being taken.

"Maybe you remember something," Uncle Hank said, more desperate this time. He ran a hand through his disheveled hair. "Anybody hanging around that summer that gave you a strange feeling? It could even be somebody who seemed like they belonged there. Lord knows you had an army coming and going. Maybe a gardener or a maid? Maybe your mom was acting nervous or scared? Something small, something off. Any small thing might be something. It could help."

"I already told you everything I remembered," I said, resentment leaking into my words. Well, I'd told him *almost* everything. And he'd betrayed me.

He was so sure that my mother was dead, so sure that I had the answer to what had really happened to her—so sure that I held the key.

"There has to be something else," Uncle Hank snapped at me. He raised his hand and for a moment I thought he might hit me or grab me, and I tried not to flinch. "There has to be something you haven't told me yet."

I didn't answer him. "Does my father know about these?" I asked instead.

"I don't know what Alistair knows or doesn't know," Uncle Hank said. "And he stopped listening to me a long time ago."

"Maybe if he saw these—" I started, but Uncle Hank cut me off.

"This isn't a Calloway matter anymore," Uncle Hank spat. "I won't go to those people again. They long ago made up their hearts and minds about my sister; they've made that very clear. I know they're your family, Charlotte, but I'll tell you the same thing I told your mother. They're—they're cold people. Grace never really understood until it was too late, and maybe you won't either, but there it is. And that's all I'll say on the matter."

I handed him back the envelope. "I can't help you," I said. "I'm sorry."

Uncle Hank reluctantly took the photographs and rubbed his chin. He shook his head at me, as if I had disappointed him. "I know you're a Calloway, Charlotte," he said. "But you're a Fairchild, too. You're one of us. Don't forget that."

His words stung. I bit my lip and looked away, unsure of what to say.

"There's this thing we do every year at your grandma's house—a party for Grace, on her birthday," Uncle Hank said, putting the envelope back into his bag, a bit resigned now that he wouldn't get anything else from me. "She would be turning forty-three this year. It would mean a lot to Ma if you and Seraphina came."

I knew about the party. My mother's family had held one every year since she left. When I was younger, I hadn't been allowed to go. My father didn't think it was a good idea. And now . . . now it was easy to ignore it since I was at school. Knollwood seemed a world away from Hillsborough, and that was part of its appeal.

"I'll think about it," I lied.

"Okay, then," Uncle Hank said, rubbing the back of his neck with one hand, as if he wasn't sure what the proper goodbye was, and I just stared back at him.

For a moment, I tried to see him the way my mother saw him. I knew he was her favorite brother. Growing up, she had told me stories—how he had taught her to drive in their dad's station wagon when she was only twelve. When she mistook the gas for the brake pedal and leveled their mailbox, Uncle Hank took the fall for her, claiming he was the one behind the wheel. He bore the brunt of three lashes from their dad's belt, while my mom watched from upstairs, peeking her head between the banisters. When she was in the fourth grade and tumbled over the handlebars of her bike, Uncle Hank had been the one to hold her hand and distract her while the doctor sewed up the stitches on her chin, and he asked for a matching ugly brown Band-Aid to wear on his chin so that she didn't feel so ridiculous wearing one by herself.

Uncle Hank and I used to share an eternity of summers, of sunburned toes, and rocky road ice-cream cones that melted in the searing July afternoon faster than you could eat them, and the slightly sour smell of lake water and sweat. There used to be so much that reminded me of Uncle Hank. But now, all that connected us was the ghost of my mother.

Strangely, that was what separated us, too.

four
GRACE CALLOWAY

AUGUST 4, 2007
4:35 P.M.

I could feel it in the air that day—the retreat of summer. The suffocating heat of July had given way to cooler August afternoons. And it wasn't just the heat that had abated; it was the girls' moods. Charlotte and Seraphina were beginning to grow restless, I could tell; the novelty of being at the lake house had started to wear off. Running barefoot through the sprinklers in the front lawn, camping in the backyard, barbecuing on the patio—once great adventures—had started to feel routine. They'd abandoned the tire swing Alistair had hung over the old elm on the edge of the lake, lost interest in racing each other out to the raft and back. The other day I'd found Charlotte and Seraphina marooned on the cold leather sofa in the den, playing their PlayStation 3.

It felt like the end of something. And it was.

I looked over from where I sat on the cushioned seats at the bow of the boat to where Alistair sat behind the wheel. He had Charlotte in his lap; he was teaching her how to steer our new twenty-five-foot Sea Ray bowrider. I couldn't hear what they were saying to one another over the noise of the motor and the sound of the waves breaking against the hull. Seraphina sat on her knees next to me, leaning out over the edge of the boat, hands splayed to catch the spray of the waves. I had one finger hooked in one of the loops of her life jacket straps at the back, anchoring her to me in the event a bumpy wave caused her to lose her balance.

The lake was just under four hundred acres. It was surrounded by woods and undeveloped land. A few houses dotted the shoreline here and there, and there was a public boat launch on the north side. We passed a fisherman in his aluminum boat at the edge of the lake. He stared out at us from under the bill of his baseball cap, and I raised my hand to wave hello.

I imagined how we must have appeared to a casual onlooker. Just a happy family enjoying a Saturday afternoon boat ride around the lake.

Now I took a mental snapshot. Seraphina's blond curls floating behind her in the breeze. *Click.* Charlotte wearing her father's Knicks hat as she peered over the wheel. The hat was too big even though Alistair had adjusted it to its tightest setting. It kept sliding down onto the bridge of her nose, covering her eyes, and Charlotte kept tilting her head back to clear her view, refusing to take it off. *Click.* Alistair, the sunlight catching in his blond hair, reflecting off his oiled, toned shoulders. My perfect, handsome husband holding our daughter in his arms. *Click.*

In college, I'd taken a photography class and there was a quote by Ansel Adams our professor had up on the wall: "You don't take a photograph, you make it." I'd always thought that a photograph was made not once, but twice. In the first and most obvious instance, the photographer made the photograph—she chose the framing, the angle of the shot, the lighting, the composition of objects. She chose what she wanted you to see. It was staged, artificial, the story she wanted told. But every photograph was made a second time when the viewer looked at it. Because you didn't just see the photograph as it was, you saw it as you were. You brought your own context to it, your own story, your own perceptions. You made the meaning. I always thought that what people saw when they looked at a photo said more about them than what was actually in the shot.

Now I held my mental snapshots up for review and I tried to erase myself, a great unmaking. I tried to see those snapshots as a stranger would. I held the images far away from my mind's eye so that all the intricacies blended together, until it became a harmless palette of colors and lines. For just a moment, I wanted things to be only what they appeared to be from a distance.

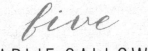

five
CHARLIE CALLOWAY

2017

They were yelling again. I could hear them through the wall. So I put a movie on for Seraphina and turned the volume up.

"Stay here," I told her, and I padded out of our room and down the hall. I peeked my head in through their half-open door.

My father's suitcase was on the bed. My mother was by the dresser, a drawer out, and she was tossing collared shirts into it.

"Just go," she said.

"Damn it, Grace," my father said. He had just gotten out of the shower. I could see the steam coating the mirror in their bathroom; his cheeks were red where he had shaved. He was dressed in a towel that was tied around his waist.

He grabbed her by the wrist, pulled her toward him so that she was in his arms.

"Look at me," he said.

"Get your hands off me," my mother snapped.

"Mommy?" I called out.

They both turned then and saw me standing there. My father let her go. I saw my mother's face—her eyes red and puckered. She quickly turned her back to me again, so I couldn't see her.

"Why is Mommy crying?" I asked.

My father came over and picked me up, even though I was getting too old for that now.

"What do you say we get an Eskimo Pie?" he asked.

"Okay," I said.

He carried me downstairs to the kitchen and dug two Eskimo Pies out of the freezer. We sat on the steps of the back patio as we ate them, looking out at the lake.

"Won't she be mad we're eating these?" I asked, licking a piece of melted chocolate off my finger. My mother never let me and Seraphina have ice cream this late in the afternoon. She always said it would ruin our dinner.

"Charlotte, I need you to be a big girl and look after your mother while I'm away," my father said. "Do you think you can do that?"

"You're going back already?" I asked.

"I have an early meeting in the morning," he said.

"Don't go," I said. "You promised you'd take me out on the boat again tomorrow."

"Next weekend, okay?" he said.

"Can I come with you?" I asked.

He was silent for a moment.

"I need you to stay here and look after your mother," he said. "Can you do that for me?"

I didn't say anything. I didn't want him to leave me there with her, but I knew there was nothing I could do to stop it.

He got up and went inside to finish packing and I stayed out on the back porch. I didn't want to watch him leave. When I heard the front door open and close and the sound of his car backing out of the front drive, I went and sat on the tire swing he had built me two summers ago.

I sat there for a while, until the sun started to dull in the sky, waiting for someone to come looking for me, but no one did.

I heard a sound in the bushes. I turned and I saw him standing there—a man. He was dressed in jeans and a dark jacket and he was holding a camera to his eye so I couldn't see his face.

I stopped swinging.

He came closer.

He was tall. I squinted at him. He seemed both familiar and un-familiar.

I opened my mouth to ask him who he was, what he wanted, but nothing came out.

He came closer, stood over me, so close I could reach out and touch him if I wanted. I looked up into the lens of his camera.

Click.

He took a picture.

Who are you who are you who are you?

The words reverberated in my mind.

Suddenly, the man stopped as if he had heard me, as if he could read my thoughts as plainly as if they were written on my fore-head. Slowly, he lowered the camera and I saw his face.

Or, I saw where his face should have been, when really, there was no face at all.

Where his skin should have been was red, raw flesh, as if it had been boiled and stripped. There were two gaping black pits where his eyes should have gone, and the seam of his lips had been stitched together. He tried to move them, his lips straining at the stitches as if he desperately wanted to tell me something, but all that came out was a terrible, painful groan.

I sucked in my breath in horror.

He reached out to grab me and I screamed. I closed my eyes and thrashed against it, the hand on my shoulder, whose grip only tightened and shook me harder.

"Charlie," a voice said. "Charlie, it's okay. It's me."

I woke with a start. There was a hand on my shoulder. I looked up and saw Leo standing over me, shaking me slightly. I screamed again.

"Easy there, cousin," Leo said. "It's just me."

"I would say that's a perfectly normal reaction for a girl to have when your face is the first thing she sees when she wakes up," Drew said. "Don't act like this is the first time this has happened to you, Leo."

"Drew, always a pleasure," Leo said, turning to look at her. "Especially this bright and early in the morning."

"Bite me," Drew said.

"Been there, done that," Leo said.

"Oh, fuck off."

I sat up in my bed and rubbed my eyes. I glanced at the clock on my bedside table. Six thirty A.M.

Drew was standing in the doorway in a robe, her wet hair tied up in a towel. Her shower caddy was slung over one arm.

"How'd you even get in here?" Drew asked.

"You left the door open when you went to shower," Leo said, shrugging.

"Well, that's the last time I do that," Drew said. She set her shower caddy down on the top of her dresser.

"What's up, Leo?" I asked. My mind felt muddled as I tried to grasp on to the remnants of my dream, which were quickly slipping away. I had dreamed of the house on Langely Lake, of the fight my mother and father had had the day my mother disappeared, of a faceless man with a camera who was trying to tell me something.

Leo sat next to me on the bed. "My first class was canceled," he said. He reached for the remote on my bedside table and flicked on my TV. Well, technically, it was Leo's TV. Aunt Grier had refused to let him keep a TV in his room because she thought it would interfere with his studies, so he kept it in my room instead, along with his Xbox. "Wanted to get some Call of Duty in."

"Get out," Drew said. "I have to get dressed."

"By all means," Leo said. "Go right ahead. Nothing I haven't seen before."

Drew threw her hairbrush at him. Leo ducked, and the brush clanked against my headboard and fell to the floor.

I held up my hands. "Hey, watch it," I said. "I don't want to get hit by friendly fire here."

"Sorry," Drew said.

"Can't you do this later?" I asked Leo.

"Duty, Charlie," Leo said, holding his controller up and shrugging as if he were powerless. "It calls."

"Whatever," Drew said, ripping open the top drawer of her dresser and pulling out a bra and a pair of underwear. "I'll just get dressed in the bathroom."

"Oh, wear the black lacy one," Leo said. "I always liked that one."

I climbed out of bed before Drew chucked a bottle of hair spray at him on her way out the door.

"Do you have to do that?" I asked Leo as I sorted through my closet for something clean to wear.

"If it were thirty percent less fun, I would try to abstain," Leo said, his eyes on the TV screen and his fingers working the controller.

None of my friends were fans of Leo's. Drew, for obvious reasons, and Yael and Stevie out of solidarity. I knew they found him conceited and cruel, and I had to admit that Leo had some hard edges. But he was family, and at one point, he had been all I really had.

When I had gone to live with Uncle Teddy and Aunt Grier in Scarsdale when I was ten, Leo had taken me under his wing. That first day at Brentley Academy, he had invited me to sit at his lunch table, which was no small thing for a new kid at school in the middle of a school year. I sat between Leo and his friend Richie Masterson, who I remember thinking was cute with his dark hair and freckles. That was, until Richie Masterson put down his ham sandwich, turned to me, and asked, "Did you help your dad hide the body?"

Oh no, I thought. Not here. Not now. Not again.

I tried to breathe but couldn't. The air scraped at my lungs.

"Charlotte's mother was a whore," Leo said.

I turned to look at him, my eyes wide and incredulous at his betrayal. We all sat in stunned silence. Richie's taunting smile froze and faltered on his lips.

"You know, a woman who sleeps with a guy for his money?" Leo explained as if we were all idiots and didn't know the meaning of the word, probably because we were gaping at him like we didn't. He took a bite of his sandwich and said casually with his mouth full, "You should know, Richie, your mother is a whore, too."

"Hey," Richie said. Heat bloomed in his cheeks. "My mother is not a—"

"Didn't she leave your father and take all his money?" Leo asked, but it was not a question, because Richie's father was a patient of Aunt Grier, and Leo's favorite pastime was to sit just out of sight but within earshot of the study when his mother was with a patient and collect secrets. "See? She was a whore. But nobody cares to talk about it because you're not important enough. You're just an unimportant nobody with a whore for a mother. Charlotte's mother was a whore, but at least people care enough about her to talk about it, because she's a Calloway. She matters."

Richie bit his lip; I could see the tendon in his neck straining and I could see the war he was waging within himself—the war I had waged a hundred times with myself and lost—the war not to let the tears come, not to show any of us watching that he was about to break. I almost felt bad for him. Almost.

And that was the last time anybody at Brentley ever brought up my mother. That was the day that Leo saved me not just from the other kids, but from myself. Because he taught me to hate her. And that anger was a beautiful gift. Before, I had felt a lot of things. Dr. Malby had helped me to name them: Grief. Loss. Guilt. Shame. But never anger.

For the first time, I was in control. I had vowed to never give that up.

But now there was Uncle Hank, again, and those photographs. And that one photograph I had no memory of being taken, with one word on the back: *STOP*. Stop what?

"Come get waffles with me," I said to Leo, pulling on my navy Knollwood blazer. "I'm hungry."

"Fine," Leo said, putting down the controller. "For you, cousin, anything."

In my mailbox that morning, I found another note. It was my first ticket from the A's, printed on thick card stock.

Item #1: Nancy Reagan's collar
To be returned to its new owners on Friday night at midnight.

Although Headmaster Collins had three children, his pit bull, Nancy Reagan, was his pride and joy. The first time I learned of Nancy's existence, we were in his office, and he had pointed to a picture of his family as he talked.

"They say they're not supposed to be fully cognitively developed at that age, but I can just tell, my Nancy, she's as smart as a whip. She can't talk, of course, but when you look her in the eye, you can just tell she understands."

I thought he was talking about his infant daughter.

"I have a cousin around that age, Clementine," I'd said. I swear I said "cousin," but Headmaster Collins must not have heard me.

"What do you find works best for her diet?" he asked.

It was an odd question, and it should have raised flags, but I'd only just met the man, and I figured he was a little eccentric.

"My aunt Grier is a real health nut," I said. "Vegan and gluten free and all that. She's doing this whole farm-to-table thing right now. Grows her own vegetables and purees them and everything. So I assume Clementine is subsisting on a diet of pureed home-grown organic carrots."

"Farm-to-table," Headmaster Collins said, scratching his chin. "Yes, yes. I will try that. I bet that makes her coat shine."

It was about at that point that I caught on to my mistake, and I pretended from that point on in the conversation that Clementine was a dog. He still asked me about her, even two years later, and still, I continued to lie.

There were framed pictures of Nancy in the headmaster's office; rumor had it that there was even a life-sized oil portrait of Nancy in a gilt frame over the mantel in his house. Marcus Lansbury had sworn he saw it when he was asked to tea with his uncle at the headmaster's house last fall.

Of course, everyone knew about Nancy's collar. It was encrusted with diamonds and it had been gifted to Nancy last Christmas. Mrs. Collins had raised hell when she opened her biggest present: a state-of-the-art vacuum cleaner.

In the evening, I went to the library with Stevie to study. We both had American Literature together and were working our way through Plath's *Ariel*. I read aloud the first two stanzas of the poem "Daddy" and then set my book down.

"Well, I have no idea what it means, but at least it rhymes, sort of," I said.

"She's talking about how repressed she feels," Stevie said. "Like she's living in this little box where she can barely breathe."

"Then why can't she just say that?" I asked.

"Because, sometimes the words we have aren't enough," Stevie said. "You need things like metaphor and sound and rhyme to get at the full weight of it."

"I guess," I grumbled, turning the page.

"I'm going to go dig up Plath's unabridged journals," Stevie said, getting up from the table. "Maybe they'll give us a good historical context that we can use to analyze the poems."

"Sounds thrilling," I said.

I kept reading. Suddenly, I got the distinct feeling that someone was watching me, and I glanced up to see Dalton standing there, across the table from me.

"Coming to pay me homage for my ungodly poker skills?" I asked, raising an eyebrow at him.

"Something like that," Dalton said. He fished an envelope out of the pocket of his blazer and slid it across the table toward me. Then, to my surprise, he sat down.

"You know," he said, "if someone—not mentioning any names here or anything—but if *someone* had been playing by the rules last night, things might have turned out differently."

"Yes, well, *someone* regrets nothing," I said, opening the envelope and sorting through the cash.

Dalton laughed. "Are you really going to count it in front of me? Don't you trust me, Calloway?"

"I trust you about as far as I can throw you," I said, tucking the envelope into my American Literature textbook. "And I probably wouldn't even be able to lift you."

"Is this distrust specific to me or to all guys in general?"

"Oh, all of you," I said. "Don't flatter yourself."

Dalton laughed again. "How did we get such a bad rap?"

"Have you met my cousin Leo?"

"I sincerely hope that your whole perception of the male populace is not based on Leo," Dalton said.

I laughed. "Unfortunately for you, I have firsthand knowledge of the inner workings of the male teenage mind, and it doesn't bode well for any of you. You're all gross."

Dalton leaned forward and tapped on my textbook. "Doing a bit of light reading?" he asked.

I held up the textbook so he could see. "American Lit," I said. "We're deconstructing poems from Plath's *Ariel*. I can't make heads or tails of it, but we have to write some big paper."

"Who do you have?"

"Mrs. Morrison," I said.

Dalton nodded. "I could help you with that."

"Oh yeah?" I said. "You a big Plath junkie?"

He laughed. "Hardly," he said. "Literature's probably my worst subject."

"Well, with that ringing endorsement, I might just fend for myself," I said.

Dalton looked stealthily side to side, as if checking to make sure no one was close enough to hear. He leaned forward again and lowered his voice. "I was talking about the A's cache," he said.

"The A's cache?" I repeated, as quietly as I could.

"Yeah, we have sort of a . . . *repository* of essays, exams, et cetera, for every teacher, every class, going back, like, decades. Every A contributes to it and every A is free to use it at their discretion. It's what got me through Mrs. Morrison's American Literature class last year with a solid A minus. Mom and Dad were so proud, they sprung for new rims for my Porsche."

"But aren't you afraid you'll get caught?" I asked.

Knollwood's zero-tolerance policy when it came to cheating meant automatic expulsion. Plus, Mrs. Morrison and a lot of other teachers had recently started running every paper that was turned in through an online service that automatically checked the essay for plagiarism, analyzing the paper against material on the web and other papers previously turned in to its database.

"We're working on a way around that," Dalton said. "It's just software, and you can beat it if you know what you're doing."

My mind instantly went to Jude Bane—the computer nerd who was one of my fellow A initiates. Was that why the A's had included him? Were they looking for him to hack the system?

"But in the meantime, as long as you use papers from far enough back, you should be fine. They're too old to be in the database, and it's not like Mrs. Morrison is going to remember every paper on Plath that she's ever read."

"True," I said.

Dalton leaned back in his chair. "Any plans for homecoming?"

"My whole family is coming in for the game against Xavier," I said. "My dad is an alum. My uncle Teddy is too—well, sort of. I think Uncle Teddy technically got expelled before he graduated, but my grandmother Eugenia doesn't like to talk about it. But anyways, my cousin Piper is checking out Knollwood because she might go here next year, so her whole family is coming. What about you?"

I spotted Stevie out of the corner of my eye, coming around the nearest bookshelf. She stopped short when she saw Dalton at our table and did an excited happy dance, bouncing up and down on the balls of her feet. I discreetly shook my head at her, and she busied herself pretending to look for a book in the stacks while she very obviously eavesdropped on our conversation.

"My mom's an alum, too," Dalton said. "But she won't be able to make it, probably. Work keeps her pretty busy."

"Oh, that's too bad," I said.

Dalton shrugged. "Actually, though, when I was asking about

your plans for homecoming, I was referring to the dance, not the game."

I heard Stevie squeal and then try to cover it up with a coughing fit. I ignored her.

"Oh," I said.

"Are you going with anyone?"

"Well, I always go stag with the girls," I said. I pointedly turned my head a fraction so I couldn't see the frantic gestures Stevie was making in my direction, like she was trying to land a plane.

"The girls?" Dalton asked.

"Yeah—Drew, Stevie, Yael. It's always kinda been our thing," I said.

Freshman and sophomore year, the four of us had gone to homecoming together. We'd gotten ready together, we'd danced together, and when the dance was over, Stevie and Yael had dragged their mattresses into my and Drew's room and slept on our floor. Not that any of us got much sleep. Mostly, those nights consisted of our staying up until dawn laughing and drinking cooking sherry that Drew had co-opted from the dormitory's kitchen.

"What about you?" I asked. "Who are you taking?"

Dalton shrugged. "Haven't asked anyone yet. Maybe I'll try the whole stag thing."

"Psh," I said, and rolled my eyes. Royce Dalton without a date? I couldn't picture it.

"What?" Dalton asked, the corner of his lips twitching up sheepishly. I tried not to think about how cute he was when he smiled, the way it made my stomach drop like I was standing on top of a high ledge glancing down. "You don't think I can hack it for one night alone?"

"I think there are at least a hundred girls at Knollwood who are dying to go to the dance with you, and to not ask a single one of them seems a little rude."

"Oh, so I need to ask someone for the greater good?"

"Oh, please," I said. "Don't act like you wouldn't enjoy yourself. There's gotta be at least one girl at Knollwood you'd want to go with."

"Well, I was going to ask you, but you already have three dates, so it appears I'm too late," Dalton said.

I rolled my eyes again. Dalton was such a flirt. I pitied the girl who took him too seriously.

"Yes, it's too bad," I said. "But you can't really mess with tradition."

After Dalton left and meandered across the library to sit with Ren and Darcy, Stevie returned to our table with her book.

"He was totally asking you to the dance," Stevie said, exasperated. "And you completely shut him down."

I sighed. "He was not, and I did not," I said. "It's amazing to me that someone who's so great at deconstructing Plath's esoteric poetry could so completely misread a normal conversation that plays out right in front of her in plain English."

"Okay, Cleopatra," Stevie said.

"Cleopatra?"

"Queen of Denial," Stevie explained.

I chucked my pencil at her.

I tried not to let my gaze flicker across the room to Dalton every time I looked up from my reading, but I couldn't help myself. I found myself watching him as he read, wondering what he was saying every time he leaned over to talk to Ren or Darcy. When I looked up later and found that their table was empty, that Dalton had left, I felt a sharp pang of disappointment.

"Does this one look okay?"

Yael turned sideways and glanced at herself in the mirror, taking in the angles of the dress.

Dress shopping with Yael was hellish because everything looked good on her tall, slender frame. Currently she was wearing a short, high-necked, sleeveless dress in dark blue. There was a sheer overlay that was embellished with hundreds of beads and crystals. The style accentuated Yael's tiny waist and her legs that went on for days, and the color popped against her porcelain skin.

"I hate you," I said, and I was only half joking.

It was Friday afternoon and Yael, Drew, Stevie, and I were at Delphine's, the only boutique in Falls Church, shopping for our homecoming dresses. I had been dragged there against my will and despite many protests. I found my dress in about two minutes. In fact, it was the first and only dress I tried on: a short wine-colored silk dress with a low back. Simple yet elegant. It was the only dress there that didn't scream Pretty Pretty Princess. The other girls tried on dresses made of soft chiffon, or frothy lace, or full skirts of tulle in soft pastels: rose, mint, periwinkle. I had dutifully held their hangers and fished through the racks for different sizes and offered second opinions for the past hour, but my patience was wearing thin. A dress was a dress, and they were all starting to look the same to me. Currently, I was draping myself over the chair in Yael's dressing room and fiddling with my phone as she undressed.

I couldn't help but think about that night: the first item for the A's was due by midnight. The first challenge, and they had given us just two days to complete it.

I had done my homework: I had a basic understanding of Nancy's schedule—where she would be, and when, and who would be with her. The other afternoon, I had staked out a place on the quad with a good view of the headmaster's house. My spot was on a hill, so I could see over the fence into the backyard. I did my trigonometry homework as I tracked Nancy's comings and goings. I felt more than a little ridiculous stalking a dog.

"Do you like this one?" Drew asked, opening Yael's dressing room door without knocking. She had on a champagne-colored high-low chiffon dress with a sweetheart neckline.

Yael shifted her weight to her back leg and carefully considered the dress, standing only in her bra and underwear but seemingly unconcerned with her state of undress.

"Turn," Yael instructed, and Drew did a slow revolving circle in front of us.

"The high-low style is a little last season," Yael said.

I noticed something red on the tag of the dress and I reached out to read it. "No wonder," I said, taking a closer look. "This dress *is* last season. It's been marked down."

Drew quickly grabbed the tag back from me. "Whoops, somebody must have accidentally put this on the new-dresses rack. I hate it when sale items get mixed in with the good stuff."

"There's nothing wrong with a good deal," Stevie said, peeking her head over the divider. She was in the dressing room next to Yael's, but she was standing on a chair and leaning over, so I could only see her from the elbows up.

"I do kind of like it," Drew said. "I can pull off vintage, right?"

"Are you feeling okay?" I asked jokingly, touching my hand to her forehead to measure her temperature. Drew's mom was high up at some women's fashion retailer, so Drew typically had a taste for high-end fashion. The newer and more expensive, the better. She was not one to dig through the discount rack.

Drew pushed my hand away.

"Ignore her. You look hot," Stevie said.

"Hot enough to make Crosby break up with Ren?" Drew asked.

"Are they back together again?" Yael asked.

"I can't tell," Drew said. "But he hasn't asked me to the dance yet, so I figured they were."

"I thought we were all going together," I said, looking up from my phone, a little annoyed. "Or are we just your backup?"

"Re-lax," Drew said, drawing out the syllables. "You girls are always my first choice. But, you know, you don't appreciate me in a dress the way the boys do. And also, I love you all dearly, but I really don't want to make out with you."

"Dalton asked Charlie to the dance," Stevie cooed.

"What? When?" Drew chirped.

"You didn't tell me that," Yael said, and she gave my forearm a pinch.

"Ouch," I said, rubbing my skin.

"It happened in the library the other day, and she turned him down," Stevie said.

"You turned down Royce Dalton?" Yael asked, her eyes wide.

I glared at Stevie. "Apparently, sarcasm and humor are lost on some people," I said. "He wasn't serious."

"He was too serious," Stevie said. "I bet you could get him to ask you again if you encouraged him a little. He seemed so heart-broken when you blew him off."

"I don't know," Drew said, biting her thumbnail and consider-ing. "I heard he was going with McKenna St. Clare. She was going on and on about what boutonniere to get him to match her dress in French class this morning."

"Oh," Stevie said, deflated. She looked at me with soulful eyes, like she felt sorry for me—like I cared that Dalton was going to homecoming with McKenna St. Clare instead of me.

McKenna St. Clare was a sophomore—the prettiest girl in her class. She was tall and waiflike, with green, almond-shaped eyes.

"Yeah," I said, making a big show of rolling my eyes. "He sounds like he was really heartbroken that I turned him down. He must have waited a whole two minutes before asking someone else."

I was trying to sound nonchalant about the whole thing, but my joke landed wrong. I sounded bitter, which was unfair, because I wasn't bitter. I wasn't.

Yael bit her lip. "Royce Dalton would make a poor dance partner anyway. He's too tall for you."

"Yeah," Drew echoed. "He's just so . . ."

She trailed off, searching for a derogatory adjective to make me feel better. When she couldn't find one, she deflected.

"Hey, help me out of this dress, will you?" she asked me, turning around.

I tugged at her zipper.

I couldn't stay there and listen to their pity, their lousy but well-intentioned attempts at making me feel better that I wasn't going to the dance with Dalton. Especially since I didn't want to go to the dance with him anyway. I didn't.

"I have some errands to run in town," I said, throwing my phone in my purse. "I'll catch up with you guys later, okay?"

"Want me to come with you?" Stevie asked, her voice all soft and cushiony, like I was some fragile creature about to break.

"No," I snapped.

She visibly jerked back as if I had slapped her.

"I mean, no, thanks," I said, forcing myself to smile. "I'll just see you later."

"Sure," she said.

I left, knowing they would probably start talking about me in pitying tones as soon as I was out of earshot, which was really annoying. And what was even more annoying was that they honestly thought I would go for someone like Royce Dalton in the first place. Royce Dalton—the biggest man-whore at Knollwood. Did they honestly think I would go to the dance with him and we would do all that sappy couple stuff? Dalton had practically written the smooth operator playbook. I was sure he would get me a corsage that perfectly matched my dress. When he was walking me home, he would notice that I was cold, and he would take off his jacket and drape it around my shoulders. And when we got to my door, we would make awkward small talk until he kissed me. We would have a nice time, I could picture it.

But, unlike my friends, I could also picture what would happen next. As soon as I let my guard down, Dalton would move on to the next pretty girl, and I would be just like Harper Cartwright, making the stink eye at him from across the way at A's meetings. No, thank you. Hard pass. McKenna St. Clare could have him, for all I cared.

At Mimi's, the local grocery store, I put a pound of raw bacon and a box of Ziploc baggies on the checkout counter and called my sister in Reading.

"Is everything okay?" Seraphina answered my call slightly panicked. It was rare for us to call one another, when texting took such little effort.

"What are you doing tomorrow?" I asked.

"What is it, Saturday?" she asked. I could picture her lounging on her dorm bed, picking at her fingernails. "Hopefully, practicing my two favorite deadly sins: gluttony and sloth," she said. "Why do you ask?"

"Uncle Hank called me the other day," I said.

I lied because I didn't want to alarm her by telling her that he had come to see me, or mentioning the pictures.

"That wacko?" Seraphina asked. "What did he want?"

"Well, you know how Grandma and Grandpa Fairchild always have that thing every year for Mom's birthday?"

There was a pause.

"Yeah," she said.

"He wanted me to come," I said. "Actually, he wanted both of us to come."

There was another pause on the line, this one longer. The lady behind the counter rang up my items slowly and put them in a paper bag.

"Seraphina, you still there?" I asked, holding the phone between my chin and shoulder as I handed the cashier a twenty from my wallet.

"I don't understand why you want to go, I guess," Seraphina said.

I mouthed, *Thanks,* to the lady behind the counter and headed out the front of the store onto the sidewalk with my purchases.

It was a fair enough question, and the truth was, if it weren't for the pictures, I wouldn't have wanted to go. But I *had* seen the pictures, and those pictures had unsettled me. I wasn't sure what they were all about, what they meant, but they raised questions. Questions I couldn't leave unanswered. But I didn't know how to make Seraphina understand that without telling her everything, and I didn't want to do that over the phone.

"I just think it's time," I said. "I mean, they're still our family, whatever our mother did."

The thing was, I had to go back to Hillsborough. I had to go back to the house on Langely Lake. I had to talk to my mother's oldest friend, Claire. And maybe if my sister was there, and I could explain everything to her, we could do this together.

"I don't know," Seraphina said. "I'm fine seeing them at Christmas and stuff, but it feels weird to go to something that's all about *her.* And Dad would be pissed if he found out."

"It's just for one night," I said. "If we hate it, we can leave, I promise."

There was a sigh. A long drawn-out breath.

"If I figure out the train schedule, will you come?" I asked. "I can pick you up in Hillsborough."

"I suppose I can practice my deadly sins another time," Seraphina said.

"You are the picture of virtue, my good sister," I said.

Drew knelt next to my desk drawer and worked the lock with the ends of two large paper clips.

"Fuck," she said. "It broke."

She tossed the broken paper clip on the floor and reached for a fresh clip from the pile next to her.

"Don't push so hard," I said as I sat on my bed and pulled on a pair of black booties. Drew had to steal Ren's sealed file from the counselor's office for her ticket, so she was practicing on my locked desk drawer. I'd overheard enough of the lock-picking tutorials she'd watched on YouTube to get the gist of the process.

"Yeah, yeah, okay," Drew said as she inserted two fresh paper clips into the drawer's lock and tried again.

I glanced at the time on my phone. It was nearing eleven o'clock. In my closet mirror, I checked my all-black ensemble: black jeans, black booties, black tank, black pullover. How convenient that all black was both practical for late-night burglaries and stylishly classic.

There was a loud click and I looked over to see Drew pulling my desk drawer open.

"Nailed it," she said.

"Told you."

I got the package of bacon from Mimi's out of our mini fridge and pulled several strips from the pack. I placed them in a Ziploc bag, which I folded and tucked into the pocket of my pullover.

"So, I'll see you at the Ledge in an hour?" I asked as I headed toward our window.

Drew pursed her lips and smacked them loudly, a kiss goodbye.

Nancy was just where I knew she'd be: in the backyard of the headmaster's house, lounging in the shadow of an elm. It was lucky for me that things had gone down the way they had last Christmas with Nancy's diamond collar and Mrs. Collins's vacuum cleaner. Mrs. Collins's unabated wrath over the whole thing was the reason Nancy was driven to sleep outside in the yard when the weather was nice enough instead of slumbering on a silk pillow at the foot of the Collinses' bed.

Getting up and over the fence was an easy enough job. Nancy didn't even stir from her place beneath the elm. She just lifted her head and watched me lazily. The Collinses' back porch light came on, triggered by my movement, and I went very still and crouched down, in case one of the Collinses happened to look out. I made my way toward Nancy slowly, crawling along the ground.

When I got closer to her, Nancy growled, a low rumble in the back of her throat. She stood, her muscles rigid, as if at any moment she might lunge at me. I stopped where I was, just a few feet from her.

"Easy, girl," I said.

I slowly pulled my phone out of my pocket and clicked open the dog-whistle app I had downloaded earlier that day. Just as Nancy sprang toward me, I hit the button.

Of course, I couldn't hear anything, so for one terrifying moment, I thought it might not have worked. But then Nancy froze. She sat back on her haunches and whined, cocking her head to the side. I clicked the button again to silence the whistle.

"There's no reason we can't both get what we want here," I said.

I withdrew the Ziploc bag of bacon from my pocket and opened it. Nancy sniffed at the air. Her tongue lapped at the sides of her mouth. I took a few strips out and laid them on the ground at my feet. Nancy came forward eagerly and started to feast.

"Sorry about that pureed-carrot diet they have you on," I said. "I'm afraid that's my fault."

I leaned down cautiously. I could see the buckle clasp for Nancy's diamond collar at the nape of her neck. I imagined reaching for it, and Nancy whipping around and catching my hand in her razor-sharp teeth. I shook the thought from my mind. Nancy would have to take a few of my fingers before I'd risk failing a ticket and being excluded from the A's.

I reached forward slowly until my hands were on the back of Nancy's neck. She didn't growl or draw away from me; she was so preoccupied with the bacon that she didn't seem to notice me at all. I made quick work of the clasp and slid the heavy collar off her neck and into my pocket.

"Good girl," I said.

Nancy looked up at me then, and something seemed to shift behind her eyes. I noticed she had finished the bacon, and I fished nervously in the Ziploc bag for the last few strips. I threw them on the ground at her feet, but Nancy didn't seem to notice them.

A low growl ripped through her belly. The folds around her eyes drew back across her forehead; she bared her teeth and let out one mean bark. I tried to reach around in my pocket for my phone and the dog whistle app, but my fingers were slippery with bacon grease. Instead, I turned on my heel and I ran as fast as I could toward the fence.

As close as I was, I knew I wasn't fast enough to beat Nancy with her four legs to my two. I could feel her teeth in the flesh of my ankle as she lunged and nipped at my feet. I let out a gasp at her bite and stumbled forward.

I was at the fence now. I got my footing in the railing and lifted myself up and over before Nancy could bring herself to strike again. Still, I could hear her pacing there, just on the other side of the fence, waiting to see if I'd come back.

I limped a few feet from the fence and pulled up the leg of my jeans to survey the damage. In the stray light from the Collinses' backyard, I could make out the pink half moon of flesh in the shape of Nancy's front right incisor just behind my right anklebone.

When I was a safe distance away, I chanced a glance back into the yard. Nancy had returned to her place beneath the elm, where she was quickly devouring the only evidence I had left behind of my presence there that night: the last strips of bacon from Mimi's Supermarket.

Out of the eight initiates, seven of us made it to the Ledge by the deadline. We laid our spoils on a picnic blanket on the hood of Ren's car:

> One diamond collar stolen from the neck of the headmaster's
> prized pit bull
> One set of the janitor's keys
> One framed picture of Mr. Franklin, the trig teacher, shaking
> hands with President Nixon after returning from service
> overseas
> One file on Ren Montgomery stolen from the school counselor's
> office, still sealed
> One pass code to the academic dean's computer
> One set of hall passes, signed by the headmaster
> One beige scarf with a distinctive red wine stain

I never found out what Auden was supposed to steal. He never showed.

six

GRACE CALLOWAY

AUGUST 4, 2007
7:52 P.M.

The phone rang. I stubbed my toe on my nightstand trying to reach it before the second ring. I didn't want it to wake the girls. I had a fleeting thought as I answered it—*What if it's him?* But Claire's voice greeted me instead.

"I saw Alistair's car whipping down Main as I was coming out of the grocery store," she said. "He was headed toward the freeway. Everything okay?"

Claire knew our routine well—Alistair drove in on Friday evening and left late Sunday night. It was only Saturday, and after this week's events, she was quick to check up on me.

"Everything's fine," I lied. "He had to leave early. He has a golf thing with a client early tomorrow."

The first lie I'd told when this whole thing started—weeks and weeks ago now—had stuck to the back of my tongue. But now I found that the more lies I told, the easier they came out. Sometimes they slid out without my meaning them to, without my even knowing. I wondered sometimes if I fooled even myself.

"Giving up a family day to go swing a stick around with another guy ignoring his family? How nice," Claire said dryly.

Her dislike for Alistair bordered on hostile. I didn't respond.

"It's supposed to storm later," Claire said, changing the subject.

"Want some company? I could come over. I've got a bottle of Pinot in the fridge."

"I told the girls we'd have a game night," I said. "Thought I'd get in some quality mother-daughter time while Alistair's away."

"Okay, if you're sure," Claire said, obviously disappointed.

"I'll call you tomorrow," I said.

In truth, I'd put the girls to bed early. Being on the boat all day had drained them. They'd fallen asleep on the living room sofa watching television, and I'd carried them, one by one, upstairs to their room on the second floor.

I glanced out the window toward the lake. Claire was right—it looked like it would storm. There were clouds billowing overhead. The sky looked heavy.

It had become my routine this summer to take a nightly solo swim out on the lake. I did laps out to the raft and back, my preferred form of exercise. But I hadn't swum in days due to the injury to my shoulder.

Now I longed to slip into the water, to feel my muscles lengthen and pull with each stroke, to close my eyes and hold my breath, if only to experience the respite of breaking the surface and gasping for air.

I passed the suitcases open on my bed and went to my dresser to get my swimsuit. I had time for one last swim.

seven

CHARLIE CALLOWAY

2017

The drive from Knollwood in New Hampshire to the Fairchilds' house in Hillsborough, Connecticut, was supposed to take four and a half hours, but I did it in three and a half, zipping along those New England freeways in my Mercedes. The party started at seven, but I had two stops to make first: one at the train station to pick up my sister, Seraphina, who was coming in from her boarding school in Pennsylvania, and the other at the supermarket so I didn't show up empty-handed.

Hillsborough was a small, blue-collar town in Fairfield County, Connecticut. Its main industry was an old lumber mill my grandfather had worked at before he retired. My father had built a house there on Langely Lake for my mother two years after they were married. Most of the houses in Hillsborough were graying, vinyl-sided boxes with gravel driveways and slouching carports, but the house my father built wasn't anything like that. It sat on the edge of town, right on the lake, with a paved driveway that wound its way from the road through a long green yard, ducking in and out of the shade of towering elms. Near the house was a stone fence, bordered by five-foot hedges. But still, you could see the house from a great distance, towering into the sky, three stories tall, with large arched windows gaping at you.

When I was a child, I spent my summers in that house. My

mother, Seraphina, and I would walk around barefoot in thin cotton dresses and large straw hats. We'd sleep late and have picnics on the lawn. In the afternoons, we'd swim out to the raft and lie spread-eagle on it, letting the sun lick us dry. In the evenings, we'd camp out in a tent and tell ghost stories, the canvas top of the tent so thin we could see the stars. On the weekends, my father would come up from the city. We'd run out to meet him when we heard his car turn down the drive and he'd pick us up and swing us around until we laughed with dizziness. He'd grill swordfish for us on the back porch and read poetry to my mother. I could still see her in my mind—her feet propped up on a chair, her eyes closed but her head tilted in the direction of my father's voice as he read to her and I chased Seraphina, squealing, through the sprinklers.

At the train station, while I waited on the platform for the six thirty train from Reading, my phone rang. It was my sister.

"Don't be mad," she said by way of greeting.

"Did you miss your train?" I asked.

"No, not exactly," she said.

"Where are you?"

"In Reading," she said.

"You haven't even left yet?" I asked.

"Here's the part where I need you to not get mad. I'm not coming."

"Seraphina, what do you mean you're not coming?"

"Listen, I just . . . I changed my mind, okay?"

"Are you worried about what Dad will say when he finds out?" I asked.

"It's not about that."

"Then tell me what it's about."

"You need to let her go," Seraphina said. "*They* need to let her go. What you're all doing, it's not healthy for anyone."

It wasn't her fault, I told myself. Seraphina was only five when our mother left; she was too young to remember the good stuff.

She only remembered what everyone else told her to remember, or rather, forgot what they told her to forget.

The Fairchilds lived on the other side of town from the train station, near the hospital, in one of those graying vinyl-sided houses on a narrow yard. I parked in the street because the gravel driveway was full. I saw Grandpa Fairchild's old station wagon near the house, the same car my uncle Hank had taught my mother to drive in when she was only twelve years old. Someone's minivan was parked behind it, and at the end of the driveway, its tail end sticking into the street, was Uncle Hank's rusting truck.

Every light in the house was on, and I could hear the roar of a football game and Grandpa Fairchild's staccato curses from the den as I stepped onto the front porch. My ankle still smarted from Nancy's bite, and I limped a little as I made my way to the door. I had stopped at the Kmart on the way over to pick up some prepackaged cookies and I held the plastic tray in front of me like a shield as I rang the doorbell.

It took a while for someone to answer. But then the door swung open and he leaned against the door frame, a beer in one hand: Greyson Rhodes. He was wearing a UConn sweatshirt and a pair of worn jeans, his blond hair long and slightly wavy, a good week of stubble shading his sharp jawline. And those gray eyes. I hadn't seen Greyson since we were kids. I had the biggest crush on him when I was little because he was tall and thick in the shoulders and played football. His mom, Claire, was best friends with my mom, and he used to babysit me and Seraphina and his younger brother, Ryder, when they would go out.

He squinted at me and then I saw recognition dawn on his face.

"Did you really just ring the doorbell?" he asked, as if my being there wasn't weird at all, as if it had only been a week since we had last seen each other instead of years.

"What are you, like, the welcome committee?" I asked, raising my voice a bit so he could hear me over all the noise of the game and people talking inside.

"Kinda the opposite, actually," Greyson said, taking a swig of his beer. "We thought you were a salesman or something. Or worse, the Mormons. I was elected to send you away diplomatically."

"We don't want any!" someone yelled from inside.

"I brought cookies," I said, lifting the tray toward him.

"How very Martha Stewart of you," he said.

"Greyson, who is it?" someone called, and this voice I recognized. It belonged to my grandma.

"It's Charlotte," he called over his shoulder.

There was a pause and then my grandma appeared behind him, gaping at me like I was some alien creature she was trying to make sense of.

"Charlotte," she said after she had recovered herself. "Charlotte, you don't need to ring the doorbell like a stranger. Just come in, come on in."

She put an arm around me and ushered me into the house. She kept patting my arm as if she thought I might just be a figment of her imagination and she needed to reassure herself I was really there.

"This is a surprise," she said. "A good surprise. It's so good to see you. Everyone, look. Charlotte's here."

There were people in the living room I didn't recognize and I wondered for a moment if I should recognize them, or if they were just my grandma's neighbors. I recognized my aunt Caroline, Uncle Lonnie's wife, who was sitting in the La-Z-Boy, bouncing a baby up and down on her lap. I wondered if I had another cousin I hadn't met yet. Aunt Caroline stopped talking when her eyes met mine and hiccupped a little in shock. I gave a vague, half-hearted wave to the room.

"Hi," I said.

Maybe I should have called ahead or something to tell them—warn them—that I was coming.

"You brought cookies! How thoughtful of you, Charlotte," Grandma said warmly as she took my pathetic cookie tray and led me into the kitchen.

Grandma rearranged my store-bought cookies onto a platter and set them on the counter, which was crowded with all sorts of delicious, homemade food—a giant pot roast, gleaming buttered ears of corn, potato salad, and sourdough rolls.

Two of my younger cousins ran through the room, and my great-aunt Jane, my grandma's sister, who was balancing a tray of chips and dip on her hip, yelled after them to not run in the house. Someone called in from the den for another Bud Light.

This was how my grandparents' house always was, how I remembered it as a child: full of people, constant motion, everyone talking all at once.

"These are your grandpa's favorite," Grandma said, plucking a few of the cookies I had brought and putting them on a small plate. She smiled at me as if I had known this and bought those particular cookies on purpose, though they'd just happened to be arranged at the top of the kiosk in the bakery section.

Someone threw an arm around me and gave me a little squeeze. When I turned and saw who it was, I stiffened.

"How are things, doll?" Claire Rhodes asked.

It'd been years since I'd last seen Claire. When I was little, she'd been one of my favorite adults because she always talked to me like I was one of the grown-ups, or "one of the girls." She was always at the house on Langely Lake during the summers, and she and my mom spent a lot of time together. She still sent me and Seraphina cards on our birthdays. But for all of her charm and ease and well wishes, I couldn't help but be wary of her now. I knew Claire knew more about my mother than she was letting on. If anyone would have known that my mother was planning to leave, or if anyone was in contact with her now, it would be Claire.

Claire leaned forward on the counter and scooped some potato salad onto her plate.

"Things are good," I said. How did one sum up the last ten years of one's life cordially in a few sentences? "I'm going to boarding school up in New Hampshire now. Just started my junior year."

"How's the boy situation?" Claire asked as she took a bite of the potato salad. "And the parties? God, tell me about the parties."

"Claire," Grandma said, chastising her. "I'm sure Charlotte takes her studies very seriously."

"Yeah, but a girl can live a little," Claire said. "You miss things if you always have your nose stuck in a book. I remember how Grace and I were at your age, Charlotte. The things we got up to."

"Grace had her rebellious moments as any teen does," Grandma said. "But you don't want to give Charlotte the wrong idea. Grace was a good student."

"I'm not saying Grace wasn't smart," Claire said. "Grace was sharp as they come. But she wasn't satisfied with being stuck in a classroom or sitting still. Charlotte, your mother, she wanted to be out there, living life. The adventures we had together. This one time, sophomore year, we stole this pack of hall passes from the principal and we left school in the morning and drove down to the boardwalk in Seaside Heights. We spent all day on the beach, our toes in the sand, drinking warm beer we'd gotten from a stranger in a parking lot."

"Charlotte," Grandma interrupted. She handed me a plate of the store-bought cookies. "Why don't you take these to your grandpa in the den?"

"Sure," I said, taking the plate. Behind my grandma's back, Claire smiled at me and mouthed, *We'll talk soon.*

The den was dimly lit. My grandpa was in his recliner, a beer in his hand and a bag of Lay's potato chips in his lap. He sat up suddenly and raised his beer angrily at the TV. Some of the chips spilled out of the bag and into his lap.

"You call that a fumble?" he yelled. "Get your damn eyes checked!"

My uncle Lonnie, the youngest of my uncles, sat on the couch, next to Greyson and Greyson's younger brother, Ryder, who was a teenager now. I guessed he was around Seraphina's age. My cousin Patrick, who was a few years younger than me, was sprawled out on the floor in front of the TV, and my uncle Hank sat at the card table behind the couch. The color drained from Uncle Hank's face when he saw me, and I quickly looked away. I knew he probably hadn't told them about coming to see me up at Knollwood, or about the pictures he had found in his little breaking-and-entering stunt at the lake house. He'd probably thought I would never actually show up when he invited me.

"Um, hey, Grandpa," I said.

Grandpa's eyes flickered away from the TV to my face for a second, and then he glanced back quickly, looking slightly alarmed. I knew what it was. I knew for a second, he thought I was her, my mother. I had always taken after her but lately, the resemblance was uncanny.

"Charlotte," he said after a moment. "What are you doing here?"

He gave me a smile but there was a sadness lurking there behind his eyes, and I remembered again why it was so hard to come back here, to be around them. He heaved himself out of his recliner and wrapped his arms around me. We Calloways were not ones for physical displays of affection, but I didn't want to be rude, so I awkwardly tried to hug him back with the cookie plate still in my hands.

"I brought you your favorite cookies," I said when he released me.

I held out the plate as proof.

"Don't tell your grandma," he said, taking the plate and giving me a conspiratorial wink. "She thinks all this sugar is making me fat."

He patted his large gut.

"It's not the sugar that's making you fat, it's that chair where you sit all day," my uncle Lonnie said with a laugh. He stood to hug me and I stepped around the coffee table so he could. "It's good to see you, kid," Uncle Lonnie said. "Hank, look who's here."

Uncle Hank gave me a little nod from the foldout table. "Hey there, Charlotte."

"Hi, Uncle Hank," I said.

"There's a spot for you right next to Ryder," Uncle Lonnie said, nodding toward the end of the couch. "Why don't you take a seat and watch the game?"

I settled into the seat on the far end of the couch, near the wall.

"Hey, Ryder," I said. "It's been a while. You grew."

The last time I had seen Ryder, he was five years old, short and scrawny, just a mop of blond curls. He had been a funny kid, this little ball of energy, always cracking jokes and making mischief. Now he was sprawling and lanky; he slouched on the couch and his long legs disappeared underneath the coffee table. He looked tired.

"Yeah," Ryder said without taking his eyes off the TV. "Growth spurt."

"Nice," I said. "I'm still waiting for one of those myself."

Ryder just nodded.

"Prepubescent teenagers, tough crowd," Greyson said, leaning forward a bit and giving me a shrug.

"I'm not prepubescent, asshole," Ryder said.

"Language," Greyson said.

There was another controversial call in the game that got everyone riled up, and then Uncle Lonnie was asking Greyson about

UConn's lineup that year, and I sat quiet and forgotten. I felt like an alien, a stranger. I didn't know what to do with my hands, so I tucked them into the crooks of my elbows. For the hundredth time since I'd walked through the door, I regretted coming here at all.

I glanced at the wood-paneled wall of the den, at all the picture frames that were sporadically lit up by the glare of the television. They were mostly pictures of Hank, Will, Lonnie, and my mother when they were younger. Hank as a lifeguard at the community pool; Will in his Marine Corps uniform at Parris Island; Lonnie on his skateboard; my mother standing on the podium next to a pool in some gymnasium, a "State Champion" sash around her shoulder, her hair still wet, beaming proudly at the camera. There were other pictures of my mother: In one, she had ice cream all over her face and she was laughing, her mouth open so wide it almost looked painful; in another, she was all dressed up for a high school dance in a scarlet dress, her hair pulled back. A young dark-haired man in a suit and tie had his arms around her, pulling her close.

My mother was the only girl; she grew up among a band of brothers. I thought this made her tough. I could tell from looking at the pictures that before she was a teenager, she was kind of a tomboy, always chasing after her brothers, trying to keep up, all skinned knees and dirty palms. When she got older, she became more feminine, with makeup and crop tops and the occasional dress. But I realized looking at these pictures that there had never been anything soft about my mother. That last summer that we spent together, I remembered her with her chin up, shoulders squared, as if she was always looking for a fight.

Around ten o'clock, we all piled into the kitchen around the table. There were too many of us to all fit in the room at once, and so some of us leaned in doorways or stood on tiptoes to see over the crowd from the den. My grandma pulled me to the front of the table. She put her arm around me to keep me there. She had baked a birthday cake for my mother and frosted it herself. "Happy Birth-day, Grace," it said in purple frosting, and two numbered candles, "4" and "3," slouched in the frosting. Everyone sang a discordant chorus of "Happy Birthday," with Lonnie crooning, "How old are you, how old are you, you look like a monkey, and you smell like a zoo," at the end. And then they all looked at me, and my grandma whispered in my ear with her arm still around me, "Blow out the candles, Charlotte."

As they looked at me, I knew they couldn't help but see her. I leaned forward and took a deep breath to put out the candles, and I imagined my mother on a white-sand beach somewhere a world away, doing the exact same thing. Together, we took a breath, and together, we extinguished the flames.

eight
GRACE CALLOWAY

AUGUST 4, 2007
8:48 P.M.

By the time I reached the water, it had started to rain. I walked in up to my waist, the sandy lake bottom giving way beneath my feet; I sank a little deeper with every step I took. The water was still lukewarm, even though the sun had disappeared. I took a deep breath, filled my lungs with air, and dove.

In high school, I could break a minute in the hundred-meter breaststroke. I'd always been a natural swimmer; I felt a strange kinship with the water, which was one reason it was so shocking when my boyfriend Jake drowned in a cold ravine up in northern New Hampshire.

When I heard the news, I didn't say much. Death doesn't make any sense when you're sixteen. Death doesn't make any sense when you're older either. It just becomes a familiar stranger, a presence you've grown used to. But when you're sixteen, you're stubborn enough to demand answers. Death is a dark abyss that you shout down into. You throw rocks into its belly and listen for the echo, trying to figure out its dimensions. But there isn't any knowing.

The next week at school I skipped fifth-period econ and snuck into the high school pool. On the bleachers, I stripped down to my underwear and I jumped into the deep end. I let myself sink, down and down and down.

I wanted to know what it felt like. My heart beat like a drum in my ears. I held my breath until I grew light-headed and my lungs screamed in my chest. I opened my eyes and they burned against the chlorine.

Now I was on top of the water, sprinting across the surface, my breath quick and hard. Bobbing in and out as I worked my way across the lake, out to the raft, and back to shore. Then back to the raft again, until I felt that sweet sense of utter exhaustion fill me. The cuts on my shoulder ached.

It wasn't until my final lap that it happened. As I turned toward the house, the back porch light went out. I was suddenly sheathed in darkness, with only the gentle glow of the moon above me to illuminate my way. The moonlight caught along the water, the edges of the house, and I stared hard into the darkness, trying to make out if there was anything—anyone—there.

Don't be silly, I told myself. Of course there wasn't anyone there. We were all alone out there; there wasn't anyone for miles. The back porch light must have burned out.

But still, some small primal part of me stood on edge. Suddenly, I heard a shrill shriek and my head jerked hard in the direction of the noise. It was coming from the backyard; I saw a dash of movement near the waterline. Something heavy, dark, lumbering. My gut twisted, and I sank down lower in the water, which suddenly felt colder. I shivered, tracking the moving object with my eyes, my heart hammering in my chest.

The shriek came again, and this time I recognized it. It was the metal chain tied to the old elm, and the mysterious object I was so carefully tracking was the tire swing, blowing in the wind. I laughed at myself. There was nothing dark and ominous waiting for me out there. It was just my mind and my nerves playing tricks. There was nothing to be afraid of.

I looked up at the night sky. The rain was coming down harder now; the storm was picking up. I had better head in. I took a deep steadying breath and plunged once again into the water, back toward the house.

CHARLIE CALLOWAY

2017

The next morning I woke up in my mother's old bedroom. It was in the attic of my grandparents' house, with walls that sloped in the middle to the ceiling. Next to the bed was a small circular window that looked out over the driveway and a basketball hoop. I imagined my mother being woken up on Saturday mornings by my uncle Will and uncle Hank playing a game of H-O-R-S-E.

My mother's bedspread was a patchwork quilt that my grandma had made. Next to it was a rocking chair, and a white dresser with a mirror overlooking it, and dozens of pictures stuck into the edges of the mirror. The snapshots were faded now: school pictures of my mother's friends and classmates, a picture of my mother and Claire as teenagers at the boardwalk in Jersey, my mother sitting next to a dark-haired boy on the front porch steps, laughing. There were shelves in the far corner of the room that held rows of trophies and ribbons from my mother's time on the swim team in high school, and an easel and an old smock next to them.

It struck me then that I hadn't known her at all, really. For a long time I had tried to forget her, or to hate her. And before that, she wasn't a person but my mother. She was the woman who braided my wet hair into plaits after my baths. The woman who sat up with me all night when I was sick, feeding me push-up ice pops to ease my sore throat and watching *Wild Hearts Can't Be*

Broken again and again and again until the DVD was scratched and would no longer play. But my mother had been a person before she had been my mother. A person with her own friends, her own likes and dislikes, her own memories and adventures and heartaches. She had lived a whole life before I came along. Maybe if I tried to understand a little bit of that, I could understand why she left.

I figured the best place to start was where Uncle Hank had left off: at the house on Langely Lake. He had found the pictures there, which surely were some kind of clue. I hadn't been to the lake house in years, but maybe if I went back now, saw the place with fresh eyes, I would find something, or maybe I would at least remember something that could be useful.

When I came down to the kitchen, Grandma was at the stove cooking pancakes. There was bacon frying in a skillet. Her smile fell a little when she saw that I was fully dressed and had my overnight bag slung over my shoulder.

"Leaving already?" she asked.

"I thought I'd get an early start," I lied. "I have this big trig exam tomorrow that I still need to study for. But I can stay for breakfast."

"Wonderful," she said. "Pull up a chair and I'll get you a plate."

I sat at the kitchen table as she made up a plate of bacon and eggs and pancakes and sat down next to me with a cup of coffee to watch me eat.

"Your grandpa is having a bit of a lie-in," she said with an exasperated smile. "The man's seventy-five and doesn't know his own limits."

"Is that bacon I smell?"

I looked up to see Uncle Hank wandering in from the den, in the same jeans and rumpled plaid button-up he'd been wearing the night before. He was suffering from a serious case of bedhead.

"Speaking of children who don't know how to grow up," Grandma Fairchild said.

I didn't really want to be around my uncle Hank, and I was a little afraid of what might happen if my grandma left the room for any reason and Uncle Hank got me alone. Would he start in again with the questions and his theories? So I ate my pancakes quickly, before he had the chance.

When I went to stack my plate in the sink, I noticed piles of washed Tupperware containers on the counter. Each pile had a little sticky note with a name on it, and I saw one with Claire's name. I hadn't had a chance to really talk to Claire last night at the party, but if I could get her alone, probe her a little, maybe she could give me some insight into the photos that Uncle Hank had found, among other things.

"Hey, Grandma," I said. "Do you want me to drop these by Claire's? It's on my way."

"Are you sure you remember where it is?" she asked. "I'll jot down the address for you, just in case."

She wrote the address down on another sticky note and hugged me a little longer than was comfortable in the doorway.

"Don't let it be another year before you come by again," she said. "It was good—so good—to have you here."

When she pulled away, I could see there were tears in her eyes. She turned her head to try to hide them.

The Rhodeses lived in a blue two-story house on Maple Street. There was a green hatchback in the driveway when I pulled up. I stood on the front porch and rang the doorbell with the Tupperware containers stacked in my arms.

Greyson answered the door. He was wearing jeans and a light V-neck T-shirt. His hair was still wet from the shower. He smelled like citrus and nutmeg.

"Martha Stewart, nice to see you again," he said.

"Is Claire here?" I asked. "My grandma just wanted me to drop these off on my way out of town."

But Greyson didn't reach for them. Instead he held the screen door open for me and motioned for me to come inside.

"She took the boys swimming," he said. "It's a rare quiet and peaceful morning in the Rhodes house."

I tried to hide my disappointment.

"Oh," I said. "Well, do you know when she might be back?"

"It'll probably be a couple hours," he said. "Come on in."

I didn't know what else to do so I followed him inside to the kitchen.

"You can just set those on the counter there," Greyson said. "I'll put them away later."

He opened the fridge and ducked his head in. "Want a soda or something to drink?"

"No, thanks," I said. "I've actually got to get going. I have this philosophy test tomorrow I need to study for."

"Philosophy, huh?" Greyson said as he took a drink from his water bottle. "Who are you studying? Aristotle? Descartes? Nietzsche?"

Shit. "Um, Foucault actually."

"Oh, I wrote a paper on Foucault's theory of panopticism," he said, yawning and stretching his hands over his head. I tried to ignore the way his shirt rode up and exposed his tight, muscled abs.

"Right," I said, swallowing the lump that had risen into my throat. What was wrong with me? I averted my gaze. "Panopticism— that's what I have to write my paper on," I said.

Greyson narrowed his eyes at me. "I thought you said you had to study for an exam."

Shit.

"Yeah, well, the exam is a paper. But I need to study up a little to write it," I said.

Take that, jerk-off.

He was smiling at me now.

"What?" I asked.

"You're up to something," he said. "You're doing that thing where you scrunch up your face like you're concentrating really hard or something. It's the same face you made that time I was babysitting you and you and Ryder disappeared together and when you came back and I asked you what you were up to you said, 'Nothing,' but then I went upstairs to find you had TP'd my bedroom."

"Yeah, well, maybe someone should have been paying a little more attention to babysitting than playing Donkey Kong on his Nintendo."

"I was on level nine. I was about to save the princess."

"Whatever," I said. "I really have to get going."

"To write your paper on Kant's theory of panopticism?"

"Yes, to write my paper on Kant's theory of panopticism."

"Nice try, but panopticism was Foucault's theory, not Kant's," Greyson said.

Shit.

"See, this is why I need to study," I said.

"Charlotte, just tell me what you're up to."

I sighed. "Fine," I said. "But you can't tell Claire."

"Perfect. My favorite things to do are the things I can't tell my mother about," Greyson said with a smile.

"What are you even doing here anyways?" I asked. "Didn't you just graduate from college? Shouldn't you be out there in the real world like a grown man?"

Greyson picked up an apple from the fruit bowl on the counter. He took a bite and answered me with his mouth full. "I did graduate," he said. "I even have a grown-up job. But it's hard to beat free rent and home-cooked meals."

I rolled my eyes. "So, basically, you're a man-child?"

"Not all of us have trust funds," Greyson said.

I only shrugged in response. I never felt ashamed when people brought up that I came from money I didn't earn, just as I never thought people who didn't come from money should be ashamed of the fact that they didn't have it. In my mind, you were dealt the cards you were dealt, but it was how you played them that mattered.

"Actually, do you have a flashlight I can borrow?"

"You can borrow it if I can come with you," Greyson said.

"Fine," I said. "Meet me in the car. You have two minutes, and then I'm leaving with or without you."

In the car on the way to the lake house, I told Greyson about the pictures Uncle Hank had found. It was actually nice to tell someone about them, and Greyson was the perfect audience. He knew enough about my mother and me and my family not to need a lot of background, but he was also as impartial a party as I could find. It was probably a good idea to have someone come with me to the lake house, anyway. I was a little nervous about going there by myself. And it was better to have two pairs of eyes. There was a better chance we would find something.

"How are we going to get in?" Greyson asked when I told him where we were going. "Is this a breaking-and-entering situation? And is it really considered breaking and entering if it's your own place? Should I google this?"

He smiled at me and ran his hand haphazardly through his hair again.

"Stop doing that," I said.

"Doing what?"

I exaggerated running my hand through my hair and flipping it over my shoulder. "That," I said.

Greyson laughed. "I'm sorry, am I distracting you with my beautiful man mane?"

"Hardly," I said. "And don't google it. Uncle Hank found a way in, and he didn't have a key. We'll figure it out."

I signaled right and we started down the long winding driveway to the house. From the outside, the house looked just as we had left it years ago. My father had hired a groundskeeper to look after the property and you couldn't tell from the outside that the house was unlived in. The lawn was neatly mown, the flower beds weeded, the bushes trimmed.

Getting in was a lot less difficult or even interesting than Greyson or I had imagined. The spare key was where we had hidden it when I was a kid: in the frog statue by the back kitchen door.

Inside, the house looked dark and forlorn: the floorboards were coated with a thick layer of dust, the curtains were drawn tight, and the furniture was sheathed in large white sheets. It would have been bright enough to see if we had drawn back the curtains, but we opted to keep them closed and used our flashlights instead.

The pictures still hung in their places on the walls. There was a picture of my mother at the Jersey Shore. She was dressed in a red bathing suit, standing ankle-deep in the water. She looked over her shoulder at whoever was taking the picture (my father?) and smiled, as if they'd caught her in some private moment. It struck me how young my mother was in some of these pictures—perhaps only a few years older than I was now. And the resemblance between us was striking—the same wide gray eyes and heart-shaped face. The same dark brown hair and pale skin. She had the same slightly crooked smile, the same dimple that peeked out of her right cheek.

There were so many pictures. Pictures of my mother and father in Grandmother Eugenia's garden at the Greenwich house, pictures of my sister and me playing in the Fairchilds' backyard on my mother's old swing set. A candid shot of my father holding my mother in his arms and her looking up at him. Snapshots of who my family used to be.

Hanging next to these pictures was a family portrait in a heavy gilt frame. Seraphina was only a baby, and she was sitting in my mother's lap. I stood beside her, in front of my father, Alistair Calloway. He was tall and lean and handsome in that Calloway way, with his blue eyes and blond hair and high forehead. It was strange, but except for his hair, which was now graying at the temples, he looked the same now as he did then, as if he hadn't aged a day.

"It was the one reckless thing my father ever did," I said. "Marrying my mother."

"How'd they even meet?" Greyson asked, and it was a fair question.

"They met in the ballroom of the Carlyle Hotel," I said. I'd been told this story a hundred times. "At some benefit my grandparents were hosting. My father was working at the Calloway Group. My mother was twenty-two."

"So Grace was what—like, a cocktail waitress at the party?"

"No," I said, glaring at him.

"What?" Greyson said. "There's nothing wrong with being a cocktail waitress."

I glanced back at the portrait of my mother on the wall—how elegant she looked there, how happy. It had never occurred to me as a child to ask what my mother had been doing in the ballroom of the Carlyle Hotel. In my mind, she appeared in a ball gown and my father danced with her, swept her off her feet. But now, I had to admit her presence there seemed strange.

"Your father always kind of scared me," Greyson said, staring up at the picture. "I mean, he's kind of an intimidating guy."

I didn't say anything. I remembered the night after my mother left. My father had gone to the police station to file a report.

Grandma Fairchild came over to stay with us. She fell asleep in the upstairs guest bedroom. Late in the night, Seraphina climbed into my bed crying, and I didn't want to wake our grandma. I was seven, and I was the big sister, and I wanted to help.

"Don't cry," I told Seraphina. "We'll build a fort and we'll crawl into it, away from it all."

We stripped the sheets and pillows from our beds, pulled the cushions from the couches in the downstairs living room. We raided the linen closet, collected fluffy bath towels and thick down comforters and kitchen tablecloths. We draped them over chairs and lamps and tables, Scotch-taped their ends to the walls, and secured them in the edges of doorways—through the living room, the dining room, the upstairs hall. With a flashlight, we crawled through the labyrinth of passageways we had created, naming the rooms and their purposes, and we fell asleep tucked into the space between the coffee table and the couch in the downstairs study.

Sometime in the night, our father came home. I heard the creak of the front door opening, and I saw, through the thin curtain of the sheet draped overhead, a light turn on. I heard my father's expletives from the front hall, heard him call our names, heard the ripping of tape from the walls, the sharp edges of chairs biting into the hardwood floor as they were overturned.

"Go," I whispered to my sister. "Go, go, go."

Go where, I didn't know. But we crawled, one after another, through the living room, as the soft ceilings of our fortress fell around us. The wood floor was hard and unforgiving under the bare knobs of our knees, the heels of our hands. I led the way into the dining room, took refuge under the big oak table.

He found Seraphina first. Pulled her from underneath the dining room table by her ankle—I saw it all. He sat down not four feet from me, pulled her onto his lap, tugged her pajama bottoms down to her thighs. I heard the sharp slap of his hand against her bare bottom. Once, twice, a third time. My sister was staring right at me, her face red and puckered, her eyes dripping and wet. She wailed, but she didn't call out my name, didn't give me away.

I scooted back farther under the depths of the dining room table. I covered my mouth with both hands, tucked my fingers into my lips so that he couldn't hear me breathe, couldn't hear my dry gasps for air.

Now I looked up at the portrait of my father, tall and smiling, his arm around my mother.

"I guess he wasn't around that much, right?" Greyson said.

"He was around," I said.

"Huh," Greyson said. "I just don't remember seeing him that much, is all."

"Well, it's not like you were here all the time," I said.

"Sure, I guess," Greyson said.

When we reached the second-floor landing, I didn't turn right and go to my old bedroom. I knew what I would find there; I could navigate it with my eyes closed even after all these years: the giant bay window looking out onto the lake, the pale pink walls, the twin canopied beds where Seraphina and I slept, my old dollhouse in the corner. Instead, I turned left and headed to my parents' room on the other end of the house. The door was closed but not locked. It was dark inside, the dying light of the day filtering in through the cracks in the curtains. I threw the curtains open and coughed at the waves of dust that unfurled themselves from the window dressings.

My mother's vanity was draped in sheets, but I brushed them off and sat in her chair, just as I had when I was a little girl and I would play with her makeup. I opened her jewelry box and started going through the velvet cases. There were so many—all gifts from my father, I presumed. A pearl necklace for her birthday, diamond earrings for an anniversary, a sapphire ring on the day of my birth, a platinum tennis bracelet for Valentine's Day.

I wondered why my mother hadn't taken any of her jewelry with her. When she left, her SUV was still parked in the front driveway; her purse with her keys, wallet, and phone was sitting on her bedroom bureau. It took days before anybody noticed her luggage was missing—two paisley-print suitcases that she normally used to cart her belongings back and forth between the city and the lake house. Some of her things were missing too—her toothbrush, her comb, her favorite summer dresses, a pair of sandals. It bothered me at first, trying to figure out the importance of what she had left behind and what she had chosen to take with her. And then the investigator found the bank tapes and it all made sense: my mother hadn't wanted to take anything that would be missed, anything remotely traceable. She didn't want to be found.

I remembered there was a rip in the inner lining of one of the suitcases. Seraphina and I had found it once while packing, and we thought it was special, like a secret compartment. We used to keep little things in there when we were traveling, our most prized possessions. That summer, Seraphina had stored one of her horse figurines in there, and I had stowed away the bracelet my father had gotten me on a business trip to Barcelona. As a little girl, I would sometimes lie in bed awake at night and imagine my mother, wherever she was, unpacking her things and discovering the treasures that Seraphina and I had hidden there. A part of me liked knowing that my mother carried a piece of us with her. I wondered if they brought her some small comfort.

In the bottom drawer of the jewelry box, I came across a worn drawstring pouch. Inside I found a cheap gold necklace with a crab pendant. The body of the crab was a fake ruby and the claws were clutching artificial diamonds. I remembered my mother wearing this necklace often. It had been one of her favorites; she wore it almost every day. I had always assumed my father had given it to her, but under closer inspection, I realized how inexpensive it was, the gold chain faded, the fake ruby cloudy and plastic. This definitely was not a gift from my father. I wondered why she had worn it so often, and why she kept it in her jewelry box with all her good jewelry. I didn't know why, but something made me take it. I slipped the pouch into my pocket.

"Hey, what are you doing in here?"

I turned around on the vanity seat and saw a man in coveralls standing in the doorway, a flashlight in his hand. Greyson froze where he was in my parents' walk-in closet.

"This is my house," I said. "What are *you* doing in here?"

"I'm calling the police," the man said as he took a phone out of his pocket and started dialing. He pointed a finger at me. "I saw you take something from that jewelry box. You better put it back."

"Hey, man, this is Charlotte Calloway, all right?" Greyson said as he stepped out of the closet and came to stand by my side. "Her dad owns this place. He's the one who pays your bills. It's probably best not to piss him off by calling the police on his daughter."

The man hesitated. "You're Mr. Calloway's daughter?"

"Yes," I said. "And I can prove it."

I fished my driver's license out of my purse and held it out to him. He came toward me and picked it up, squinting at the name and the picture and then back at me.

"Your turn," I said when he handed my license back. "Who are you?"

"Frankie Martin," he said, running a hand along the back of his neck. "I've been keeping up the grounds here for half a decade. The first time I've ever actually been inside, though. No one told me anyone was coming up to the house today."

He was still squinting at me like he wasn't sure I should be there.

"Look, you or I can give my father a call if you really want," I said, and I reached into my purse and held up my phone for emphasis. "But he's in Aruba on business and I can tell you he's not going to be very happy to be bothered." I pulled up my father in my contacts and hovered my thumb over the "call" button.

My father wasn't in Aruba. It was Sunday and he was either at home in the city or on the golf course with my grandfather. But I really didn't want to explain to him why I was at the lake house.

"No, no, that's all right," the man said, scratching the back of his neck again. "Just be sure you lock up when you leave. It will be my ass on the line if you leave a door unlocked and someone gets in here."

"Will do," Greyson said.

After Mr. Martin left, Greyson and I combed the house methodically, room by room, but it was impossible to search every nook and cranny. When it started to get dark out, we agreed it was time to leave.

"I'll drop you off on my way out of town," I said.

"Thanks," Greyson said.

I paused. I had never gotten to have that conversation with Claire.

"Actually, I'm kind of hungry," I said. I glanced sidelong at him. "Do you think Claire would mind if I stayed for dinner?"

"The more the merrier," Greyson said, leaning forward to adjust the air-conditioning. "And lucky you, Sunday night is sloppy joe night."

"Oh boy," I said.

At dinner, Nolan, the youngest, recounted jumping off the high board at the community pool, and Ryder grunted one-word answers any time he was asked a question. When we were done eating, I stayed to help Claire with the dishes as Greyson took Nolan upstairs for his bath and Ryder ambled away to play video games in his room.

"So, what were you and Greyson up to today?" Claire asked as she filled the sink with hot water. Steam peeled off the edges of the sink. "Please tell me he didn't hold you captive in the den watching football all day."

"No," I said. "We were out, mostly. He took me to Mandy's Ice Cream Parlor on Third. We took a little walk around the park."

Shit. Was Mandy's still there? I hadn't been there since I was . . . like, seven. I peeked a glance at Claire to see if my lie had landed. She was nodding and reaching for the soap.

"Thanks," Claire said. "For getting Greyson out of the house for a bit, getting his mind off things. He really needed that."

Getting Greyson out of the house? Getting his mind off things? What, did Greyson not have friends or something? I mean, I guess it wasn't that surprising. He was kind of obnoxious even if he was sort of cute.

"Um, yeah, sure," I said.

"And I wanted to thank you for coming to your grandparents' party for your mom the other night," Claire said. "I know it meant a lot to them to have you there."

"Yeah," I said. "It was . . . nice . . . to be there. To be a part of it."

"Hand me that plate, will you?" Claire asked, and I handed her the first dirty plate off the stack on the counter.

"Claire, speaking of my mother," I said.

"Yeah?"

"Well, I was wondering . . ." I hesitated. "I don't know, it's just that, from everything you told me the other night about my mother, she seemed like a free spirit. Do you think maybe she got tired of being tied down? Maybe she wanted to make a clean break, you know? It's not impossible, right? Do you think that's why she left?"

Claire was quiet for a moment as she scrubbed the plate with soapy water. Then she set it down in the sink and turned off the running faucet. She turned to face me, her hands still red and wet from the hot water.

"Your mother didn't leave you and Seraphina, Charlotte," she said. "I knew your mother better than anyone and she would never have done something like that."

"So she never mentioned leaving?" I asked. "Like even hypothetically? She never wanted something different?"

Claire chewed on her bottom lip as if she were having some internal debate.

"Claire," I said. "Please."

She sighed and looked at me. "Your mother always tried to keep this from you and Seraphina, but she and your father used to fight."

"I know," I said. "I saw them."

"This was different, Charlotte," Claire said. "Not just arguments. It got physical."

"Are you saying . . . are you saying my father used to hit her?" I asked. My stomach clenched and I felt dizzy. No. No. I shouldn't have been asking these questions. I didn't want to know this.

"I believe he did, yes," Claire said.

"You believe he did, or you *know* he did?"

"Your mother was very protective of your father and their relationship," Claire said. She reached for a towel and dried her hands. "She didn't want people to know that they weren't happy. There was this one fight, a few days before she disappeared, that got worse than the others. Grace showed up at my place one night with bruises up and down the left side of her body and a gaping cut a few inches wide on her shoulder. I bandaged her up myself."

"My father did that to her?"

When I reached for the counter to steady myself, I realized my hands were shaking.

"Grace told me her version of events," Claire said. "There was a disagreement. Things got heated. She said she fell."

"So it was an accident," I said. People fight. People lose their tempers. Accidents happen.

It didn't make sense. None of this made sense. Claire had gotten the story wrong, somehow. If something like that had happened, I would have known.

"He would never do something like that," I said again. "He wouldn't."

"Grace—she was an outsider," Claire said. "She didn't come from their world. She wasn't one of them. They always treated her like she didn't belong. They were cold—his whole family was cold to her."

"That's not true," I said, because it wasn't. I would have known. "My father loved her."

"Maybe so," Claire said. "I know he used to, in the beginning anyway."

It had been stupid of me to start this line of questioning, because what did Claire know about my parents' relationship? She hadn't really been there; she hadn't really seen anything. Not the way my mother would perch on her tiptoes so she could reach to straighten my father's tie before he left for work. Not the way my father slid his hands into the back pockets of my mother's blue jeans as she grilled the potatoes on the back patio, the way she leaned into him. If Claire had seen the things I saw, she wouldn't ever be able to believe my father would raise a hand against my mother. He loved her. He loved her. And it ruined him.

"So, even though you believe all of that—that my mother was unloved, mistreated, and physically beaten—you still think she didn't leave us?" I asked.

"When I found out about the safety-deposit boxes, I wasn't shocked," Claire said. "If you ask me, she withdrew all that money with the intention of leaving your father, but she was going to take you and Seraphina with her, start a new life."

"So then why didn't she?" I asked.

"Because Alistair Calloway isn't a man you just leave," Claire said. "Especially when you're a working-class girl from Hillsborough. I think he found out what she was planning. He found out and—well, he punished her for it. He made it so she could never leave."

Her words turned me to ice. She was no better than Uncle Hank with her crazy theories. No, she was worse than Uncle Hank, because she said it out of jealousy. She hated my father. She was jealous of the way my mother had loved him.

"They may not have found Grace's body when they searched the woods or dragged the lake," Claire said. "No, Alistair is too smart for that. But somewhere, your mother's still out there, waiting to be found. And when we find her, he won't be able to hide what he did anymore. The whole world will know what he is."

"You're a liar," I said. "You're lying. Why don't you just tell the truth? I saw you. I saw you that night with my mother by the lake."

I had never told anyone that. Not the police when they did their initial investigation, or my father, or even Uncle Hank. I had told them everything but that.

There had been a storm the night my mother disappeared, I remembered. The whole day, the sky had been gray and dull, the clouds heavy. My parents had a fight late in the afternoon; my father left. Around seven thirty, my mother put Seraphina and me to bed in the room we shared on the second floor, and then she went out back to take her nightly swim in the lake, a towel tossed over her shoulder, a rubber cap concealing her hair. I fell asleep but woke to rain slicking the windowpanes. I had the distinct memory in my dream of my mother calling out to me. I got up and went to the window. And I saw them, down in the water, my mother, and her—Claire.

Claire was facing my mother, so her back was to me, but I recognized her familiar blond hair, tied up in a knot at the back of her head. I didn't think it was strange that she was there. She and my mother were constantly together and it was not unusual for the two of them to sit out back on the screened-in porch on an evening like that, and drink a glass of wine. But there was something in the way they were holding each other—how desperately they clung to one another in the water—that made me look away, embarrassed. I felt something twist in my gut.

It didn't mean anything, I told myself, the way they were holding each other. My mother loved my father. She loved him. She had screamed, and he had left, but she hadn't really meant it. I knew she hadn't meant it. I climbed back into bed.

In the morning, I woke to see that the storm had ravaged the yard—tree branches littered the back lawn—and had whipped the lake into a placid pane of glass. I got up and padded down the hallway to my parents' room, looking for my mother, but she wasn't there. Her bed hadn't been slept in.

"I saw the two of you together that night," I said. "I saw you in the lake. I know that you and my mother . . . you weren't just friends."

Claire leaned back against the sink as if she needed its support to keep upright. "Charlotte," she said, "I honestly don't know what you're talking about."

"You don't need to lie to me," I said. "I'm not going to tell anyone. I just need to know."

"The last time I saw your mother was a few days before," Claire said. "I never came to the house that night."

"Just tell me the truth," I said. "Please. Tell me what you were doing there. Tell me what the pictures meant."

"What pictures?" Claire asked.

"You know," I said. "I know you know."

"Charlotte," Claire said, "I don't know what you saw that night— or who you saw—but whoever it was, it wasn't me."

She reached out as if to comfort me, and I took a step back. My hand knocked against a glass on the counter and it fell to the floor and shattered.

"Charlotte," Claire said.

"I have to go," I said.

I blindly grabbed my purse from the table and stumbled toward the front door. I was in my car and backing down the driveway before I really registered what was happening.

Claire was lying; she had to be lying.

Only, the thing was, I wasn't so sure she *was* lying.

part two

ten
ALISTAIR CALLOWAY

FALL 1996

Every November, between Halloween and Thanksgiving, my family hosted a charity ball at the Carlyle Hotel. All proceeds went to whatever obscure and ridiculous cause my sister Olivia picked out. One year we raised money for the United States Flora Ethics Committee, which was fighting for a Bill of Rights for plants. Olivia believed that broccoli should have rights, too. The food that year was awful—seven courses of wild-caught herbs and vegetables and chicken, and wine made of grapes that had been "humanely" fermented. Another year, we raised money for prosthetics for three-legged dogs. But the cause du jour was just a front, because there was only one cause the great Calloways had ever really believed in, the only thing that we took great pains to raise awareness of: ourselves.

As usual, I arrived promptly at eight o'clock, clean-shaven, dressed sharply in a suit, my fiancée Margot Whittaker on my arm. I looked around for my younger brother, Teddy, who wasn't there. Teddy was, as usual, not prompt, and would probably arrive after the main course had been served, with a thick stubble on his chin, and dressed in some sort of calculatedly inappropriate attire like a Tommy Bahama shirt and flip-flops, despite the weather. Teddy's eternal quest in life was to push the limits of my father's patience and my mother's blind adoration. My father had very little patience to begin with and would have disinherited Teddy years ago if it were not for my mother, but Teddy had yet to bottom out on the depths of her love for him.

As usual, Eugenia had spared no expense (Eugenia was my mother, and I had always called her Eugenia, even as a child, because she felt the term "mother" prematurely aged her). The pale violet orchids in the centerpieces had been flown in from Bogotá; the wines were from a cellar in Tuscany; the steaks that would be served during the main course had been dry-aged in the finest butcher's cellar in the city for the past three weeks. And no detail was overlooked. The tablecloths were starched and pressed, the water glasses were set exactly one inch from the tip of the dinner knives; Eugenia had gotten out a ruler to check the measurements herself.

"Alistair, you look dashing," Eugenia said, greeting me with a kiss on both cheeks.

Eugenia had always been coolly indifferent toward me. I think she found it boring that I was always where I was supposed to be, doing what I was supposed to do. She didn't have to scold me, or worry about me, or coddle me like Olivia and Teddy. But I was my father's favorite. He found Olivia foolish and frivolous and Teddy unruly and rebellious. I was always there, a quick study and duty-bound to prove myself, and so my father put me through the fire again and again and again, molding me into a man whom he'd find worthy of being handed the Calloway legacy one day.

"Margot, dear," Eugenia said, "you're here."

Eugenia was severely disappointed that I had chosen to marry a girl who was not pretty, flighty, or rich. In short, that I had not chosen someone more like her. And she was annoyed that I had given Margot the family ring: an eighteen-carat flawless emerald-cut canary diamond, flanked by two half-moon-cut diamonds on a platinum band. The ring had belonged to my grandmother. My mother had her eye on it for Teddy, but my grandmother had bequeathed it to me in her will, and I had given it to Margot. Ever since, my mother had been a complete bitch to Margot, hoping to scare her off, and Margot always responded with a smile, not retreating an inch.

"Eugenia, it's lovely to see you," Margot said without a hint of sarcasm. "You must tell me who you're wearing. That dress is stunning."

"Oh, I would, dear," Eugenia responded to Margot, and I knew then that the reply would not be nice, because "dear" was not a term of endearment with Eugenia. Whenever I heard my mother say this I heard "pond scum" or "white trash" in its place, because that's what she really meant, but those weren't terms one could use in polite company. "But you probably wouldn't be familiar, since you're not knowledgeable about fashion. Your dress is tolerable. Did Alistair pick that out for you?"

"Yes, it was a gift," Margot said.

"It's Versace," I said. "From their fall line. I thought you would approve."

"Maybe on a different frame," Eugenia said, eyeing Margot up and down while she took a sip from her wineglass. "Yes, a different frame would elevate it."

I opened my mouth to respond, but Margot put her hand on my arm.

"I'm parched," Margot said. "Let's get a drink, shall we? It was a pleasure talking to you, Eugenia. We'll catch up more later."

My mother smiled wanly at us as Margot steered me across the room.

"You let her get to you," Margot whispered disapprovingly to me.

"How can you *not* let her get to you?" I whispered back.

Margot shrugged. "Because I have nothing to gain from that. And it's amusing to me. It's a little game I'm playing. The nastier she is, the sweeter I'll be. I'll break her down eventually. One day, she'll leave me her shares in the Calloway Group, and I'll know I've won. I'm going to make that bitch love me."

"Eugenia doesn't love anybody—except herself and Teddy."

"Yeah, how do you think Teddy managed that exactly?" Margot asked, taking two wineglasses from the tray proffered by a waiter and handing me one.

"He's a wounded little bird," I said, taking the glass. "He's broken, and so Eugenia feels the need to fix him."

"Interesting," Margot said, and I could practically see the gears clicking in her head as she formulated some plan. "I never thought weakness could be perceived as desirable. I can use that."

I took a sip from my wineglass and glanced at my fiancée. Margot was a mosaic of strong, distinctive features all warring with one another for prominence: a tall forehead, a sharp chin, high cheekbones. If she'd had only one of these features she might have been quite striking, but the effect of all of them together was that they washed each other out, making her rather plain.

Plain girls have always interested me more than pretty girls. Pretty girls have never had to work for anything, but the plain ones, they've been working at everything their whole lives. They've had to make people notice them. They've had to work at being funny, or being smart, or being daring. The pretty ones, they just sit there and smile at you and are either so damn nice and so damn agreeable all the time that you want to pull them aside and tell them some ugly truth to wipe that stupid smile off their faces, or they're so damn disagreeable and hard to please that you want to knock them around a little bit, remind them that they bruise and break just as easily as anybody else.

Margot was smart. That was the thing she had chosen to work at. And not just book smart—though she was that, too. She was in her first year of medical school at Columbia. But she was also streetsmart. She was ambitious, and cunning, and manipulative as hell. In truth, I was 99 percent sure Margot was a sociopath, or at the very least, she displayed strong sociopathic tendencies. That was one of the things that connected me most to her. I had been raised by a sociopath (my father) and a narcissist (my mother), so at the very least, it felt familiar.

Having strong sociopathic tendencies was practically a prerequisite to exist in my world. "Normal" people (a.k.a. weak-willed pansies) could talk about how having a conscience was what made us human, but to me, a conscience was a whiny little bitch voice I liked to hit the mute button on. A conscience wasn't going to run a successful billion-dollar real estate company. It couldn't make the hard cost-cutting decisions; it couldn't fire Monica, the single mom with three kids at home, or Jerry, the guy whose wife had stage-three breast cancer, when that's what was best for the bottom line. A sociopath could smile and ask Monica about her kids in the break room and nod consolingly as Jerry nearly lost his shit recounting how the doctor said the last treatment didn't take, and then turn around and tell Monica and Jerry that they needed to box up their offices and ship out because they hadn't been meeting their sales goals and they were trying to run a business here. A sociopath didn't lose sleep over how Monica was going to pay her kids' orthodontist bills that month, or how Jerry and his wife were going to manage without health insurance.

Here it was plain and simple: a conscience would strangle you. Normal people could have their sensitivity and vulnerability and *feelings* and live their pretty little lives, but that was all they were ever going to be. Normal. Average. And I'd never wanted to be average. I was a Calloway. I wasn't born and bred and raised to be average. I didn't see the appeal. I'd had the average beat and starved out of me, and I was better for it, stronger.

Margot put a hand on my arm. She was staring across the room, back toward the entrance.

"That little shit," she said. "What game do you think he's playing now?"

I turned and followed her gaze. To my astonishment, there was Teddy. Not only was he practically on time, but he was wearing a suit; his hair was neatly cut and gelled, and on his arm, he had a respectable-looking date: some dark-haired beauty wearing a simple satin off-the-shoulder gown with a sweetheart neckline. Nothing gaudy or loud. Nothing that screamed for attention. So unlike the leggy blond dates in tight, low-cut gowns that Teddy normally brought to family functions.

"What's his angle—being all punctual and parading around some boring prude?" Margot asked, narrowing her eyes at Teddy and his date as we watched my mother gleefully embrace them both.

I downed my wine. "I don't know, but I'm going to find out," I said, handing Margot my empty glass.

I started off across the room toward my brother.

My deepest fear was that one day Teddy would get his shit together and try to prove himself to our father. That he would somehow weasel his way into managing the Calloway Group even though it had been me busting my balls all these years. It had been me who had graduated first in my class at Knollwood Augustus Prep. It had been me who had graduated summa cum laude from Columbia. Me, again, who had spent every summer interning at the Calloway Group, working my ass off in the mailroom like some nobody, because my father believed in learning the company from the ground up. I had kept my nose to the grindstone all these years, while Teddy had partied and done whatever he damn well pleased. He had gotten thrown out of three boarding schools. My parents had had to buy his way into Princeton, and now that he was there, he spent more of his time drinking and taking lavish trips with his friends than in the classroom. It was all a big joke to him, which was how I preferred it. I didn't want him to try, because if he did, I knew he had a huge advantage as my mother's favorite, and that my father would pit us against one another until one of us broke. I was under no delusion that my father favored me for any other reason than that I tried the hardest.

I found my brother by the hors d'oeuvres table, loading up a small plate.

"Slow down," I said. "I know by the time you usually get here, there's only dessert left, but there are actually seven courses to this thing, so you can pace yourself."

"Oh, fuck off," Teddy said.

"Who's the skirt?" I asked.

Teddy peered over his shoulder as he took a bite of his salmon puff.

"Her name's Grace," he said.

I glanced back at the girl, who was still standing by the entrance with my mother, deep in conversation. Grace. The name suited her. It was soft and old-fashioned and Grace did indeed look like an old world beauty, quiet and demure. What was someone like that doing with my brother?

"She doesn't seem like your type," I said.

"What? Leggy? Blond? Easy?"

"Well, yes."

"That's the whole point," Teddy said, popping another salmon puff into his mouth and talking over it as he chewed. "It wouldn't feel so gratifying if there weren't any challenge to it."

"Don't tell me you're still playing that stupid game," I said. "Bingo for Dingoes?"

I was annoyed, but also relieved to hear that Teddy's appearance here, his punctuality, his crisply ironed suit, were all part of a silly game, and one that had nothing to do with me or the Calloway Group.

"It's called the Board of Conquests," Teddy corrected me. "And I'm about to get four in a row."

"Is that right? And what box is Grace checking for you?"

"We've added townies to this round," Teddy said. "I met Grace at the public library."

"What in god's name were you doing in a library?"

"I got lost," Teddy said.

"Every time I've convinced myself you've gone as low as you can go, you find a way to sink to new depths."

Teddy clapped me on the back and smiled. "Well, we're always trying to outdo ourselves, aren't we? It's the Calloway way. Come on, I'll introduce you. I've got this whole 'heart of gold' shtick going. You know, I love my family, we're so close, yadda yadda yadda. You can play the part of doting big brother and help me sell her on it."

"Sounds exhausting, and I'm tired," I said.

Now that I knew what my brother was up to, I was bored. I had no interest in playing his stupid little games.

"What if I make it worth your while?" Teddy asked.

"What were you thinking, exactly?"

Teddy looked as if he were deep in thought. "Next summer when Dad asks me to intern at the office, I'll blow him off. I've got this friend with a boat off the coast of Uruguay. We'll be off the grid for two months at least."

"Let me get this straight," I said. "Your idea of doing me a favor is blowing off a crappy office job to go hang out on a yacht all summer?"

"Or," Teddy said, "I could pull Dad aside right now, have a real heart-to-heart. You know, tell him how I've really been thinking things through lately and how sorry I am for the way I've acted. How I'm going to start taking my classes seriously, and how I'd really like it if I could start learning the ropes at the office."

Most of the time, it seemed like Teddy was a complete idiot, but then there were moments like this, when I knew it was all just an act, and underneath all the feigned laziness and stupidity, he really was one of us: sharp and shrewd and cutthroat. He was a Calloway through and through.

"Fine," I said. "Introduce us."

Teddy slung his arm around me and pulled me over to where Grace and Eugenia stood.

"Grace," Teddy said, "I'd like you to meet Alistair, my brother. He's a Columbia alum; he works at the Calloway Group with our father."

Grace looked at me. There was something about her that seemed familiar, but I couldn't put my finger on it. Her eyes were gray, with swirls of pale yellow. I hadn't been able to tell what color they were from across the room. But up close, they were stunning.

"Nice to meet you," Grace said. "Teddy's told me so much about you."

It took me a moment to realize she had extended her hand in my direction.

"Oh, right," I said, and took her hand. It felt so different from the meaty fists I was used to shaking all day at the office. It was small and warm and fragile in my palm, breakable.

"Alistair, this is Grace Fairchild," Teddy said. "She's a painter."

"Well, not professionally," Grace said. "I've never actually sold any of my paintings."

"A lot of great artists weren't appreciated initially," Teddy said. "Van Gogh, for instance, only sold two paintings in his lifetime, and now his work goes for millions. It's extraordinary, really, how long it can take people to recognize the value of something right in front of them."

He slipped his arm around Grace's slim waist. It bothered me to see how easily he touched her—as if she already belonged to him.

"Yes, well, Teddy finds a lot of things extraordinary," I said. "A suit. A clean shave. Showing up on time. But I guess, to be fair, we all found that extraordinary."

Teddy glared at me.

Shit. Doting older brother. I forgot.

"Would you care to dance?" I asked Grace.

Grace looked like I had taken her by surprise, but she recovered herself quickly. "Sure," she said. "Of course."

She slid out of Teddy's arm and gave me her hand again. Something in my stomach tightened.

I led her out onto the dance floor, past several other couples, so we could no longer see Teddy or my mother.

Grace leaned her head close to my ear and whispered, "So, I'm going to tell you a secret, because you're going to find out in just a moment anyway. But I don't really know how to dance."

I smiled and bent my lips close to her ear. "Your secret is safe with me. Don't worry, just lean into me and I'll lead you through it. No one will be any the wiser."

I took her in my arms then, one hand at the small of her back, the other holding her palm in mine. I drew her close and we danced.

"This isn't so bad," Grace said after a moment. "Thanks for making me look good."

"That's hardly a challenge," I said.

Heat bloomed in Grace's cheeks, but she laughed to cover it. My eye caught on the crab pendant of her necklace, which rested against her throat. I wondered if Teddy had gotten that for her.

"Teddy told me the two of you met in a library," I said. "That's some extraordinarily bad luck you had. The library should have been the one place you'd be safe from a travesty like that."

Grace laughed. "Well, I work there part-time, so I'm there a lot. Painting's really more of a hobby than anything else. I just do it because it makes me happy—I don't really expect it to ever pay the bills."

"So, what's next for you then, if not painting?" I asked.

"To tell you the truth, I'm still trying to figure out what I want to be when I grow up," Grace said. "What about you? Did you always know you wanted to follow in your father's footsteps and take over the family business?"

"I always knew I'd do it," I said with a shrug.

"That's not the same thing," Grace said.

She looked at me, really looked at me, and there was something—*unsettling? comforting?*—in her gaze. She looked at me like she already knew me. Even the parts I hadn't meant to show her, the parts I never showed anyone.

"You're exactly the way he described you," Grace said.

"Teddy?" I asked.

"No, not Teddy," Grace said. "Jake Griffin."

The name struck me, ran through me, like an electric shock. I stopped cold. It was a name I hadn't heard in years.

"I'm sorry," Grace said. "Maybe I shouldn't have said anything. I debated not saying anything, but it seemed strange not to mention it."

I realized I was standing still, so I started to move again, stiffly, with Grace in my arms.

"How did you know Jake?" I asked.

"We were dating when it happened," Grace said. "Before that, we grew up together."

"You're *that* Grace," I said. It clicked then. I knew why Grace seemed so familiar. I hadn't met her before—but I had seen her.

"He talked about me?" Grace asked.

I nodded. "He had this picture of you on his desk in his dorm."

I remembered that picture even now, almost six years later.

Grace was sitting on some front porch steps in a pair of cutoffs and sneakers. It was summertime in the photo and Grace had a half-eaten ice-cream cone in one hand; the rest was smeared all over her nose, her chin, and she was leaning forward, mouth open in laughter. I remembered picking up the frame once, wondering what had made her laugh like that.

"It was this candid shot of you with this ice-cream cone, but there was more ice cream on your face than in the cone," I said.

"Isn't that how you're supposed to do it?"

I wanted to ask her about the picture—about who had taken it and what she had been laughing at at the time—but when I looked up, I saw Teddy standing behind her.

"May I cut in?" he asked.

Grace looked up at me with those wide-set doe eyes.

"Yes," Grace said. "Of course."

I realized I was still holding her even though we had stopped dancing, my hand on the small of her back, my other hand clasping her palm. Reluctantly, I let her go.

I meandered over to the nearest waiter holding a tray of wineglasses and took one, turning my back to the dance floor. I didn't want to watch them together.

Margot found me there.

"So, anything to worry about?" Margot asked.

"What?"

"Teddy and the total Virgin Mary with him?" Margot asked.

"Oh," I said. "No. Just some stupid game he's playing."

"Hm," Margot said. "Typical."

"It's the strangest thing, though," I said.

"What is?"

"The girl—Grace. She used to date Jake Griffin."

My gaze flickered to Margot and then away. I wanted to gauge her reaction.

"Who?" Margot asked. There wasn't a hint of recognition in her eyes. She didn't remember at all.

It was strange that a name that had haunted me for the past six years had such little effect on Margot. There were times when we were lying next to each other at night in the dark, and I'd want to speak that name into the void. I wanted to know if she was thinking about it, too. If it haunted her like it haunted me. If I wasn't alone.

I thought I knew what Margot would say if I told her about the times I couldn't drown out that whiny little voice in the back of my mind, and now, looking at her unaffected reaction to Jake's name, I knew that I was right.

You let it get to you again, she would say disapprovingly.

How can you not let it get to you? I would ask. Because she knew. She had been there that night. *How can you not feel the smallest bit of guilt?*

Because I have nothing to gain from that, she would say.

And she'd be right.

It was weak of me to feel guilt or remorse. It was weak of me to think of it at all.

"You remember, Jake Griffin from Knollwood Prep," I said finally, with a shrug that I hoped would appear indifferent. "The boy who killed himself."

"Oh, Jake," Margot said finally. "Small world, I guess."

"Yeah," I said, because she was right.

I turned and looked back out at the dance floor. I found them there in the middle of it—Teddy with Grace in his arms.

Most of the time the world felt big, boundless, full of possibilities—everything was there for the taking, everything was waiting to be conquered, and Margot and I were poised for the conquering. What was there to be afraid of? What was there holding us back? Nothing could touch us; we wouldn't let it.

But tonight, for the first time in a long time, the world felt small, and I felt small in it.

eleven
CHARLIE CALLOWAY

2017

In trig, I fingered the plastic crab pendant that hung at the base of the necklace I wore around my neck and stared out the window at the trees, which were beginning to redden. Trig was supposed to be a senior class, but I'd always had a head for numbers, for tricky equations, for figuring things out.

That was all this was, I told myself. A tricky equation. My mother's disappearance. The assumption (by some) that my father had killed her. It seemed intimidating when you first looked at it—all those complex differentials and variables. But if you broke it down, part by part, it always made sense in the end—the equation always led to a logical answer.

"Who has the answer?"

I jerked my head away from the window, back toward the dry-erase board at the front of the room. I was playing a dangerous game zoning out in trig. Old Mr. Franklin, or "sir," as he had us address him, was ex-military. He had served in Nam. He believed in hierarchy, in reverence for authority, and in torturing and humiliating any poor soul who couldn't cross-multiply and divide fast enough to come up with the answer when he wanted it.

Trig was the only class at Knollwood Prep, besides Mr. Andrew's Introduction to Photography class, that didn't follow the Harkness method. It was easy to see why—sitting in a circle, teachers and students on the same footing, with students encouraged to speak their minds whenever they felt like it? That flew in the face of everything Mr. Franklin held dear. Instead, our desks were in neat rows, squarely facing the front of the room, and instead of an open discussion, Mr. Franklin spent every class lecturing at us from the dry-erase board, shouting out problems and demanding the correct answers when you'd barely had time to put pen to paper. Here, there was no getting away with thought-provoking, open-ended bullshit answers, because there was always only one answer. So, I shot my hand in the air, even though I hadn't even heard what equation we were supposed to be working out, because the surest way not to get called on in Mr. Franklin's class was to look like you knew the answer. Mr. Franklin always zeroed in on the kid who was feverishly still trying to work out the equation in his notebook, or the kid who was pointedly averting his gaze, praying to the gods that his time had not yet come.

"Mr. Kensington," Mr. Franklin said. "You look like you have the right answer."

Al Kensington didn't look like he had the right answer at all. He looked like Mr. Franklin had just kicked his dog.

"Um, x equals thirty degrees?" Al said.

Mr. Franklin glared at him.

"Sir!" Al said, blushing down to the collar of his shirt. "Sorry, x equals thirty degrees, sir?"

Mr. Franklin held out his dry-erase marker. "Come up here and show us how you got to that answer."

That, of course, meant that Al had gotten it wrong. Mr. Franklin was a firm believer in learning from others' mistakes, so he made sure to make them as public as possible and to walk through the errors, line by line.

Al took his paper and stood, walking unsteadily toward the front of the room, shaking in terror. As he passed Auden Stein's desk—he was the only other junior in the class—Auden brought his balled hand to his mouth and coughed discreetly into it.

"Forty-five," he coughed.

Al stiffened and paused for a moment and then continued forward.

"What was that, Mr. Stein?" Mr. Franklin asked.

"What was what, sir?" Auden asked innocently.

"It sounded like you were trying to give Mr. Kensington a number as he passed by your desk," Mr. Franklin said.

Behind him, at the board, Al was quickly scribbling his work onto the dry-erase board, trying to figure out where he had gone wrong in the equation and make out forty-five before Mr. Franklin returned his attention to him. If Mr. Franklin had been paying attention to Al, he would have seen that he'd started the equation from the end, with the answer, and was working backward.

"No, sir," Auden said.

"I take cheating very seriously," Mr. Franklin said. "I'm sure you're aware of Knollwood Prep's zero-tolerance policy?"

"Yes, sir," Auden said.

"So what was that?"

"What was what, sir?"

At this point, the throbbing vein in Mr. Franklin's forehead looked like it might burst. "What did you say to Mr. Kensington as he passed by your desk?"

"I didn't say anything, sir," Auden said. "I coughed. My mother's always told me I have a funny-sounding cough, that it sounds like I'm saying—"

"Forty-five!" Al shouted, jumping away from the board and lifting his arms in triumph. "Forty-five. The answer is forty-five." He pointed to his work on the board. "You can use a trig identity to get a quadratic in cosine."

Mr. Franklin let out his breath slowly. "Another teachable moment—gone. Mr. Kensington, you may take your seat."

"But I can explain it," Al started, "I understand it now. What you have to do is—"

"Mr. Kensington, take your seat!" Mr. Franklin snapped, and Al drew back as if he had been slapped.

If Auden had been anyone else in the class, Mr. Franklin would have called him to the board and given him an impossible equation to solve in front of all of us. But Auden was too smart—he was some sort of math prodigy—and Mr. Franklin wasn't about to provide Auden with a stage on which he would shine.

"Is this your idea of a practical joke, Mr. Stein?"

I glanced back up toward the front of the room, toward Mr. Franklin, who was squinting at the picture on the edge of his desk like he had never seen it before, when it'd sat there for as long as I could remember. It took me a moment to realize that was *the* picture—the picture one of the A initiates had stolen for their first ticket. The last time I remembered seeing it was at the Ledge a week ago. Had it been on Mr. Franklin's desk this whole time, and if so, what was it doing there? Had the A's returned it? And if they had, what had been the point of taking it in the first place?

"I asked, do you find this amusing, Mr. Stein?" Mr. Franklin repeated himself, a deep fury in his throat.

Everyone turned to look at Auden.

"Do I find what amusing, sir?" Auden asked.

"The defacement of my personal property," Mr. Franklin said. "Is this your idea of a joke?"

Auden shifted in his seat. "I'm sorry, sir, but I'm not sure what you're talking about."

Mr. Franklin turned the picture around so he could see it. At first, I didn't notice anything different about the picture at all—

there was Mr. Franklin in uniform in the Oval Office. There was President Nixon, shaking his hand. I leaned forward in my seat so I could see it better. And then I gasped.

Someone had photoshopped Auden's grinning face onto Mr. Franklin's body. The juxtaposition of those two things—Auden's silly grinning face on Mr. Franklin's stern, uniformed body—was so ridiculous I had to choke back a laugh. In the seat next to me, Sheila Andrews was losing the battle of being discreet, trying to cover her giggles with a coughing fit.

"Sir, I didn't—" Auden said.

"To the headmaster's office this instant, Mr. Stein," Mr. Franklin said, his mouth so tight I barely saw his lips move.

"Sir, that wasn't me," Auden said. "I mean, that is me—in the picture. But I didn't do that."

"Mr. Stein!" Mr. Franklin growled, and the whole class fell silent.

For one long moment, Auden sat and stared at the back of Dalton's head, as if willing him to turn around and look him in the eye. Dalton was sitting in the front row, staring nonchalantly forward, as if nothing interesting were happening at all. Finally, Auden gathered his things and marched out of the room, shutting the door so forcefully in his wake that the wall shuddered.

Mr. Franklin followed him without even bothering to dismiss us. When he was gone, Sheila collapsed forward on her desk, laughing and gulping for air.

"That—was—classic," Sheila said to me.

I almost couldn't hear her over the roar of the room. People were turning around in their desks to talk to one another. There was a buzz of energy, a sense of excitement, which felt foreign to Mr. Franklin's trig class.

"How long do you think Auden's been planning that one?" Sheila asked. "I mean, genius. I wish I had that kind of balls."

I wanted to tell Sheila that she didn't even know the half of it, that she had only gotten part of the joke, and only fourteen students in the whole school would get the full joke—that Auden had been framed, literally and figuratively.

I glanced over at Dalton, who was talking to Crosby. Crosby had a wicked grin on his face. I tried to make out what they were saying, but they were too far away.

The A's had made their first move of the year—a prank that had simultaneously taken everyone's least favorite teacher down a peg and reprimanded the one initiate who had failed to retrieve his first ticket—a prank that everyone on campus, from students to faculty, would be talking about for the next week, and I hadn't been a part of it, hadn't even known it was coming. Why? Why had I been left out? Were any of the initiates involved? After all, we—or at least one of us—had done the heavy lifting. Shouldn't we, at the very least, have been allowed to know what we were stealing the ticket items for?

I tore out a sheet of paper from my notebook, balled it up, and chucked it at the back of Dalton's head. It missed him by a mile. I called out his name but he didn't hear me over the noise of the classroom. I crossed my arms, slouched in my chair, and stared in Dalton and Crosby's direction, willing them to look my way, to give me some kind of clue as to what was going on, but they didn't.

None of us moved from our desks until the bell rang. We were all too nervous to leave in case Mr. Franklin came back and found our desks empty while class was still supposed to be in session. But he didn't return. I should have known then that my annoyance at Dalton and Crosby and the rest of the senior A's was the least of my worries—that a bigger storm was brewing. But I didn't. I spent the rest of class looking idly at the spot on Mr. Franklin's desk where the picture had sat. I couldn't help but wonder how long that picture had been there, waiting for Mr. Franklin to notice. I wondered if it had been there since the morning after the A's meeting, just sitting there like a bomb waiting to explode.

"Knock, knock."

I opened my eyes and craned my neck toward the open door of my dorm room. Leo was standing there, leaning against the door frame. He was still dressed in his football practice jersey, which hung off his tall, muscular frame, and he had his gym bag slung over one shoulder. His blond hair was slicked back with sweat, his cheeks red and heated.

My mind was still groggy with sleep. I must have dozed off while studying. My laptop was warm on my stomach, the screen glowing and the cursor blinking in the middle of a sentence deconstructing Plath's poem "Daddy." I had the USB drive that Dalton had given me with the A's cache of old literature essays from Mrs. Morrison's class. There were several on Plath's *Ariel*, and reading through them and "borrowing" some ideas was definitely making my essay a whole lot easier to write.

"What time is it?" I asked, my voice scratchy. The sky outside was a soft pink, like sherbet.

"Almost five thirty," Leo said, setting his bag down at the end of my bed and sitting.

I nudged him with one of my socked feet. "Don't sit there," I said. "You're all sweaty."

His response to this was to climb onto the bed and spread out next to me.

"Is that lavender I detect?" he asked, smelling my pillow. "'Clean linen' perhaps?"

"Not anymore, thanks," I said, pushing him away.

"I'm so tired," Leo said, yawning and laying his head on my pillow. "Coach had us running suicides for, like, an hour. I could sleep for days."

I turned my head and glanced over at him, hogging the other side of my pillow. He had his eyes closed, and I could see his long, girlish lashes fluttering against his cheekbones as he took slow, measured breaths.

"Hey, don't get too comfortable," I said, giving him a little shove.

His eyelids fluttered open and I saw the bright turquoise of his eyes. He smiled and sat up, running a hand through his trademark Calloway blond hair.

"Did you hear about Auden?" Leo asked.

"I was there when it happened," I said. "We have trig together."

"No—I know that," Leo said. "Did you hear what they found in his room?"

"No," I said. "What?"

"What was left of Mr. Franklin's original photograph," Leo said. "They searched his locker in the field house, too. They found a set of the janitor's keys, the ones that were reported missing last week."

The janitor's keys—another item from the Game. A sour sense of foreboding settled in my stomach.

"The school has him on charges of theft, trespassing, destruction of personal property, and harassment of an instructor," Leo said. "They're saying he's going to be suspended. He's meeting in front of the Student Ethics Board at the end of the week."

I sat up. "Did you know about this?" I asked. The set of the janitor's keys had been Leo's ticket, after all. "Did you know the A's were going to do this?"

"No," Leo said. "They didn't tell me a thing."

"So they're—what—punishing Auden for not showing up? For not playing the Game?" I asked.

Leo shrugged. "Looks like it."

"I never knew that was part of it," I said.

I knew the consequences of snitching on the A's—of giving up their secrets—but I had never suspected that we would be punished for failing to get a ticket item or for quitting the Game. I didn't even know if Auden had actually quit playing or if he had just not been able to get his item in time. Maybe to the A's, it didn't matter either way.

At first, the photograph in Mr. Franklin's room had seemed like a harmless prank—a small slap on the wrist. Maybe Auden would get a few detentions. But the planted janitor's keys? Suspension? The A's were messing with Auden's future, his academic record. And for what reason? It seemed strange, because just last week, Auden had played poker with Dalton and Crosby and me and Leo. He was one of us.

"It's like they're sending a message," Leo said. "Not just to Auden, but to the rest of us."

"Yeah," I said. When it came to the Game, not only could we not get caught, but we couldn't stop playing.

"So I was thinking," Leo said, "that we could form an alliance. When we get our next item, I'll help you with yours and you help me with mine. Double our chances. The first ticket was hard enough, and I have a feeling they're not going to get any easier."

"Sure," I said. "An alliance sounds great."

It was kind of a relief actually, not to be doing this alone, especially when I had this whole thing going on with my mom, and I was doing that alone. I didn't have much of a choice on that front. I couldn't exactly confide in Leo because I knew exactly how he felt about my mother; his was far from an unbiased ear.

I leaned back against my headboard and glanced over at Leo, who was lying on my pillow with his eyes closed. He must have drifted off to sleep.

When we were little, we used to sleep like this—side by side—every night. That was after the fallout with my uncle Hank, when Seraphina and I had gone to live with Uncle Teddy and Aunt Grier for a while. I had my own room on the second floor. It was a lovely room. They let me pick the color of the walls and filled the bookcase with all of my favorite books. But at night, lying there alone in my own bed in the dark, that room felt infinite and I felt infinitely alone. The house made noises I had never heard before—the furnace in the basement groaned and roared; I listened to the horrifying gurgle of the water flowing through the pipes when the upstairs toilet flushed. The darkness began to take on shapes—I was sure that there was something moving behind the mirror of my vanity, behind my bookcase, and I couldn't sleep. Most nights, I would go into Leo's room, crawl under his blue bedspread, and curl up behind him, sticking my cold, bare toes into the warm flesh of his calves, burying my nose in the nape of his neck, curling into him as far as I could get—away from the darkness, away from the noises I did not recognize, away from the terrifying fantasies of my mind. And he always let me. It was the only way I could fall asleep.

"Charlie?" Leo asked softly now, and I jumped. His eyes were still closed. "Can I ask you something?"

"Anything," I said.

"What do you think of Royce Dalton?"

There was something strange about the way he said Dalton's name—maybe it was the way he said his whole name instead of just his last.

"Why?" I asked, suspicious. Had he heard something? Had Dalton asked Leo about me, or told Leo he was interested?

"Just be careful," Leo said. "He's not very nice when it comes to girls. I mean, he's very nice at the beginning—but not at the end. And there's always an end."

"I thought the two of you were friends," I said.

"We are," Leo said. "But that's because we've never dated."

"Ha," I said.

"I'm serious though, Charlie," Leo said, and he opened his eyes to look at me. He was being incredibly earnest, and Leo was rarely earnest. "Promise me you won't date him."

"I won't date him," I said. It was an easy promise to make because 1) I had gone seventeen years without a boyfriend, and it was a streak I didn't intend to break any time soon, and 2) I would have been an idiot to date the womanizing Royce Dalton.

"Good," Leo said, and he closed his eyes again.

We stayed like that for a long time, side by side on my bed, until long after I heard Leo's breath deepen as he drifted off to sleep and I followed close behind him.

In Mrs. Morrison's American Lit class the next afternoon, I was copying down the definitions of "assonance" and "dissonance" off the board when Ren came in with a yellow hall pass and handed it to Mrs. Morrison. Mrs. Morrison glanced at it and then at me.

"Charlie, you're wanted in Headmaster Collins's office," she said.

I froze. My mind went immediately to Nancy's diamond collar. I'd heard through the grapevine that Headmaster Collins had thrown a fit when he'd found out his beloved dog had been robbed. The gardener had torn their yard apart trying to find it, thinking perhaps the collar had merely come loose and fallen off somewhere. Had Headmaster Collins somehow figured out it was me? Had I unknowingly left behind some form of incriminating evidence? Or was Auden behind this? Was he throwing all of the A's under the bus to get himself out of trouble?

"Did Headmaster Collins mention what this is in regard to?" I asked.

Mrs. Morrison glanced at the note, but the reason line must have been blank because she looked at Ren expectantly.

Ren just shrugged. "I just deliver the passes. Headmaster Collins doesn't tell me anything; he *doggedly* preserves students' privacy." She shot me a warning look when she said this that I'm sure Mrs. Morrison didn't notice because she had already returned her attention to the dry-erase board.

Fuck.

I gathered my books, slung my bag over my shoulder, and followed Ren out into the hallway. I was trying to concoct some plausible explanation in my mind for why I would have taken Nancy's collar—preferably one that wouldn't result in my expulsion—when I noticed Darcy leaning against a set of lockers just a few paces away, smiling at me.

"I was just fucking with you, Calloway," Ren said, giving my shoulder a playful nudge. "Headmaster Collins is at a dentist appointment."

"We're breaking you free," Darcy said. "Thought it was high time for a little R & R."

Darcy put her arm around my shoulder as we exited the arts building and steered me left, toward Rosewood Hall.

Some upperclassmen had free periods. Sometimes they would use them as study halls and take up residence in the library; other times they'd serve as an assistant for a semester to one of the faculty. The third option for a free period was to be the runner for the headmaster's office, which meant you got to run errands for the headmaster himself, or sit on the couch outside the headmaster's office and do your homework if it was a particularly slow day. Being a runner was a very coveted position at Knollwood because you literally had a place inside the administration. You knew things that nobody else knew. You delivered the hall passes for students pulled into disciplinary meetings, you caught snippets of conversations with guidance counselors who popped in to air their grievances, and you overheard phone calls between the headmaster and disgruntled parents. Sometimes you'd be asked to pull a student's personal file for the headmaster and of course you weren't supposed to look but sometimes your eyes were bound to stray and stumble upon intimate details of another student's life. Like the fact that Andrea Forrester had once been hospitalized for an eating disorder. Or that Frankie Lewandowski had a DUI. Things that might be useful or interesting to know. Great fodder for dining hall gossip. When you were the runner, you had your finger on the pulse of the school.

This semester, Ren was the runner. I remembered now the pack of stolen hall passes at the last A's meeting, all stamped with Headmaster Collins's signature. It had been one of the other initiates' first ticket item. I guess I was finally starting to reap some of the fun.

The dormitory was empty since it was the middle of the day; the halls felt lonely and forlorn. I followed Ren and Darcy to the end of the hall on the first floor, where all the seniors' rooms were. Ren slid her key card in and held the door open for me.

Ren's room was messy. She was a senior, so she didn't have to share. There was a single bed against the window, unmade, with a plain black Parachute duvet and linens in disarray. There were a chair and desk by the door, and literally every inch of the desk's surface was covered—a clunky hair dryer with its cord snaking off the edge, a silver Miu Miu leather card case, a statistics and probability textbook, a half-drunk bottle of Diet Pepsi. And there were clothes everywhere—hanging from the chair, littering the floor so that it was impossible to walk without stepping on something.

"God, you're such a slob," Darcy said as if it were an endearing quality.

"There's an order to my madness," Ren said. She leaned down and removed what looked like a cosmetics case from underneath a pile of T-shirts. She sat on her bed and opened it; inside was a grinder, an eighth of weed in a little baggie, and a vape pen.

"Make yourself at home," Darcy told me as she shut Ren's door and took a seat on the other end of Ren's bed.

I found a beanbag chair buried under some discarded blue jeans, so I cleared it off and sat. Darcy tossed me the latest issue of *Cosmo* from a stack of magazines on Ren's nightstand and I absently thumbed through it, my eyes sliding over the glossy images and article titles: "Choosing the Perfect Lip Gloss for Your Skin Tone," "5 Tricks to Try in Bed That Will Blow His Mind," "The Absolute Must-Have Trends This Fall."

I'd never had an easy time making girlfriends. I didn't particularly like the things a lot of girls liked—I didn't care for makeup or make a big deal about clothes and shopping; I'd never had a boyfriend. But, more than that, it was that girlfriends took a lot of work. When I hung out with boys like Leo, everything was refreshingly easy and transparent. You played video games or cards or whatever, and sure, boys could be crass or give each other a hard time, but you always knew exactly where you stood. With girls, so much happened beneath the surface; there was so much subtext that had to be read and analyzed, so many unspoken rules that you had to pay attention to. And there were *feelings* to account for. Part of the reason Drew and I got along so well is because we operated without all the BS. Yael and Stevie were part of the package deal, but even with them I often found myself saying or doing the wrong thing.

"So, find anything good?" Darcy asked Ren.

"I wouldn't worry about it," Ren said as she focused on pouring the ground buds into the vaporizer. "She got a B minus on her physics test last week, which is bringing down her class average. And it looks like she hasn't taken statistics yet, and you know Mr. Wong only gives out like two A's a semester. You've already taken that, so you have a huge leg up next semester."

I didn't ask who they were talking about, but I knew enough to guess. It was common knowledge that Darcy Flemming and Stella Ng were neck and neck for valedictorian this year. Was Ren using her privileges as runner to keep an eye on Stella Ng's academic record and give Darcy the inside scoop on her competition? I was a little surprised though that they would talk about it so openly in front of me. Did this mean they considered me part of their inner circle now, that they trusted me with their secrets?

Ren took a drag on her vape pen.

"I hope so," Darcy said. "I wanted to compete in the Maclay Finals this year, but with things being as tight as they are, my mom was adamant I take a break from riding and focus on my studies."

"Horses are stupid," Ren said, exhaling.

"Do you ride?" Darcy asked me.

"No, but my sister does," I said. "That's why she chose to go to Reynolds actually. They have a stable and a competitive equestrian team."

"Your family has a place on Martha's Vineyard, right?" Ren asked me.

"Yeah," I said. "In Edgartown."

"I thought so," Ren said. "I thought I saw you at L'Étoile this summer."

"Yeah, we go there a lot."

"My father has a place in Chilmark on the water," Ren said. "We have a big party for the Fourth every year. You should stop by some time."

The Montgomerys' annual Fourth of July party was legendary. Guests dined on oysters and lobsters in hundred-foot-long white tents on the estate and danced under the stars to a live band. Last year, the Montgomery family had put on a fireworks show on the beach that was rumored to have cost over a hundred grand. My fling at the time, Cedric Roth, had attended. He'd told me all about it.

"Sounds fun," I said.

"Here," Ren said, tossing me the vape pen.

The first time I'd smoked was that past summer in the room

over the boathouse with Cedric Roth, where he hid his bong far from the prying eyes of his parents.

"Breathe," he'd instructed, and I'd leaned forward, putting my lips to the glass barrel.

He showed me how to inhale, how to hold the smoke in my lungs. My throat burned. It felt like it was on fire, and I instinctively coughed, but then I couldn't stop coughing, harder and harder. I remembered the way my body loosened and my mind unraveled and everything around me felt different, how I could taste the air on my tongue for the first time.

Now, when I took a drag on Ren's vape, the smoke tickled my throat but I held back the cough. My eyes started to water.

We weren't allowed to have candles in our dorms, but Ren had an electric wax warmer plugged in on her desk. She got up and took a meltable wax square out of its packaging and placed it on top.

"Harvest Apple," she said.

I stared at Ren's walls, which were white and bare. Most girls hung posters of their favorite bands or put up bulletin boards covered in ribbon and pinned with photographs, or strung up string lights, but Ren hadn't bothered.

Maybe, I thought, things could be as easy with Ren and Darcy and the other A's as they had always been with Drew.

I took another drag on the vape pen. I could feel the weed starting to take effect as I stared at Ren's blank walls. They stretched open and bright white before me, full of possibilities.

Disciplinary hearings conducted by the Student Ethics Board were always open to the public. They were held in Bleeker Hall, in the largest lecture room that Knollwood Prep had—a room usually reserved for when important speakers came to campus or for large, school-wide meetings, because it was the only room besides the auditorium that could seat the whole school if everyone decided to show up. Usually, the only people who attended were the students on the ethics board themselves, the student facing punishment, and Headmaster Collins. But because of the public nature of Auden Stein's offense, dozens of students and even some faculty were present on the day of his hearing.

Crosby, Dalton, and Ren sat in the row behind Drew and me. Crosby kept poking Drew in the back of her neck with his pencil, and Drew kept giggling and acting annoyed and turning around to swat him. I had my feet propped up on the back of the seat in front of me. My ankle itched and I was trying not to scratch it. I'd put more triple antibiotic ointment on Nancy's bite mark last night and a fresh Band-Aid. Now I peeled back the edge of the bandage to sneak a peek. The bite had scabbed over; there would definitely be a scar.

"Some townies are having a bonfire tomorrow," I heard Ren say to Dalton. She was talking about the high school kids from Falls Church, who would sometimes have parties in the woods between town and campus. Sometimes upperclassmen from Knollwood would go because there was always lots of beer and pot. "You going?" Ren asked Dalton.

I glanced behind me and saw that Ren was picking at her nails. She looked bored, as if someone had dragged her there against her will.

"Maybe," Dalton said. "Could be a good time."

"Hardly," Ren said. "What do I have to do for a little excitement around here, slit my wrists?"

"Jesus, Ren," Dalton said.

"I'm just saying . . . did they have to build this school in the middle of fucking nowhere? Nothing interesting ever happens here."

Crosby reached forward to poke Drew again and Ren smacked his hand away.

"Stop that," she said. "We're not five. Or apes."

In the front of the room, Stevie, the president of the Student Ethics Board for two years running, stood up to read the board's verdict for Auden's punishment. The legs of her chair squealed against the wooden floorboards of the lecture hall as she stood. She read the charges against Auden: Theft and destruction of personal property. Harassment of a faculty member. It was enough to suspend him for two weeks. Or, at least, that's what the Knollwood Augustus Prep Student Book of Conduct demanded, but the official punishment was always recommended by the Student Ethics Board and then carried out by Headmaster Collins. Always, always, the Student Ethics Board handed down the harshest sentence possible, because they wanted the faculty to take them seriously. They didn't want to look like a group of weak-willed kids giving preferential treatment to their peers. And also, because only total Goody Two-shoes nerds were on the Student Ethics Board.

"The board recommends that Mr. Stein be suspended for two weeks for indecent conduct unbefitting of a student at Knollwood Augustus Prep," Stevie read. "Furthermore, we recommend that, at the conclusion of Mr. Stein's suspension, he be required to meet with a guidance counselor, who will assess Mr. Stein's readiness to reenter this institution."

I rolled my eyes. Mr. Franklin, who was seated on the lecture stage across from the Student Ethics Board's table, crossed his arms and coughed, clearly feeling that the punishment was not harsh enough. I'm sure he had pushed for Auden's expulsion.

"Thank you, Miss Sorantos," Headmaster Collins stated. He sat behind a large wooden table that had been set up in the middle of the room, squarely facing the stadium-style seats of the lecture hall. He scratched his chin, looked down at the folder open on the table before him, and gave a little flick of his hand to Auden, who promptly stood up.

Headmaster Collins paused for a moment and then looked out at the audience of students and faculty.

"For the first time in my tenure here at this fine institution, I find myself in disagreement with the Student Ethics Board's decision," Headmaster Collins said.

Stevie gasped and dropped her pencil, which rolled loudly across the table and clattered to the floor.

"I'm afraid there's a larger issue at stake here than the disappointing ways in which Mr. Stein has chosen to conduct himself, which the board has failed to address. And I must take part of the blame on myself," Headmaster Collins said. "There's been a weed we've allowed to grow among us for many years. And if we don't commit ourselves to rooting it out now, eventually it will spoil the whole garden.

"Tradition. What is tradition? We have a great many traditions here at Knollwood Augustus Prep. We have a tradition of graduating some of the best and brightest young minds in this country, who go on to the best schools in this country, and become part of the best institutions in this country. We have a tradition of fostering excellence, integrity, and innovation. But for many years now, we've also fostered a tradition of catering and cowering to a select few students who take it upon themselves to facelessly harass and bully students and faculty into letting them have their way or merely for the purpose of their own entertainment. These self-proclaimed vigilantes fly in the face of what this institution values—they champion crude and selfish aims, like the cancellation of Saturday morning cultural enrichment classes, often at the expense of something much more dear, like a man's reputation.

"Tradition. That has been a word many alumni—and even faculty and students, at times—have used to protect this group, and for a long time, too long now, I have stood silently by. But when this *tradition* threatens the traditions that are essential to this institution, I will bear it no more."

Headmaster Collins looked at Auden now.

"Mr. Stein, while you are bearing the blame for the disgraceful events that occurred in Mr. Franklin's classroom, I do not believe you acted alone. And so, while I believe two weeks' suspension is the proper punishment for these offenses, I do not believe we have the math quite right yet. For it is not two weeks for one person, but two weeks for each person who took part. And since tradition suggests that there are at least a dozen members of this illicit group, then the full term of this punishment is two weeks for each of these twelve students, or, if you choose to be their scapegoat, twenty-four weeks' suspension for one."

I sucked in my breath. A murmur of heated whispers filled the room.

"Did he just say twenty-four weeks?" Drew asked me.

I didn't answer her. I was looking at Auden. His eyes were wide as he absorbed the full weight of what Headmaster Collins was saying. Two weeks' suspension was bad enough—a black mark that would go on his permanent academic record. None of the top schools would want him now. But twenty-four weeks' suspension? He would have to repeat the year. He would be held back.

"So I will ask you again, Mr. Stein, but this is the last time I will ask," Headmaster Collins said. "Give me the names of the students who acted along with you, and have the punishment evenly divided amongst you, or take the full weight of the punishment on your own head. The choice is yours, Mr. Stein, but you must make it now."

Drew stiffened and went still beside me. I knew what she was thinking of: Wellesley, and how being named for this sort of misconduct would cost her her admission. She was thinking about her parents, George and Fern, whom she was always waging some form of emotional warfare against to get their attention, but how this would get her the worst kind of attention, the kind she didn't want.

But I wasn't thinking about college or about how my father would react. I was thinking how the whole tradition of the A's—which had been in existence for nearly as long as Knollwood itself—hung tenuously in the balance. I hadn't had a chance to be a part of it yet, hadn't had a chance to leave my mark. It couldn't be over yet. It hadn't even started.

Auden opened his mouth and then closed it again like a fish sucking at air.

I remembered that first night at the Ledge so clearly—Auden following Ren into the dark woods, head bowed, hands buried deep in his pockets. What did the A's have against him? And was it enough?

"I—" Auden started. He looked out at the auditorium. For a moment, his eyes rested on me. Then he looked away.

"It was just me," he said. "I acted alone."

Drew exhaled loudly next to me.

Headmaster Collins sighed. He looked disappointed. "Very well," he said. "Mr. Stein, you are hereby suspended from Knollwood Augustus Prep for a period of twenty-four weeks, effectively immediately. And you—" Headmaster Collins pointed a meaty finger out at us in the audience. He had an uncanny ability to make you feel like he was looking directly at you while staring at everyone at once. "You know who you are. Take this under advisement: in the past, this has been an administration with a bark and no bite, but no more. There will be no more warnings, no more preferential treatment given to those who threaten the traditions of this institution. Put a stop to your illicit constructions, or I will make it my mission to put a stop to you myself."

"How's that for a little excitement, Ren?" I heard Dalton whisper behind me.

I couldn't be sure, but I thought I heard Ren bark softly in reply.

twelve
GRACE FAIRCHILD

FALL 1996

When I graduated from high school, I got a small swimming scholarship to attend Trenton State College in New Jersey. No one in my family had ever gone to college, so it was no small thing for me to pack up the Oldsmobile my mom had passed down to me and drive the two hundred miles south to my dorm room in Travers Hall.

The thing was, nobody ever left Hillsborough. People were born there, they grew up there, and then they married their high school sweetheart, bought a house down the street from their parents, and repeated the cycle. But that was never going to be me. I had always wanted something more out of life. I could feel it tugging at me from the inside, almost like some sort of physical force pulling me out of Hillsborough's orbit.

Jake was like that too, which was one reason we got along so well. He was just different from most of the people that I knew. He had big dreams, and he was really smart and driven. In high school, he got a full ride to a fancy boarding school in New Hampshire. We had an unspoken understanding between us that he would go, and that even though he was no longer living in the house down the street, the distance wouldn't change anything between us, and it didn't.

Jake and I were like two jigsaw pieces that fit together—alike in

some ways, different in others, but our differences always comple-
mented one another. Jake had grown up with two younger sisters,
so he was sensitive in a way most guys weren't. I'd grown up with
three older brothers, so I had a toughness beneath the surface that
I think took most people by surprise. Jake was book smart, while I
was artsy, always sporting paint smudges on my baby-doll dresses
and Doc Martens, my fingers perpetually stained with clay. And
while I was quiet and reserved, Jake was the type who put you instantly at ease. He was my best friend and I loved him, more than
I had ever loved anybody, but then he died.

Only, he didn't just die, he killed himself. That was maybe the
hardest part—that Jake's being dead was not some tragic accident,
but his own choice.

The other hard part was that I hadn't even seen it coming. It
happened near the end of the fall semester of my sophomore year,
his junior year—right before he was supposed to come home for
winter break. We had talked for the last time two nights before it
happened and he had sounded so normal, so happy. I didn't know
then that that was the last conversation we would ever have or I
would have paid more attention to it. I had just gotten out of the
shower when he called and I was preoccupied with some fight my
friend Claire and I were having; I let him go earlier than I normally
would have to finish an art project that was due in the morning.

Later, when I found out that Jake was dead, I played that conversation over and over in my mind trying to figure out what I had
missed. He'd seemed excited to come home; we'd made plans for
how we would spend our days—sledding down Martha's Hill, ice-
skating on Langely Lake, drinking root beer floats at the old A&W.
Where, in all that, was a cry for help? Where, in all that, was Jake's
goodbye?

I questioned a lot at first. I wanted to see the suicide note they'd found in the typewriter in Jake's dorm room. I pored over it, trying to poke holes. The night after the funeral, I called Jake's mom, and I asked her, what did Jake mean when he admitted in the note to stealing that exam? Jake had always been a straight-A student; why would he have needed to cheat? It didn't make any sense.

My mother took me aside the next morning.

"I know you're hurting," she said, "but you have to have some compassion for poor Mrs. Griffin. She's lost her child. You're picking at a wound that's trying to heal."

I realized that part of what my mother was saying was true. My questions, they were coming from a selfish place. A part of me was angry with Jake for what he'd done, but a bigger part of me was angry with myself. Because Jake knew me better than anyone—I had confided in him my smallest triumphs and my greatest defeats. He had patiently listened and built me back up again when I was down. But somehow, I hadn't done the same for him. He had been hurting, he had desperately needed me, and I wasn't listening hard enough to know. I had failed him in the most profound way a person can fail anyone. And as long as I questioned things, as long as Jake hadn't really killed himself, as long as there was some other explanation, I wouldn't have failed him as profoundly as I thought I had.

But the other part of what my mother said was wrong—I wasn't picking at a wound that was trying to heal over, because the grief I felt would be with me always. Jake had been a part of me, and now a part of me was gone. I was never going to get it back; I was never going to be whole again. I understood that somehow, even at sixteen. And I understood it at nineteen, when I dropped out of college to focus on my art. And I understood it at twenty-two, when I'd been living in Trenton for three years and I met the next man I would fall in love with.

His name was Teddy Calloway. I was shelving returns at my part-time job at the local library (my art didn't really pay the bills), and I had my headphones on so I could listen to my mix tape in my Walkman. As I pushed my cart forward, I felt it hit something, and then I heard a muffled cry of pain. I looked up to see a young man wincing at the other end of my cart. Several books fell off the cart and made a loud clatter as they hit the floor.

"Shit," I said.

The man looked up at me, startled, and chuckled. I didn't know what he found so funny; I was a little preoccupied with how attractive he was. He had beautiful, piercing blue eyes and he was tall—at least a foot and a half taller than me. He put a finger to his lips in a "shh" gesture, and I realized with horror that I still had my headphones on and I must have just yelled "shit" in the quiet library, or at the very least, spoken it at an inappropriate volume.

Sure enough, an elderly woman poked her head into our aisle and said pointedly, "Please keep your voice down."

When she was gone, I had to bite back a laugh. I looked back at the amused young man on the other side of my cart, took my headphones off, and silently mouthed, "Shit."

He laughed.

I made my way around the cart and knelt to start picking up the books that had spilled. The man leaned down to help me.

"You're kind of a mess, aren't you?" he whispered.

"You're kind of direct, aren't you?" I whispered back.

He smiled at me.

"I'm sorry about your foot," I said. "I wasn't paying attention."

"It's okay. I wasn't really using that foot anyway," he said with an easy smile. "What were you listening to?"

"A little bit of everything," I said as I stacked the fallen books in my arms. "Nirvana, Pearl Jam, Smashing Pumpkins."

"Smashing Pumpkins," the guy said, nodding in approval. "I saw them the other year at Lollapalooza. You listening to stuff from their last album?"

I nodded.

"What's your name?" he asked.

"Grace Fairchild," I said. "Yours?"

"Teddy," he answered. "Teddy Calloway."

And my first thought was of Jake.

The thing was, I recognized Teddy's last name. Jake had been good friends with a Calloway at his boarding school. He had talked about him all the time and I had seen pictures. I remembered fragments of those photographs: tall, blond, ice-blue eyes, a smug smile. The boy I had seen in the pictures looked like the boy kneeling next to me now, in between the dusty stacks in the library.

"You went to Knollwood Prep," I said.

Teddy looked surprised. "Yeah, actually, I did. I'm sorry, do we know each other? Did you go there?"

"No," I said. "A friend of mine used to. Jake Griffin. Did you know him?"

"No," Teddy said. "But I was only there a few months my freshman year. I spent most of my time at Andover, actually."

"Oh," I said.

"But maybe you're thinking of my older brother, Alistair?" Teddy asked. "He spent all four years there."

Alistair. Yes, now I remembered. That was his name.

"Oh, yeah, I think you're right," I said.

"So, what overpriced prep school did you go to?" he asked.

"Me? None of them. I just went to public school."

"Lucky," he said.

I shrugged.

"Do you go to Princeton?" he asked. Princeton was only about twelve miles up the road from Trenton.

"No, I'm just a local," I said.

His face lit up. "Really?"

"What other perfectly ordinary things about myself can I impress you with?" I asked.

"No, it's just refreshing, that's all," he said. "Here, let me get those for you."

I passed him the books I was holding and as I did, my hand grazed the bare skin of his forearm, and I felt a little buzz of electricity where we touched.

"What are you doing tonight, Grace?" he asked as he stacked the books back on the cart and I stood.

I fingered the pendant that hung at the end of my necklace. It was the necklace Jake had bought me off a vendor's cart on the boardwalk in West Haven the last summer that we were together. The pendant was his zodiac sign and birthstone: a ruby crab clutching two diamonds in its claws.

I brushed my hands on the thighs of my jeans and looked up at Teddy, biting my lip.

"I don't know," I said brazenly. "What are we doing tonight?"

Teddy picked me up at my apartment at eight, and he took me to an old mom-and-pop shop in town. He did old-fashioned things like hold the door open for me, and pull out my chair at the dinner table, and put his jacket around my shoulders when I was cold.

Two weeks after we went on our first date, he took me to his family's charity ball at the Carlyle Hotel in New York City.

This was my first foray into Teddy's world. In Trenton, we mostly hung out in my world—Teddy would come by the library, or he would hang out at my apartment, or we would go see a movie. I never met him on campus, never went by his eating club, never met his friends.

I had always known that Teddy and I were different, that we came from different worlds. But it wasn't until that night at the Carlyle Hotel that I felt it. When I walked into that ballroom for the first time, it was like nothing I had ever seen before. The crisp suits and the glittering evening gowns and the crystal wineglasses and the seven-course dinner. And there I was, in my simple gown that I had found while sifting through racks at the thrift store down the street from my apartment. People kissed one another on the cheek in greeting like fancy Parisians in a movie, and they talked about restaurants and chefs and designers and hotels and cities I had never been to before, like they were speaking some foreign tongue. And all the while I just stood there, trying to smile, and wondering what to do with my hands.

The only okay thing about the evening was meeting Teddy's brother, Alistair. Seeing him was like seeing a familiar face in a crowd of strangers, which was odd, because I'd never actually met Alistair before—I had only seen his picture and heard Jake talk about him. But, I don't know, he felt familiar to me, like we were old friends picking up where we had left off after a long time apart. It felt easy, comfortable, dancing with him, even talking to him about Jake.

I got through the rest of the evening the same way I had gotten through those last two years in Hillsborough after Jake died: I drank more than I should have until I felt a little bit brave, I laughed at things I didn't understand, and I smiled when I really wanted to cry. I was who I thought everyone around me wanted me to be, and I hated it.

After it was all over, a car drove us from the city back to New Jersey and Teddy leaned over and put his head in my lap in the backseat. He was the slightest bit drunk himself. I ran my fingers through his hair and I tried to memorize the lines of his face even though it was nearly too dark to see.

"Did you have a good time?" he asked, looking up at me.

"Yes," I lied.

"My mother really liked you," he said.

"I could tell she really loves you," I said. And that was true.

If it were just me and Teddy all the time, like it had been, I could do this, I thought. There wouldn't be a doubt in my mind about us. But it wouldn't just be me and Teddy in our own little world. There would be his world, too, sooner or later, and I didn't think I could do that—feel so out of place and small all the time. I couldn't go back to the very thing I had run from in the first place—pretending to be someone other than who I was, pretending to feel a way I didn't really feel, to make other people comfortable. There was a gap between us I didn't know if we could overcome.

When we got to my apartment, Teddy walked me to my door. He leaned against the door frame as I searched my purse for my keys.

"Can I stay over?" he asked. "I'm a little drunk."

"I don't think it's a good idea," I said, not quite meeting his eyes.

"I probably shouldn't drive myself home," he said with a sloppy smile. He took my glove off and kissed the bare skin at my wrist.

"You're not driving yourself home," I said, tugging my wrist away. "You have a driver."

"What's wrong?" he asked, taken aback that I wasn't playing along like I usually did.

I bit my lip and forced my eyes up to meet his. "I just don't think we should prolong the inevitable, that's all," I said.

The backs of my eyes stung and I hated myself. I didn't want to cry in front of him.

"Prolong the inevitable?" he said. "Grace, what the hell are you talking about?"

"Come on," I said, my voice hitching and betraying me. "I know you see it, too."

"See what?" he asked.

"We're just—we're different. Too different."

"Is this about tonight?" he asked. "I thought you said you had a good time."

"I didn't," I said. "Okay? Is that what you want to hear? I didn't have a good time. I felt like some—like some—I don't know. And I didn't like it."

He reached for me and wrapped his arms around me and I stood there stiffly, refusing to let myself sink into his touch or be consoled.

"Grace," he whispered into my hair as he held me. "I'm sorry."

"It's not your fault," I said. "Don't apologize. You didn't do anything wrong."

He drew back, his hands on my shoulders, and he was shaking. I thought maybe he was upset about our breaking up; it took me a moment to realize he was laughing.

"What on earth is so funny?" I asked, a little pissed.

"It's just . . . ," he said, and then he laughed some more. "I only brought you tonight to impress you. I didn't expect—I didn't expect you to hate them as much as I do."

"You're really drunk," I said.

"No," Teddy said. "I mean, yes, I am. But that's because that's the only way to get through an evening with those people."

I chuckled despite myself. "Yeah," I said. "That's kind of truc."

"They're awful," Teddy said. "The whole thing—the food, this suit, the vain look-at-me conversation, and whoever the hell Francisco Trivoli is."

"Only the chef-patron of the Ivy," I said, mimicking the haughty accent of the woman who had not been able to shut up about Francisco Trivoli all night. "Apparently, he's got three Michelin stars."

"Fuck him," Teddy said.

I laughed.

"Please let me come in," Teddy said, burying his hands in his coat pockets and bouncing from one foot to the other. "My balls are shriveling it's so cold."

"Fine," I said. "But don't get any funny ideas. You and your balls are sleeping on the couch."

"Scout's honor," Teddy said, holding up one hand. "Cross my heart, poke my eye out, that there won't be any funny business."

I laughed. "That's not quite how that goes."

In the end, I let him in. We polished off an old bottle of Pinot I had in my cabinet, and Teddy, true to his word, slept on the couch. Only, I slept there too, snuggled in his arms, the glow of my old television set lighting my living room like some adult night-light as we both faded from consciousness. And as I drifted off to sleep, I felt the faint stirrings of something I hadn't felt in years—not since Jake had passed away. It was the feeling that maybe—just maybe—there was actually someone out there who saw me, and got me.

thirteen
CHARLIE CALLOWAY

2017

Homecoming at Knollwood Augustus Prep was practically a Calloway family reunion. Grandfather and Eugenia came up, as did my uncle Teddy, who had gone to Knollwood for a bit when he was my age, and my aunt Grier, and their daughters, Piper and Clementine. My father would have come, because Knollwood was his alma mater, but at the last minute he had decided to visit Seraphina instead, since it was her homecoming that weekend as well and he didn't want her to feel left out, or so he told me over the phone. I was disappointed, of course, but part of me was also relieved.

After everything Claire had told me the other weekend, I wasn't sure I was ready to face my father. I knew I would measure every look, every gesture, every breath he took, terrified that I might see something hiding in the shadows of his features—something I hadn't noticed before, or maybe, something I hadn't *wanted* to notice.

That was the thing that got me, the dark thought I turned over and over again in my mind at night as I lay, unsleeping, in my bed. Was it that my father was incapable of the things Claire claimed, or was it that I didn't want him to be capable of those things?

"I can't for the life of me understand why Sera chose Reynolds over Knollwood," Piper said, craning her neck to see over the tall man sitting in front of her in the bleachers. "Knollwood is superior in every way that matters—academics, extracurriculars, good-looking boys."

It was Friday afternoon of homecoming weekend, and the whole school had turned out to see the Knollwood Lions take on our rivals, the Xavier Panthers. Piper sat next to me. On my other side was Eugenia, who had brought her own blanket and cushioned seat and wine and cheese basket. Every few minutes, she'd call down the row to my aunt Grier or my uncle Teddy, who sat on the other side of Piper with my cousin Clementine in his lap, and ask whether they would like a slice of Brie on a wheat cracker. At halftime, she took a full bottle of wine out of her designer wine carrier bag and poured herself a long-stemmed glass. When I said under my breath, "Eugenia, you can't drink on school property," she just smiled at me and said, "No, darling, *you* can't drink on school property."

Grandfather did nothing to stop her, but then, Grandfather could never really tell Eugenia to do anything she didn't want to do, and so he rarely tried. Besides, he was in good spirits because Leo was quarterback, and he was having a good game. There were just two minutes left to go, and we were ahead by seven points.

"Well, Reynolds has a stable on campus where Seraphina can keep Peppermint," I told Piper. "And for Seraphina, that trumped everything."

Piper tossed her long blond hair over her shoulder. She was a Calloway, through and through, from her bright blue eyes to her tall forehead.

"Mama made me look at Reynolds, and Andover and the Putney School, but I told her not to hold her breath." Piper was twelve, and next year she would start at boarding school. That was the reason why Piper and her parents were here now—they were considering Knollwood.

"Ah, my little fish," I said, leaning into her shoulder.

"Fish?" Piper said, scrunching up her face like she smelled something bad.

"Yeah, you know, fish. Like freshman. The little fish in the big pond."

"I'll never be a fish," Piper said. "I'm a Calloway."

The Knollwood Lions scored again, with Leo carrying the ball triumphantly into the end zone, and we were all on our feet, cheering.

After the game was over, Eugenia suggested that she and I wait for Leo to shower and change, and everyone else would head to Falls Church to grab a table at Fiona's. Fiona's was the only nice restaurant in town, and so there was always a mad rush to get a table on weekends when families were in town, like homecoming or graduation. As they were leaving, Uncle Teddy pinched my arm playfully and said under his breath, "Don't let the old broad drive."

When everyone was gone and it was just Eugenia and myself, I buried my hands deep in the pockets of my jacket and braced myself for the inevitable. Eugenia was always very direct and she didn't shy away from prying into the particularities of our lives. For the past several years, she had taken a keen interest in my and Leo's dating activities. Freshman year, I had made the mistake of teasing Leo about Drew in front of Eugenia, and Eugenia had somehow proceeded to gather Drew's entire family history, and when she discovered that Drew's aunt played tennis at the same club, she invited her and her husband to play doubles. A few weeks later at a family dinner, Leo was forced to admit to Eugenia that his relationship with Drew was short-lived, and Eugenia had told Leo, in front of the whole family at dinner, that Calloways did not engage in dalliances and it was not becoming for a man to appear loose. I had nearly choked on my tomato bisque and Leo went red in the ears and stared down at the table. We'd vowed from that point on to keep our lips sealed when it came to who we were dating (or more, I promised not to let slip who Leo was involved with, since I didn't date).

So it took me by surprise when instead of asking about my romantic endeavors, Eugenia folded her box of crackers neatly back into her wine bag and said, "Your father told me you were at the house on Langely Lake last weekend."

"How did he—?"

"The groundskeeper phoned him," she said. "It's been a while since anyone's been at the house. You and your friend gave that poor gardener quite the scare."

"Sorry about that," I said.

She didn't ask me what I had been doing at the lake house, or what I had been doing in Hillsborough, even though there was only one reason I would ever go to Hillsborough: my mother.

"Your mother's family—they've always wanted to control the narrative," Eugenia said. "They don't want to believe Grace is the type of person she turned out to be. It is a great tragedy to lose a child, and an even greater tragedy to lose your good opinion of your child—and so the Fairchilds told themselves a story they could live with. I don't blame them for that. But I do blame them for trying to drag you and everyone else down that twisted, delusional path with them." Eugenia sighed. "Charlotte, there is something you have to understand," she said. "Your whole life, people will try to tell you who you are and what to believe about yourself. Don't let them."

I looked out at the now empty football field. The sky overhead was shot through with pink and orange. It was the kind of sky that came at the end of summer; the kind of sky that marked the end of days where there was more daylight than darkness; the kind that announced the cool chill of autumn.

"The truth is, your mother was unhappy," Eugenia said. "She was always unhappy. A quiet, reserved, skittish thing. Prone to moods and outbursts. She struck your uncle Teddy once, you know. Nearly broke his nose," she said, shaking her head.

"She hit Uncle Teddy?" I asked. I had never heard that story. I couldn't recall my mother and Uncle Teddy ever being hostile toward one another. In fact, I barely remembered them interacting with one another at all. "Why?"

"There's hardly a provocation that could justify physically assaulting someone in public," Eugenia said, waving away my question. "I sometimes wonder if your mother had some sort of chemical imbalance that made her act the way she did."

This new sliver of information dropped like a pebble into the pool of my mind, creating a ripple through the memories I had of my mother. Was what Eugenia said true? For a moment, it seemed to obscure everything I thought I knew about my mother, casting every image in a slightly different light.

I remembered one morning at the lake house, going to my parents' bedroom door and finding that it was locked. It was a weekday and my father was away in the city. I stood there for a long time, twisting the knob and calling for my mother, but she never opened the door. After a while, Claire showed up. I remembered her telling me that my mother wasn't feeling well, but that she was there to take me and Seraphina out for breakfast.

Were there other things that happened that I hadn't really understood at the time?

"For years your mother was very withdrawn with the family," Eugenia said. "And those last couple of months before she left, she even became distant with Alistair. It nearly killed him, what she did."

At that moment, Leo came out of the field house with one of his teammates. He raised his hand and waved at us in the distance. Eugenia stood and adjusted the wine bag on her shoulder.

"I've kept my mouth shut about your mother for years out of

respect for your father. But I thought you deserved to know the truth," Eugenia said before turning away from me.

Yael leaned over the porcelain sink next to me toward the mirror and concentrated hard as she drew the liquid black liner across her lower lid. Then she leaned back to admire her handiwork: a perfect, thick black line.

"Do mine next," Drew said. "You always do the best smoky eye. Somehow mine always end up making me look like the walking dead."

"That's because you put way too much on," Yael said. "Less is more."

I stared blankly at my wan complexion in the mirror and my damp, freshly washed hair. Usually I enjoyed getting ready for the homecoming dance and spending time with the girls, but today I was having trouble feeling anything but this suffocating weight on my chest. Ever since Eugenia had told me those things about my mother, I couldn't really think about anything else. My mother may have had some sort of manic-depressive mood disorder. My mother's family was spinning the narrative about her disappearance because they couldn't accept the person she'd turned out to be. Surely some of what Eugenia said was true—but which parts, and how much?

"Earth to Charlie," Stevie called out.

"Hmm?" I asked.

"Are you using that?" she asked, pointing at the tube of red lipstick balanced on the lip of the sink in front of me.

"Oh, no, here you go," I said, handing it to her.

"You okay?" Stevie asked as she reached for it. "You've been kind of in a funk all day."

"I'm fine," I said.

Yael came over and put her arm around me. "It's okay, Charlie,"

she said, leaning her head on my shoulder and glancing meaning-
fully at my reflection in the mirror as if she understood. "You don't
have to hide it from us. I know what's going on."

She knew?

I had never talked to Yael or Stevie about my mother. I had almost talked to Drew about her once—on one of our first Saturday
nights at Knollwood as freshmen. The subject sort of thrust itself
upon us. Drew and I had gone to the grocery store in Falls Church
with our roommate, River. We were loading up on junk food for
a movie night in our dorm room, which was supposed to be a fun
bonding experience but was proving instead to be a tortuous crash
course on a subject Drew and I would become begrudging experts
on over the rest of the semester: Things River Could Not Eat.
(Throughout the rest of the semester, Drew and I would also become reluctant experts on other subjects, like Things River Found
Misogynistic and Things River Left Lying Around the Room That
Looked Like Trash but Were Not Trash So Why Did You Throw
That Away?) I had made the mistake of plucking a bag of gummy
bears off the shelf when we first came into the store, and River had
batted the bag away from the cart like she was a goalie defending
her net.

"What gives?" I asked.

"Gummy bears are made of gelatin," River said, her face puckered in disgust.

"Yeah, okay, so?"

She raised her eyebrows at me. I looked at Drew, who looked as
confused as I felt.

"Is that like super fattening or something?" Drew asked.

River scoffed. "Gelatin is made from collagen, which comes from
ground-up animals."

Drew and I looked at each other.

"Okay, so that's a no for gummy bears," I said. I eyed the other candies on the shelf and picked up a bag of M&M's. "Are you more of a chocolate girl?" I asked, hopeful.

River rolled her eyes. "Those hard candy shells come from a resin excreted by bugs," she said.

"I guess they don't sound so appetizing when you put it like that," Drew said.

"Yes, I find it difficult to find the torture of innocent animals appetizing in general," River said.

I grabbed a bag of cinnamon-sugar pecans.

"Okay, what about some nuts?" I asked.

River leveled me with a death glare.

"What? You're not one of those people who consider plants sentient beings, are you?"

"They're coated in *sugar*," River said. "a.k.a. bone char."

"Is there anything in this store you can eat?" I asked.

"I'll check the produce section," River said, grabbing the cart from me and pushing it determinedly down the aisle.

Later, when we were waiting in line to check out with our cart full of organic kale and fresh fruit, I skimmed the magazines displayed next to the boxes of gum and York Peppermint Patties, and I saw it: on the cover of the *Star Enquirer* was my mother. She was wearing a pair of thick sunglasses and a hat and she was sprawled out on a beach chair. She held up her hand as if to block the photographer's shot of her face. BILLIONAIRE'S WIFE GRACE CALLOWAY SPOTTED IN BUENOS AIRES WITH SECRET LOVER, the tabloid read.

The color drained from my face. I glanced up and caught Drew's eye, and I knew from the expression on her face that she had seen it, too. I opened my mouth to say something—to cut it off before it could even start—to explain to her that it was all a lie, that none of it was true, when Drew beat me to it.

"Oh my god," Drew said.

"What?" River asked as she moved a bag of oranges from the cart to the conveyor belt.

"These blueberries aren't organic," Drew said.

"What?" River asked, reaching for the carton of blueberries in Drew's hands.

"I don't eat GMOs," Drew said. "Can you grab the organic ones for me? Please?"

River sighed. "Fine," she said. "I'll be right back."

When she was gone, Drew picked up the *People* magazine next to the *Star Enquirer* and flipped through it casually.

"Another one bites the dust," Drew said, clucking her tongue at some celebrity breakup. I didn't see who it was—I was too busy trying to word the explanation calmly enough in my head so that she wouldn't think I sounded crazy.

That photograph—the one of my mother on the cover—had been taken on a family vacation in St. Thomas when I was six. I knew this because I was the one who had taken that picture. My mother had put her hand up to block the shot because she had just woken up from a nap dozing in that beach chair, and I had startled her. I don't know how the *Star Enquirer* got ahold of that picture, which family album they had raided, which family member had sold it to the highest bidder. But it wasn't the first time something like this had happened, and it probably wouldn't be the last.

No, my father did not drive my mother off or kill her or whatever else the tabloids were saying. No, I didn't want to talk about it.

But Drew didn't ask. She didn't give me a condescending smile or a pitying glance. She just placed the *People* magazine back in the rack, but this time over the *Star Enquirer* so the picture of my mother was completely covered, hidden from view, and went back to unloading the cart. That's when I knew we would be best friends.

That was the closest I had ever come to talking to someone at

Knollwood about my mother. I had wanted to keep that part of my life in the past, to move on. So, how did Yael know? How had I been so transparent?

"It's Dalton, isn't it?" Yael asked. "You're totally dreading seeing him tonight."

Dalton. In truth, I had forgotten all about him these last two days.

I stared back at Yael's reflection. She was looking at me so earnestly—with so much concern. Maybe it would be nice to tell someone who wasn't involved in any way in my family drama—someone who could just listen and offer a fresh perspective if I needed it. Maybe it would be nice not to be so alone in all of this. For a moment, I contemplated telling them everything. But then I realized, I would have to tell them *everything*. I would have to go back to the very beginning of all of it, which felt overwhelming. And what if—what if I did choose to trust them, and that came back to bite me in the ass, as it had in the past?

"Right," I said after a moment. "It's Dalton."

"Don't let him bum you out," Drew said, coming over and giving my shoulder a squeeze. "Here, let me do your hair for you. I have an idea for an updo that would look killer on you. When Dalton sees you, he'll forget all about that slut McKenna."

"Sure," I said, trying to give her a smile that I hoped she would think was genuine. "Thanks."

String lights were draped overhead in the gymnasium and a live band was playing on the stage that the student council had set up. Stevie, Yael, and Drew were all out on the dance floor, gyrating in one big clump with most of the other students who had shown up to the dance, but I had made an excuse about needing something to drink half an hour ago and retreated to an empty table by myself. I'd been trying to be sociable and normal all night, but I was reaching my limit. After keeping up a steady stream of conversation at the dinner the school had catered for us on the front lawn, I'd done a solid hour of swaying and jumping up and down with my hands in the air with everyone else (which was no easy feat in four-inch Manolos). Now, I was contemplating my exit strategy even though it was still pretty early.

My phone vibrated and I pulled it out of my purse. To my surprise, I saw Greyson's name come up on the screen with a text message.

GREYSON: Nice Irish exit on Sunday.

His text made me smile. I typed back a quick reply.

ME: Sry I didn't say goodbye.:/
GREYSON: No worries. My mom filled me in. She's worried about you, tho.

I bit my lip and put my phone down. I didn't want to talk about how I felt or how worried Claire was. But then I remembered what Eugenia had said—how my mother had struggled with depression. If that were true, surely Claire would know. I picked up my phone and texted Greyson back.

ME: Did Claire ever say anything to you about my mom being depressed or having weird violent outbursts?
GREYSON: No. Why? What's up?
ME: My grandmother told me that my mom went through these weird moods and may have had some sort of chemical imbalance. Idk. Do you think that could be true?
GREYSON: Idk.

"Who's Greyson?"

I looked up to see Drew standing over me, slightly out of breath, a sheen of sweat glistening on her forehead.

"No one," I said, and I lowered my phone beneath the table so she couldn't see the screen. "Just an old friend."

"A cute old friend?" Drew asked, raising an eyebrow at me.

"It's not like that," I said.

"All right, Ms. Secretive, I won't grill you," she said, sinking into the seat next to mine. "Are you hydrated yet? You went to get a drink, like, forever ago."

"Sorry," I said.

She leaned forward and started unbuckling the straps of her heels. "These bad boys are killing me. I don't know why I thought three-inch heels were a good idea."

I felt my phone vibrate and looked down to see another text from Greyson.

GREYSON: Do you know who the private investigator was who worked on your mom's case? Like, have you ever seen any of the stuff he had on her?

The private investigator—I hadn't thought about him in ages. I had met him once, when I was seven. He had interviewed me. And then I remembered seeing him on occasion the year after. He would come by to visit my father, and they would go into my father's study and close the door.

ME: Hmm. No. But I could look into it.
GREYSON: There might be something there.

"Come dance with us," Drew said. She was on her feet again, barefoot this time, holding her hands out toward me to pull me up.

I glanced out at the dance floor and saw Yael and Stevie near the edge of the stage. Yael waved at me; Stevie wrangled an invisible lasso over her head and threw it at me, attempting to lasso me back onto the dance floor. I laughed. Then the song that was playing ended and a slow song came on.

"May I have this dance?" Drew asked.

"Of course," I laughed.

She took my hand and dragged me out onto the middle of the dance floor. We both put our hands on each other's shoulders and held each other at arms' length, swaying back and forth like we were at some middle school dance and giggling like we were five.

Around us, real couples slow-danced and held each other close. I caught sight of Crosby holding Ren around the waist. Drew saw them too. She rolled her eyes and made a gagging sound. I laughed. But then I saw them: Dalton and McKenna.

Honestly, I didn't think it would affect me so much, not with everything else that was going on. But it did. I felt it in my gut, like someone had blindsided me with a punch.

McKenna was wearing a backless, red, floor-length dress that looked stunning. Dalton had his arms wrapped around her; he leaned down to whisper something in her ear and she leaned her head back and laughed. I looked away.

What if that were me? That was a silly, stupid thought, but I couldn't help but wonder. What if I had said yes to Dalton? What if that were me there with Dalton instead of McKenna—me who Dalton was holding, my ear that Dalton was whispering in? My heart felt heavy.

When the slow song ended, a loud, upbeat song came on. I leaned forward and yelled so Drew could hear me over the music.

"I'm gonna go pee," I said.

"Want me to come with you?"

"No, no, stay," I said. "I'll be right back."

"Okay, come find us," she said.

I took off toward the girls' bathroom, which also happened to be on the way to the exit, which was where I was really headed. I couldn't be there anymore. I would make some excuse to Drew later—I would tell her I had gotten sick, that I hadn't wanted to ruin everyone else's night, so I just ducked out.

Outside, the air was crisp and chilly. I hugged my bare arms to my chest and ran my fingers over them to keep from shivering.

I could hear voices carrying across campus. The school had erected a large tent on the football field for the alumni, where they had their own catered dinner and entertainment, and the Falls Church municipal orchestra was playing in the auditorium. The path I was on would meander by there. I wondered what time it was exactly, and whether I would be passing by the entrance to the auditorium as the performance let out. I didn't want to risk running into Grandfather or Uncle Teddy and have them see me walking home from the dance alone. It would raise too many questions I didn't feel like answering. It would be best to turn back and loop around Acacia Hall, go the long way. I turned around briskly and walked right into someone.

"Sorry—" I said, startled, and looked up into Dalton's chocolate-brown eyes. I was close enough to smell his cologne—a citrus scent mixed with spices and wood.

He had his hands on my arms to steady me. For some reason, he was smiling at me. "Hey there, Calloway," he said.

"Hi," I said dumbly. What the crap was Dalton doing out here?

"I saw you take off back there and I wanted to make sure you were okay," he said.

"I'm fine," I said.

"Oh, okay, good," he said.

He still had his hands on my arms. Why did he still have his hands on my arms?

"Is that all?" I asked, glancing pointedly at his hand on my arm.

"You're leaving . . . just because?" he asked, finally letting go of me and burying his hands in his pockets.

"Yeah, I'm tired," I said. "What's with the third degree?"

"You're upset?" he asked, confused.

I didn't know why I was snapping at Dalton when just a second ago I had been fantasizing about being in his arms, but all of a sudden I was so annoyed I couldn't help myself.

"What do you want, Dalton?" I asked.

"Can I walk you back to your dorm?" he asked.

"You want to walk me back to my dorm?"

"Yes."

"Why?"

"Why not?"

"What about McKenna?" I asked.

"What about McKenna?" Dalton asked.

"Are you a parrot or something?" I asked. "Are you just going to repeat everything I say?"

"Sorry," Dalton said, taken aback. "So, you're mad at me?" he asked after a moment.

I rolled my eyes. "I just don't understand what you're doing. Go enjoy the dance with your date."

"You're mad that I brought McKenna to the dance?" he asked.

"No," I said. "I don't care who you go to the dance with."

"Okay," Dalton said. "Because I remember asking you to the dance, and I remember you telling me to ask someone else, which is what I did. But now you seemed pissed off about it."

Yes, that's exactly right, I thought.

"No," was all I said.

For some reason, he was smiling. Why was he smiling? Was he laughing at me? Did he find this funny?

"Stop smiling before I hit you," I said.

"Charlie," he said. "I'm going to tell you something, and I want you to listen, and then I want you to tell me the truth in return."

"Fine," I said.

"I like you," he said.

"Well, obviously," I said.

Dalton laughed. "See, this is exactly why I like you, Calloway. You're not like other girls."

I held up my hand. "I'm going to stop you right there, before you get to the follow-up cliché line of the century, 'I've never felt this way before.'"

"Hell, you don't make this easy, do you?" Dalton said, rubbing the back of his neck. "It wasn't a line—you aren't like the other girls here. Other girls would have taken that as a compliment, but I say it to you, and you basically tell me to piss off."

"Okay, geez, sorry," I said. "What did you mean then, if you weren't being cliché?"

"I meant, you're not like other girls, because other girls travel around in these packs, like they're scared to be alone," Dalton said. "But you're by yourself a lot. Not because you don't have friends, but because you're just comfortable that way. You're also, like, the master of bullshitting teachers. And you invite yourself to guys' poker night, and then soundly beat all of us. Though your tactics were a bit unfair. And while most girls—and guys for that matter—are obsessed with who they're hooking up with, I've never seen you with anyone. You're just—I don't know—different. And I like that. I like you. And that isn't a line, it's just the truth."

I was quiet. I'd always had a way with words. I was quick with witty retorts. I was an expert at deflecting teachers' questions with observations so long-winded they'd forget what their question was by the end of it. But now, I couldn't think of a single thing to say.

"Say something," he said.

I exhaled. It was cold enough out that I could see my breath.

"You're all right, too, I guess," I said after a moment.

"Okay then," Dalton said, as if that settled everything. "Here," he said, shrugging out of his jacket and wrapping it around my shoulders. "You're shivering."

"I'm okay," I said, but I wriggled into it anyway. It still had his warmth.

"Come on," Dalton said, and he took my hand. "There's something I want you to see, and I don't want us to miss it."

We turned back down the path that led past the auditorium and started walking. As we walked, I heard the bell tower over the campus church strike the hour. Ten o'clock. I almost stopped; I almost turned back. The orchestra would just have finished playing—and sure enough, the doors to the auditorium ahead of us were opening, and people were pouring out. I wanted to turn around and go back the other way to avoid the hassle of the crowd of alumni, but then I saw it.

In front of the auditorium was a row of busts on short pillars. On one side were busts of every headmaster who had served at Knollwood for the past one hundred years. At the end of this row, of course, was Headmaster Collins's bust, which had just been put in the previous year. It usually stood out because it was slightly whiter than all the other busts. The elements hadn't weathered it yet to the same sepia shade as the others. But tonight, it stood out for an entirely different reason. Under the floodlights from the auditorium, you could see it even from a distance—Nancy's diamond-encrusted dog collar around Headmaster Collins's neck. The diamonds caught and sparkled in the light. But it wasn't just the dog collar or the leash attached to it that drew attention. A balloon had been glued to the bust's lips, with "Bark! Bark! Bark!" written all over it. And on the pillar, someone had spray-painted the words "Heel, Collins. Good boy."

This has been an administration with a bark and no bite, but no more, Headmaster Collins had said at Auden's disciplinary hearing. He had threatened the A's. And when Dalton had asked Ren what she had thought of the headmaster's challenge, Ren had barked. I had thought it strange at the time.

Now someone from the alumni group had seen Headmaster Collins's graffitied bust; people were gathering around it. I could hear the excited fervor of the crowd. And there, making his way hurriedly to the bust, the crowd parting in front of him like the Red Sea, was Headmaster Collins himself.

"It's embarrassing, that's what it is," Grandfather said, sawing into his stack of pancakes. "How a grown man can't command the respect of a bunch of teenagers when that's his fucking job is beyond me."

"I wish I'd gotten to see it," Piper said for the hundredth time that morning, sighing into her glass of orange juice. "I wish I'd been there instead of back at the hotel watching the baby."

"I'm not a baby," Clementine said, slamming her fork onto the table.

"Stop that," Aunt Grier said, picking up the fork and handing it back to Clementine.

Rosie's Diner was always busy on Sunday mornings after church let out, but it was especially busy today with most of the alumni still in town for homecoming weekend. I spotted at least half a dozen people I knew from school and their families, all with the same idea to have one last meal together before everyone hit the road.

I sat on the outside of the booth only half listening to the conversation. I couldn't get the text conversation I had had with Greyson out of my head. I had turned his suggestion over and over in my mind last night. It seemed so obvious. Why hadn't I thought of it before as the best place to start? I had questions, and somewhere in some dark, dusty storage closet, there was a box full of answers.

"He should be fired," Grandfather said. "I'm going to give Fred Eakins a call when we get home. He's on the board. I'm sure he's already heard about it."

"Don't give yourself an aneurism," Uncle Teddy said. "When it comes down to it, it's really just some spray paint and a balloon and some kids having some fun. We got up to much worse in my day."

He winked at me across the table.

"Teddy, please, they're going to think we condone this type of behavior," Aunt Grier said, wiping at the corner of Clementine's mouth with a Wet-Nap.

"Getting into some trouble is good for your complexion," Uncle Teddy said. "Leo, Charlotte, I want you to know that if you don't call me sometime before your teen years are up asking me to bail you out of jail, I'll be a little disappointed."

"Teddy," Aunt Grier said.

"Get it all out of your systems before it goes on your permanent record," Uncle Teddy said.

"No proselytizing at the breakfast table," Eugenia said.

"Yes, Mother," Uncle Teddy said, just to annoy her.

Uncle Teddy excused himself to go to the restroom. I waited a moment after he had left and then crawled out of the booth and followed him. Rosie's Diner had only one unisex bathroom, at the back of the restaurant. So I waited, leaning against the back hall wall. I heard a toilet flush, then the sound of the sink running.

I told myself not to be nervous about asking him. In many ways, Uncle Teddy was like a second father. If there was anyone within the family I would confide in besides Leo, it was him.

The door to the washroom opened and Uncle Teddy flipped the light switch off.

"Oh, sorry, didn't see you there," he said. He took a step back and held the door to the washroom open for me, flicked the light back on. "It's all yours."

I took a step forward, held the door.

"Actually, there was something I wanted to talk to you about," I said.

"Okay, what's up?" Uncle Teddy asked.

"It's about my mom," I said. I swallowed nervously. "I know that's not anyone's favorite subject."

Uncle Teddy's smile wavered for a moment, but then he said, "What do you want to know?"

"Well, first, Eugenia mentioned something strange the other day," I said, tucking an errant strand of hair behind my ear. "She said that my mom hit you once. That she almost broke your nose."

Uncle Teddy looked past me, as if he were remembering something and was someplace else altogether. After a moment, he seemed to recover himself. "Your mom has a mean right hook," he said, feigning a smile.

"So it's true?"

"Listen, all of that is ancient history," Uncle Teddy said, slightly irritated. "I have no idea why my mother is even bringing that up."

"She found out I was at the house on Langely Lake the other week," I said.

Uncle Teddy frowned. "What were you doing down there?"

I hesitated. "If I tell you something, do you promise not to bring it up to my father?"

"Charlotte—"

"I can't tell you if you're going to talk to him about it. He made it clear he didn't want him involved."

"Who made that clear?"

I hesitated. "Promise my father doesn't find out about this?"

Uncle Teddy sighed. "Fine. You have my word."

"My uncle Hank—do you remember him? He's my mom's oldest brother?"

"We've met."

"Well he came to see me the other week," I said. "He told me he had to talk to me about my mom—about what happened to her. And he showed me these photographs he found in the lake house. These photographs—Uncle Teddy, if you had only seen them. He thinks they have something to do with what happened to my mom. I don't know."

"What's in the photographs?" Uncle Teddy asked.

"Some pictures are of my mom with a strange guy in a diner," I said. "And then there are other pictures of me and Seraphina and my mom from that summer. Like, creepy stalker photographs. As if someone were following us around Hillsborough that summer."

Uncle Teddy's brow creased in concern. "Do you have the photographs with you? Can I see them?"

I shook my head. "Uncle Hank has them. Listen, I know our family and theirs haven't always seen eye to eye, and I don't know what to make of the photographs, but I have to admit they're strange," I said. "I know this is a huge favor to ask, but do you think you could get me whatever information my father's private investigator found on my mother? I need to know the whole story. Or, at least, what there is to know."

Uncle Teddy was quiet for a moment.

"I can get you the PI case folder," he said. "It'll be our little secret."

"Thank you, Uncle Teddy," I said, letting out a sigh of relief.

"Of course," Uncle Teddy said, and he put his arm around my shoulder as we headed back to our booth. "What's a little secret between blood?"

fourteen
ALISTAIR CALLOWAY

1996

In late December, my family gathered at my parents' house in Greenwich for the holidays. As usual, Eugenia outdid herself. The whole house smelled of evergreens. A twenty-foot Christmas tree stood in the entrance hall near the grand staircase; the banisters were wrapped with holly and ribbon. Festive garlands dripped from every mantel, and paintings of snow-covered landscapes hung proudly on the walls while white lights twinkled from every bough of the trees on the front lawn.

We all brought someone home with us for the holidays because we Calloways would go crazy if we stayed cooped up with just ourselves. I brought Margot, as I had the Christmas before last. Olivia invited her friend Porter from Vassar, who wore argyle sweaters and horn-rimmed glasses and liked to talk in long run-on sentences about art and Sartre. I figured Teddy would show up half-drunk the day after Christmas with one of his eating club cronies in tow; instead, he showed up three days before Christmas with Grace.

Margot and I had been out at Bergdorf's all afternoon making our wedding registry and so I didn't see my brother and Grace until that evening when we all sat down together in the parlor.

There was a fire lit in the hearth; Teddy and Grace were sitting next to Margot and me on the large sofa, and Eugenia was getting us drinks from the wet bar.

"When was the last time you had your hair cut?" Eugenia asked, fussing over Teddy as usual as she handed him his scotch.

Teddy ran a hand subconsciously through his hair, patting at his unruly cowlick. "I've been busy," he said.

"I'll give Robert a call," Eugenia said. "He can come by and give you a proper cut and a shave."

I leaned forward and ran the sharp wire of the cheese cutter through the pale rind of the Parmigiano-Reggiano that Eugenia had laid out on the coffee table. I imagined the block of cheese was Grace's pale slender neck as I sliced it.

I was irritated that Grace was there. In our last conversation, it was like she had picked at a scab that had long ago healed over, and now I had to deal with it all over again. I was having this recurring dream now where I was standing atop a tall ledge in the dark. It was so dark I couldn't really see anything around me—I just instinctively knew where I was, and what lay below me. Every time, I tried to navigate away from the ledge. I'd be sure it was in front of me, so I'd take a step back. Or I'd be sure it was behind me, and I'd move forward. And every time, I was wrong. I fell—down and down and down until I hit the water. It engulfed me, cold and dark, and I'd try to swim out of it, but I could never reach the surface in time. No matter how hard I tried, how fast I swam, I could never find my way out of it. I'd wake up gasping for breath, drenched in a cold sweat.

Twice, Margot had been sleeping next to me when it happened. She was alarmed enough that she urged me to see a doctor. I scheduled an emergency appointment with my physician, Dr. Carmichael, and he ran a full physical, countless blood tests. Everything came back normal.

"You have a perfect bill of health," Dr. Carmichael had told me at our last appointment.

"Then why do I wake up at night drenched in sweat?" I asked.

"Anxiety," Dr. Carmichael said. "Has any stressful event occurred in your life lately? Anything out of the usual?"

I thought of Grace. *We were dating when it happened,* she had said.

"I'm getting married," I said instead. "In September. At the Vineyard."

"That would do it," Dr. Carmichael said with a chuckle. "Classic case of prewedding jitters."

He prescribed me Xanax; I popped that shit like candy, just so I could get some fucking sleep.

And now there Grace was again—sitting in my family's parlor like she was a member of the goddamn club. It was annoying, to say the least. What was she even doing there? Was Teddy still playing that stupid game of his?

"It's called Two Truths and a Lie," Eugenia was saying to the group. "It's a little game we like to play."

"I want to go first," Olivia said, perching on a chair near the fireplace.

"We need to explain the rules of the game first," Eugenia said, settling into her armchair with her glass of red wine. "And Grace should get to go first, since she's our guest."

Olivia leaned back in her chair and sighed. "That's hardly fair. Since we know practically nothing about her, she has a huge advantage."

"Do we have to play this?" Teddy whined. "Can't we be normal and play charades or something?"

"You're just saying that because you always lose," Olivia said. "He's not very good," Olivia said to Grace.

"Well, considering this game champions pathological liars, I'll take that as a compliment," Teddy said. "It's no wonder you're so good at it."

Olivia stuck her tongue out at him.

Olivia and Teddy always fought when they played this game.

Last time, it had ended with Olivia throwing her glass of wine in Teddy's face—the whole glass, not just the wine.

"Each person makes three statements—two of them are true, and one of them is a lie," Eugenia explained to Grace and Porter. Margot had played with us before. "The rest of us have to guess which one is the lie."

"And we can ask you things to try and figure it out," Olivia said. "And you can lie all you want to try and trick us."

"If we guess wrong, you remain in the game," Eugenia said. "And if we guess correctly, you're out. Everyone takes a turn until there's only one person left."

"And the winner gets a prize," Olivia said. "It's always something good. What's the prize this time, Eugenia?"

"The prize," Eugenia said, "is my watch."

She unclasped the white-gold band from around her wrist and held it up for all of us to see. It was a Rolex with a pavé-diamond dial.

"Oh, let me see," Olivia said, reaching out her hands to take the watch. "It's beautiful."

"So, Grace," Eugenia said. "You get to go first."

"Okay, three things," Grace said, clutching the stem of her wineglass.

"You don't have to play, if you don't want to," Teddy said.

"Yes, she has to play," Olivia said. "Why wouldn't she have to play?"

"It's fine," Grace said, putting her hand on Teddy's knee. She bit her lip for a moment, deep in thought.

"The first thing is, I used to swim competitively in high school, and I won a state champion title," she said after a moment. "The second thing is, I never finished college. And the third thing is, I have four brothers."

"What did you swim in high school?" Margot asked.

"Breaststroke," Grace said.

"Funny," Olivia said. "Teddy was also a champion of stroking breasts in high school."

"Shut up, Liv," Teddy said.

Margot tilted her head and considered Grace. She fingered the band of her engagement ring, as she often did when she was thinking. "Could be true," she said. "She's short, but she does have somewhat of a swimmer's build."

"Yeah, no chest," Olivia said.

"What the hell, Olivia?" Teddy said.

Grace's cheeks reddened.

"What are your brothers' names?" I asked.

Grace turned her eyes on me. It took her a moment to answer. "Lonnie, Will, Phillip, and Hank," she said.

"Jeez," Olivia said. "Are your parents Catholic or something? Do they not believe in birth control?"

"Mother, can't you, like, muzzle her or something?" Teddy complained. Teddy was the only one who could call Eugenia "Mother."

"Olivia, try to be civil," Eugenia chastised.

"Tell us something about each of your brothers," my father said.

"Well, Lonnie is the youngest," Grace said. "He's sort of the family clown. And Will is the middle one. He's always been the brave one, the adventurer. Phillip is the brains of the family. He's in law school. And Hank is the oldest—he's sort of rough around the edges but has a good heart."

"Which one's your favorite?" Olivia asked.

"I love all of my brothers," Grace said. "But I guess I'm closest with Hank."

"Why didn't you finish college?" Porter asked.

Grace shrugged. "For a lot of reasons," she said. "I felt like I didn't have a clear sense of what I wanted to do. And I don't think a classroom or a degree can teach you the things you really need to know in life. I guess I wanted to be out in the world, living."

"Those are stupid reasons," Olivia said.

"Okay, I think we're done playing," Teddy said, clapping his hands together. "Charades, anyone?"

"What?" Olivia said. "If someone gives a stupid answer, I'm allowed to say so. It's part of the game."

"She's right, Teddy," my father said. "Don't be so sensitive."

The tips of Teddy's ears reddened and he stared down at the coffee table.

"What were your brothers' names again?" my father asked Grace.

Grace was quiet for a moment. "Lonnie, Will, Hank, and Patrick," she said after a moment.

"You said Phillip before, dear," my father said. "Not Patrick."

Grace's eyes widened slightly. She looked down at her hands. "Did I?"

"Who votes that that was the lie?" Olivia said to the room. "Grace doesn't have four brothers."

We all raised our hands except for Teddy.

"Yes, you're right," Grace said with a small smile. "That was the lie. I guess I'm out."

"Don't give up so easily next time," Olivia said, clearly annoyed. "You could have tried to convince us that Dad just remembered things wrong."

"Not likely," our father said, giving Grace a wink. "I have a mind like a steel trap."

"My turn now," Olivia said, sitting up in her chair like a proud peacock.

Grace was mainly quiet for the rest of the game; Teddy silently seethed beside her. When it was Teddy's turn, his three things were: "My sister, Olivia, is an asshole; I hate my sister, Olivia; and

I do not hope that Olivia dies a horrific, painful death." In the end, my father won the game, and he picked the gold wristwatch out of Olivia's claws and gave it back to my mother.

Later that evening, I meandered down the hall and into Teddy's room. I sat casually in the armchair next to his bed and watched him unpack.

Teddy didn't acknowledge my presence, so I picked up the small rubber stress ball on his nightstand and threw it up in the air, caught it, and threw it up again.

"What?" Teddy finally asked when he could no longer ignore me.

"Nothing. It's just . . . a surprising choice of guest, is all," I said, setting the ball back down. "Is it really taking you this long to fuck her?"

Teddy stopped unfolding his shirts. His back was rigid; his ears went red.

"It's not like that anymore," Teddy said, not looking at me. "Not that it's any of your business."

"So you're what? Serious about her?"

"Would it be so terrible if I was?"

"Teddy, she's a poor choice," I said. "She's very . . . average."

Teddy gave a dark laugh. "*Average.* You say that like it's the worst possible thing a person could be. And you're wrong. You don't know her like I do."

"Listen," I said, standing and clapping my hand on my brother's shoulder. "You may think I'm being unfair, but I'm just trying to look out for you. You can be many things and make it in this family. Be stupid, be rebellious, be frivolous, be vain. But you can't be average. And Grace is average. She won't survive us. So do everyone a favor, and just fuck her and get it over with."

It happened very fast: one moment I was standing there with my hand on my brother's shoulder, and the next, he grabbed me by the collar of my shirt and slammed me up against the wall. He was red in the face and breathing all heavy, and I saw the fury in his eyes.

I laughed.

"Careful, Teddy," I said. "Your feelings are showing."

Eugenia had finally given in to the fact that I was going to marry Margot. I think the thing that helped her to get over it was her love of planning an event where the Calloways would be the main attraction. Wedding planning gave my mother plenty to focus on besides her dislike of the bride.

When I woke up the next morning, I found my mother and Margot sitting side by side at the breakfast table. Fabric samples were spread out in front of them.

"What are my favorite two women in the world up to?" I asked.

"Hey," Olivia said, offended. She was sitting a little ways down the table with a fashion magazine and glass of OJ in front of her. I ignored her.

"We're picking our color palette for the wedding," Margot said brightly.

"Oh, can I see?" I asked, reaching for one of the swatches in front of them on the table.

My mother swatted my hand away. "You're a man; you don't get an opinion," she said.

"Why not?" I asked.

"Because you're color-blind."

"I am not color-blind," I said.

My mother sighed and held up two swatches of white fabric. "What color are these?" she asked.

"White," I said.

"Precisely what I'm talking about," she said. She pointed to the swatch on the left. "This is egg cream," she said. "It has a yellow base." She pointed to the swatch on the right. "And this is moonlight. It has a blue base. Honestly, it's like night and day."

I squinted at both of them to get a better look. "They look the same to me," I said.

"Precisely," my mother said, and clucked her tongue. "Colorblind."

"Fine," I said, conceding. I picked up the pitcher of coffee and poured myself a cup. "I'll just get my coffee and be on my way then."

Margot and my mother ignored me, already tittering away about the color of the tablecloths. That's when I glanced out the window and saw them: Teddy and Grace on the front lawn. They were snowshoeing. Grace had on a pale cream peacoat and a wool hat pulled low over her ears. The tip of her nose was red with the cold. Teddy pushed her down into the snow. She laughed. She looked ridiculous lying there on her back with the giant webbed shoes strapped to her feet, sticking up. She pulled on Teddy's leg and he fell down next to her.

Grace started to move her arms and legs back and forth, forming a snow angel. It was like a fucking Hallmark card or something.

Then, Teddy leaned over, tucked Grace's hair back behind her ear, and kissed her. Something tugged in my gut, and I looked away.

fifteen
CHARLIE CALLOWAY

2017

It was tradition at Knollwood for upperclassmen to spend the first weekend in October at a retreat at Camp Wallaby in Maine. I had never been to camp as a kid, but I pictured melting marshmallows over an open campfire, and singing "Kumbaya" with a long-haired hippie with an acoustic guitar, and spending the day canoeing and braiding friendship bracelets. Cheesy, harmless stuff. But Harper Cartwright was quick to set us all straight on the bus ride up: this was no relaxing weekend retreat we were headed to.

"It's more of a 'get your shit together' wake-up call," Harper said, leaning back in her seat.

Apparently, everyone was forced to meet one-on-one with a guidance counselor, who reminded you that you were about to make one of the biggest decisions of your life.

"They basically remind you there are only, like, ten schools worth going to, and statistically how unlikely it is you'll get in, and if you don't get in, how you might as well just kill yourself. They get bonuses for making students cry," Harper said.

"It's not that bad," Dalton said. "They help you strategize. You know, what extracurricular might round you out, or what classes you should take to stand out as an applicant."

"They brought in someone from the admissions office at Harvard last year to speak," Crosby said, flicking Drew playfully on the knee. Somehow, Drew had finagled her way into sitting next to him and Ren was glaring at her from across the aisle.

"I'm feeling kind of carsick," I told Leo, who was sitting next to me. "I think I'll go lie down in the back and try and take a nap."

"Feel better," he said.

I found an empty bench at the back of the bus and lay down, using my messenger bag as a pillow. But first, I got out the old 1990–1991 Knollwood Augustus Prep yearbook I had stolen from the library the other day. After the conversations I'd had with Claire and Uncle Hank, I'd gotten to thinking about my father. There must have been snippets of his time there, glimpses of who he had been when he was my age.

I cracked open the hard cover of the book, which was in classic Knollwood colors: navy blue and gold. The pages were slick and glossy inside. The first one was an "In Memoriam" page for a student who had passed away.

JAKE GRIFFIN

July 8, 1973–December 21, 1990

Beloved son, brother, friend, and an invaluable
member of the Knollwood Augustus Prep family.

It didn't say how Jake had passed away. (Was it some sort of chronic illness? A car accident? Or something more sinister, like suicide?) There was a large school portrait of Jake in the middle of the page. He was wearing the Knollwood school blazer and tie. He had been a handsome kid, with dark hair and kind features. His wide smile seemed genuine and infectious.

Around the portrait was a collage of pictures of Jake at Knollwood—

Jake presiding over the student council, gavel poised to signal the beginning of a session; Jake standing on a foldout chair to hang streamers for the homecoming dance; Jake extended in the air, racket raised over his head as he delivered the winning serve at a tennis tournament. I was about to turn the page when I noticed it—a picture of Jake on Healy Quad, his arm slung over the shoulder of another boy. Beneath the picture was a caption: *Jake Griffin and Alistair Calloway*. I almost hadn't recognized the seventeen-year-old version of my father standing next to him, but when I really looked at him, I could pick out his familiar features—the blond hair, cut short; his blue eyes; his long forehead and sharp chin. Yes, that was my father.

My father often talked about his time at Knollwood and the friends that he had made there; he remained close with many of them. They were the people he golfed with on Sunday, the families we dined with in the summer on Martha's Vineyard—even, occasionally, the people we vacationed with. But he had never mentioned Jake Griffin. That wasn't a name I recognized. And yet, here the two of them were, arms around each other, beaming at the camera.

But perhaps it wasn't that strange that my father had never mentioned Jake. Maybe they weren't as close as the picture suggested, or perhaps they were close, and the memory of Jake was painful, so my father preferred not to bring it up.

I turned the page. The senior portraits came next, in alphabetical order. I quickly found my father's portrait near the front. Alistair Calloway. He had been voted "Best All-Around" by his classmates. His quote was from an unknown source: "Never look behind. What's done is done. Be wise and look ahead."

Flipping through the pages, it was easy to see the kind of boy my father had been: good-looking and well liked, smart and athletic. Captain of the tennis team, head of crew, president of the senior class, valedictorian. But then again, what other story was a yearbook supposed to tell but the happy one, the one that everyone wanted to remember?

One of the great joys of Camp Wallaby—and there were many, including the cabins that lacked A/C, and the intensive nonstop team-building exercises in which everyone jockeyed to be the leader, and the forced fireside chats in which students passive-aggressively complained about other students' passive-aggressiveness—was the fact that we were forbidden to bring our cell phones or any other technology that would connect us to the outside world. So, not only was I cut off from hearing about any progress my uncle Teddy may or may not have made into tracking down the PI's files on my mother's case, but I was also cut off from talking to Greyson, the only person who had an inkling of the mind-fuck I was going through on a daily basis.

At the moment, the group of twelve I had randomly been assigned to was at the volleyball court. Our counselor, Kirk, was a twentysomething who was overly enthusiastic about his lot in life.

"Okay," Kirk sang, clapping his hands together. "This afternoon, we're gonna play some volleyball. I'm going to assign two team leaders. These are two people who really excelled at trust falls this morning."

I raised my hand to ask how it was possible to distinguish oneself at something as passive as falling, but Dalton was standing in front of me, and his height blocked Kirk's view of my hand.

"Sheila and Zachery, come on up here and pick your teams," Kirk said. "And let's give them all a hand for their performances this morning."

I slow-clapped while others around me applauded.

"Let's hear it for gravity," I said. "To be honest, it did most of the work."

Dalton turned his head and chuckled at me. At least I amused someone.

"I'll take Crosby," Sheila said.

Crosby jogged past me to stand next to Sheila on her side of the net. They high-fived each other.

Zachery called Dalton. Sheila called Harper Cartwright. When it was Zachery's turn, Dalton leaned down and whispered something in his ear.

"Come on, man," Zachery whined. But still, he raised his hand and pointed at me. "We'll take Charlie."

I couldn't blame Zachery for his reluctance in choosing me. I had never been into sports, really. I just never got the appeal of sweating, or shortness of breath, or the way it made your body ache. It had never been fun to me, and I had never been particularly well coordinated.

"All right, Calloway," Dalton said as I made my way up to them. He raised both hands above his head in the air and I had to raise myself onto my tiptoes to reach them.

"Yeah, um, go team," I said.

"It figures," I heard Harper say over my shoulder, and I turned to see her rolling her eyes and making a kissy face, which was annoying, but nothing I would have really cared about if Sheila hadn't laughed right along with her, as if they were in on the joke together.

When the teams were picked, I stood next to the net in front of Dalton, who was serving. Across from me, on the other side of the net, was Harper. She was nearly as short as I was, so we were fairly evenly matched in that regard. She flipped her curly blond hair over her shoulder and dubiously toed the dark sand court.

Dalton delivered a razor-sharp serve that sliced over the net and landed on the other side of the court, untouched in a cloud of dust. My team applauded.

"It's all right, it's all right," Sheila said, trying to rally her team. "We'll get the next one."

"Anyone awake over there?" Zachery chided as Harper tossed the ball back to Dalton under the net.

"Send the next one my way, Dalton, if you think you're so fierce," Harper said.

"Whatever you say, Miss Cartwright," Dalton said with a smile.

His next serve whizzed through the air, just over the net, and Harper jumped up and spiked it back over.

I realized too late that the ball was coming directly toward my face, and that I was not positioned correctly to be able to take a step back in order to hit the ball. So I ducked out of the way. The ball hit the court behind me with a dull thud.

"That's what I'm talking about," Harper yelped, and Sheila gave her a loud, smacking high-five.

"You know you're supposed to hit the ball, right?" Zachery asked me.

I suddenly found myself wishing that volleyball was a contact sport. "Can I pretend your face is the ball and practice?"

"Easy, tiger."

Sheila served next. She scored a point before turning the ball over. I realized with a sinking feeling as my team rotated that I was up next to serve. I had the upper-body strength of an eight-year-old boy.

I tried the underhand serve. The ball didn't make it over the net, but it did nail Zachery in the back of the head, which was a small, if humiliating, victory. Across the court, Harper let out a loud snicker. My only consolation was that it was an ugly through-the-nose snicker that kind of sounded like she'd snorted.

"It's okay, good effort!" Kirk yelled, and clapped his hands loudly, which, of course, only made things a million times worse than I already thought they were.

I was determined to redeem myself. I bent my knees and leaned forward. I watched Dalton on the next play, the way he didn't clasp his hands together until he reached the ball, the way he leveled his forearms before he bumped it. I could do that. When the next ball came over, I was ready. It was coming toward my section of the court and I prepared myself to hit it.

"Got it!" Dalton said, and I barely had time to step out of the way before he barreled into the very spot I had just been in and popped the ball into the air. Zachery spiked it over.

"Hey," I said.

But Dalton only gave me a little wink, like he had done me a favor. "Don't worry; I've got you."

I scoffed but he was too busy bumping chests with Zachery and making some sort of caveman hoot to see it.

I knew my performance thus far hadn't done much to give him any confidence in my abilities, but still.

When the next ball came my way, I catapulted myself to it.

"Got it!" Dalton and I yelled at the same time, right before we collided. Dalton fell and I fell right down on top of him.

"You okay?" Dalton asked when the dust had settled around us.

I swatted his chest.

"Ouch," Dalton said.

"That was my ball," I said.

"I was just trying to help," he said.

"Well, don't."

I picked myself up and dusted off my knees, which were covered in sand.

"You okay, Dalton?" Zachery asked. "Did she hurt you?"

"Hey, he's the one who ran into me," I said.

"When Dalton says he's got it, you get out of the way," Zachery said. "He's our LeBron James. You always let LeBron James take the winning shot."

"You really don't want to take another step toward me right now, Zachery," I said.

"Control your girl, Dalton," Zachery said.

"What did you just say?" I asked, but Dalton held out his arm and caught me around the waist.

"Just ignore him," he said.

At that point I didn't really have much of a choice, because the next ball was coming over the net. This ball wasn't coming remotely toward me; it was going to fall just over the net. But I didn't care. I launched myself across the court. Right before I leapt into the air and pulled back my hand to spike the ball over, I saw her. There, on the other side of the net, waiting, was Harper Cartwright. As I my palm made contact with the ball, all I could think was, Dive, bitch. Dive. I hit that ball like it was Zachery's face.

Harper did dive, but she wasn't quick enough. The ball smacked the floor of the court. Score.

I hollered in a very unsportsmanlike manner that I'm sure thoroughly horrified Counselor Kirk. Meanwhile, Dalton picked me up and threw me over his shoulder and spun around in a victory dance.

"What now, Zachery? What now?" I yelled.

"I'm sorry to interrupt the revelry," came a voice. Dalton slowed and set me down. That's when I saw her—my guidance counselor, Mariah.

Every student was assigned a guidance counselor when they entered Knollwood, and Mariah was mine. We were required to meet with our counselors at least once a semester to go over our class schedules and talk about our "goals" and what we "wanted to accomplish," which would have been annoying enough as it was, but Mariah felt her guidance should extend beyond the academic and extracurricular realm. She was always asking me about my family, and how I was holding up, and—I swear I'm not just imagining this—elbowing the tissue box across her desk in my direction, as if at any moment I might explode in a torrential downpour of tears. I'd seen the undeniable twinkle of glee in her eye the last time I was in her office and asked for a tissue, and then the sheer disappointment when I used it to blot my lipstick.

Mariah was middle-aged and always dressed business casual—chinos and loafers, a blazer over a collared shirt. She was the type of person who insisted on all the students' calling her by her first name, and she liked to put her hands in her front pants pockets and nod when she was deep in thought. People who put their hands in their front pants pockets bugged me.

"I'm scheduled to meet with Charlie next," she said. "Is it okay if I steal her for a bit?"

"Please, take her," Zachery said.

"I got us that last point if you didn't notice," I said.

"Yeah, congratulations. You also cost us several and almost injured our star player. So you're still in the negative, if *you* hadn't noticed," Zachery said.

"Oh, Zachery, I'm really going to miss this very special time we've shared together," I said. And I reached up and patted him on the head as I walked past him.

On the sidelines, Mariah hugged me.

"So good to see you, Charlie," she said. "I'm so glad we have a chance to talk. I feel like we didn't get to accomplish all that we could in our last visit."

Give it up, lady, I wanted to say. *I'm not going to cry.*

We started walking toward the lake. Mariah buried her hands in her front pockets and started to nod.

"So, regardless of what you might have heard from your peers, the real purpose of this session is not to scare you, but to help you get where you want to go," Mariah said. "I think the best place for us to start is for you to tell me where you'd like to end up in a year and a half. For most Knollwood Augustus Prep students, that means college, but some seek out other opportunities for personal or intellectual growth—such as Outward Bound, or a year of travel, or a year of volunteer service."

"My plans haven't changed," I said. "I'm going to UPenn. To the Wharton School."

Mariah smiled at me. "I hope we can be honest with each other right now, Charlie. Don't feel pressured by what your peers might think, or what your family might think of your choices. I'm here to get a sense of where *you* want to see yourself."

"Okay," I said. "But I just told you what I wanted. UPenn. The Wharton School."

"That's a tough school to get into," Mariah said. "And the acceptance rate is less than twelve percent."

"I have good grades," I said. "And great test scores."

"Yes, and yes," Mariah said. "A three point seven GPA and ninety-ninth percentile in test scores. I'm not questioning your intellectual chops, Charlie."

"So, what's the problem?"

"Well, a school like UPenn wants students who show they can handle the academic rigors of their program, but they also want to see well-rounded individuals. Students who are going to take an active interest in the university outside of their classes, forge their place in the school and out in the world. And you don't have any extracurricular activities, which is very unusual for a Knollwood student. No social clubs or sports or special interests."

"I was going to write my college essay on that," I said. "How the very fact that I don't conform to the conventional mold is what makes me a unique, well-rounded individual. The average student's résumé today is on steroids. Everyone is in orchestra and plays on the tennis team and serves on the student council. Not because they're actually interested in all of those things, but because they feel they have to check all these boxes to prove their worth to their dream school. But I don't need to be defined by my participation in a club or a sport. And that makes me a freethinking individual who will forge her own path at a school like UPenn and in the world thereafter."

"I was expecting that type of response from you," Mariah said.

"And what type of response is that exactly?"

"Manipulative," she said. She stopped and looked at me, hands in pockets, head nodding. "You're smart, but I think that's a detriment in your development, because you've learned to use your intellect to twist things to your advantage. You know how to play people."

Heat pooled into my cheeks. Mariah had never talked to me like this before. "Excuse me?" I said.

"What concerns me is that you've even learned to manipulate yourself," she said. "You genuinely believe what you just told me."

I didn't respond. She had backed me into a corner. I could either say I believed it and be deemed a manipulator, or I could say I didn't believe it and be deemed a liar.

"I'd love to hear your take on things," I said. "If I've twisted the facts, then untwist them. What's the real reason I'm sorely lacking in extracurriculars?"

"You lack empathy," Mariah said. "You don't connect easily with other people because you don't trust anyone, and because you've been taught to think you're better than everyone else. And you've been taught to exploit others for your own gain. In short, you suffer from narcissistic personality disorder."

I felt like the wind had been knocked out of me. "Shit," I said, because fuck manners at this point. "Tell me what you really think. Please, don't hold back on account of my feelings, because apparently, I don't have any."

"On the contrary," Mariah said, "narcissists have deep feelings, but mostly about themselves. And I'm not trying to hurt you, Charlie. I'm trying to help you."

"What exactly does this have to do with UPenn?" I asked.

"This has to do with your future, Charlie, with the type of person you want to become. It's not too late to change, to turn things around."

Mariah took a piece of paper out of her shoulder bag and handed it to me. It was Knollwood Augustus Prep's Club Day poster, the one I had found in my mailbox a few weeks ago.

"Take a look at the opportunities Knollwood is offering you," Mariah said. "Pick something that matters to you—if even a little bit. It's still open period to join. Just try it. Try to open yourself up to a new experience, to new people. You may surprise yourself."

At campfire that evening, Counselor Kirk took out his guitar and started to lead everyone in a round of "Save Tonight" by Eagle-Eye Cherry. I didn't have much of a singing voice, and I really didn't feel like being around anyone, so I snuck away by myself to the edge of the space still lit by the campfire. I lay down behind a fallen tree and stared up at the night sky, at all the stars that were visible on a cloudless, moonless night.

I couldn't help but think about everyone whose voice drifted over me. I knew all of my friends' dream schools and career plans. Lately, it was all they talked about. I knew that Leo was planning on going to Harvard, where he was a legacy on his mother's side, and that Drew had her heart set on studying political science at Wellesley, Hillary Clinton's alma mater. Stevie had her eye on Berkeley, where she would be premed, and Yael was leaning toward Columbia, mostly because she wanted to be in the city. They were all so sure; they had their minds made up and their futures laid out, like me. I wondered if their counselors had shit all over their dreams like mine had—and not just their dreams, but them personally.

I couldn't help but think that it was just me. That there was something wrong with me. That what Mariah had said about me was true.

A twig snapped just above my head and I looked up to see Leo standing over me.

"Sorry," he whispered. "Didn't mean to scare you. Just thought I'd join." He lay down beside me on the ground.

"Hey, cuz," I said.

"I can't wait for college," Leo said, sighing. "Or just to get back to campus where there's some fresh meat. I've hooked up with every upperclassman over a six already. There's nothing here for me anymore."

"That is a problem," I said sarcastically.

"I found myself actually considering Sheila Andrews just now," Leo said. "I caught myself looking at her over the glow of the camp-fire with Kirk's sultry baritone crooning in the background and I thought, Maybe. And then I decided I'd come over here before I did something stupid."

"I'm pretty sure Sheila Andrews would cut off your balls if you messed with her," I said. "So, I'd steer clear."

"What about Stevie?" Leo asked, wiggling his eyebrows at me. "It's always the uptight prudes who turn out to be the most fun in bed."

"Fat chance," I said. "Stevie is too smart to give you a second glance, much less her virginity."

"I like a challenge," Leo said. "Maybe you could put in a good word for me? Wear her down a little bit?"

Something occurred to me then, and the smile slid off my face. I sat up. "Tell me you didn't put Stevie in your stupid game."

I'd never betrayed Leo's confidence and told anyone about the Board of Conquests—not even Drew. But if he'd put Stevie on his board, I'd be forced to warn her. I couldn't just sit back and let her get played.

"Relax, I was joking," Leo said. "Though, I have to admit, putting Little Miss Priss in the game would certainly make things interesting."

"Promise me you didn't put any of my friends on the board," I said, because I had to be sure.

Leo looked at me and rolled his eyes, annoyed I hadn't found his joke as funny as he did. "I promise," he said. "So, how'd things go with your counselor?" he asked, changing the subject.

"Really, really good," I said in a mock-cheerful voice as I lay back down. "Apparently I'm a horrible person."

Leo laughed.

"No, really," I said. "She flat-out called me a narcissist."

"You're a Calloway," Leo said. "We're all narcissists. It's, like, genetic."

I laughed. "I guess," I said.

Then I was silent and closed my eyes and tried to communicate like we had when we were children—the way we each used to feel what the other was feeling, even when we didn't have the words to convey it.

I'm not a bad person, am I? I wanted to ask. *We Calloways are selfish and manipulative and we have hard edges, but—but—but we'd never hurt anyone, not in any significant way, not in a way that really mattered. Right?*

It was stupid, the kind of thing I was glad I didn't have to say out loud. But also, the kind of thing I liked to think Leo might have understood if I had said it. I lay there for a moment, my eyes still closed tight, and wondered if he had heard me. Then, in the darkness, I felt him take my hand.

sixteen
GRACE FAIRCHILD

CHRISTMAS EVE 1996

For the third night in a row, I couldn't sleep. Teddy's parents' house was easily the largest house I'd ever been in, but it didn't feel like a home. Everything was cold and polished and untouched. It didn't feel lived in. There were fresh flowers in the vase on my armoire in the morning, and at night when I returned to my room everything was tidied—my dirty clothes washed and folded and returned to my suitcase, the minty smear of my toothpaste wiped clean from the sink, the bedspread perfectly creased and turned down by the maid. Every trace of me neatly erased. It was so different from the house where I had grown up, where we were always leaving bits of ourselves behind—the old sofa in the garage that reeked of Lonnie's pot; the smear of fingerprints on the wall by the front door where we'd balance ourselves as we leaned down to take off our winter boots; the permanent stain on the kitchen ceiling from when Will's volcano experiment prematurely erupted; the dimples in the baseboards from our illicit kicking the ball around indoors.

And it wasn't just the house that felt foreign; it was the people. Eugenia had been welcoming, asking me question after question about myself. Did I ride horses? *No.* Ski? *No.* Where was my favorite place to vacation? *I haven't traveled much.* In her relentless quest to find some common ground, she had only proved we had none. Teddy's father was reserved; Olivia and her friend Porter were too self-involved to pay anyone else much attention. Margot couldn't be bothered to remember my name—she had called me "Gaby" once, and then "Gina." Alistair was aloof—we'd been seated next to one another at dinner and he'd barely spoken two words to me, choosing instead to engage Porter in a convoluted conversation on existentialism and art. Even Teddy was different somehow. When it was just the two of us, he was fun and easygoing. But around his family, Teddy became a caricature of himself—lazy and flippant, as if he wanted to refute any expectations they might have of him and at the same time prove he didn't care what they thought.

I couldn't seem to navigate the strange world I had entered into. At dinner, we were served foie gras in duck jus. I didn't know what it was, and I was too embarrassed to ask, so I ate it. I'd never tasted anything quite like it before—it was light and buttery and melted on my tongue, a little slice of heaven. Olivia abstained from the foie gras and had a salad instead. When I asked if she was a vegetarian, she said she didn't find the torture of animals appetizing. She explained, in excruciating detail, that the ducks were gavaged. They had a tube stuck down their throats twice a day and were force-fed corn boiled in fat until their livers grew to ten times their natural size—that was what gave the duck liver such a delicious taste and texture. When she finished, I set my fork down, horrified. I couldn't stomach the cheese course or the dessert, a decadent chocolate soufflé.

And tomorrow morning would be the worst of all. We would open presents after brunch. I'd enlisted Teddy's help in picking out gifts for his family. He had taken me to Barneys, where he'd done all of his shopping. We'd stood at the counter and he'd shown me the sterling silver cufflinks he'd bought for his father (half my month's rent) and the Hermès handbag he'd picked out for his mother (half a year's rent). I'd had to settle for thoughtful gifts instead—a coffee table book on gardening for his mother, a shaving set for his father. I dreaded sitting in front of them as they opened them tomorrow—the feigned "ohh"s and "ahh"s and thank-yous, especially in the wake of the extravagant gifts they had probably gotten me.

Deciding I could no longer lie there and stew, I threw back my bedsheets and got up. I pulled my swimsuit and goggles out of my suitcase, put the swimsuit on, and grabbed a spare towel from the bathroom. In the dark, I navigated my way through the cavernous hallways to the indoor pool Teddy had shown me after dinner.

I'd lost count of my laps when I looked up and saw that I was no longer alone. Alistair Calloway was sitting on the far edge of the pool, near the chaise lounge where I had left my towel, his pant legs rolled up, his ankles dangling in the water. He lifted his beer in greeting when he saw me notice him, and I took off my goggles and swam over to where he was.

"Fancy seeing you here," he said.

"Couldn't sleep," I said, pinching my nose to get the water out.

"Room not to your liking?"

"No. I mean—yes, it's lovely. It's just . . . it's like staying in a museum," I said.

"'Homey' isn't really Eugenia's style," Alistair said, taking a sip of his beer.

It was the deep end of the pool, so I grabbed on to the edge to keep myself up. We both fell into an awkward silence. I wondered what he was doing here—if he was having trouble sleeping too, and if he usually came to the pool by himself late at night to unwind. But he wasn't wearing a swimsuit; he was fully dressed. Had he followed me here?

Alistair was the most difficult member of Teddy's family to read. He had been kind and charming at the charity ball, easy to talk to. He'd been exactly the way Jake had described him to me years ago when we'd sat in our tree house above Langely Lake and he'd spread out his yearbook on the plywood boards and told me about his friends, pointing to their pictures. I remembered Alistair's portrait—his light blond hair and ice-blue eyes; he was quite handsome and striking in his school blazer. There was something haughty in the way he looked out at you, the tilt of his chin. I almost hadn't believed it when Jake had told me Alistair was one of his first friends at Knollwood, how Alistair had taken him under his wing in tennis. But the other night, Alistair had barely looked at me when we were playing Two Truths and a Lie, and tonight at dinner, he'd ignored me. I didn't understand what I could have done or said to put him off.

"You said you used to swim in high school?" Alistair asked.

I was surprised he'd been paying attention.

"I won state champion in breaststroke," I corrected him.

Alistair whistled. "I wasn't aware I was in the presence of greatness."

I bit my lip and sent a spray of water in his direction.

He laughed and stood.

"I'll race you to the other end," he said. He pulled his shirt off over his head, revealing his flat muscled abs. I looked away as his hands moved to his belt buckle. "Let's make it interesting. Let's wager something."

"Why does everything in your family have to be a competition?" I asked, half joking.

"Where's the fun if you don't stand to lose something?" he asked.

"Fine," I said. An idea had dawned on me. "If I win, you have to trade me one of the gifts you got for your mom—a good one. And you can give her my coffee table book instead."

"A coffee table book?" Alistair teased. "You drive a hard bargain."

He slid into the water next to me in his boxers.

"All right," he said. He exhaled deeply, adjusting to the cool temperature of the pool. "And if I win," he said, "I'm going to kiss you."

I couldn't tell by the way he said it if he was joking, if I was supposed to laugh.

"You're going to kiss me?" I said, waiting for the punch line.

"Yes," he said.

"Why?" I asked.

"Because I want to."

"You shouldn't want to." It was the only thing I could think to say.

"And you shouldn't make a wager you don't intend to win," Alistair said. "Or don't you think you can beat me?"

He had that haughty look in his eye—the same one I recognized from that old yearbook photo. I narrowed my eyes at him.

"On the count of three, then," I said, lowering my goggles onto my nose. "One, two, three."

I pushed off hard from the wall. I was a little tired from all the laps I'd swum, but I had the advantage of being warmed up, while Alistair was going cold into a full sprint. I propelled myself forward as fast as I could, my breath in hot short gasps. In my peripheral vision, I could see Alistair keeping pace with me. My strokes were faster, but he had the advantage of height. He took one stroke for my every two. At the last moment, he reached out and tagged the wall a half second before me.

I stood. We were in the shallow end now. I was breathing hard, my breaths racking my body. Next to me, Alistair appeared winded, too. Smug, but winded.

"You're faster than I thought you'd be," he said.

"Not fast enough, unfortunately," I said.

When we'd both caught our breath, Alistair scooted closer to me along the wall so that we were almost nose-to-nose. He looked at me. He had blue eyes, just like his brother, but there was something different about them—darker, colder. While Teddy's eyes were like a bright cloudless summer day, Alistair's were like the Arctic Sea.

He leaned into me, and at the last moment, I turned my head. I felt the stubble on his jaw as his lips grazed my cheek.

When he pulled back, anger flashed in his eyes.

"That wasn't a kiss," Alistair said.

I shrugged. "You weren't very specific in defining it," I said. "But that's hardly my fault."

I started back across the pool, this time at a slow, leisurely pace. A few seconds later, I heard the movement of the water behind me as Alistair followed.

I was about halfway across the pool when I felt Alistair reach out and grab my ankle. He pulled me toward him, against the hard warm panes of his chest. I could smell his scent—a hint of spice and something exotic and sweet, like tuberose blossoms. He looked down at me, and I knew he was going to kiss me before he did. He tilted my chin up to meet him. He grazed my lips gently, and then his hand slid into my hair, and he pulled me harder toward him. He opened my lips with his tongue and kissed me roughly. I was breathless, my heart hammering in my chest, the apex of my thighs aching.

When it was over, he looked at me, his eyes hooded.

"That," he whispered against my lips, "was a kiss."

seventeen
CHARLIE CALLOWAY

2017

When I returned from Camp Wallaby, there was a large box waiting for me on my dorm room bed. Inside was a letter from Uncle Teddy.

As promised, kiddo, here is everything from Mr. Lynch, the private investigator.

There were stacks of thick manila envelopes with labels like "Phone Records" and "Credit Card Bills." I found a drive labeled "Interviews" and plugged it into my laptop. Several folders popped up instantly with names and dates. Nearly everyone on both sides of my immediate family had been interviewed, as well as close friends of the family and employees. My father's family was at the top of the list because it was in alphabetical order. I wondered whose interview I should listen to first. I had already heard what Eugenia had to say—that my mother struggled with depression and that might have had something to do with her disappearance. I clicked on my aunt Grier's folder. She was my aunt by marriage and a psychologist. She had gone to Harvard and gotten her doctorate at NYU. If anyone were to weigh in on my mother's mental state and how it may have related to her disappearance, it would be my aunt Grier.

I clicked on the audio file and it started to play. I put on my headphones in case Drew came into our room.

"State your name, the date, and your relationship to Grace Calloway," came a male's voice. It was a deep, rough voice that I assumed belonged to Mr. Lynch.

"Grier Calloway. October twenty-second, 2007. Grace Calloway is my sister-in-law."

October 22, 2007—that was more than two months after my mother went missing, and a few weeks after the bank tapes were discovered.

"Mrs. Calloway, would you say you and your sister-in-law are close?"

"Not particularly," Grier said. "Given her history with my husband, I think it's only natural."

What did that mean? Did Uncle Teddy not like my mother for some reason?

"But we were cordial enough, and we saw each other at family gatherings and over the holidays quite a bit," Grier's voice went on.

"And what is your impression of her character?"

"That's a complicated question," Grier said, "because my impression of Grace was influenced by events that transpired before I even met her. But I would say that, looking at her history, Grace is a creature of habit. She exhibits similar patterns of behavior— namely abandonment—and seems driven by a singular desire."

"And what desire is that?"

"Well, on the face of it, money. But of course, there's always an underlying cause for this desire. Maybe to Grace, money represents a sense of freedom or security she never had in her working-class family. Maybe money gave her a sense of power. I couldn't tell you; I didn't know her well enough."

"When you say Grace is a creature of habit, can you give me an example of what you mean?" Mr. Lynch asked.

"Well, take what she did to Teddy," Aunt Grier said. "It was no coincidence that Grace settled near Princeton and met Teddy. She was clearly hunting for an affluent partner. Teddy was a good catch—he came from a well-established, wealthy family, and so Grace invested her time in him, in their relationship. And then when she met Alistair, who was obviously the favored heir, someone who was already positioned for leadership at the Calloway Group, she latched onto him. When she saw an opportunity to secure him, she did. She saw it as trading up."

I could hear my heart beating in my chest. I felt dizzy. My mother dated Uncle Teddy? She left him for my father? Was this true?

"And you see both of these relationships as primarily motivated by money?" asked Mr. Lynch.

"Yes," Aunt Grier said. "Everyone is acting as if Grace taking this money and running off is some kind of surprise. But if you look at her history, it's a behavior she's exhibited repeatedly. Grace is, like most people, a creature of habit. Here she had a chance to get Alistair's money without any of the obligations or entrapments—no more husband, no more children, nothing tying her down. Grace saw an opportunity, once again, to trade up, and she took it."

I slammed my laptop shut. I didn't want to hear any more. I couldn't. My mother had used Uncle Teddy and my father for their money, and then, as soon as she had the chance, she just ran off with it? This whole time, she had just been manipulating all of us? And what did that make me? Just some by-product of her greed—some entanglement, or "obligation" or "entrapment," that stood in the way of what she really wanted?

Not to mention—what other dark secrets about their past were my family hiding from me?

Maybe listening to these interviews and going through the case files was a bad idea. What if I found out things that didn't only ruin any nice memory I had of my mother but tainted my relationship with the family I had left? Did I really want to know? Was it really worth it?

"She's the worst," Drew said, sighing heavily as we made our way across Healy Quad, back toward Rosewood Hall. "Quantum physics? Trig? Is she serious? I almost fell asleep just reading the course descriptions. How am I supposed to survive a whole semester of the actual classes?"

Drew was upset because Mariah had told her she needed to take some upper-level math or science courses next semester to round out all the art, history, and language classes she was taking.

"I want to study *political* science in college," Drew said. "Not actual science."

"Speaking of scheduling for next semester," I said, lowering my voice, "Dalton told me he could get all of the junior A's preferred enrollment for the spring."

Normally, only seniors had preferred enrollment, which meant they got to register for their courses first, giving them first pick of spring classes. Apparently, Jude Bane had been able to hack the registrar and trick the system into thinking the junior A's were really seniors, effectively allowing us to skip right to the front of the line when enrollment opened.

"Hallelujah," Drew said. "I'm going to sign up for Miss Horvath's Yoga and Mindfulness seminar. I've been wanting to take that since I started here but it's always full by the time I register."

"We need to get our course lists to Dalton by the end of the week so he can input them into the system," I said. "Maybe we can coordinate so we can have similar schedules?"

"Of course," Drew said. "Oh, so, you never told me, what terrible things did Mariah say to you?"

"Apparently, I lack empathy and suffer from a severe case of narcissistic personality disorder," I said.

"Psh. Show me a teenager who doesn't meet that description," Drew said, unimpressed.

"Did she call you a narcissist, too?"

"No, but Stevie told me Mariah said her perfectionism was borderline obsessive-compulsive and recommended counseling."

"Harsh."

"Yeah."

"How's Stevie taking it?"

"She's creating a spreadsheet of psychiatrists within a fifty-mile radius who are covered by her parents' insurance, complete with what schools they went to and their specializations, before she makes any decisions."

"Maybe Mariah had a point about that one."

"A little," Drew said.

"Mariah told me I'm more likely to get into UPenn if I join some extracurricular activities," I said.

"I've been saying that since freshman year," Drew said. "You should join fencing. I swear it will help you work out all that pent-up aggression you have inside you."

I thought about my recent volleyball match at Camp Wallaby. "I'm not exactly very coordinated," I said.

"Fair point," Drew said. "What about the debate club? Physical sparring might not be your forte, but verbal sparring is definitely your thing."

"Yeah, but the debate club? I'd rather not get into UPenn than be a master debater."

"Fine. Fine." Drew stopped suddenly and held out her hand to stop me too, which caught me hard in the gut.

"Ouch," I said. "Hey, I'm walking here."

"I have the best idea," Drew said, and she started walking again.

"Can you have good ideas and walk at the same time?" I asked, pressing my hands to my aching stomach.

"Shh," Drew said. "Listen. This is genius. You should join the *Knollwood Chronicle*."

"The school newspaper?" I asked, dubious.

"Yes," Drew said. "You could write for, like, the Opinions column. The newspaper has way more clout than the Debate Club. It's not quite on par with joining a sport, but it's close."

"I don't know," I said.

"UPenn would eat that sort of thing up," Drew said. "And it would get Mariah off your back."

"Maybe," I said.

"Ladies," Leo said, coming up behind Drew and me on the quad and putting one arm around each of our shoulders.

Drew shrugged out of his grasp. "Gross," she said. "I just showered."

"Where've you been lately?" I asked Leo. "Your Xbox is getting lonely."

"Sorry, my *extracurriculars* have been keeping me busy," Leo said. "Speaking of which, how's round two looking for you guys?"

"When did—?"

"This morning," Leo said. "Check your mailboxes."

"How'd you make out?" I asked.

Leo removed his hand from around my shoulder and reached into the pocket of his blazer. "Just swimmingly," he said.

Drew and I both stopped to read the card he handed me.

Item #2: One fish sculpture from the Poseidon Fountain

Drew pursed her lips together into a fish face.

The Poseidon Fountain sat on the north lawn in front of the theater. It was a large stone fountain with Poseidon in the center, riding a frothy wave, brandishing his trident in the air. Five large bronze fish sculptures surrounded him, jumping out of the sea, their mouths pursed open and water pouring forth. Stealing the fish would be a tricky job if Leo didn't have someone helping him, as I'm sure the fish sculpture was probably pretty heavy for one person. Luckily, Leo had me.

"Not bad," I said, handing the ticket back to him.

Leo followed us into the mailroom of Rosewood Hall. He leaned against the wall next to my box.

"Wanna take bets on what you'll get?" Leo asked. "The secret recipe to Mrs. Wilson's biscuits?"

"Mmm," I said. "Or Headmaster Collins's prized pit bull—the whole dog this time?"

I withdrew the card from my mailbox and read.

Item #2: One compromising photo of you with Mr. Andrews

My stomach twisted.

Drew leaned over to read mine as she unlocked her own box.

"No fair," she said. "You get to seduce Mr. Andrews for your ticket? I'd do that just for fun."

"What'd you get, Reisling?" Leo asked.

Drew opened her box and withdrew her card.

"Fuck," she said, reading it.

"That bad?" I asked.

"See for yourself," Drew said, handing me her ticket.

I took it and read while Leo read over my shoulder.

Item #2: Mr. Franklin's trig midterm

Leo let out a low whistle.

"Damn, Reisling," he said. "Who'd you piss off to get landed with this?"

Drew and I both looked at each other. *Ren.* All of Drew's flirting with Crosby hadn't gone unnoticed. Ren was using the Game to carry out her revenge.

Stealing an exam would have been bad enough because of Knoll-wood's zero-tolerance policy when it came to cheating. If Drew were caught trying to steal an exam, she'd be expelled, no questions asked. But this particular exam was even tougher, because Mr. Franklin always wrote the exam fresh the day before it was given. There would be no easy shortcut, like getting an old exam from a previous student or sneaking onto his computer to print a copy. No, this would be some serious *Mission: Impossible* stunt.

"I'm not sure," Drew told Leo. "But someone up there hates me."

As I stood outside the door to the room that housed the *Knollwood Chronicle*, I imagined all the things I'd rather have been doing at that very moment.

Eating a jar full of raw jalapeños until my throat blistered.

Having another heart-to-heart with Mariah about my personality disorder.

Running a marathon on a searing August afternoon, with heat pooling on the pavement.

None of these things sounded fun, exactly, but they were all more appealing than what I was about to do. Still, I told myself to suck it up, exhaled deeply, and pushed open the door to the newsroom.

My view of what a high school newsroom would look like was largely and improbably shaped by old films like *His Girl Friday* and *Citizen Kane* and *All the President's Men*. I imagined a kinetic room where editors—clad in glasses and sweater vests, each with a pencil tucked behind one ear—chased their reporters down narrow rows of desks, demanding to know where they got their scoops, the reporters always vowing steadfastly to never divulge their sources. I imagined journalists hunched over typewriters, and endless piles of Styrofoam cups nesting stale coffee, and the sound of phones ringing.

The *Knollwood Chronicle*'s room looked like most other classrooms around campus—the same bland, taupe-colored walls, the same gray carpet. A few desks and computers and chairs. An old patched-up couch at one end, and at the other, a steel filing cabinet. It was quiet, mostly—there were only a handful of people, mainly sitting at desks, clicking away at their keyboards, and another small group in the corner on the couch.

"Can I help you?"

I turned and saw a girl with pale skin and dark hair sitting behind the desk closest to the door.

"Is this the *Chronicle*?" I asked.

"In all our glory," she said. She stood and leaned over the computer on her desk to shake my hand. "I'm Penn Franklin, the editor in chief," she said.

Penn was a senior. We'd never officially met, but I had seen her around.

"I'm Charlie," I said. "I was hoping to try the *Chronicle* out for Open Period. If you have any spots left."

She raised her eyebrows at me. It wasn't just that I was wandering in in the last week of Open Period asking for a spot. It was also that I was an upperclassman who had never stepped foot in the *Chronicle* before. Most students who did Open Period were underclassmen, freshmen eager to find their place at the school, carve out their niche. And most juniors, well, they had already found their place. Most of them had climbed to the upper rungs of whatever club or sport they had joined as freshmen. Drew was cocaptain of the volleyball team. Stevie was president of the Student Ethics Board. Leo was president of the junior class. I was title-less.

"What department are you interested in?" Penn asked. "Writing, photography, layout, marketing, sales?"

"Writing," I said. "Definitely writing."

"Most of our beats have been given out already," Penn said, tucking a sheet of hair behind her ear. "I'll have to check and see if any of our editors have room to take you on."

"I can take her."

I knew the voice before I turned around and saw her shiny, perfectly coifed blond curls. Harper Cartwright.

"We have a spot in Features," Harper said, smiling at me.

I instinctively gritted my teeth.

"Perfect," Penn said before I could edge my way out of it with some bullshit excuse. Because I knew what this would be, what I was getting myself into. As a new writer, I expected to be hazed a little, to do coffee runs, to get the shitty stories that nobody else wanted. But this would be something else entirely. This would be placing myself directly under Harper Cartwright's thumb, something I was loath to do given she was Dalton's most recent ex and she probably suspected Dalton and I were more than friendly.

"Perfect," Harper said, and I saw the evil gleam in her eye. "We're just wrapping up pitching, if you want to sit in."

"Sounds great," I lied.

I followed her over to the corner of the room, where a group of students sat around an old coffee table, and took the only spot left on the patched-up couch. Harper sat in an armchair facing the couch, a notebook in hand.

"This is Charlie," Harper said to the group. Looking around, I realized I didn't know a single person there, which probably meant they were all underclassmen, mostly freshmen. They looked so doe-eyed and young. "Charlie's a junior," Harper said. "She's new to the paper so you guys will have to show her the ropes."

I almost cringed under the weight of her condescension but managed a little wave and smile to the group.

"Finn, you're up next, I believe," Harper said, glancing down at her notebook.

"Well," Finn said, sitting up straighter in the seat next to me. "Picture this. Title: 'School Uniforms.' Subtitle: 'The Great Equalizer or the Great Divider'?" He gesticulated widely, as if writing the invisible title in the air in front of him with his short, stubby fingers. "The title needs some bedazzling, some sparkle, for sure, but the meat of the piece is a quasi-fashion, quasi-political story on these hideous uniforms we're forced to wear."

It was then that I noticed the perfect creases down the legs of his pants, the way his blazer was neatly pressed. He had added a bright pink silk handkerchief that was folded in his breast pocket. It took all that was in me to refrain from rolling my eyes. Not another clothing-obsessed prep up in arms because he had to wear a polyester blazer to class. Please, kill me now. I'd known coming here was a mistake.

"Sounds fascinating," Harper said, nodding and jotting something down in her notebook. "There seems to be a lot to chew on there, so I'm going to pair you with Charlie."

"Me, Charlie?" I asked, both hoping and knowing it was useless to hope that there was another Charlie in the group.

"Yes, you, Charlie," Harper said. "The two of you can share a byline."

I had to share my first byline with a freshman? And I had to put my name next to some stupid article on stripes versus polka dots that the whole school would see? And UPenn was supposed to be impressed by this?

Uh, hell no.

"Actually," I said, "I have a really great idea for a story."

"I'm sure you do," Harper said, "and we'd all love to hear it—at the next pitch meeting. But, as of now, our pages are full."

Harper closed her notebook with a snap and smiled at the group.

"Great job this week, everyone," Harper said. "I'm really looking forward to reading your work. Don't forget to get me your drafts by the end of the day on Friday."

As everyone shuffled away their notebooks and pens and laptops, Finn shifted in the seat next to me. "Do you want to go grab some coffee?" he asked. "Maybe we can sketch out an outline together for the article?"

"I can't right now," I said. "I have somewhere I need to be."

As in, anywhere but here.

"Okay," he said. "Well, we should exchange numbers or emails so we can plan to meet up later."

Harper was headed toward the door. I had to talk to her before she left, sweet-talk her into letting me have my own article.

"Sure," I said. I ripped the corner off a loose piece of paper in my bag, scribbled down my school email address, and handed it to him as I stood. "Here, just email me yours."

I was across the room and out the door before he could respond or protest.

"Harper," I called out. Harper stopped halfway down the hallway and turned.

"Hey, Charlie," Harper said. "I'm so excited you decided to join the *Chronicle*. I had no idea you were interested in journalism."

Oh, I'm not, I wanted to say. *I just wanted an excuse to spend more time with you. Maybe later we could paint our nails together and braid each other's hair?*

But I bit my tongue. I had to play nice.

"Yeah," I said. "I was just thinking, maybe I could sit this round out and come back next week for the pitch meeting?"

"Could you tell me exactly what your concerns are about doing this story with Finn?" Harper asked, shifting the strap of her bag from one shoulder to the other. She creased her brow as if she truly cared about my answer.

"Come on, Harper," I said. "School uniforms? It's a stupid fluff piece. I couldn't think of anything less interesting to write about if I tried."

Harper cleared her throat; her glance flicked to just beyond my left shoulder. I turned and saw Finn standing in the hall behind us. His ears were beet red.

"Excuse me," he said.

I didn't say anything; I just stepped out of the way so he could pass.

Harper and I stood there silently, listening to his footsteps echo back to us as he turned the corner. In the distance, we heard a door open and close.

Harper smiled. "I'm afraid this is the last week of Open Period," she said. "So, if you want a spot on the paper, you'll have to share this byline with Finn."

I sighed. "There's really nothing else you can give me?"

"I need a thousand words by Friday," Harper said.

Then she turned on her heel and left, and I watched any chance I had of making this extracurricular activity work disappear with her.

The first thing we did was kill the lights in the fountain. It was a dark, moonless night, but when the Poseidon Fountain was lit up, we knew Old Man Riley—or anyone else strolling across campus at two in the morning—would be able to see us from hundreds of yards away.

Leo had a set of the janitor's keys, which opened every door on campus. The A's had made a copy before planting the original set in Auden's locker. So, he was able to get to the control switch in the theater and turn off the lights.

Under the cover of darkness, I undressed and slid into the basin of the Poseidon Fountain in only my underwear. It was October now, and there was a cold bite in the air. Goose bumps erupted up and down my arms and legs as I waded to the middle of the fountain where the drain was at the base. With the fountain full, the water came up to my waist.

I had never particularly liked being in the water. I was a late bloomer when it came to learning to swim, which had disappointed my mother, because she had been a natural swimmer.

When I was four, my parents taught me to swim in the indoor swimming pool at my grandparents' house in Greenwich. I remember my mother holding me as I lay on my belly, kicking and paddling, but as soon as she would let go, I would sink and cling to her in the water, and she would pull me up, gasping and screaming.

"She's never going to learn if you coddle her like that," my father had said, sitting on the edge of the pool with his legs in the water.

"She'll get it when she's ready," my mother said, setting me on the edge of the pool next to my father. She climbed out and patted herself dry with a towel. "I learned to swim when I was barely out of diapers," she said. "It's in her genes. She'll get it."

She reached out and ruffled my hair.

"I need to call Hank back before dinner," she said, tilting her head to one side to get the water out.

"We'll be here, won't we?" my father said to me. "Looking at the pretty pool, thinking how nice it would be to swim."

"Don't rush her, Alistair," my mother said, ducking down to give my father a kiss on the cheek. "She's just a late bloomer."

When she was gone, my father slid into the water. He took a few steps away from the edge of the pool and then turned to reach his arms out toward me.

"Come on, Charlotte," he said. "Swim to Daddy."

I stared at him for a moment, unsure.

"Jump," my father said. "Jump and I'll catch you."

I stood on the edge and looked at his outstretched arms. They didn't seem that far away. Surely, with a leap, I would reach them. So I did it. I jumped.

I felt my feet break the surface of the pool and then my head went under and I waited, I waited for my father's arms to reach down and pick me up, to rescue me, but they didn't.

My first reaction was to cry out for help, and so I did. I opened my mouth to call for my father, and it filled with pool water.

My next reaction was to panic, and I started to kick and thrash in the water in a desperate attempt to swim as I sank instead. I opened my eyes and they burned with chlorine. I looked up through the water and saw the blurry figure of my father standing there, above me, just out of reach. I stretched out my arm toward him and he took a step back. I could hear his disembodied voice. It sounded like he was calling my name, but I couldn't hear him clearly under the water.

I could feel my heart—it was pounding, hot, in my ears. My lungs ached. I couldn't breathe.

And then something grabbed me from behind and pulled me to the surface.

I was crying, screaming; I couldn't see as I gulped at the air. It took me a moment to realize it was my mother who was holding me. She pulled me out of the pool and wrapped me in her towel, which was already wet, and cradled me in her arms.

"Jesus, Alistair," my mother said over my shoulder. "What the hell were you thinking?"

"She would have swum," my father said. I couldn't see him because he was still behind me in the pool. "She would have figured it out, if you just let her. She would have been fine."

Now I felt around the bottom of the fountain with my feet until I found it—the plug. Then I took a deep breath and lowered myself to the bottom, and pulled the stopper out.

"It's a nice night for a swim," Leo said when I returned to the surface. He was beside me now in the water and we sat there together, waiting for the water to slowly drain around us.

When the fountain was empty, we dismantled one of the fish sculptures. It took both of us to carry the sculpture, slow and waddling, to the theater, where we hid it in the old prop room, covered in a sheet.

It was Thursday evening, and, not surprisingly, Finn had never emailed me about getting together to write our draft of the article. I couldn't say I blamed him, really, but I also wasn't about to let him write a story by himself that my name was going to go on, or worse, report to Harper that I hadn't helped write the article and give her an excuse to drop me from the paper. Since Harper wasn't going to let me write my own piece, my only recourse was to convince Finn to take the article in a different, less lame direction. So, when I spotted him across the dining hall at dinner, I grabbed a tray of pizza and soda and marched across the dining hall to his table.

Drew caught my eye as I passed my usual table, where she was sitting with Yael and Stevie and a bunch of the guys—Leo, Dalton, the whole gang—and headed toward the south side of the dining hall, where the freshmen sat.

"Where are you going?" she called out to me.

To my social ruin and the pinnacle of humiliation, probably, I wanted to say, but instead I just shrugged my shoulders at her and rolled my eyes.

I marched up to Finn's table. He was sitting with some sweaty, pimple-faced freshman boys, who were talking animatedly but fell silent when they saw me standing there.

"Hey, Finn," I said.

Finn looked up and his ears turned red again when he saw me. He looked back down at his tray, fiddled with some pasta at the end of his fork. "Hey," he said.

"Long time, no see," I said.

"Yeah," he said, still not looking at me, and I almost felt bad. Partly for him—for the things he had heard me say in the hallway— but also for myself, for having to put up with this. Because regardless of whether I had hurt his feelings, what I'd said was true.

"Do you think we could meet up later?" I asked. I didn't even say *to work on the article*—because, hey, I was throwing the kid a bone. Let his friends think we were meeting up for other reasons. Let them think he had some hot date with an upperclassman.

But Finn only shrugged. "I don't know. I'm kind of busy later."

Oh, hell no.

I shrugged right back at him. "That's okay," I said. "Now works, too."

I took a step forward and set my tray down at the table across from him, and his friends scooted over to make room for me.

"Hey, guys, I'm Charlie," I said as I opened the tab on my soda.

"Declan," the kid sitting next to Finn said, giving his head a little shake to clear his long mop of hair out of his eyes.

"Luke," the boy sitting next to me said.

"Finn and I are writing an article on uniforms for the *Chronicle*," I said.

I sucked on the tip of my thumb where some soda had sprayed on me and dug out my laptop from my shoulder bag.

I decided it might actually be to my advantage that Finn's friends were there. Maybe by discussing the article in front of them, Finn would come to see how silly it was and he would understand that we needed to find a new angle or a new topic with more meat.

"We could use some quotes for the piece, actually," I said as I opened my laptop. "How do you guys feel about the uniform? Are you pro-polyester or anti-polyester?"

"Honestly," Finn said, rolling his eyes, "this goes beyond how ludicrous it is to line a blazer with polyester. I wanted to take it a more political route."

"What exactly is political about blazers?" I asked.

"Think about it," Finn said. "At Knollwood, the point of uniforms is to eliminate the socioeconomic divide—but that's such a narrow context focused on the microcosm of our campus. If we think of the larger communities we're a part of, Falls Church, for example, or New Hampshire, or even the United States, the Knollwood uniform becomes not an equalizer but a status symbol."

Hmm. Not where I had thought he was going to go with it. I actually had never spent much time thinking about the uniform I wore, about how it might look to other people, what it meant. And how that meaning might change depending on where I was and who I was with.

"That's deep, bro," Declan said.

"It doesn't suck as much as I thought it would," I said. "Actually, it might not suck at all."

"I know," Finn said. "It's hardly a stupid fluff piece."

I cleared my throat and opened a new document in my word processor. "Yeah, definitely not fluff. Have you started an outline?"

Finn took a sip from his water glass and then daintily patted the corners of his mouth with his napkin.

"Yeah," he said after a moment. "I was actually going to head to the library for a bit before it closes to finish up, if you want to come."

I glanced at my wristwatch. It was going on seven o'clock.

"Sure," I said, shutting my laptop and wrapping my slice of pizza in a napkin so I could eat it on the way. "Sure, let's go. Nice to meet you, Declan, Luke."

"Likewise," Declan said, and as I stood to pick up my tray, I swore I saw Luke give Finn some kind of wink.

Finn and I walked our trays to the conveyor belt at the far side of the cafeteria, where we set our dishes down, and then headed out through the French doors that led to the cafeteria patio and the pathway on the back lawn that led to the library.

"We should do some interviews with students on campus and people outside campus," I said. "We could do some freeform-association thing, where we ask people to give us the first three words that pop into their minds when they think of Knollwood's uniform. You know, dig into the subconscious perception a bit, see what connotations pop up."

I took a bite of my pizza and almost ran directly into Finn, who stopped suddenly in front of me and turned to face me.

"Look," he said. "I didn't want to say this in front of my friends and look like a jerk, but I'm not sharing this byline with you. I wrote the article already, and your name isn't going on it."

I almost choked on my bite of pizza. I swallowed the piece that was in my mouth only half-chewed, and it scraped at the back of my throat as it went down. My eyes watered.

"Is this because I told Harper I thought your article was fluff?" I asked. "Because, that wasn't really about you. I just wanted to write my own story, that's all. I'm not good at the whole . . . *collaboration* thing."

"I wasn't exactly looking forward to sharing my story and my first byline with someone else, either," Finn said. "Especially someone who came in weeks after Open Period started and missed Hell Week. But I wasn't a jerk about it."

"What's Hell Week?" I asked.

"They made all the newbies wear these stupid paper dunce hats. And not just in the newsroom, but everywhere. And we had to run a lap around the building any time we wrote in the passive voice and do the whole senior staff's laundry. Stuff like that."

"Ew," I said.

"Yeah," Finn said. "So for you to just march into the pitch meeting, all holier-than-thou, and demand your own story and then call my piece 'fluff' when I get stuck with you—well, it's just a little rich, if you ask me. Even if I am a freshman and you're—you."

"I'm—me?" I asked. "What does that mean?"

"You know, you're *Charlie Calloway*," Finn said, and I could see the italics in the way he said my name, as if it meant something.

"Look, let me help write this article and I'll do something for you," I said. "There has to be something you want. You can tell your friends we made out if you like."

"I'm gay," Finn said.

"Oh," I said. "I just thought that your friends thought we were . . . I don't know. I'm pretty sure your friend Luke winked at you back there."

"Luke's an idiot," Finn said.

"It's just that I—I sort of need this," I said. "If I don't have this byline, Harper will kick me off the paper. And I need this paper to get into UPenn."

"I'm sorry," Finn said.

For a second I thought he was apologizing, that he had changed his mind about the article.

"'I'm sorry,'" he said again. "Two words. You should try using them sometime."

"What?" I asked.

"It's called an apology. Contrition. Feeling bad when you've done something bad."

"I know what 'contrition' means," I said.

"Do you? Because I didn't hear any kind of apology. All I heard was you telling me what you need and what you want and how you might manipulate me to get it. And I'm sure that usually works for you. But this isn't one of those times," Finn said.

"Finn," I said. "Please."

He turned and started walking back up the path. "I'm sorry," he called over his shoulder.

But he didn't sound sorry at all.

eighteen
ALISTAIR CALLOWAY

SPRING 1997

In the conference room, my father and our lead architect had the building plans for our latest development project in Murray Hill spread out on the table. They were going over the neighborhood planning codes. I'd just come from my walk-through of the shell of a tenement with my design consultant. It was the first official project that I was heading at the Calloway Group. I had found the building and helped broker the deal, and now I would oversee the extensive renovations that would turn that sad dilapidated mess into luxury rental apartments that rising young professionals would pay through the nose for.

My father looked up as I entered the room.

"Where's Teddy?" he asked.

"He's not here?" I said, glancing at my watch. It was going on half past two. Teddy should have been there half an hour ago. He was in the city on spring break and my father had instructed him in no uncertain terms to stop by.

Normally, I'd have been pleased that Teddy was a no-show. But that was before my father had made him my de facto second-in-command on the Murray Hill project. Teddy was supposed to shadow me when he graduated in May. My father had already cleared out an office for him. Apparently, Teddy was getting a seat at the table whether he fucking showed up or not.

"I'll call him," I said. "I'll be right back."

"Rosie," I called as I passed her desk on my way to my office, "get me Teddy on the phone."

It was no surprise that Teddy was late. He and Grace were staying at my apartment on the Upper East Side and they spent their days traipsing around the city, taking in the sights. I'd avoided them as much as possible, leaving for the office early every morning before they woke up. I'd even stayed two nights at Margot's, but her apartment was small and uncomfortable—a third-story walk-up that she shared with two other med students in Brooklyn. So, the other night, I'd slept at my place. I heard them come home late in the evening as I was lying in bed. Grace's laughter floated down the hall, and then I heard their bedroom door creaking closed. I put a pillow over my head and tried not to picture them together in the dark.

"I have Teddy on line one for you," Rosie called from the doorway.

I picked up my phone.

"Where the hell are you?" I asked. "You were supposed to be here to go over plans for the new rental property half an hour ago."

"Hold on a sec," Teddy said. His voice became muffled. "Yeah, medium rare, please. And a glass of Chardonnay when you get the chance." I heard static and then my brother's voice again. "Sorry, I'm back. What's up?"

"Tell me you're not literally out to fucking lunch right now," I said.

"Well, the early showing of the movie was sold out, so we had to go to the later one. And that pushed lunch back, and then there was a wait to get a table so we're just now ordering," Teddy said.

"Get your ass in a cab and get down here," I said. "Now."

"Listen, you don't really need me there," Teddy said. "Can't you just fill me in later on what I missed? I mean, I'm on vacation."

"Please," I said. "Your whole life has been a fucking vacation. The fun's over."

"All right, *Dad*," Teddy said.

"I'm serious, Teddy," I said. "Enough with your pranks. If Father and Eugenia want to hand you consolation prizes your whole life just for existing, that's their choice. But this is my project, and I'll be damned if I'm going to let you fuck it up."

"You sound a little shrill," Teddy said. "Maybe it's just the connection. Anyway, my appetizers are here."

"Listen here, you little shit," I said, "don't you even think about—"

But before I could finish, Teddy hung up.

My phone rang. I fumbled for the light on my bedside table.

"Mother of Christ," Margot muttered next to me. She held up a hand to shield her eyes from the lamp.

"Sorry. Go back to sleep," I said, squinting at the clock.

2:18 A.M. Who the hell would be calling at this hour? I grabbed for my phone. The number on the screen was Teddy's. Fuck him.

I turned off the light and rolled over, tucking my arm around Margot's warm body and pulling her to me. She ran her fingertips along my forearm and settled her body against mine.

A few seconds later, my phone rang again.

Margot groaned and pulled a pillow over her head to muffle the sound.

I grabbed for my phone again and answered it.

"You better be dying in a ditch somewhere right now," I said.

Only, it wasn't Teddy's voice that answered me. It was Grace's.

"Alistair?" she said.

I sat up.

"Alistair, I'm sorry to be calling," she said. She sounded slightly breathless. "I know it's late," she said, "but I didn't know who else to call."

"What's wrong?" I asked.

"It's Teddy," she said. "He's fine—he just, he had a lot to drink, and then he got sick in the cab, and so the driver pulled over and made us get out, and nobody else will take us when they see the state he's in. He's a mess, and I don't think I can get him down to the subway by myself—he's too heavy, and he keeps falling."

"Where are you now?" I asked, rubbing the sleep from my eyes.

"The West Village," she said. "Seventh and Greenwich."

"Stay there," I said. "I'm coming to get you."

Half an hour later, I'd driven to Lower Manhattan. I spotted them almost immediately, Teddy huddled on the sidewalk and Grace standing in her winter peacoat, breathing a fog of warm air into the cold March night, looking lost and uncertain. I pulled over.

Grace called my name when she saw me. "I've never seen him like this before," she said. "I tried to get him to go home hours ago, but he wouldn't leave the bar."

Her lips were blue and she was shivering. I wanted to hurt my brother for making her stand out in the cold in the middle of the night like this.

"I'll help you get him in the car," was all I said.

I could smell my brother before I reached him. He had the remnants of vomit down the front of his coat and he smelled like sour Chinese food and wine. Grace took Teddy gently by one arm, and I took him by the other, perhaps a little roughly, and shuffled him toward the idling car.

"I know it's spring break," I said to Teddy. "But this isn't fucking Cancún."

Teddy crawled in and crumpled in the backseat. Grace got in after him, and I went around front to get in the driver's seat. As I put the car into drive, I looked at Teddy in the rearview mirror.

"What was the occasion?" I asked dryly.

Teddy just kept his eyes closed and hugged himself, groaning in discomfort.

"It was your father," Grace said. "He called Teddy about missing that meeting, and I don't know, it didn't go well."

"He's a prick," Teddy moaned, leaning his head against the window. "I don't feel good."

"Then stick your head out the window," I said. "I'm not paying to have the car detailed because you can't hold your liquor."

Grace leaned over and rolled Teddy's window down for him. The icy spring air filled the car.

"It's too cold," Teddy whined, his words sloppy and running together.

"The cold air might do you good," Grace said, rubbing Teddy's knee. "Your dad did seem like he was being a little hard on him," Grace said to me.

"Don't let Teddy's sad act fool you," I said. "He deserved a lot more than a few harsh words."

Teddy leaned toward Grace and put his head in her lap. His eyes drooped closed. Grace ran her fingers through his hair and hummed a gentle tune I couldn't place.

I'd never envied my brother anything. But I envied him this.

Teddy mumbled something I couldn't make out.

"What'd he say?" I asked.

"Something about a rosebush?" Grace said.

"It's just like the rosebush," Teddy said sloppily. After a few minutes, he went still and silent; I think he had fallen asleep.

"What does he mean about the rosebush?" Grace asked me quietly.

My eyes met hers in the rearview mirror. Then I looked away.

"When we were kids, my father told me to go cut down Eugenia's prized rosebush," I said. It was Eugenia's favorite, the one that had won the Hartford Flower and Garden Show three years running. I remembered that day—how hot it was, sweat dripping into my eyes, and the way the thorns bit at my palms as I hacked at the base of the rosebush with the gardener's shears.

"As I was cutting it down, I looked up, and there was Teddy," I said, "running toward me, screaming at me to stop. I didn't, of course—Father had given me a job to do, and I was going to do it. Anyway, we fought."

I remembered that fight, the two of us rolling around in the dirt, answering a kick to the shin with a swift, hard punch to the gut.

"I cut the rosebush down, and that night at dinner, Teddy wasn't allowed at the table."

"Because of the fight?" Grace asked.

"No," I said. "Because my father had told him to save the rose-bush, and he'd failed."

"I don't understand," Grace said. "I thought your father told you to cut it down."

"He did," I said. "He told me to cut it down and he told Teddy to save it."

"But why?"

"I guess he wanted to see which one of us would prevail."

"That's cruel."

I shrugged. I knew Teddy saw it that way, too, but I didn't.

My great-grandfather had come to this country a penniless tai-lor. He'd saved his money and bought a factory in the Meatpack-ing District and built up a sizable fortune. My grandfather, the youngest of his six brothers, had outwitted his brothers to take their inheritance, and with it he had started the Calloway Group. My father had taken that company and built it into one of the larg-est real estate companies in New York City. He didn't want Teddy and me to just sit on our asses and carry on what he had done; he wanted us to make more of what we were given, the way his father had, the way he had. To carve out our own legacies.

"Father's a Darwinist," I said. "He believes only the strongest survive and the rest will be wiped out."

"And is that what you believe, too?" Grace asked.

I met her gaze in the rearview mirror again. When I was a child, I looked up to my father. I wanted to be exactly like him. He taught me to be selfish, to go after the things I wanted with a stubborn, unrelenting tenacity. That was the only way to win, to get ahead, to accomplish something close to what he had accomplished. I thought about all the things I'd sacrificed on the altar of that belief. Things I could never undo. Who was I—what was I—if I no longer believed in that?

"He's not wrong," was all I said.

Grace's reflection held my gaze. She looked thoughtful, almost sad.

"Maybe," she said after a moment. "But it seems like an awfully lonely way to live."

nineteen
CHARLIE CALLOWAY

2017

I woke to a blindingly bright light. I glanced over at the door and saw that Drew had flipped on the light switch. Panicking for a second, thinking that I had slept through my alarm, I looked at the clock on my nightstand. It read six thirty A.M. I threw up a hand to shield my eyes.

"Jeez, Drew, kill the light, will you?" I asked, my voice scratchy.

I heard two bounding leaps and then felt Drew jump onto my bed.

"I'm so proud of you!" Drew chirped. "My very own Edward R. Murrow."

"What are you talking about?" I asked, sitting up.

"You," she said. "Your article."

Drew was dressed in her workout shorts and a T-shirt, her hair thrown up in a messy bun from her morning run. Her cheeks were still flushed. She handed me the newspaper she was holding.

"I saw it this morning when I was getting my coffee," she said. "It's soooo good, Charlie. Really. I read it twice."

I took the paper from her and read.

IN THE EYE OF THE BEHOLDER
By Finn McIntire and Charlie Calloway

Finn had included me in the byline. But why?

"I'm going to take a quick shower," she said. "And then let's grab breakfast, 'kay?"

"Sure," I said, rubbing the sleep from my eyes.

Drew grabbed her towel from the hook on the back of our door and picked up her shower caddy. She hummed as she left the room. I waited until she left and then I started to read.

"Charlie, why don't you go next?" Harper said, pen poised over her notebook.

The Features team was sitting around the coffee table in the *Chronicle*'s room. I sat on the patched-up couch again. Finn was on the other side of the table, sitting in a swivel chair he had pulled over from one of the desks. He hadn't looked at me all meeting. I knew because I had been staring at him practically the entire time, trying to catch his eye.

"Sure," I said. "I want to do a piece on Knollwood's urban legends. You know, unpacking the mythologies around campus. Where did they come from? What might they reveal about us? Why do these particular stories persist?"

"Interesting," Harper said. "Do you have an example?"

"Everyone knows about the Knollwood ghost," I said. "But no one really knows if a student actually died on campus, or when these stories started."

Ever since I'd seen the "In Memoriam" page in my dad's old yearbook, I couldn't stop thinking about the kid who had passed away, Jake Griffin. What had happened to him exactly? Could the Knollwood ghost—the specter that haunted campus—be him?

"I like it," Harper said. "Well, I think you just got your first solo byline, Charlie."

"Actually," I said, "since this piece involves a bit of research, I was wondering if I could work with Finn again."

I glanced at Finn. His eyes flickered toward me and then away again immediately when we made eye contact. His ears turned red.

"We made a pretty good team last time," I said.

"Sure," Harper said. "Sounds good."

When the meeting was over, I stuffed my notebook into my bag and then made my way over to Finn, who was still putting his things away.

"The byline," I said quietly so that no one else would hear. "You didn't have to do that."

Finn shrugged. "Your free-association idea was good. I used it. And I just didn't feel right not giving you any credit."

"Thank you," I said.

Finn looked at me.

"You don't have to share this byline with me," he said.

"I want to," I said. "It's called recompense. You know, making amends when you mess up. Unless . . . unless you don't like the story and you want to work on something else?"

"No," Finn said. "I like it. I think it could be really good. Besides, who doesn't like a good ghost story?"

The next afternoon, after Introduction to Photography, I lingered as everyone filtered out of the classroom. Mr. Andrews was always the last one out because he had to shut down his PowerPoint and put away his equipment. As I slowly tucked my laptop into my shoulder bag, I glanced at the clock that hung above the door. It read 4:15. Leo had promised he would be in position outside in the courtyard by 4:25, ready with his iPhone to catch my steamy embrace with Mr. Andrews through the classroom window.

"Do you mind taking a look at some of the stills I shot last weekend?" I asked, standing at one of the tall lab tables, the stills in front of me on the tabletop. I made sure to keep my back to the window. I didn't want my face to be distinguishable in any of Leo's shots.

"Sure," Mr. Andrews said, coming over to stand next to me. He leaned over to study them. His arm brushed mine and I didn't move it. I just stood there, pressing my arm to his.

In that moment, I felt powerful. Was this how guys felt when they were going after a girl? Like they were the hunter, and the girl was the prey?

"I tried to incorporate the rule of threes you were telling us about in framing," I said. I took a step closer to him, and when he stood up all the way, he was between me and the lab table, facing the window.

"I can see that," he said. "You did a nice job."

"Thanks," I said, looking up at him through my eyelashes. "I learned from the best."

I lifted myself onto my toes and kissed him, reaching my arms around his neck. He didn't move.

"Charlie—" Mr. Andrews said when I drew back; he removed my arms from around his neck. "I think you've gotten the wrong idea here. I'm your teacher."

"I know," I said. I leaned into him, fingered the top button of his shirt, and gave him one of those crooked, flirtatious smiles I had seen Drew give Crosby a hundred times. "And I feel like you have a lot to teach me."

When I looked into his eyes, I expected to see that look that Cedric Roth had always given me last summer when I was squeezed into the seam of the couch in the study and he was on top of me. That eyes-half-closed, mouth-half-open, I-want-you look. But it wasn't there. Instead, Mr. Andrews looked disappointed.

"Don't do that, Charlie," Mr. Andrews said. "Don't sell yourself so short. You're a whole lot more than—than this."

Slowly, he separated himself from me. And as I turned to glance at the window, where the eye of Leo's iPhone camera gaped at me through the glass, I didn't feel powerful anymore. Instead, I felt something I hadn't felt in a very long time.

Shame.

In the dining hall that evening, I sat at a table with just the girls and pushed my food around my plate. After that afternoon's events, I'd lost my appetite. I couldn't figure out how a little harmless flirting had somehow turned into something that made me feel like the lowest of the low. Suddenly, I realized that both Stevie and Yael were looking at me expectantly.

"What?" I asked.

"Told you she wasn't listening," Stevie said.

"You know, just because your male counterparts aren't present doesn't mean the two of you can check out of the conversation," Yael chided.

I glanced across the table at Drew, who also seemed to be doing a lot of food rearranging on her plate without much fork-to-mouth movement.

"Sorry," I said. "I'm just tired."

"Relax, we're just giving you a hard time," Yael said. "Anyone down for fro yo?"

"Me!" Stevie said, shooting her hand in the air.

"No thanks," Drew said.

"I'm good," I said.

I waited until Stevie and Yael left before I nudged Drew under the table.

"Hey, so Dalton needs our lists," I said, my voice low.

"What list?"

"For preferred registration," I said. "I sent you my list last week but I never got yours."

"Oh, right," Drew said. "Sorry, I haven't looked at it yet."

"Um, okay," I said. I didn't understand why she was being this way. Here was our one chance to get our top class choices next semester and ensure we had matching schedules, and she was completely blowing it off.

"Why don't you just give your list to Dalton so you don't miss the deadline?" Drew asked. "I've got your list so I can build my schedule off that."

"Is everything okay?" I asked.

"Hmm?" Drew said, distracted. "Oh, yeah. I just have a migraine."

She was being weird, evasive. Her migraine excuse was as transparent as my tired excuse.

"Hey," I said casually, "did you figure out how you're going to get Mr. Franklin's trig exam yet?"

"Oh yeah, I think so," Drew said.

"Need any help?" I asked.

"No, I've got it covered," Drew said. "Thanks, though."

"So, that's it?" I asked. "You're not even going to give me any details?"

"You guys, you're not going to believe it," Stevie said, sitting back down at the table, juggling three bowls of fro yo. "Mocha Midnight Madness is back."

She scooted one of the bowls across the table toward me and elbowed the other in Drew's direction.

"I got spoons!" Yael said, dumping a handful of silverware on the table.

"Yum," Drew said, but I could tell her smile was feigned. She reached for a spoon and averted her eyes from me. I had the strange feeling that even if Stevie and Yael hadn't come back to the table just then, she would have found a way to avoid answering my question.

Later that night, I was in Dalton's room doing research for a report we had been paired together on in Mr. Andrews's Introduction to

Photography class. We had to write about a modern photographer who was doing something innovative in the medium.

Girls were allowed in the boys' dormitories during study hours, which were after dinner and before curfew (seven to nine o'clock on weekdays). But we had to leave the door ajar and have three feet on the floor at all times. I sat on Dalton's bed next to him, my back leaning against the dormitory wall and one foot tucked under me, one dangling on the floor. I was trying to stay focused on the task at hand, but my mind kept wandering to Mr. Andrews. I wanted to ask Dalton about the compromising photo (what did the A's want with it?), but I didn't know how to broach the topic. Dalton wouldn't be allowed to tell me the purpose behind the compromising photo without betraying the A's confidence, and I didn't want to put him in that position.

On the one hand, Mr. Andrews seemed like a decent human being, and blackmailing him or undoing him with these misleading pictures seemed cruel. But on the other hand, I didn't have a choice. If I failed, would the A's release the photographs they had of me and Leo? Forget the public humiliation I would suffer—Leo would suffer too, and he had done nothing wrong. I couldn't do that to him.

"Earth to Charlie."

I looked up to see Dalton staring at me.

"Hmm?"

"You seem a bit distracted," Dalton said. "Everything all right?"

"Yeah," I lied. "Everything's fine."

"What do you think of this guy?" he asked, and I leaned closer to him to get a better look at his laptop screen. My shoulder leaned into his shoulder and I felt him stiffen beside me.

"Um, so this photographer uses all natural light in his photos," Dalton said. "They're showing his latest exhibit in the West Village next Wednesday. He's even doing a Q & A afterward. Maybe we could go? Get bonus points for getting a quote from the artist for our paper?"

"Sounds good," I said. "And I can ask him about his thoughts on the line between the public and the private in his art," I said sarcastically.

"Interesting line of thought, Ms. Calloway," Dalton said, clearly mocking my exchange with Mr. Andrews that first day of class. "Ethics and art is always an enlightening discussion."

I turned to laugh and caught Dalton smiling at me. There were barely three inches of space between us. My breath caught in my throat and Dalton leaned forward and kissed me.

"I've wanted to do that for a long time," he said.

"How long?" I asked.

"Pretty much since you were a freshman and you called Libby Winkler Libby *Wanker* right to her face in the dining hall because she was being snooty."

"She was so full of herself," I said. "Everybody secretly hated her."

"Still, it was a pretty ballsy move for a freshman to call out a senior like that."

He moved his laptop off his lap and skimmed his fingers along the edge of my jaw until they were on the nape of my neck, and he pulled me forward and kissed me much less gently, his fingers wildly clutching in my hair. It was painful and exciting at the same time and when he drew back it felt like he had sucked the oxygen from my lungs. I had never been kissed like that.

"And I wanted to do that from the first day in Introduction to Photography," Dalton said.

"Oh, yeah?" I said, and cocked an eyebrow at him. I was a little breathless but trying to hide it. I didn't want him to know the effect he had on me. I wanted to keep the upper hand. I reached forward and playfully unbuttoned the collar of his shirt. His mouth was slightly open; I saw the want in his eyes. "And what did you want to do to me after I beat you at poker?" I asked.

"You only beat me because you cheated," Dalton said, smiling, his voice low.

"It wasn't very gentlemanly of me," I said. "But maybe if you were less of a gentleman, you would have won."

"I'm not always a gentleman," Dalton said.

"I'll believe it when I see it," I said.

He pushed me down on my back on his bed and pinned my wrists above my head in one of his hands. He was on top of me, kissing me, his other hand trailing down my neck, skimming my collarbone, grazing my breasts, my belly button. Then his hand slipped underneath my shirt, warm skin to warm skin.

The door to his room slammed shut, and Dalton bolted off of me.

"Shit," he said.

He went over to the door and opened it and stepped outside, glancing up and down the hall. I sat up and ran a hand over my hair to smooth it.

"That was weird," Dalton said when he came back in. "It was probably a draft or something."

"I should get going," I said. "Now that we have our project figured out."

I reached for my laptop and started to gather up my things.

"Yeah, I'll walk you back to your room," Dalton said.

Drew wasn't back yet as it wasn't quite curfew, so I sat on my bed with my laptop taking some notes on the photographer Dalton and I had picked for our project. The USB drive with the interviews from my mother's case file was still sitting on my bedside table, and it kept catching my eye.

Maybe my mistake was not in listening to the interviews, but in listening to the wrong ones. I put in the USB drive and clicked on Grandma Fairchild's audio file and put on my headphones. The first half of the interview covered the same ground as my aunt Grier's—basically, my mother's personality and character—but of course, Grandma Fairchild painted a very different, much more pleasant picture of my mother. Then Mr. Lynch asked about my parents' relationship.

"Grace cares for Alistair a great deal," Grandma Fairchild said. "It was kind of a quick, whirlwind affair when it all started, which was unusual for Grace. She had a hard time opening herself up to anyone after Jake."

"Jake?"

"Yes, Jake Griffin, her high school boyfriend. He grew up down the street. They met when they were children."

Jake Griffin. That name sounded so familiar. Where had I heard it before?

"He was a good kid, a smart kid," said my grandmother. "He went to boarding school up in New Hampshire, I think it was. On a full scholarship. But he passed away very young. Grace was still in high school—oh, she must have been sixteen or so when it happened. Very young. She was devastated. It took her a long time to get past it."

A boarding school in New Hampshire? A boy who passed away? A cold shiver ran down my spine. Jake Griffin. I hadn't heard that name before, but I had seen it. In the front of my father's senior yearbook, on the "In Memoriam" page. Jake Griffin, the boy who had died, the one in the picture with my father on Healy Quad, their arms wrapped around one another, smiling at the camera. *Jake Griffin and Alistair Calloway,* the caption had read.

I tried to put all of the pieces together in my mind, to make them fit. What did it mean that:

1. My mother had dated this boy
2. At the same time my father was friends with him
3. In the same year this boy had died, and
4. Seventeen years later my mother disappeared into thin air?

Because what were the chances it didn't mean anything?

twenty
GRACE FAIRCHILD

SPRING 1997

I sat with Teddy's family and Margot during the ceremony. When Teddy walked across the stage in his cap and gown and received his diploma, we all stayed politely seated, unlike most of the other families, who popped up to snap a photo. Eugenia had hired a photographer to sit close to the stage and document everything. She had also made all of us arrive two hours before the ceremony so that said photographer could take pictures of us with Teddy in his cap and gown at the most scenic spots on campus. That way, we wouldn't have to jostle for pictures with all the other graduates and their families. I also secretly suspected Eugenia wanted the pictures taken when her hair and makeup were freshly done, rather than after she had sat through the hour-long ceremony in the blistering sun.

I'd bought a new outfit for the occasion—a pale pink dress on discount at Saks Off 5th. It was a designer I'd heard Olivia mention once. The dress was formfitting but had a modest neckline and hit a few inches above my knees. I felt pretty in it, but as I was posing for pictures, I had a disturbing thought—what if the dress was too sheer? I hadn't thought so when I'd stood before the mirror in the dull fluorescent lights of the dressing room, but standing in the bright sunlight, I wondered how much people could see and cursed myself for not thinking to buy a slip, just in case.

Now, as the band played and the graduates marched proudly down the aisle with their diplomas in hand, Teddy's father leaned toward me.

"We're going to miss our reservation," he said, frowning at his watch. The ceremony had started late and was now threatening Eugenia's perfectly laid plans.

"Alistair, stay behind and wait for your brother," Eugenia said, fanning herself with her program. "We'll go ahead to the restaurant and hold our table."

Margot put a hand on Alistair's elbow and fanned herself furiously with a program with the other. "I'm going with your parents," she said. "If I stay in this heat one more minute I'm going to get heatstroke."

"I'll wait with you," I volunteered.

Alistair nodded. "Go corral the troops," he told me as he stood, his hands in his suit pockets. "I'm going to find a restroom."

It took me a few minutes to find Teddy on the mall with all the other families and graduates. But eventually I spotted him off to one side, standing with some of his friends in a half circle, facing the other direction, toward the stage. I recognized two of them: Graham Park and Nick Cheng. Teddy and I had met them for a late movie downtown and gone out for sushi a few times. They were nice guys, always very polite. The third boy was tall and gangly, with freckles. He was half turned toward me so I could see his profile. I tried to place him in my mind, but I couldn't remember ever meeting him.

"I still contend that Teddy here is the true champion," Nick said, clapping Teddy on the back.

"Nick pointed her out to me earlier, over by the fountain," the tall one said. "I saw that little pink dress she's wearing. There's no way she hasn't put out."

I stopped walking. The realization that they were talking about me hit me hard in the gut. I suddenly felt like I wasn't wearing any clothes. It was like one of those horrible dreams where you suddenly realize you've been walking around naked and everybody is staring at you.

"Like I said, I'm bowing out this round," Teddy said.

"Bullshit," Graham said. "I'm not winning by default. Let's review the plays. Nick?"

"Teddy went to first with that Zeta Sigma, rounded second with that French foreign exchange student, and made third with the econ TA," Nick said, counting each of Teddy's conquests off on his fingers. I wondered when these encounters had taken place—were they while we were together? Before?

"And you hit a home run with the townie," the tall gangly one said.

Townie. I didn't even have a name.

"Come on, just admit it," he went on. "You've tapped that."

Teddy shrugged. He was laughing. I could tell by the way his shoulders shook, even though I couldn't see his face.

"I plead the fifth," Teddy said.

Witnessing Teddy divulge one of the most intimate details of our relationship to this gangly freckled boy and his other friends made me feel sick. And the fact that it was all some kind of joke, some kind of game.

Nick raised Teddy's arm triumphantly in the air. "I declare a winner."

"We're not worthy, oh great one," the gangly freckled boy said, giving Teddy a mocking half bow.

As I stood there, willing myself to leave but unable to move, Teddy turned and saw me.

The expression on my face must have told him everything I couldn't say, because his smile faltered, and all his color drained away.

"Grace," he said.

I turned and walked quickly away from him, stumbling slightly as my heels poked into the grass. He chased after me and grabbed me by the arm, forcing me to stop.

I saw his friends a few paces back, still standing in their half circle, looking at us.

"Don't touch me," I said. I tried to tug my arm out of Teddy's grasp, but his grip only tightened. His fingers dug into my forearm, sharp and bony. I winced.

"Grace, just let me explain," he said, as if he had the words to make things right, to put us back together. But he couldn't possibly. Those words didn't exist.

"I said, get your hands off me," I repeated.

"I don't know what you heard," Teddy said, glancing back at his friends and then lowering his voice. "But don't listen to those idiots. They were just dicking around. They're jerks. They didn't mean anything."

"No, *I* didn't mean anything," I said. "I was just—what? Some kind of joke to you? A stupid game?"

"No," Teddy said vehemently. "That's not true. You weren't—it wasn't." He stopped and took a deep breath. He looked at me so earnestly it hurt. "It was real. You and me. I swear to you it's real. Grace, I love you."

I did it just like Hank had taught me in the backyard when I was ten. Knuckles clenched, thumb on the outside, weight on my back foot, and then I threw it forward, right into his face. My fist sang with the impact. I heard the wind go out of him; he released me instantly and doubled forward.

"Fuck," Teddy said, clutching his nose. "Fuck."

I didn't wait to see if he was all right. I just turned and ran.

I could barely see straight. As I rounded the corner of the nearest building, I ran straight into someone, hard. I felt the hot, sharp pain of my ankle twisting in the strap of my heel as I fell, and then someone reached out to steady me.

"Whoa there, you all right?" the man asked.

When I looked up, I saw that it was Alistair. We seemed to recognize each other at the same time. I saw the way his face lit up from within, that flicker of light in his eyes. "I was just coming to find you," he said.

And then he seemed to register the emotion in my eyes, and his face clouded over.

"Are you okay?" he asked.

I hardly knew how to answer that question.

"It wasn't real," I said. "None of it was real."

I knew I was babbling but I couldn't stop.

I grabbed my ankle, which stung, and then slowly stood and shifted my weight to it. It was fine. I'd only twisted it—I could walk.

I heard my name in the distance, and I looked back over my shoulder. It was Teddy, trying to figure out which way I had gone. There was blood on the collar of his shirt. I had busted his nose.

I looked back at Alistair.

Alistair nodded as if he understood. "Go," he said. "I'll make sure he doesn't follow you." His voice was tight, laced with fury.

It was the second time that Alistair had saved me, and for the second time, I was too distracted to thank him. I just turned the corner and ran, without a backward glance.

twenty-one
CHARLIE CALLOWAY

2017

I stayed until Ms. Stanfeld did her nightly curfew check and then I grabbed a duffel out of my closet and hastily packed. I threw in a change of clothes, my laptop, and everything I could fit from my mother's case file.

"Can you please level with me?" Drew asked as she watched me from her bed. "Just tell me what's going on."

"I don't know what's going on," I said, grabbing my toiletries bag and throwing in all my stuff from my shower caddy. "But I sure as hell am going to find out."

"Okay," Drew said. "But you're kinda scaring me. Can you at least tell me where you're going?"

"I'm going to Hillsborough," I said. "But you can't tell anybody— not even Leo. I need you to cover for me in case I don't make it back by curfew tomorrow, okay?"

"Okay," Drew said.

I lowered myself out of the window first and then Drew tossed me my duffel.

"Promise me you'll be careful," Drew whispered down to me.

"I'll try," I whispered back.

I drove through the night and got to my grandparents' house at two in the morning. My uncle Hank's truck was in the driveway and the house was dark. I didn't want to wake them, so I reclined my seat and closed my eyes. I expected sleep to elude me, but I woke to a loud rapping on my window.

"Charlotte?"

I sat up, rubbing the crust from my eyes. I groaned when I felt how stiff my neck was from dozing in the car.

My grandma opened my car door.

"Charlotte?" she said again. "Dear, what are you doing out here?"

"Hi, Grandma," I said. I blinked at her in the early morning light. "What time is it?"

She was dressed in her bathrobe and slippers and she had the morning paper in her hands.

I must have looked really lost, because she didn't press me about why I was there again. Instead, she said, "Let's get you inside. I'll make you something to eat."

I followed her into the house and folded myself into a chair at the kitchen table. I could smell coffee brewing and looked around for the source. Grandma greased a pan and set it on the stove.

"Pancakes and eggs sound good, sweetheart?"

"Mhm," I said.

"Here," she said, pouring me a mug of coffee and setting it down in front of me.

She busied herself beating the eggs and whipping up the pancake batter but I could feel her constant worried glances. I sipped at my coffee and tried to arrange a coherent thought.

Jake. Jake Griffin. Jake Griffin and my mother. I needed to know about them. What happened to Jake? How did he die? And what was the connection between Jake and my mother and my father? Because there had to be something that connected them. I knew I had the pieces; I just had to figure out how they all fit together.

I was about to open my mouth to ask about Jake, to tell my

grandma I had listened to her interview in the PI's files and I needed to know everything there was to know right that instant, when my uncle Hank came in.

He stopped dead when he saw me. As I raised my hand to wave hello at him, his face took on an ugly, terrifying look.

"What the hell is she doing here?" he asked.

My heart plummeted into my stomach. What?

Grandma stopped mid–pancake flip and turned to face him. "Now, Hank, this is my house, and I say who's welcome here, and Charlotte is always welcome."

"After the shit she pulled?" Uncle Hank spat. He pointed a finger at me; his eyes were wild with anger. "She's not Grace, Ma. She may look like her, but she's not her. She's one of them. She's always going to be one of them."

"What's going on?" I asked.

"You know exactly what you did," Uncle Hank said, seething. "I thought you were that little girl I remembered. But you're not. You grew up to be as slimy and manipulative as any of them. I trusted you. God, I trusted you. What a mistake that was. But I won't make it again."

There were tears stinging the backs of my eyes. What could I have possibly done since the last time I was here to make him hate me so much? I was sure it had to be some kind of misunderstanding.

"Uncle Hank—" I said, but he held up a hand to stop me.

"Don't you dare," Uncle Hank said. "Don't cry like we've hurt you, when you don't give a damn about us. When you lied to my face."

"I don't—" I looked at Grandma for help. She was clutching her elbows, hugging her arms to her chest. Tears streamed down her cheeks.

"You went to him after I told you not to," Uncle Hank said.

"Who?" I asked.

"Your father," Uncle Hank said.

"I didn't."

"Then why did your uncle come to me? How did he know about the pictures?"

"Uncle Teddy contacted you?" I asked.

"He demanded I give him the pictures I found," Uncle Hank said. "Threatened to charge me with breaking and entering if I didn't."

"I didn't know," I said. "I didn't know he would do that."

"Just get out," Uncle Hank said. "Whatever you've come for, we're not interested. You didn't come here for us. You're here because you want something, and whatever it is, we're not about to give it to you."

I looked from him to my grandmother. I waited for her to say something in my defense but she didn't. She just looked at me like I had broken her heart.

"I'm . . . I'm sorry," I said, and I rushed past Uncle Hank and out the front door before my legs could give out from under me.

In the car, I told myself I wouldn't cry. I drove to the only other place I thought I might still be welcome in Hillsborough: the Rhodeses' house.

It was around seven thirty in the morning. I knew it was a little early to be stopping by unannounced, but I rang the doorbell anyway.

Greyson answered. "Hey there, Martha Stewart," he said.

I was trying really hard not to lose it. There was a huge lump in my throat, and I felt heavy and weighed down. *They hate you now,* I told myself. *They hate you.*

It was difficult not to feel the huge disparity between the warmth and love I had experienced the last time I was at my grandparents' house and the utter coldness with which I had been chased from the house this time. And my grandmother had just stood there.

She'd just stood there and let Uncle Hank say those awful things and she looked at me like . . . like she agreed with him.

I would never be welcome there again. I would never sit in the den with everyone and watch a football game on a Friday night. I would never sleep over in my mother's bed. I would never belong there again.

"Charlie, are you okay?" Greyson asked. The humor and smile had slipped from his face, replaced by a look of concern.

"Is Claire here?" I asked. "I really need to talk to her."

"She took the boys to school," he said. "And then she has a shift at the hospital."

I looked at him again and noticed he was all dressed in a suit and tie. It was a weekday. Of course he was on his way to work. How had I not noticed that before? My mind was hazy from lack of sleep.

"I shouldn't have come here," I said. "I'm sorry."

I turned to go.

Don't cry until you get in the car, I told myself.

"Charlie, wait—" Greyson called, and he rushed after me down the sidewalk. I started to run to my car but he beat me there and stood in front of the driver's-side door, blocking my escape. "Charlie, what's going on?" Greyson asked.

Then he did the unforgivable. He wrapped his arms around me and I broke apart. I started to cry. Like really cry. Giant, heaving sobs.

He rubbed my back and held me tighter.

"It's okay," Greyson said. "Everything's going to be okay."

And his words comforted me, even though I knew they weren't true.

When I woke up, I didn't know where I was. I looked around the room. The curtains on the window were shut, and I was lying in a bed, but it wasn't my bed, and it wasn't my room.

It was a queen-sized bed with dark plaid sheets. There were a television and an Xbox sitting on a black dresser, and a desk and laptop against the other wall. And there were football trophies sitting on floating shelves, and pictures. Pictures of a boy with blond hair. Greyson. I was in Greyson's room.

I sat up. I remembered now—what a colossal wreck I had been, and how Greyson had held me in his driveway until I couldn't cry anymore and I just felt raw. How he carried me to his room and tucked me into his bed like I was a child, closing the curtains tight, telling me to get some sleep, and how I fell asleep almost as soon as my head hit the pillow.

I padded downstairs. Greyson was in the kitchen cooking something on the stove. It smelled savory and delicious, and I was hungry in spite of myself.

"What are you making?" I asked.

"Breakfast burritos," he said. "They're the best grief hangover food."

"It smells amazing," I said.

"You look like you're feeling better," he said.

"I am."

I sat down on the stool at the island, and he fixed me a burrito and slid the plate across the counter to me. I ate like I was famished and licked my thumbs and fingers when I was done. Then I accidentally burped. I clamped my hand over my mouth and blushed. Shit.

"Compliments to the chef?" I said.

"That's the highest form of compliment," Greyson said, and I laughed despite myself, a deep sidesplitting laugh. Greyson laughed, too.

When we recovered ourselves, Greyson asked, "So, I take it your uncle gave you the PI's files?"

"He did," I said, and I filled him in on everything—from my

aunt Grier's revelation that my gold-digging mother had apparently been hunting for a husband in the Calloway family, to the discovery of Jake's mysterious death in my father's yearbook, to my grandmother's interview, to my uncle Hank's reaction when I had shown up at my grandparents' house this morning.

"Jeez," Greyson said. "Forget my grief burritos. If I had known all that, I would have made you my post-traumatic stress omelet."

"Yeah, I'm feeling a little overwhelmed, to say the least," I said.

"What can I do to help?" Greyson asked. "Put me to work. What can I do?"

"I need to talk to your mom, actually," I said. "She would know about Jake. How he died, how he might be connected to my mother's disappearance."

"I'll get my keys," Greyson said.

Greyson sat next to me in the ER waiting room. We had paged Claire about ten minutes ago. Suddenly, the double doors to the hallway flew open and Claire rushed in in her scrubs.

"Greyson, what's wrong? Is Ryder okay? Is it Nolan?"

Greyson stood. "No, everyone's fine, Mom. But there's someone here who had to see you."

He motioned at me behind him and I stood too.

Claire took a deep breath when she saw me and then turned and nudged Greyson firmly in the chest.

"You don't page someone nine-one-one in the ER unless you're bleeding from the head," Claire said.

"Trust me," Greyson said. "We're sort of at that level here. Metaphorically."

Claire looked at me. "What is it, Charlotte?" she asked, not unkindly. "Is everything okay?"

"It's about my mom," I said. "I need you to tell me everything you know about her and Jake Griffin."

Greyson, Claire, and I sat on a bench outside near the entrance to the hospital.

"Jake Griffin, now there's a name I haven't heard in a long time," Claire said. "What made you want to know about Jake?"

I tiptoed around the truth, which was something I was becoming quite good at.

"My father gave me access to the interviews the PI conducted, and Jake's name came up," I said. "I'm just trying to fill in the holes in my understanding."

Claire nodded. "Okay," she said. "But Jake doesn't have anything to do with your mother's disappearance. That was decades ago."

"I know," I said. "I'm just trying to understand her better, is all."

"Well, there's not too much to tell," Claire said. "Your mom and Jake grew up together. The Griffins lived right down the street from your grandparents' house—in that blue Craftsman home on the corner. They were always together, and sometime in middle school that turned into dating. But Jake—he was a dreamer. He wanted something more than what Hillsborough had to offer, and in high school he transferred to some fancy boarding school out of state on a scholarship.

"Your mom and Jake did the whole long-distance thing. And for the most part, it worked out for them. I mean, they had their squabbles, like anyone."

"What did they fight about?" I asked.

"Normal stuff," Claire said. "Like not spending enough time together. But they worked it out. And then, Jake's junior year, right before he was supposed to come home for winter break, he killed himself."

"Why?" I asked.

"To tell you the truth, we were all pretty shocked by it," Claire said. "Jake was this bright-eyed kid. He always seemed happy. But, I guess it just goes to show that you never really know what's going on with someone. I guess Jake was struggling at school. They found a stolen exam in his room. They found a note, too. Jake wrote that someone had found out that he cheated and they were going to turn him in. Cheating would have meant expulsion. I think he thought that everything he had worked so hard for was about to be taken from him. When you're that young, I guess that would seem like the end of the world. Tore your mom to pieces. She never saw it coming."

"What about my father?" I asked.

Claire looked confused. "What about him?"

"The boarding school Jake went to was Knollwood Augustus Prep," I said. "They were friends."

"Jake and your father knew each other?" Claire asked.

"Yes," I said. "My mother never mentioned that?"

"No," Claire said. "No, she didn't."

Was it possible that my mother was unaware of the connection? Or perhaps it was just a weird coincidence that they had met years after Jake had passed away?

But there was a feeling that nagged at me in the pit of my gut. A feeling that even though I couldn't yet figure out how things were related, they somehow fit together. The connection was important. I just had to figure out why.

"Maybe it's like that six-degrees-of-separation thing they talk about," Greyson said. He leaned forward to turn up the dial on his radio. The Red Hot Chili Peppers were playing. "Like I know someone, who knows someone, who knows someone, who knows someone who knows Tom Cruise," Greyson said. "It's a smaller world than you think. A couple of summers ago, I was backpacking around Europe with some buddies, and we were standing in front of Buckingham Palace waiting for the changing of the guard and I look to my right, and who is standing next to me but Mrs.

Chavez and her husband, who live across the street from us. Clad in fanny packs and everything. Like, what are the chances that I would travel halfway around the world and somehow be in the same place at the same time as my neighbors?"

"Yeah," I said. "That's weird, I guess."

I balanced my feet on his dashboard. It was midafternoon now and we were headed back to Greyson's house. We stopped at a red light and I glanced out the window. There was a homeless man sitting on the bench near the bus stop. *Uncover the Facts. Discreet and Confidential,* the sign behind him read.

As the light in front of us turned green and we started to move, the man shifted in his seat and lay down on the bench. When he moved, I saw the whole bench ad. Under the title *Hindsberg & Thornton Investigations,* there was a shot of two men in suits, from their shoulders up. They looked straight on and smiled confidently. A shock of recognition ran through me.

"Stop!" I shouted. "Stop the car."

Greyson ground his Corolla to a halt in the middle of the intersection. I jerked forward in my seat. The driver in the car behind us laid on his horn.

"What?" Greyson asked. "Charlie, what is it?"

The man on the right in the bench ad was older than when I had last seen him. His hair had receded at the temples, and he had gained some weight in his face. But it was him. I was sure it was him.

"Look," I said, pointing at the bench. Greyson's gaze followed the direction in which my finger was pointing. "It's him," I said. "The man in Uncle Hank's photographs. The guy in the diner with my mother. That's him."

twenty-two
ALISTAIR CALLOWAY

SUMMER 1997

The Hillsborough art gallery was in an old brick building off Main. Inside, it was crowded. I squinted at the bright recessed lighting that reflected off the white walls and concrete floors, scanning the room for the only familiar face I could expect to see there, but Grace was nowhere in sight.

I'd received the flyer about the gallery show for local artists in the mail a week ago. Grace's return address was on the envelope. She had scribbled a short note on the flyer: "Alistair—In case you're interested . . ." I'd put the note in my top desk drawer, out of sight. I wasn't interested. Well, I *shouldn't* have been interested. But this morning, I'd taken the flyer out again. Before I could think better of it, I'd thrown on a button-down shirt and called down to the valet to pull around my car.

I meandered idly around the perimeter of the gallery by myself, looking at all the artwork in different media that hung on the walls—photographs, oil paintings, drawings. I spotted her finally. Grace was standing across the room by the hors d'oeuvres table, talking to a group of people I didn't know. The man next to her placed a hand casually on her back and Grace went on talking like it was the most natural thing in the world for this guy to be touching her. Something tightened in my chest.

I shouldn't have come. It had been an idiotic, impulsive decision, made all the more asinine by the fact that I should have been working. We'd fired our lead design consultant for the Murray Hill project, and I should have spent the afternoon going through the résumés HR had sent over for his replacement. I glanced at my watch. Without traffic, I could be back in the city in an hour and a half. I was contemplating where I might stop off for a bite to eat, when I looked up and saw it—Jake's eternally youthful face staring right at me.

It was an abstract oil painting on canvas. The bright colors on his features were startling—yellow, orange, blue. Such vibrant, happy hues, and yet something about his gaze was somber. The paint was thick and textured on the canvas, spread by a palette knife, making each angle of his face, his sadness, palpable.

"You came."

I looked over to see Grace standing next to me. She smiled and held out a glass of white wine.

"I got your note," I said, taking the glass.

Grace nodded. "I never got to thank you for, you know," Grace said.

I cleared my throat and looked away. I hadn't seen or talked to Grace since Teddy's graduation ceremony. That image of Grace as I reached out to steady her in the corridor between buildings, her eyes slightly teary, her ankle twisted, as she babbled on about Teddy and his stupid game, still haunted me. "Teddy's an idiot," I said.

"Yeah," Grace said, nodding. "It just took me a while to figure that out."

She turned and gestured at the canvases on the wall.

"So, what do you think?" she asked, changing the subject.

I glanced back at the wall. I had only noticed the canvas of Jake at first, but now I realized there was a series of abstract portraits—a middle-aged woman who looked vaguely like Grace (Grace's mother perhaps?) standing at a kitchen sink; a long-limbed teenage boy skateboarding; a young blond woman on a beach, her shoulders sunburned. Each portrait was in the same bright colors as Jake's, with the same texture, but they seemed lighter somehow, happier.

"They're really something," I said.

"You know, I looked back through all these pictures I had of him, trying to find the right one to paint," Grace said. "I picked my favorite memories—Jake out on the lake in the summer, Jake at the boardwalk, Jake hanging out on my porch. And somehow, they all came out looking like that—no matter how bright the colors I used, somehow the mood stained it. It's not how he was, but it's how I remember him now."

We were silent for a moment. We both looked at each other. Over Grace's shoulder, I saw the man she had been talking with earlier looking at us. Something in his stare seemed territorial and not exactly welcoming. He nudged the guy he was talking to and nodded in our direction, like he was asking who I was. I returned my attention to Grace.

"I don't want to take you away from your friends," I said.

"You're not," Grace said.

"Well, I think your boyfriend isn't too keen on you talking to me."

"My boyfriend?" She turned around to see who I was talking about. "That's my brother Hank," Grace said, laughing.

I felt the tightness in my chest instantly ease and I laughed too.

"He's just being protective," Grace went on. She paused a moment. "I don't—I'm not seeing anyone at the moment."

I nodded and couldn't quite meet her eyes.

"Jake mentioned you a lot, you know?" Grace said, looking back at Jake's portrait. "When he'd talk about Knollwood and his friends there, yours was the name that came up the most."

"Really?"

"Yes," Grace said. "He looked up to you."

I only nodded. I didn't know what else to say. I hadn't talked about Jake with anyone for years. When he'd first passed away, it had been difficult not to talk about Jake, not to think about him. But now, after all this time, the words eluded me.

"I get that you don't like to talk about him," Grace said. "So we don't have to. But I just have one question first before we never talk about it again. I never got to see Jake at Knollwood—he talked about it all the time, but I never got to go visit, to actually see it. And I always wanted to know what Jake was like at school. Did he seem happy there?"

"Yes, he seemed happy," I said.

"I thought he was," Grace said. "He always sounded happy."

"Everybody liked Jake," I said. "He was hard not to like, even though you kind of wanted to hate him, because the bastard seemed to be good at everything."

Grace chuckled knowingly.

"He was an ace in the classroom and an ace on the tennis court—definitely gave me a run for my money," I said.

"That's the thing that always got me," Grace said. "He seemed to be doing so well. But I guess that was all a lie. I never knew how much he was struggling."

"Knollwood is a very competitive school," I said. "All of us struggled from time to time."

"He never said anything to you about falling behind?"

My throat constricted. I didn't want to talk about this anymore. I opened my mouth to answer her but couldn't. I simply shook my head.

"He never said anything to me about it either," Grace said.

I had to put an end to this line of questioning before things went too far.

"I can tell you a lot of things about Jake," I said. "But if you're looking for an answer as to why, I don't have one."

Grace was quiet for a moment. "This may be horrible for me to say," she said, "but it actually makes me feel better to hear you say that. I just—for a long time, I felt like I had failed him by not seeing it. And it's just comforting to hear, that I wasn't the only one who didn't see it coming."

I instinctively reached forward and grabbed her hand. She looked surprised by the gesture, but she didn't draw her hand away.

"Listen to me, Grace," I said, slowly and deliberately, because it was important that she heard me. It was important she understood. "What happened to Jake, that wasn't your fault. You had nothing to do with it."

She just looked at me—her eyes wide and searching and so full of loss.

"It wasn't your fault," I said again.

She put her other hand on top of my mine then, and gave it a little squeeze.

"It wasn't yours either," she said back to me.

I recoiled at her words. I couldn't stomach them. But she held my hand firmly between her own.

I cleared my throat and looked away from her.

"I, um, have to be getting back to the city," I said, reaching to scratch the back of my neck to free my hand from hers.

"Do you have to go right now?" Grace asked. She sounded disappointed. "Can you spare half an hour? There's something I would really like to show you."

I looked back at her. She seemed insistent.

"Okay," I said.

Grace broke into a smile. "Okay," she said back to me.

In my car, Grace sat in the front passenger seat and gave me directions. A few minutes outside of town, she instructed me to pull over near a thick stand of trees. We parked in the grass near a split elm that lightning had cut nearly clean down the middle. Grace took my hand and led me into the woods. Through a break in the trees, I saw the lake.

"Langely Lake," Grace told me.

She gestured at a thick oak near the water's edge. There were several long boards lying flat in the arc of the tree where the trunk had split. Smaller boards had been nailed to the face of the trunk as a makeshift ladder.

"We built that, Jake and me, when we were kids," Grace said. "It was our special place. No one else knew about it. I know it doesn't look like much now, but it was something to us."

Grace climbed the makeshift ladder into the tree house and I followed her. We sat on the boards with our legs dangling below us, over the water.

"The first time I ever saw you was in this tree house," Grace said. "Jake laid his yearbook out right here on these boards that first summer he was home. He pointed to your photo and told me your name. You looked like such a snotty little asshole in your school blazer I couldn't believe it when Jake told me you were friends."

I laughed. "It's not my fault," I said. "Everybody had to wear those blazers. We all looked liked pretentious dicks."

"Trust me, it wasn't the blazer," Grace said. "It was you. You had this look like you just knew you were better than everyone."

"Well, I've always made an excellent first impression," I said. "Funny enough, the first time I saw you was in a photograph, too. I think I mentioned it when we first met—there was this picture of you with an ice cream cone that Jake kept on his desk."

"Ah, yes," Grace said. "The one where I have ice cream smeared across my face? See, I make a great first impression, too." She bumped her shoulder against mine and looked out at the lake. "I thought you were a pretentious jerk and you thought I was some heathen who hadn't mastered the art of eating."

"No," I said. "I didn't think that at all."

"Oh yeah?" Grace said. "Then what did you think?"

"I thought—I thought, you looked like happiness," I said. I didn't know how to put into words the way I'd felt when I saw her picture—the way something inside of me had shifted. "Not that you looked happy, though you did, but that you were happiness personified. I thought, I have to meet that girl."

There was a painfully long moment before Grace turned her gaze away from the lake and looked at me. There were so many things I felt that I should tell her. Instead, I took her into my arms and kissed her. She didn't pull away. Instead, she kissed me back.

She tugged on the collar of my shirt, pulling me down with her onto the boards of the makeshift tree house, and my hands were in her hair, unbuttoning her blouse, skimming the hem of her skirt.

Afterward, I took her hand in mine, and Grace leaned her head against my shoulder and together we stared out over the lake and watched the sun disappear into the trees on the other side, like the flame of a candle flickering out.

part three

twenty-three
CHARLIE CALLOWAY

2017

He wasn't just a nameless man in a photograph anymore. I knew his name, his occupation, his whereabouts. Peter Hindsberg. He was a private investigator, one half of Hindsberg & Thornton Investigations, which he ran with his partner, Ron Thornton. Their website listed an address for their office near the outlet mall across town. In their short bios, I read that Peter Hindsberg had served as an insurance fraud investigator for Hartco Insurance for several years before starting his own investigation firm with his longtime friend Ron Thornton, a former police officer in Stamford. A quick Google search didn't reveal much further information, aside from an engagement announcement in the *Hillsborough Chronicle* from 2004 between Peter and a Miss Lucy Hale, a pretty brunette who taught kindergarten at a local elementary school.

"Do you think your mom thought your dad was cheating or something?" Greyson asked, leaning over my shoulder to get a better view of his computer screen as I scrolled.

"Why do you say that?" I asked.

Greyson pointed to a spot on the screen. "Just looking at the list of services here."

I scanned it. Under surveillance, background checks, missing persons, civil and criminal research, pre-litigation, legal preparation, and subpoena service, there were listed: cheating spouses, alimony, and child custody.

"Or is it possible your mom was thinking about divorce?" Greyson asked. "Maybe she wanted to get all her ducks in a row before going through with it?"

I bit my lip. I couldn't help but remember what Eugenia had told me—how unhappy my mother had been, how withdrawn. And what Claire had said: *Alistair Calloway isn't a man you just leave.* The last time I had seen my parents together, they were fighting. My mother had screamed at my father not to touch her. What if my mother had told my father she wanted a divorce, or what if my father had found out somehow that my mother was planning to leave him? What if that was the reason for their fight?

I picked up the landline on Greyson's desk and started dialing.

"What are you doing?" Greyson asked.

I held up a hand to silence him. The phone was ringing on the other end.

"Hindsberg and Thornton Investigations," a woman's voice said. "How may I help you?"

I opened my mouth to say something and then froze. I hung up the phone.

"What was that?" Greyson asked.

"I think I need to go see him," I said.

"Peter Hindsberg?" Greyson asked. "What are you going to say?"

"I don't know," I said. "But I have to find out exactly what he was doing for my mother."

"All right," Greyson said. "I'll drive you."

The offices of Hindsberg & Thornton Investigations were in an un-kempt office complex across the street from a Rite Aid. Inside, the reception area was empty. I went up to the middle-aged woman sitting behind the front desk with Greyson close behind me.

"Can I help you?" the woman asked. I could tell from her voice that she was the same woman who had answered the phone earlier when I called.

"I'm here to see Peter Hindsberg," I said.

"He's not in."

"Well, when will he be back?" I asked.

"A week from Monday," the woman said. She glanced back at her computer screen. I could see in the reflection in her glasses that she was playing solitaire. "He just left for Jamaica. Family cruise."

This. Was. Not. Happening.

"Well, I really need to speak to him," I said. "It's important."

The woman glanced back up at me. "Are you a client?"

"Yes," I said. "I need to talk to him about my case. It's urgent."

"Name?" the woman asked, her fingers poised over her keyboard. I realized then that she was going to look me up in the system, and that she would quickly see I wasn't there.

"What I meant is, I'm a new client," I said. "I need to find someone, and when I spoke to Mr. Hindsberg over the phone the other week, he said he could help me. Maybe I could just get his cell number?"

"Mr. Thornton is handling all of Mr. Hindsberg's caseload while he's on vacation," the woman said. "If it's really urgent, I could see if he has a few minutes to meet with you."

"Sure," I said, glancing behind me at the empty waiting room. "Yeah, that would be great. Thank you."

"One moment," the woman said. She pushed back her chair and stood and disappeared down the short hall behind her.

"What are you doing?" Greyson whispered.

"I need you to distract her," I whispered back.

"Distract her?"

"Like make conversation," I said. "Keep her occupied."

"Charlie, what's going on?" he asked.

In the distance, I heard a curt knock on a door and then low, indistinct voices.

"I have a plan," I said. "Just trust me."

I didn't have time to say any more, because the receptionist had returned to her desk. "Mr. Thornton will see you now," the woman said. She sat and gave a little nod at the hallway behind her. "Second door on your right."

"Thanks," I said.

I gave Greyson a subtle wink as I left him at the receptionist's desk and turned down the hallway. There were three doors along the hallway, one on the left and two on the right. The receptionist had left the second one on the right slightly ajar. The other doors were closed.

"So, are you a Huskies fan?" I heard Greyson ask the receptionist behind me. "Big into basketball?"

Face palm. What was I thinking relying on Greyson's social skills for a reliable distraction?

"No," the woman said.

"Football?"

"No."

I glanced behind me to be sure the receptionist wasn't looking my way. She wasn't. I grabbed the handle to the first door on the right, praying it wasn't locked. It twisted in my palm. So far, so good. I opened it as quietly as I could and peeked inside. It was dark but I caught my reflection in the mirror above the counter. Bathroom. Not what I was looking for. I closed the door and continued down the short hall.

I stopped in front of the door on the left. With one more glance behind me to make sure the receptionist wasn't looking, I pushed the door open as quietly as I could. It was dark because the shades were drawn on the far window, but there were a desk, a couch, and a couple of filing cabinets. Peter's office. Score. I slipped inside and closed the door quietly behind me.

I grabbed my phone from my back pocket and turned on my flashlight. I surveyed the filing cabinets, which were arranged along the right wall a little ways behind the desk. The first set of drawers was labeled with business items: "Accounting," "Bank Records," "Contracts," "Permits and Licenses." I moved on to the second cabinet. This one contained client files arranged alphabetically. The cabinet on top read "Clients: A–C." Bingo. I reached out and tugged on the handle, but it was locked. Crap.

I looked around me for something to pick the lock with, trying to remember everything I could from all those tutorials Drew had watched on YouTube in preparation for her first A's ticket. From what I remembered, I'd need two large paper clips—one to use as the pick and the other to put tension on the lock. I rummaged around Peter Hindsberg's desk and found a pair of paper clips in his wire mesh desktop organizer. I unfolded the clips and fashioned a small hook at the end of the clip I would use as the tension wrench. Then I stuck the tension wrench into the bottom of the lock and turned it to the right slightly, applying pressure in the direction the lock should go. I held it there and inserted the pick into the top of the lock, raking the pins until they set. It took me several tries to get all of the pins set, and then I felt the lock give and I was able to turn it with my other paper clip. I was in.

I eased the drawer open slowly and held my phone light close as I searched through the files. There were at least a hundred files packed tightly together in the drawer, some fat and some thin. I skimmed through the A's and the B's, searching for the beginning of the C's. Then, near the back, I found it: "Calloway, Grace."

The file was light. It contained a few pieces of yellow legal pad paper, full of chicken-scratch notes, and a smaller envelope. I opened it, and dozens of photographs slid out onto the floor of the office. I picked one up, shone the light of my phone on it, and gasped.

It was my father.

He was just a teenager in the photograph; his face still had the roundness of a boy's. He had a beer in one hand and his other arm was slung around the shoulder of a boy I recognized. Jake Griffin.

It was nighttime and the picture was dark. The red time stamp in the bottom right corner of the photograph read, *9:32 P.M. December 21, 1990*. In the picture, Jake beamed at the camera and held up his own beer in salute to whoever was taking the picture. A girl stood on Jake's other side, posed to give him a kiss on the cheek. I recognized Matthew York, one of my father's friends, standing to my father's right.

I reached down and picked up another photograph off the floor. This one was of a slender blond girl I didn't recognize. In the photograph, she was naked, and she stared at whoever was taking the picture with a steady, unabashed gaze. Her body was marked up all over with red permanent marker with derogatory words and descriptions. Parts of her were circled and labeled: her nose, which someone had marked "beak," her stomach, which someone had marked "fat." The time stamp for this one was months earlier: September 22, 1990.

Through the wall, I heard the phone ring in the front office and the receptionist answer.

"Hindsberg and Thornton Investigations," she said. "Oh, hello, Peter. How was your flight? Hmm. Okay, let me see if I can find it for you. Let me transfer the call. One moment."

Next to me, the phone on Peter Hindsberg's desk rang and I jumped.

I heard Greyson's voice through the wall next, loud and panicky, as if he were trying to alert me to the fact that I was about to be discovered.

"Um, real quick, can you show me where your restroom is?" he asked. "I really have to go. Like, I HAVE TO GO NOW. Sorry, it's these burritos I had this morning. They didn't really agree with me."

Shit. I closed the cabinet drawer and dropped to my knees, trying to gather all of the photos that had spilled and put them back in the file.

"Oh, is this it?" Greyson asked. "Okay, thanks. Um, the toilet paper looks a little low. Do you have more in the back or something? Sorry, just trying to be prepared—I have this condition and things can get—oh, you keep them here, right under the sink? Jeez, that's a lot of toilet paper. I bet you have a Costco membership. You know, I've been thinking about getting one of those, but I can't decide between the standard and executive memberships. Which one do you have?"

I had just enough time to slam the folder shut and climb underneath Peter Hindsberg's desk before I heard the door open. I snapped off the flashlight app on my phone and held my breath.

"Standard, I think," the receptionist said, flipping on the office light.

"Standard, eh?" Greyson said. I could tell by the sound of his voice that he had come closer and was standing in the doorway. He hesitated a moment, probably sweeping the room with his eyes, looking for me.

I saw the receptionist from the waist down as she walked around behind the desk and I scooted farther back into the desk's knee-hole hugging my legs to my chest.

"I'm sorry, I have to get this," the receptionist said.

"Sure, sure," Greyson said. "I'll, uh, just go take care of my business then."

I heard the bathroom door across the hall close and then the receptionist leaned over the desk and picked up the phone.

"Now, where did you say you'd left it?" she asked.

I swallowed and tried to quiet the sound of my breathing. I was painfully aware of the loud thumping of my heart in my ears, of the sound my breath made as I drew it in through my nose and then let it out again. Was my breathing always this loud?

Then, I saw it—a stray photograph. It was about an inch from the toe of the receptionist's right shoe. If she looked down and saw it, my cover was blown. Maybe I could lean forward very slowly, reach out my hand, and grab it before she could see it. But what if that drew her attention?

"Sure, I'll get this out today," she said. "Take care. And tell Nancy to use sunscreen this time. We don't want a repeat of the Florida Keys trip."

The receptionist laughed and set the phone down and I sat very still, staring at that photograph. I willed her not to look down. Don't see it, don't see it, don't see it, I thought.

She seemed to stand there for an immeasurably long moment, and then she moved away from the desk. The light went out and I heard the door close behind her. I exhaled loudly and grabbed for the lone photo.

I tucked the file against my chest underneath my jacket and stuffed the photos in my front jacket pockets. I slid out of the office quickly and shut the door behind me quietly. The bathroom door across the hall was still closed and I could see the light on underneath.

As I came around the receptionist's desk, I kept my hands stuffed in my jacket pockets, praying she wouldn't notice the bulge there.

"Are you all set, dear?" she asked me, looking up. "Do I need to set a follow-up appointment with Mr. Hindsberg when he gets back?"

"No, thanks," I said. "I got everything I needed."

"All right then," she said. "Your friend just went to the restroom." She leaned forward and lowered her voice, seeming very concerned. "Are you sure he's quite all right?" she asked.

Before I could answer, I heard the toilet flush and the bathroom door flew open. Greyson came out. He looked relieved when he saw me.

"We should go," Greyson said. "I'm not feeling well."

He grabbed me by the arm and steered me toward the door.

"I wouldn't go in there," Greyson told the receptionist over his shoulder. "Give it at least half an hour, to be safe."

And we made a beeline for his car, leaving the startled receptionist in our wake.

twenty-four
ALISTAIR CALLOWAY

SUMMER 1997

Margot opened the door on the first knock. She was wearing sweat-pants, her hair up in a loose bun. She had her reading glasses on, which I took to mean she was studying, but when I walked into the apartment, I saw the seating arrangements for our wedding scattered across the kitchen table, not textbooks.

"I just made some tea, do you want some?" Margot asked as she padded into the kitchen.

I had my hands in my pockets, but that was a sign of weakness, of nerves. So, I took them out, folded them across my chest. No, that wasn't natural either. Shit, what should I do with my hands?

"Alistair?" Margot called from the kitchen.

"Hmm?"

"Tea?" she asked again.

"No, thanks," I said.

Get it together, I told myself. I just had to say it, straight and simple, and get it over with: Grace and I were married.

We had married at a courthouse outside New Haven on Friday. The judge and his secretary were the only witnesses to our vows. Grace wore a pale yellow sundress and flip-flops, her hair loose around her shoulders.

Afterward, we sat on the empty, moonlit beach and went swimming in the ocean in the clothes we had on. Back in our hotel room, we laid our wet clothes on the heater to dry and climbed under the bedsheets to get warm. I tented the covers over us and kissed my wife. Grace's hair was still wet and it clung to her forehead and the sides of her face, but as she stared up at me through her lashes, I thought she had never looked more beautiful. I knew I would remember that moment until the day I died.

"I'm glad you're here," Margot said as she came out of the kitchen with her mug of tea. She sat at the table. "These seating charts are giving me a migraine."

Now, I had to do it now.

I sat down next to her.

"Margot," I said, "I need to tell you something."

She blew on her tea to cool it and took a sip. "What's up?" she asked.

"For the past few weeks, I've been seeing someone else," I said.

"You've been seeing someone else?" Margot repeated slowly, as if she wasn't sure she had heard me right.

"Yes."

"Does this person have a name?" Margot asked.

I sighed and didn't answer.

"Do I know her?" Margot asked. "Please tell me you're not cliché enough to be fucking your secretary."

"It's Grace Fairchild," I said reluctantly.

"Who?" Margot asked.

Margot's mind was like a steel trap—she remembered dates and names easily, when she felt they were important enough to remember. But Grace clearly had not made an impression.

"You've met her several times," I said. "She used to date Teddy."

"You're fucking your brother's ex-girlfriend?" Margot laughed.

I didn't respond.

"That little Virgin Mary?" Margot asked. "Well, I guess she was a little more Mary Magdalene than I gave her credit for."

"I ran into Grace at this gallery I attended a couple months ago," I said. "Neither of us meant for this to happen, but it did."

I didn't mention that Grace was pregnant. I didn't know whether that would infuriate Margot more, or if it would help her see how impossible it was for us to be together.

"So do you feel better now?" Margot asked.

"Feel better?" I asked.

"Now that you've gotten your little indiscretion off your conscience?" she said. "Can we move on?" She took a sip of her tea. "Don't expect me to be so cavalier about future infidelities," she said. "But I get it. You're under a lot of pressure with the wedding coming up, and you needed to let off some steam. Okay, fine. But you won't always get a free pass."

She looked down at the seating arrangements spread out on the table in front of her.

"I could really use your help with some of this," she said. "Was it your aunt Veronica who isn't speaking to your second cousin Harold? Your mother mentioned there was some bad blood on that side of the family. So, I was thinking about putting Cousin Harold at table eight with your family from Cambridge, and sticking Aunt Veronica at table eleven with the Bridgeport cousins."

"Margot," I said softly. Shit, this was going to be harder than I'd thought. "There's not going to be a wedding," I said.

She looked up at me. I had her attention now.

"What do you mean there's not going to be a wedding?" she asked.

"I'm not telling you about me and Grace because it's over," I said. "I'm telling you, because, well, the wedding's off."

"I don't understand," Margot said.

"Grace and I, we got married this past weekend," I said. "I wasn't golfing all weekend with my father like I told you. I was with Grace."

Margot didn't say anything. She stared down at her mug of tea.

I was quiet for a moment. I didn't know what to say, sitting there with Margot amid all the reminders of our upcoming nuptials.

Margot bit her lip and subconsciously fingered the band of her engagement ring like she often did when she was deep in thought. My eye caught on my grandmother's canary diamond on her finger. That was going to be the other difficult part about all of this. I knew it was the gentlemanly thing to let the jilted fiancée keep the ring in the event the groom called off the wedding. But the ring was a family heirloom.

"You don't need to worry about anything," I said after a while. "I'll take care of the cancellations—the venues, the guests, all of it. You don't need to do anything."

"That's noble of you," Margot said dryly.

"But," I said. *Christ, this was hard.* "Well, there is one thing."

"What?" Margot asked. "What could you possibly want from me?"

I let out my breath slowly.

"I need my grandmother's ring back," I said.

What made this a hundred times worse was that the broken engagement would change Margot's financial prospects drastically. It would have made me feel the tiniest bit better if, at the very least, I could have left her with something that would ease that burden.

"I could get it appraised," I said. "I can give you whatever the value is."

Margot scoffed. "I don't need your handouts, Alistair," she said, prideful. She twisted the ring off her finger and set it on the table between us. "You and I, it was never about the money."

I let the ring and that lie sit there between us, and I felt the weight of both. Margot and I had never been about the money exactly. I knew it had been more than that. It had been about my family, the Calloway name, which I wore like a brand. It had been about our shared ambitions and what we could accomplish together. But the money was always a part of it.

Margot had always wanted to be a surgeon, an expensive and arduous career choice in itself, but she didn't plan to stop there. Margot dreamed of opening a center for surgical discovery and research—a facility dedicated to developing and testing new surgical tools and techniques, a place that would bring surgeons, engineers, and innovators together. But a research center like that didn't happen without a large financial backer, and without a name like mine behind it.

We sat there in silence for a while. There was no crying, no tears, no tantrums, no throwing of hard objects, no vague, irrational threats. But this was Margot—cold, analytical Margot. Of course my life-altering declaration was met with a steely calm.

"Why her?" Margot asked. She had that look on her face, like she was trying to figure out some complicated algorithm. "Why her and not me?"

"Margot—"

"No, I just want to understand," Margot said. She ran her finger around the edge of her mug. "She's pretty, sure, but marrying someone for their looks is a poor investment. So it's got to be something else . . . but what, exactly?"

I sighed. I picked at my loose thumbnail.

"She's working-class," Margot went on. "She's poorly educated, she doesn't have an ambitious bone in her body, and she's soft. By every calculation, she's a poor match for you."

I knew Margot was wrong; Grace was so much more than that. But sitting there and extolling Grace's virtues wouldn't help matters.

"You can't always rationalize these things," I said. "You love who you love."

When I looked up at Margot, she had that look of deep disappointment on her face, one I had seen there once before. It was something like disgust mixed with pity, and I couldn't help but look away. I had that feeling in the pit of my stomach—a deep, burning, gut-twisting sense of shame.

"Love," Margot said. "You're throwing away what we could have had for love?"

I didn't answer her.

"You're a fool," Margot said. "Love is only ever the first act. It doesn't last forever. And what comes after?"

I reached out and pocketed the ring. "I wish you all the best, Margot," I said. "I really do."

As I was leaving, she called my name and I looked back, my hand on the door.

"You and I—we could have built something together," Margot said. "But you and Grace, you'll only ruin each other. You'll see. When it's too late to do anything about it, you'll look back at this moment and know that I was right. Every great tragedy started with love."

twenty-five
CHARLIE CALLOWAY

2017

I snuggled deeper into my red bomber jacket and tried to keep up with Dalton. What to him was a leisurely stride was a brisk pace to me. I had even worn heeled boots to try to alleviate the height difference.

Dalton put his arm around me and leaned into my ear. "Want a coffee?" he asked.

I nodded and we ducked into a crowded coffee shop in the West Village and waited in line. Both of us had been granted overnight passes to attend David Tower's exhibit and then spend the night with our parents in the city and drive back to Knollwood the following day. We'd left campus early this morning. Dalton drove. We'd stopped briefly outside Hartford for coffee and breakfast sandwiches. It was kind of nice to get away from campus for a while, and I was enjoying being in Dalton's company. It was a pleasant distraction from my current preoccupation, which lately included a lot of obsessing over the photographs I had found in my mother's case file.

What were those photographs? Where did they come from? What did they mean? And most importantly, what were they doing there? I had examined the pages torn from a yellow legal pad that had also been in the file, but they contained mostly illegible chicken scratch. I could make out a date at the top: July 14, 2007. That was three weeks before my mother went missing. The only other words

I could make out with any certainty were "Knollwood" and "Jake Griffin."

So, three weeks before my mother went missing, Peter Hindsberg had been helping my mother with a case. A case that somehow involved her dead ex-boyfriend who also happened to go to my school with my father.

And then there were those other photographs—the ones Uncle Hank had found underneath the floorboards of my parents' bedroom at the house on Langely Lake. The photographs of Peter Hindsberg and my mother, and the note that accompanied them: *I KNOW.* And that one word on the back of my picture: *STOP.*

Had someone found out about whatever case my mother and Peter Hindsberg had been working on together? If they had found out, and they were threatened enough to send those messages to my mother, what else might they have been threatened enough to do? Maybe my mother had gotten scared and run off. Or maybe she hadn't had the chance.

A shiver ran down my spine and I shook my head to clear it.

Dalton offered his credit card to the barista and insisted he pay for my coffee. I opened my mouth to object, but Dalton gave me a look that meant he wasn't going to budge.

"Thank you," I said instead.

"My pleasure," he said, smiling.

Anyone looking at us would have thought we were a couple. That Dalton was just a nice, normal boy (which he was) and I was just a nice, normal girl (which I wasn't).

Ever since we had kissed in Dalton's room, I had noted a subtle change in the way he treated me. He had become protective, possessive in a way. The boys had started to sit with me, Drew, Yael, and Stevie at dinner. That had rarely happened before, but suddenly, it was like we were part of the group. Sometimes, Dalton would sit next to me, and he'd lean back in his seat and drape his arm casually over the back of my chair. Like we were together. Once, Walker Trefont had made some crack about my lack of coordination on the volleyball court, and Dalton had quickly quipped back about Trefont's sorry blocking skills in lacrosse. Trefont went red in the ears and didn't say anything for the rest of the meal. It was like Dalton constantly had my back.

I knew the reaction I should have had to this, the normal reaction anyone else would have had—I should have been pleased. I should have doodled Dalton's name in the corner of my notebook during trig, or talked endlessly to Drew about how sexy I found his eyes or whatever.

Instead, I found myself edging away. If Drew brought up Dalton, I would become quiet, showing no more enthusiasm than a noncommittal shrug. At dinner sometimes, I would make it a point not to talk to him or glance his way. In class, if Dalton volunteered a point in discussion, I would raise my hand and heatedly argue the exact opposite point of view. It's like I wanted him to hate me.

I knew that was crazy, because the truth was, I liked Dalton. He was smart and kind and popular. I saw the way the other girls looked at him, and I was not blind to their sudden coldness to me when it became obvious that Dalton liked me. And I was attracted to him, too. I liked kissing him in darkened hallway corners or behind the boys' locker room after soccer practice. I liked unbuttoning his jacket and sliding my body against his, warm body to warm body. But for some reason, I felt the need to hold myself back. To hold him at arm's length when I could.

Dalton's phone buzzed and he pulled it out of his pocket and checked his screen.

"It looks like my mom is running a bit late," he said. "She asked if it's okay if she meets us at your father's office."

"Sure," I said, shrugging.

His mother had been anxious to meet me, he said. I guess he

had told her we were dating. When she'd heard we were coming into the city for the day, she had asked if she could take us to dinner. Dalton had suggested I invite my father as well, sort of a kill-two-birds-with-one-stone type of thing, since he had yet to meet my father. I had debated making up some lame excuse about my father's being out of town. To tell the truth, I wasn't sure how I felt about seeing him.

I hadn't seen my father since before the school year started—since before Uncle Hank had shown me those pictures he had found hidden underneath the floorboards of my parents' bedroom. I didn't know how to reconcile all of the things my mother's family and Claire had said about my father with the man I thought I knew.

I didn't know if I could look at him the same way now. Surely, the instant we were in the same room together, he would know that I had betrayed him—that I had gone digging into his past, that I knew things I shouldn't know, that I harbored ugly doubts about him. How could we ever be the same after something like that?

But, in the end, I had agreed to the dinner and invited my father. If I was ever going to get to the bottom of what had happened to my mother, I needed to start asking my father some questions. And I had decided that the best place to start was with Jake Griffin. After seeing those photos in my mother's case file, it seemed obvious that my mother's disappearance was linked in some way with Jake. I just needed to find out how, and if my father was somehow caught up in it, too.

My father's office was on the top floor of a glassy skyscraper downtown. We had called ahead and so there were passes waiting for us at security on the ground floor. Rosalind, who had been my father's secretary for as long as I could remember, greeted us at the elevator. She was a stout woman in her fifties; she was the type of person who was all sunshine and rainbows when she liked you, but all snark and bite when she didn't. When I was a child, I'd seen her make grown Wall Street men cry. Or, at least, tear up.

"Rosie," I said, giving her a hug.

She laughed and hugged me back. "Don't say that too loudly," she said. "You're the only one who can get away with calling me that, and I don't want anyone getting it into their head that that nickname will fly around here."

Like they would dare cross her.

"And who's your tall and handsome friend?" Rosie asked.

"Royce Dalton," Dalton said, extending his hand and smiling. "It's a pleasure to meet you. Charlie speaks very highly of you."

"Well, it's nice to meet you, too," Rosie said, shaking his hand. She looked at me and winked. "He's a keeper," she whispered.

Rosie let us into my father's office and went to get us waters. Apparently, my father was finishing up in a meeting across town and was running a little behind.

My father's office was large and sparsely decorated. Something about the sparseness was supposed to make it edgy and modern, but to me it just felt cold and unapproachable, which maybe was part of the point. He had a corner office, so two sides were windows that looked out over the city below. In the middle of his office was a steel-framed desk and his computer. On the other side of the room were a black leather love seat, two armchairs, and a liquor cabinet.

Dalton sank into the couch and I stood at the window, looking out over the city. From this high up, all of the buildings looked almost small.

"Your father has good taste," Dalton said.

"Yeah," I said. I turned back to his desk and the bookshelf that sat along one wall. There were lots of pictures of my father. Pictures with clients and important people. Pictures with some of his old friends from school—there he was sailing with Freddy Heinz, there he was golfing with Matthew York. But there was only one picture of my father with me and Seraphina. We were at the beach by our house on Martha's Vineyard. Seraphina must have been about seven. She was perched on my father's shoulders. I was standing next to my father, leaning into him; he had his arm around me. I was wearing one of my father's old Columbia sweatshirts, which was way too big for me. I had worn holes into the sleeves that I hooked my thumbs through.

"Sorry to have kept you waiting," I heard a familiar voice say behind me, and I turned to see my father in the doorway, dressed in a suit and overcoat.

He came in and set his briefcase on his desk.

"Charlotte, so good to see you," he said, and he wrapped an arm around me and planted a kiss in my hair. He smelled faintly of tuberose blossoms, the scent of his favorite cologne from Barneys.

"You too," I said, a little stilted and breathless.

"And you must be Charlotte's friend," my father said, taking several long strides across the room to shake Dalton's hand.

Dalton rose from the couch, his hand outstretched.

"Royce, sir," Dalton said. "It's a pleasure to meet you. I hope you don't mind, my mother is running a bit late, I'm afraid, and she likes to make an entrance."

"Well that's certainly a fine introduction to give your own mother."

We all three turned toward the door and saw a woman standing there, finely dressed in dark linen trousers and a delicate cashmere sweater and a thick wool coat. On her arm she toted a boxy Birkin bag. There was something impressive, awe-worthy, about the way she carried herself, though she was of average stature. It was strange, but as attractive as Dalton was, I had always expected his mother to be a great beauty. Instead, I could pick out some of the features that, so attractive on Dalton's face, made his mother plain—the strong, square jaw; the wide nose; the tall forehead.

There was something else that was vaguely familiar about her, but I couldn't put my finger on it.

"I meant it as a compliment, I promise," Dalton said with a smile. "Charlie, Mr. Calloway, may I introduce my dear mother—"

"Margot," my father said hoarsely.

"Oh," Dalton said, his forehead wrinkling in confusion. "I'm sorry, I didn't realize you were acquainted."

Mrs. Dalton strode forward—there was something masculine, commanding, in her gait—and kissed my father on the cheek.

"Alistair, dear, it's been too long," she said. "And this must be your daughter Charlie," she said, turning her attention to me. Her eyes were appraising, looking me up and down. "My stars, if she isn't the spitting image of her mother. Please, dear, call me Margot."

She held out her hand and I took it, even though my heart was stuttering in my chest at the mention of my mother. No one ever brought her up in front of me. "You knew my mother?" I asked.

"Yes, I knew Grace," Mrs. Dalton said. "Your father and I went to school together—at Knollwood, and then Columbia."

And it clicked then, why she seemed familiar. I hadn't met her before, but I had seen her. Margot was the girl in the photograph—the girl stripped naked, her body marked up in red. But she had that same steady, unabashed gaze as the girl in the photograph, as if you, and not she, were the one who had been stripped bare.

"My, Knollwood seems like a lifetime ago now, doesn't it?" Margot asked my father, turning back to him with a smile. "Can you believe we're old enough now to have children there? We're old geezers, I'm afraid."

It took a moment for my father to answer. He seemed frozen in thought, dazed.

"Yes," he said. "I have a hard time believing it myself."

"Well, I hope we all like Italian food," Margot said, looking at each of us in turn and smiling. "I've made reservations at Osteria da Luca." She looked pointedly at my father. "That used to be one of your favorite spots, if I'm remembering correctly," she said.

My father only nodded.

"Superb," she said. "I have a reservation for seven thirty."

She tilted her wrist up to check the time. The sleeve of her coat fell slightly and revealed the white-gold band of her watch. It was beautiful—the watch face was pearl white, surrounded by a dozen yellow diamonds that sparkled and caught the light. Dalton's mother had good taste.

"That's pretty," I said. "Barneys?"

"Hm?" Margot asked.

"Your watch," I said.

"Oh, no, family heirloom," Margot said. She dropped her hand and the arm of her sleeve fell down and covered her watch. "I have a car waiting for us downstairs," she said. "Shall we?"

There was something off with my father. At the restaurant, I stole glances at him over my dinner plate. He was uncharacteristically quiet. I wasn't sure what had affected him so much—had Eugenia told him about the conversation we'd had at homecoming? Had Uncle Teddy broken my confidence and told him about the pictures that Uncle Hank had found at the lake house? Was he angry with me? Or was it Margot's presence that had unnerved him? And if so, why?

Whatever it was, I couldn't let it get in the way of what I had come here to do. I cleared my throat and dug my fork into the pile of risotto on my plate.

"I joined the school newspaper," I said.

"The *Chronicle*?" my father asked, for the moment at least breaking out of his reverie. "Charlotte, that's great."

He smiled and I felt the warmth of his approval surge through my blood.

"I'm working the Features beat right now," I said. "I just pitched this article on the urban myths surrounding campus."

"That sounds interesting," Margot said.

"It is," I said. "There's this one myth I'm looking into right now. It's kind of a ghost story. There's this boy—an old Knollwood student—who haunts campus. Supposedly he killed himself or something; the details surrounding it are really vague."

"Oh yeah," Dalton said. "Crosby swore he saw him one night when he was"—he paused and looked around at my father and his mother—"um, coming back from studying. At the library. Scared the stuffing out of him."

I looked over at my father.

I swallowed and then went on. "I've been looking into it to see who it might be linked to, and there are only two students who died at Knollwood in the last century. It turns out that one of them was at Knollwood at the same time as you. His name was Jake Griffin."

My father paused in sawing his knife through his steak.

"Jake Griffin." Margot said his name slowly, as if she were having trouble placing him. "Oh yes, I remember. That was *so* tragic. Happened my junior year, if I'm remembering right."

"So you knew him?" I asked.

"Yes, we were on the student council together. Jake was a really sweet kid."

"Did you know him, too?" I asked my father.

"Not really," my father said. "He wasn't in my year."

Not really? My mind flashed back to the "In Memoriam" page in the yearbook—the snapshot of my father and Jake Griffin with their arms around one another, beaming at the camera. *Jake Griffin and Alistair Calloway.* My father was lying.

"But I thought I saw a picture of the two of you together in the yearbook," I said.

My father didn't answer.

"You and Jake were on the tennis team together, weren't you?" Margot asked.

"I don't remember," my father said. He wasn't looking at me or Margot. "As you said before, all of that seems like a lifetime ago."

"But there's a picture of the two of you together in the year-book," I said again. I wasn't going to let it go. I wanted answers. I needed answers. "The two of you are standing together in Healy Quad, looking very friendly."

"Where did you say this ghost of yours pops up?" Margot asked, cutting in.

"Usually around the old upperclassman dormitories at night," Dalton said.

"I'm afraid your ghost can't be Jake Griffin then," Margot said.

"Why's that?" I asked.

"Because Jake Griffin didn't die on campus," Margot said.

"He didn't?" I asked.

"Margot, please, this isn't really suitable dinner table discussion," my father said.

"Please, I want to hear," I said. If he wasn't going to give me any answers, maybe Margot would. "For the article," I added.

"It's school-related, Alistair," Margot said. "I'm helping her with her homework."

My father sighed and went back to sawing at his steak with a renewed vigor.

"They found him in the ravine off Spalding River," Margot said. "Apparently, he got caught cheating, went up to the Ledge, and jumped. The poor boy drowned. They found his body a few days later."

"That's awful," Dalton said.

"Yeah, it really hit campus hard," Margot said. "Knollwood is a family, and Jake was one of our own. But I think it's easy to forget when you're not there, and you're not in the grind of things, how much pressure you kids are under to perform. Knollwood is a tough school; not everyone is cut out for it."

Something about Margot's words made me dizzy. It was difficult to breathe.

"Excuse me," I said. "I need to go to the restroom."

"Are you okay, dear?" Margot asked. "You look a little pale."

"I'm fine," I lied.

I stumbled out of the booth and tried to keep my legs steady as I walked, then ran, from the table. In the bathroom, I locked the stall door and leaned against it, breathing heavily.

The photographs in my mother's case file of Jake and my father and Margot and their friends. They had been taken at the Ledge. How had I not recognized it before?

It was all coming together. All the variables were starting to add up:

1. First, there was that photograph of my father with Jake on Healy Quad.
2. Then there was my father's denial that they were ever friends.
3. Next, the stolen exam—which hadn't made sense to me at first, because according to everyone, Jake had been a terrific student.
4. Finally, there was the clearing above Spalding River from which Jake had allegedly jumped.

All of these clues added up to one thing: *Jake had been in the A's.* He had been an initiate—like me. And of course, my father, Margot— they had been A's too, I was sure of it. Some of those pictures from my mother's case file—those were their initiation pictures, like the ones Leo and I had taken in the back of Ren's car.

What if the stolen exam had been Jake's ticket, and he had failed? He had been caught cheating. Facing expulsion, he had gone up to the Ledge above Spalding River. The only question was, was he alone? Had he jumped of his own volition, or was he forced to his watery grave below?

twenty-six
GRACE CALLOWAY

FALL 1999

I leaned against the stall wall until the room stopped spinning. At least I hadn't thrown up. That would have been the pinnacle of my humiliation—kneeling on the porcelain tiles of the bathroom of the Carlyle Hotel in my Oscar de la Renta evening gown as the sharp-tongued wives of the Upper East Side overheard me heave my lunch into the toilet. By the time I'd reentered the party, half the crowd would have heard that I had an eating disorder and the other half would have been vehemently proclaiming I was an alcoholic.

I hadn't wanted to come out tonight at all but it was the Calloways' annual charity ball and Alistair was giving a speech. Earlier that evening, as I'd fastened his tie for him in our bedroom, he'd practiced his speech, going over all the lines, noting where he would place emphasis and where he would pause for laughter or applause. I had thought about saying something then—telling him I wasn't feeling well, mentioning that it was probably best I stay home—but things had been so tense lately between us, and I hadn't wanted to cause another fight.

Barely five minutes after arriving, he had wandered off to talk with colleagues and socialites in low-backed evening gowns and I had been left, once again, by myself. I'd caught a whiff of the warm salmon-puff appetizer trays the waiters were proffering around the room, and my stomach had turned. I'd headed straight for that bathroom stall.

But I couldn't hide in there forever. I took a deep breath and exited the stall. I stood at the sink and held my hands under the cold running water. My pallid complexion stared back at me in the mirror. I looked as awful as I felt.

They called it morning sickness, but I felt it all day long.

I'd discovered I was expecting two days ago, sitting alone on the bathroom floor, three empty water bottles and five sticks with five plus signs lying next to me. I hadn't told anyone yet, not even Alistair.

I heard a toilet flush and a stall door open. I glanced behind me in the mirror and my heart stuttered as I caught her reflection—Eugenia.

Eugenia had taken my union with Alistair even harder than Teddy had. The Thanksgiving after Alistair and I were married, she'd disinvited us to the family festivities, and the Calloway Christmas card had arrived with Alistair's head cropped out of the photo. Her anger had only started to thaw when Teddy married a pretty girl by the name of Grier Greymouth a few months ago at the Vineyard. The Greymouths were old money; they had made their fortune in shipping. Grier's mother was a friend of Eugenia's, and Eugenia had arranged the match. Grier was currently getting her doctorate in psychology at NYU, which was one of her many accomplishments that Eugenia liked to spout on about—that, and her shiny hair and her blue ribbons in dressage.

As for the rest of Alistair's family, Alistair's father paid me no more or less attention than he had previously, Teddy had stopped speaking to me altogether, and Olivia had moved to Paris after graduating from Vassar. She was working at an art gallery on the Seine and living with a morose-looking expat thirty years her senior.

Eugenia grimaced when she saw me, which was not an unusual reaction from her.

"You're sweating like a pig," she said as she joined me at the sink. She rummaged in her clutch and handed me a blotting paper, which was the kindest gesture she'd shown me in years.

"Thank you," I said, pressing the paper to my forehead.

"Really, dear, you do look terrible," Eugenia went on. "Are you sure you're all right?"

"I think I might have caught a stomach bug," I said. "I feel a little nauseous."

Eugenia inched away from me as she washed her hands. "Yes, well, you should probably go home and lie down," she said as she reached for a hand towel. "We don't want you getting everyone else sick if you're contagious."

I could see the horrors projecting in her mind—her event taking down half the Upper East Side with the flu, me patient zero.

"I think I will," I said. "Will you tell Alistair, when you see him?"

"Of course, dear," Eugenia said. "You just go on home and get some rest."

I cut a beeline through the ballroom to the coat check in the entrance hall, but there was no one there. The coatroom girl was probably taking a smoking break. It was past the time that people were arriving and too early for anyone to be leaving. I checked my watch, wondering how long she would be.

"Leaving already?"

I turned to see Teddy standing in the dark hall behind me, a glass of scotch in his hand.

"I'm not feeling well," I said.

"Alistair will be disappointed," Teddy said. "He hasn't even given his big 'Look at me, look at me' speech yet. I hear he's gotten so good at it, he can fit his entire cock in his mouth."

Teddy leaned against the wall. I could smell the alcohol on his breath.

"I should be getting back," I said, stepping away from the coat check window.

Teddy mirrored my movement with his own, taking a step so that he was blocking my path.

"I thought you said you were leaving," Teddy said.

He was too close to me. The hairs on the back of my neck stood up.

"You look very pretty tonight," Teddy said. He reached out and ran a finger down my bare forearm. My skin erupted in goose bumps. "Look how you still respond to my touch," Teddy whispered. He came even closer, so he was whispering into my ear. "I remember the way I used to play your body like an instrument, the way I'd make you moan. I bet he doesn't do that, does he?"

I stood very still. I glanced behind him, down the dark and quiet corridor to the ballroom, the bright white lights of the chandelier, the clatter of dinner plates being laid out.

"You should get back to your wife, Teddy," I said. "She's probably wondering where you are."

"My wife," Teddy said with a laugh, and took a sip of his drink. "My wife. Your husband. Look how grown-up we sound with our permanent attachments."

"You're drunk," I said.

"Yes," Teddy said. "I am. But that doesn't make any of it less true. Just a tad more pathetic maybe."

"Yes, it is pathetic."

Teddy turned. There was Alistair, standing behind us in the dark hall, his hands in his pockets, watching us.

"Like I've told you time and time again, pace yourself," Alistair said, coming toward us. He casually took Teddy's glass of scotch. "You don't want to end up making a fool of yourself."

"Always playing big brother," Teddy said dryly. "You should take a night off. You look tired."

"Go find your wife," Alistair said, his voice like ice. "And leave mine alone."

For a moment Teddy just stood there, looking at Alistair with all the malice he'd accrued over the years, his shoulders squared. Teddy was taller than Alistair; he had at least six inches on him. But Alistair was broader in the shoulders, more sturdily built. I could feel the tension between them and I wondered for a moment if this would be the point where things boiled over and Teddy unleashed that hatred he never tried too hard to hide. But after a moment, Teddy seemed to think better of a fight and retreated back toward the ballroom. We watched him go.

"What was that all about?" Alistair asked me pointedly, as if somehow it were my fault.

"How should I know?" I said.

"Do I have to worry about the two of you now?" he asked. "Sneaking off to whisper to each other in dark hallways, all alone?"

"I didn't initiate it," I said. "I was getting my coat."

Alistair raised his eyebrows, and I realized I was still coatless.

"I was *trying* to get my coat," I amended my statement. "I was trying to leave and he cornered me."

Alistair looked hurt. "You were leaving?" he asked. "You weren't going to stay for my speech?"

"I don't feel well," I said.

"That's convenient," Alistair said.

"It's not convenient," I snapped, louder than I'd meant to. My voice carried down the hall and people seated at the nearest table turned to look. I lowered my voice to a fervent whisper. "It's not convenient to be dragged to an event you don't want to go to when you're dizzy and nauseous and tired. And it's not convenient when the person you came with abandons you at said event, and the only time he speaks to you is when he's accusing you of something you didn't do. None of it, Alistair, is convenient."

I couldn't go back in that room and sit with those people and pretend like everything was fine. I turned and stumbled down the hallway toward the lobby, my coat be damned.

Alistair followed me out onto the cold New York sidewalk.

"I'm sorry," Alistair said. "I didn't mean to ignore you."

"I know," I said. "You never mean to."

The late nights at the office, the conference calls on the weekends, the way his attention was always on some new project, none of it was done to purposefully hurt me.

"You knew this was who I was when you met me," Alistair said.

"It's not just about you anymore," I said. "And it's not just about me, either."

Tears stung the back of my eyes. This was not how I wanted to tell him, standing on a cold New York sidewalk, at odds with one another.

"What are you talking about?" Alistair asked.

"I'm—" My voice fell away. I rested my hand on my stomach. "I'm pregnant."

Alistair was silent. He looked like he'd had the wind knocked out of him.

"You're sure?" he asked.

"Yes," I said. "I'm sure."

I didn't know how he would respond. Our first pregnancy had resulted in a miscarriage near the end of the first trimester. I'd been devastated by the loss, and I suspected Alistair was too, but he'd never been one to openly talk about his emotions, even with me.

Now Alistair bridged the gap between us and wrapped his arms around me. I didn't know what to do with this unanticipated display of affection, so I slid my hands underneath his suit jacket and around his waist. He held me close, like he hadn't held me in a long time.

"You're happy?" I asked.

"Of course I'm happy," Alistair said, kissing my hair. "Aren't you?"

I didn't answer. I couldn't separate how I felt about my pregnancy from how I felt about Alistair and me. I'd never felt so much distance between us as I did now.

"I don't feel well," I said instead, which was true.

Alistair took off his suit jacket and draped it around my shoulders. "Let's get you home," he said, and he moved toward the street to hail a cab.

As he held open the door for me, I tried to give him back his jacket.

"Keep it, it's cold," Alistair said.

"But your speech," I said. He couldn't give his speech in only his shirtsleeves. Eugenia would throw a fit.

"It's fine," he said. He leaned down and kissed me on the forehead. "I'll be home in a bit," he said.

At home, I took a warm bath and sat on the living room sofa in my pajamas eating saltines and nursing a ginger ale. I watched the evening network dramas transition into late-night talk shows. I woke up at midnight, infomercials glowing on the screen. I turned the television off and went to bed alone.

The next morning when I woke up, Alistair was there. He was already dressed casually in jeans and a sweater and he came into the room carrying a steaming bowl of oatmeal. He set it down next to me on my nightstand.

"Hey there, sleepyhead," he said. "I made you some oatmeal with brown sugar—thought it might be easier on your stomach than an omelet. You should eat."

I blinked up at him and rubbed the crust from my eyes. "How late did you get in last night?" I asked.

"Eat quickly and get dressed," he said, smiling. "I want to show you something."

I could only get down a few bites, and then I felt queasy. I hurried to the bathroom to dress.

As I dressed, Alistair called down to have the valet pull around the car. It was waiting for us at the front door. I ducked in to the front passenger seat and leaned my head against the cold glass window.

"Where are we going?" I asked Alistair as the car pulled away from the curb.

"It's a surprise," he said, taking my hand and holding it. He gave me a reassuring smile. "A good surprise," he said.

We drove for over an hour, until the high-rises faded away and then the suburbs and we entered flat, open land. I closed my eyes and fell asleep. When the car jostled to a stop, I woke up. I glanced out the window, but all I could see was trees.

"Come on," Alistair said, opening the door. "We're almost there."

I took his hand and let him lead me. I had the uncanny feeling that I had been there before, but I couldn't place it at first, and then, I saw the lake. Langely Lake.

We walked for several minutes without saying anything until we came to the tree house that Jake and I had built together when we were children. The place where Alistair and I had first made love.

Alistair stopped and turned to face me.

"I know you've been unhappy," he said. "And there are a lot of things I can't change about our lives. But maybe there's a middle ground.

"This was our beginning," he said, motioning around him to the lake. "And it's going to be our beginning again. I'm going to build a house for us here. Not just a house—a home. And we're going to fill it with our children, our family. This will be our place, away from everything else. When we come here, it'll just be us."

He looked so earnest. It was as if he thought by sheer will and determination, he could hold us together, fill in the cracks, keep things from falling apart. And I wanted to believe him. Oh, how desperately I wanted to believe him. So, I didn't say anything. I just reached out and took his hand.

twenty-seven
CHARLIE CALLOWAY

2017

Dalton and I got a late start back to Knollwood the next day. Margot called ahead of us to the school to let them know we'd miss the nightly curfew check, and the administration had reluctantly consented, stipulating that we had to check in with our dormitory supervisors first thing the following morning. On the drive back, I leaned my head against the cold glass window of the front passenger seat, closed my eyes, and feigned a headache. I was too shaken by my revelation about Jake to hold up a conversation with Dalton. I wanted to be alone with my thoughts. It was like everything suddenly was clicking into place—here were the connections I had been looking for, the connections I had felt were there all along, lying just beneath the surface, waiting for me to uncover them.

But then, the more I thought about it, the more I became convinced that I was wrong. I mean, would the A's really kill someone? Even if a recruit did fail a ticket, even if a recruit threatened to expose the A's, was that really worth . . . murder? Sure . . . the A's could be dark and twisted and cruel. But murder?

And, most importantly, I didn't know how to make this fit with my mother's disappearance. So Jake and my father had known each other at Knollwood; they had been in the A's together. Maybe my father even gave Jake the ticket to steal the exam. Jake got in over his head, got caught, was threatened with expulsion, and killed himself because he thought his life was over. What could that possibly have to do with my mother's disappearance a decade and a half later?

Just when things had seemed like they were clicking into place, they fell apart again. The answers that I had been so sure of in the restaurant now seemed flimsy, ridiculous. No, it still didn't make any sense.

"Here, take this," Dalton said.

I opened my eyes and saw that he was motioning to a bottle of water in the center cup holder.

"Thanks," I said, taking the bottle. "I don't know that hydration is the problem, though."

Dalton smiled. "No, silly," he said, leaning across my seat and opening the glove compartment, his other hand still on the steering wheel. "That is to wash down *this*."

He dug out an orange pill bottle from the glove compartment and shook it at me. I read the label. Prescription painkillers.

"Where'd you get those?" I asked.

"Some leftover treats from my foot injury last year," he said, closing the glove compartment and refocusing on the road. "You know, from when the idiot from Xavier tripped me during semi-finals."

I vaguely remembered Dalton hobbling around on crutches last spring, a gaggle of sophomore girls tripping over themselves to carry his books. "Thanks," I said, taking the pills.

"I'm glad I got to meet your father," Dalton said.

"Yeah," I said.

"But I feel like I didn't really get to know him," Dalton said. "He seems like one of those people who, I don't know, it's difficult to crack the surface of."

I didn't answer him. Instead, I busied myself with taking the pills and washing them down with a big gulp of water.

But I wanted to tell him he didn't know the half of it.

We went straight to the Ledge when we got back to Knollwood. Harper made a sour face when we arrived together. We were the last ones there, and I hurriedly texted the pictures Leo had taken of me and Mr. Andrews to Ren, while the rest of the A initiates piled their items onto the hood of Crosby's car.

Despite yesterday's events, I felt a little relieved, a small sense of accomplishment, because I had done it. Two down, only one item left to go. I was practically an A. I looked across the circle and met Leo's eyes.

We're almost there, I wanted to say.

I glanced around the circle to find Drew. I wanted her to share in this moment. I couldn't wait to stay up late together when we got back to our room and hear her story about what it took to steal old Mr. Franklin's trig exam. But my gaze swept the circle and I couldn't find her. My heart skipped a beat. I glanced down at the hood of Crosby's car, searching for Mr. Franklin's exam—but it wasn't there either.

It was only then that I realized—Drew hadn't made it.

twenty-eight
GRACE CALLOWAY

JUNE 2007

"Say 'cheese'!"

The flash went off, and then Charlotte held the digital camera carefully, looking at the screen to see the picture she had just taken of her sister next to her in the backseat.

"Why do people say that—'say cheese'?" Charlotte asked.

"Because it forces people to smile," I said, glancing at her in the rearview mirror. Next to me, in the driver's seat, Alistair was talking into his Bluetooth headset. We had left the city in the early afternoon to beat the weekend traffic. It was officially summer now, and most people we knew were headed to the Hamptons, but we were headed north to our house on Langely Lake.

"Why do people always have to smile in photographs?" Charlotte asked.

I reached in my purse at my feet to grab my lip balm. "Because photographs are about capturing a moment so you can remember it, and when you look back at a picture, don't you want to see yourself smiling and happy?" I asked.

"You look *so* dumb, Sera," Charlotte said, reaching the camera across the seat so her sister could see it in her booster seat.

"Don't call your sister dumb," I said, glancing at Charlotte in the rearview mirror.

She looked like me. My mom had shown me pictures the other

week of me at Charlotte's age and it was uncanny, really, the resemblance. The same wavy dark brown hair, the wide-set gray eyes, the curve of our cheeks. She looked like me, but she was so much like Alistair. She was tough and headstrong and possessed a confidence and a composure that seemed otherworldly in someone so young.

Now, when I looked at my daughter in the backseat, I found myself wondering if there was any of my likeness in her character.

Seraphina reached out and grabbed the strap of the camera from Charlotte and then flung it hard against the side of the door.

"Hey," Charlotte cried out. She reached over and grabbed the camera. "You're such a brat."

Charlotte fiddled with the camera for a moment and then looked up at me.

"She broke it," she whined.

I turned around in my seat to take the camera from her so I could examine it. The body of the camera and the screen looked fine, but it would no longer turn on.

"I'll have to take it in when we get back to the city and get it fixed," I said.

"But what about my art project?" Charlotte asked. "I have to take pictures this weekend."

Charlotte was taking a weeklong summer art class at her school.

"We might have an old camera at the house that you can use," I said. "We'll look when we get there."

"Read me those numbers again," Alistair said in the seat next to me. "Hold on."

He tapped a button on his headset to mute himself. Then he glanced at me—the first time he had looked at me since we left the city. "Grace, can you keep things at a reasonable volume? This is an important call."

He didn't wait for my response before he looked back at the road and tapped his headset again.

"My apologies, Fred," Alistair said. "I've got the girls in the car."

He laughed at something Fred said that I couldn't hear.

I rolled my eyes so that the girls couldn't see and then smiled at them and pressed my index finger to my lips in a friendly "shhh" gesture.

Then I turned back around and sighed into my seat.

I glanced at my husband sitting next to me and I thought about how I missed the electric charge of attraction that came when you didn't know every facet of a person. When you didn't sleep next to them every night, or share a bathroom, or clean up after them when they were sick. I missed the mystery—the not knowing what comes next. That point when the other person seemed perfect because you only knew the best parts of them—the parts they wanted you to see.

That was terrible, wasn't it? Though, I wondered sometimes if Alistair felt similarly. Surely sometimes he imagined I was someone else when we made love. I knew he looked at other women—long-necked women with perfect skin that they liked to show off in low-backed evening gowns at charity events. I saw him look at them, and I saw them look back. I tried to see my husband through their eyes. I knew, to them, he was handsome: tall, piercing blue eyes, a distinguished forehead crowned with salted blond hair. It was more than that, though—it was the way Alistair carried himself, as if he owned the room. As if he didn't give a damn what anyone thought of him. I'd look at my husband in these moments—the same man I lived my life next to every day—and for a glimmer of a moment, I'd actually see him. That was the thing. It's not what you look at—it's what you see. And when you've been with someone long enough, you stop really seeing each other.

Being together for ten years was like listening to your favorite song too many times on the radio. You knew all the words but you'd lost all the feelings the song used to give you—the things that made you love it in the first place. And it's confusing, because the words are all the same and so are the beat and melody—nothing's changed. Except that now when it plays, you sort of want to change the station.

At the house, I searched the kitchen first, pulling open drawers. I knew I had a spare disposable camera somewhere from one of the girls' birthday parties. When the kitchen search proved fruitless, I moved on to the old storage closet in the front hall. Charlotte trailed after me through the house, and Seraphina followed her, bobbing along like a little duckling in her sister's wake, pigeon-toed and wobbly.

I pulled down an unmarked cardboard box from the top shelf in the closet and set it on the floor.

"What's that?" Charlotte asked.

"Odds and ends," I said.

There were old videocassettes and photo albums. At the bottom of the box, something caught my eye.

"Aha," I sang out.

"What is it?" Charlotte asked.

I held it up for her to see. It was a matte black thirty-five-millimeter film camera.

"This is a very old-school camera," I said, checking to see if it was loaded with film—it was. "This is what your Daddy and I used to take pictures with when we were your age."

I looked at the picture count at the top. There were twenty-five pictures left—practically a whole roll. I pressed the power button, which did nothing.

"It's broken," Charlotte said, disappointed.

"No, it just needs new batteries," I said. "Wait here."

I padded back to the kitchen and grabbed a pair of AA batteries from a drawer. I pressed the power button again, and this time, it sang to life. I ran back to the hall to show Charlotte.

"It's all fired up for you," I said, handing Charlotte the camera. "Be gentle with it, though, it's very old."

"Where's the screen?" Charlotte asked.

"There is no screen," I said. "You won't be able to see the pictures until we get the film developed. You have to put your eye to the viewfinder to see what you're taking the picture of."

I pointed to the viewfinder on the camera, and Charlotte raised the camera to her eye.

"Like this?" she asked.

"Like that," I said.

Her finger hovered over the button to snap a picture. I reached out a hand to stop her, but it was too late. The flash went off.

"Cool," Charlotte sang out.

I laughed. "You'll have to be selective in what pictures you take," I told her. "You only have twenty-four shots left now for the whole weekend."

Charlotte lifted the camera to her face again, but she didn't take a picture. She looked one way down the hall through the camera's lens, and then the other.

"Okay," she said.

On Sunday, before we returned to the city, I stopped by the Walgreens on the corner of Third and Main in Hillsborough to pick up Charlotte's pictures. There were two attendants in the back corner of the shop where the photo center was—an elderly man with glasses and a younger man who couldn't have been more than twenty, who wore his pants low on his hips so you could see several inches of his boxers when he turned around. The older man came to the counter to assist me.

"I'm here to pick up some film I dropped off earlier," I said, pulling out my wallet. "The name's Grace Calloway."

The younger guy who was sorting through rolls of film behind the counter dropped a canister and it clattered to the floor. He turned to look at me, and there was something like shock on his face.

"Uh, I can go grab that order, actually," he said to the older man. "I remember developing it earlier. I'll be right back."

He disappeared into the back room and the older man assisting me smiled at me as we waited. The kid came back holding up an envelope.

"Got it right here," he said. He slid up to the cash register to ring me up. He had long, greasy hair. His name tag read *Randy*.

"Let us know if you need anything else," the older man said before he walked off to assist another customer.

"So, uh," Randy said, glancing over his shoulder to ensure the older man wasn't within earshot, "we don't normally develop these types of shots. Actually, it's kind of our policy *not* to develop this stuff. But, you know, being all 'to each his own' as I am, I can sometimes be persuaded to look the other way."

"What?" I asked. What did he mean, "these types of shots"?

"You know," he said, leaning over the counter toward me and lowering his voice. "For a price."

I stared at him, confused.

He sighed. "You know, like a twenty-spot or something, and we'll call it even," he said.

"Um, are you sure you have the right person?" I asked, adjusting the strap of my purse on my shoulder. "They're just a bunch of pictures my daughter took. She's seven."

Randy looked back at the writing on the envelope. "Grace Calloway?" he asked.

"Yeah," I said. "That's me. But maybe the film got switched or something? Can I check just to be sure?"

Randy shrugged and handed me the envelope. "See for yourself," he said. "But that's definitely your film. You're in some of the
pictures."

I opened the envelope. The first shot was of me—it was the one
Charlotte had taken in the hallway when I had handed her the
camera. The lens was pointed up, and I looked tall in the frame,
my hand outstretched to block the shot. I flipped through a dozen
others—some of Charlotte and Seraphina, one of Alistair and myself on the boat at sunset. And then I flipped to the next photograph, which clearly had not been taken by my daughter.

My eye caught on the image and I stopped.

There was a face I knew well but hadn't seen in over a decade.
It was Jake. Jake Griffin.

The picture was dark; it had been taken at night. There, in the
bottom right-hand corner in red, was the digital time stamp. The
picture had been taken in September of 1990, just a few months
before Jake died.

In the picture, Jake's shirt was unbuttoned at the collar; his tie
was askew. In one hand, he held a half-drunk beer bottle. In the
other, he pointed his middle finger at the camera, a sloppy smile
on his face.

In the next picture, I could make out the ghostly white belly of
a girl lying across the hood of a car, her shirt pulled up to expose
her breasts. There was a powdery line of coke across her stomach.
The camera caught Matthew York—one of Alistair's friends—as
he leaned forward, finger plugging one nostril, midsnort.

There were other pictures. And not just of Jake, but of other kids
too. People I recognized, though they were older now. There were
Freddy Heinz, and Margot, and Marissa Saunders, and Alistair.

In one picture, Margot was naked, her body marked up with red
permanent marker—parts of her were circled or X'd out. Words
had been written on her body in a dozen different scrawls, as if

everyone had taken their turn. *Fat, slut, whore, ugly, desperate, sad, bitch.*

I didn't want to look anymore. I didn't want to know. They were terrible pictures. Why would anyone take them to begin with? Why would anyone keep them?

But I couldn't help myself. I flipped to the last two pictures. There was Jake, with his arm slung around Alistair. Margot was on his other side, on her tiptoes, leaning forward to plant a kiss on Jake's cheek. Matthew York was on Alistair's other side, mouth open, howling with silent laughter. They were standing on the lip of a cliff. The time stamp on the bottom read, *9:32 P.M., December 21, 1990.* The date stopped me cold. That was the night Jake died— just a few hours before Jake's estimated time of death, according to the autopsy report. And behind him, there was the ledge where he had jumped. But here he was, not by himself, but surrounded by friends, his face split into a smile. He looked so full of life, so happy. How could this Jake—the one staring at me in the photograph— how could he be minutes away from jumping off that ledge?

"What happened to you?" I whispered to the photograph, for- getting myself, forgetting that I was in a public place. "What hap- pened?"

My eyes slid over to my husband's boyish face. Alistair had been there that night. He had never told me that. Even when I stood next to him in that art gallery years ago and told him how I blamed myself for Jake's death. How I felt sick with guilt that I hadn't known how much pain Jake must have been in to take his own life. I had shown him my deepest, darkest pathetic bits, and he had said nothing.

No, he hadn't said nothing. That wasn't true. He had held my hand, I remembered now. It was such a soft and unexpectedly ten- der gesture. And he had said that what had happened to Jake wasn't my fault, but that he didn't have any answers.

"Pretty gnarly," Randy said.

I looked up. I had forgotten for a moment where I was. Randy was looking at me expectantly.

"Not exactly G-rated, you know?" he said. "Some of that stuff is hard to look at."

"Yeah," I said.

"So are they yours?" he asked. "I mean, you're in some of the shots."

"I'll take them," I said. I opened my purse and slid a twenty-dollar bill discreetly across the counter.

Randy pocketed the cash and then scanned the bar code on the envelope into the computer.

"That'll be sixteen dollars and fifty cents," he said, and I handed him my card. I tried to keep my hand from shaking.

There was only one thing I knew for certain. If I wanted the truth about what had really happened that night, I couldn't ask Alistair. I would have to find it somewhere else.

twenty-nine
CHARLIE CALLOWAY

2017

When I got back to my room, the light was on and Drew was there. I saw her from the branch of the elm outside our window, and when I knocked on the glass, she came over to let me in.

"I suppose you've heard?" she asked casually, extending an arm to help me. Behind her, I saw the suitcase open on her bed, half packed already.

"Just the CliffsNotes version," I said as I climbed in. "Crosby filled me in. But he wasn't really in a talkative mood."

He'd been too angry, too upset, to tell me more than the barest details—Mr. Franklin had caught Drew trying to steal the trig exam this afternoon. She'd spent all evening in Headmaster Collins's office. She was being expelled.

Drew returned to the mound of clothes on her bed. She picked up the hanger on the top of the stack and undressed it.

"Do you want this?" she asked, turning to show me the black Chloé dress I had always coveted. She had bought it in SoHo two summers ago when she was visiting me. "It looks better on you anyway."

I didn't answer her; I was still trying to process what was happening. Her wall had been stripped—the memory board, the photographs, the string lights were packed into a box open on her desk. The railing in her closet was bare.

"Shit," I said. "Shit."

"Yeah," Drew said. "Pretty much."

"I still don't understand what happened," I said. I cleared a spot on her bedspread next to her clothes and sat down, hugging my knees to my chest. "Just—tell me everything. From the beginning."

"So, you know how Crosby is a TA for Mrs. Benson?" Drew asked. Mrs. Benson was the freshman geometry teacher. I nodded. "Well, he has a pass code to get into the teachers' lounge in the math building, and he gave it to me. Anyway, since the trig exam is tomorrow, I figured Mr. Franklin would use the copier in the lounge this afternoon to make copies. I sort of hid and waited around until he came. I watched him put the exam into the copier, and then while it was printing copies, I was supposed to text Crosby to pull the fire alarm to lure Mr. Franklin out of the building. But I didn't have to because Mr. Franklin went down the hall to the bathroom while the copier was going. Or at least, I thought he did. But he must have just gone to the vending machine because he was only gone for like, a minute. He sort of caught me red-handed as I was leaving."

"There's got to be something we can do," I said, pressing my palms into my eyes, thinking, thinking. There had to be a way out of this. "I mean, you're not even in trig. Is it really cheating if you're not even taking the test?"

I looked up at Drew and she shrugged. She kept on folding clothes into her suitcase as if everything were fine. I reached out and grabbed her wrist.

"Stop," I said. "Stop packing like you're leaving, like this is a done deal. Maybe the A's can help."

"I talked to Crosby earlier," Drew said. "He says he knows someone on the board of admissions at Wellesley who might be able to get them to overlook this whole thing next year when I apply."

"I meant there's got to be a way to keep you here at Knollwood," I said. "Like maybe there's a lesser charge or a loophole in the rules."

"There isn't," Drew said.

I dug my phone out of my pocket. "Let me at least call Dalton. Maybe he can help."

"Don't," Drew said, grabbing for my phone.

I held it out of her reach. "I don't understand why you're not fighting this," I said. "It's like you don't even care."

Drew was quiet for a moment. "I haven't been completely honest with you," she said finally. She put down the hanger she was holding. I could hear the emotion, tight in her throat. "My mom lost her job a few months ago," Drew said. "Her company is filing for bankruptcy."

Her words hit me like a steel bat. My best friend had been dealing with a major family crisis all semester, and I'd been too preoccupied with the A's and my own family drama to notice. "Drew, I'm so sorry," I said. "I had no idea."

"It was a little up in the air whether I could even come back this year," Drew said. "But my parents were adamant they would make it work. I think my mom was optimistic she would find something else, but she hasn't."

Drew's dad was a history professor at a small liberal arts school in Connecticut. He hardly made the kind of money that could shoulder the steep tuition of a place like Knollwood.

"I guess they had to sell the house," Drew said. "And my tuition is next on the chopping block. They were going to pull me out midsemester. I found out a few days ago."

"Is that why you've been giving me the runaround with spring enrollment?" I asked.

"I'm sorry," Drew said. "I just . . . I didn't know how to tell you what was really going on."

"What about scholarships?" I asked.

"They give out all of the financial aid in the fall," Drew said. "I couldn't apply until next year. And anyway, it wouldn't be the same."

It hit me then. Drew had gotten caught on purpose to save face. She would rather have gone out with a bang—the whole school believing she was caught up in some big cheating scandal with the A's—than with a whimper, the whole school knowing her family was financially ruined. She'd chosen infamy over ignominy.

"Does anyone else know?" I asked. I couldn't help but wonder if she had at least confided in Stevie.

Drew shook her head. "Just you," she said.

I reached out and fingered the soft strap of the Chloé dress. I remembered that day she'd bought it like it was yesterday. Drew and I had wandered in and out of boutiques in our sundresses and sandals, delirious with too much sleep and sunburns. Drew had pretended a French accent and hit on some thirty-year-old shop clerk in broken English. She'd gotten his number, just to prove that she could. Later, at some hole-in-the wall noodle place, we'd called him. Drew told him, in the elementary French we'd learned in Madame Le Fevre's class, her favorite food (*Je mange les noodles. J'adore les noodles*), while across the table I bit my lip to stifle my giggles. I'd tried to go back to that noodle place last summer, but I'd been unable to find it again.

"You should keep the dress," I said. "You've got the legs for it, not me."

"Yeah, you are like, almost legally a midget," Drew said.

I laughed and pushed her. "You're such a brat for leaving me," I said, swallowing the ball of emotion that had clawed its way up my throat.

"Puh-leeze," Drew said. "You're going to be big shit now. You'll be the only junior living in a single. And you can push the beds together and have a queen."

"Mega bed," I said.

Drew laughed. "And mega closet if you want," she said. She shook her head. "The things I do for you."

The next day at lunch, our table was uncharacteristically somber. News had spread across campus overnight that Drew had been caught stealing Mr. Franklin's trig exam. Her parents had already arrived on campus and Drew had been called away to Headmaster Collins's office half an hour ago.

"Damn, who died?" Zachery asked as he set his lunch tray down and looked around at all of us.

"You're such a dick," I said.

"Sorry, just trying to lighten the mood," he said as he sat down.

"Can't be done," Stevie said. "This whole thing royally sucks."

"So, what are you going to do about it?" Crosby asked.

Crosby was usually the life of the party, but these were the first words he'd spoken all day.

"What do you mean?" Stevie asked.

"I mean, at the disciplinary hearing this afternoon, what are you going to say?"

Stevie grew red in the face. She looked down at her plate and moved her peas around with the prongs of her fork. "The rules are very clear on this," Stevie said. "The disciplinary hearing is really just a formality at this point."

"So basically you're going to get up there and tell the headmaster to expel your best friend."

"I'm going to follow the rules," Stevie said, "which are always the same for everyone. Or, at least, they should be."

"Maybe if you weren't such a little priss, you'd have more friends," Crosby said.

"Hey, cool it," Yael said. "None of this is Stevie's fault."

Stevie looked like she might cry. "I'm going to go get some water," she said so quietly I almost couldn't hear her.

I got up and followed her over to the drink dispenser.

"Hey, you okay?" I asked.

"I don't know why he thinks I'm in any position to do something about this," Stevie said, pulling a cup from the stack with so much vigor the whole thing shook.

"He's just upset," I said. "We all are. But I'm sorry he's taking it out on you."

Stevie held her empty cup under the drink dispenser and pushed the tab for water. "If he's looking for someone to blame, I'm not the person," Stevie said.

"What's that supposed to mean?" I asked.

Stevie slowly turned to face me and for the first time, I saw how angry she was. "Obviously Drew wasn't stealing the exam for herself—she was stealing it for someone else," she said.

"You don't actually think—" I said, and then stopped and swallowed. "Are you really saying that you think *I* asked Drew to steal that exam for me?"

Stevie shrugged. "All I know is, I've heard a lot of talk from you lately about UPenn, and I know you've been distracted with your new boyfriend—"

"Dalton is *not* my boyfriend," I said.

"Whatever," Stevie said. "I just—I can't think of a single reason why Drew would have been in that room if she weren't doing it for what she saw as a very good reason—to save you."

"Stevie, I would never ask her to do something like that for me," I said.

"It's either that," Stevie said lowering her voice, "or she was there because someone else asked her to do it."

"Someone else?"

Stevie crossed her arms over her chest. "Just tell me. Is Drew . . . is she in the A's? Are you?"

"No," I said. "Of course not."

Stevie looked like she might cry. "That's what Headmaster Collins is going to think," Stevie said. "And I honestly don't know which is worse—if you were selfish enough to ask Drew to do something so dumb, or if you guys were in that stupid, awful secret club together this whole time."

"Stevie—"

"They're horrible," Stevie said. "The A's. It's a bunch of egotistical, self-entitled rich kids running around acting like gods. It's a bunch of stupid pissing contests."

"I don't think it's exactly like that," I said.

"It *is* exactly like that," Stevie said. "I don't know why you can't see that."

Part of me wished I could tell Stevie what was really going on— that Drew wanted to leave. But I thought about the way Drew had covered for me with River when we were freshmen; we didn't even know each other yet, and still, she had kept my secret. This secret wasn't mine to tell.

She took a step away from me and then turned back. "You know, for someone so smart, you're being a complete idiot," Stevie said.

I opened my mouth to respond but just then, my phone vibrated.

I glanced down at the screen and did a double take. It was my father's office. What now? I didn't have time to deal with this, but I didn't really have a choice.

"Rosie?" I asked as I picked up.

But it was my father's voice that answered me. "Charlotte."

"Dad?" I said, more than a little surprised. My father never called me. "Is everything okay?" I plugged my other ear with my finger so I could hear him over the noise of the dining hall.

"No, it's not," he said. "I thought it imperative that I call and talk to you about the company you're choosing to keep."

"Oh," I said, taken aback. What did he know about the company I kept? Had he somehow found out about Drew? That she was about to be expelled for cheating? Then I stupidly remembered my dinner with Dalton and our parents the other night. "Are you talking about Dalton?" I asked, confused.

What the hell was going on? I turned toward the French doors on the far end of the dining hall, looking for a quiet place to talk.

"Yes, the boy you brought to dinner," my father said. "I'm not sure what the nature of your relationship is, but whatever it is, it needs to stop."

I pushed open the French doors and walked outside. It was cold out and the patio was nearly empty.

"I'm not sure I understand," I said.

Was my father really calling to demand that I break up with a boy he had met once over dinner?

"He's not right for you, Charlotte," my father said. "His family—they're not the right sort of people. And the apple usually doesn't fall far from the tree. I don't want you seeing him anymore."

"His family?" I said. I'd never heard anything bad about the Daltons, and Margot had seemed perfectly nice. "But I thought you and his mother were friends."

"Then you've been misled," my father said. "Margot—I don't want you around her. If she tries to contact you again, you are to let me know immediately and I will take care of it."

"Okay," I said. As in *Jeez, okay, why don't we all just calm down*. But I think my father took it as an acquiescence to his command.

"All right," he said, and he sounded slightly placated, and a little tired. "This is for your own good, Charlotte. Trust me on that."

"Okay," I said again.

But I didn't trust him. I didn't trust him at all.

The disciplinary hearing was just as horrible as I had thought it would be. I sat with the rest of the A's as we watched Headmaster Collins offer Drew the chance to save herself by giving us up, but she didn't take it. He gave her until the end of the day to clear out her things and leave campus.

That evening after the nightly curfew check, I lay on Drew's bare mattress and stared up at the ceiling alone in the dark. It was so quiet in our room without the sounds of her breathing, of her turning over on the bed.

It didn't matter that Drew wanted to leave, that she had gotten caught on purpose. I still felt like I had just lost my best friend.

I got out my phone and texted Greyson.

I'm gonna need you to come over and hide all my razor blades, I wrote.

But he didn't come back with a funny quip to take the edge off my anger.

GREYSON: What's wrong?

I started to type out a response and then erased it. I started again, then stopped again. Finally, I just wrote out the truth.

Everything, I said.

thirty
GRACE CALLOWAY

JUNE 2007

I checked my watch again. She was running late. I drummed my fingers on the table and glanced again at the menu.

I had picked this place because Alistair had mentioned bringing clients here, and it seemed like the type of place where she would be comfortable. The wine list was two pages long, the cheapest bottle over two hundred dollars. What I hadn't anticipated was the attentive service. It was too attentive. Nearly every time I took a sip from my water glass, someone came by to refill it, and the waiter hovered nearby. Any accidental glance in his direction or inadvertent gesture brought him over, inquiring if there was anything he could get me.

I had chosen a dark booth toward the back of the restaurant, hoping for some privacy. I didn't want us to be overheard.

At half past the hour, I looked up and saw her—dressed fashionably in a trench coat and heels, her arm bent at the elbow, carrying a Birkin bag. She had a cell phone clutched in one hand, though she wasn't on it. Her pale, straw-colored hair fell just below her shoulders in a perfectly straight cut. She was the type of person who was so well put together and who carried herself with such confidence that you almost forgot she wasn't pretty.

I got up to greet her but she waved away the gesture, so I sat back down.

"Margot," I said. "Thanks so much for meeting me."

"My surgery ran over," she said by way of greeting me before turning her attention to the waiter, who had suddenly appeared at her side. She held up a finger to him, opened the menu, and quickly scanned the wine list.

"A glass of your house Merlot," she said. "Grace?"

"Oh, I'm fine with just water, thanks," I said.

"Make that two glasses of your house Merlot," Margot said to the waiter, handing him the wine list. "Don't make me drink alone," she said to me in a not unfriendly tone as she removed her trench coat and laid it in the booth next to her. "Besides, red wine has antioxidants. It's good for your heart."

"Okay," I said, giving the waiter a small smile to reassure him as I handed him my wine list. "Thanks."

We probably looked like old friends to him—two women who met often for lunch, who were so familiar they didn't need to say hello. Just two friends who cared about each other's antioxidant intake and heart health.

When the waiter left, I turned to Margot, who was scanning the menu. I had been surprised that she had agreed to meet with me when I called her last week—probably just as surprised as she had been by the invitation. Part of me wondered if she would show up at all, but she was probably too intrigued by the call to stand me up.

"How's Oliver?" I asked. To some extent, we traveled in the same circles. We saw Margot and her husband, Oliver, a wealthy banker, at functions occasionally. I knew they had a little boy around Charlotte's age. "How's your son?"

Margot glanced up from the menu. "I don't have time for pleasantries," she said. "But you could tell me the real reason you asked me here."

"Okay," I said. I had run through this conversation a hundred times in my head, but now, I didn't know what the right words were, so instead I reached in my purse and laid the photographs out on the table.

Margot glanced at them. Her brow creased. She reached down and picked them up, flipped through them one by one.

"Where did you get these?" she asked.

"They were in an old camera in a box in the closet at the lake house," I said. "I didn't realize they were on there until I got the film developed."

Our waiter came back with our wineglasses and Margot set the photographs facedown on the table.

"Are you ladies ready to order?" the waiter asked.

"We'll need just a couple more minutes," Margot said.

When he was gone, Margot took a sip from her wineglass.

"What do you want?" she asked.

"Some of these photographs were taken the night Jake died," I said. "The red time stamp places the last photograph around the estimated time of Jake's death. And you were there. I want to know what happened that night. What *really* happened."

"Why don't you ask Alistair?" Margot said. "He was there, too."

"I don't trust his answer," I said. "This whole time, he could have told me. But he kept it from me. And I know if I ask him now, he'll just twist the truth. That's all I want—the truth. I need to know."

"What does it matter what really happened that night?" Margot asked. "It won't change anything. Jake's dead. He'll still be dead."

"It matters to me," I said.

Margot sighed and looked slightly bored. I knew she didn't care one whit about what mattered to me. That had been the wrong angle to take with her. She tilted her head and ran a finger along the side of her wineglass, thinking.

"It was an accident," Margot said, looking up at me.

"You mean he didn't—he didn't kill himself?" I asked.

"No," Margot said.

She closed her menu and motioned the waiter over to our table. I fell silent. I could feel my heart drumming in my chest. This whole time I had blamed myself for not knowing the type of pain Jake had to be in to do something like that. I had carried that guilt with me for nearly seventeen years—half my life. And this whole time—it had all been a lie.

"Are there quail eggs in the chef salad?" Margot asked our waiter. She sounded faraway—muted somehow.

The waiter responded, but I wasn't listening, wasn't processing.

"Perfect," Margot said, handing the waiter her menu. "And dressing on the side, please." Margot looked at me expectantly. "Grace?"

"What?" I asked.

"Don't be a goose and make me eat by myself," she said. "Order something."

I wasn't hungry. I couldn't imagine eating anything. But to satisfy her, I glanced down at my menu and picked the first thing I saw.

"Minestrone," I said. I couldn't even form a full sentence.

"Of course," the waiter said, sliding my menu off the table.

When the waiter left, I leaned forward and asked Margot, "What do you mean it was an accident?"

Margot took a sip from her wineglass. She looked so poised, so calm, so collected, as if we were talking about our weekend plans rather than Jake's death.

"We were in this club together at school," Margot said. "Very secretive, very exclusive." She waved her hand. "Jake and I were initiates and we had gone through this whole thing to get in. I don't much like to think of it, really, the things we did. They weren't pleasant things. Anyway, we were out celebrating one night at this place off campus called the Ledge. We were drinking, and someone had brought Percocet and was passing it around. Jake had a bad reaction to the mixture. He went into respiratory arrest."

"He stopped breathing?" I asked.

"Naturally, we all panicked," Margot said. "I mean, we were just kids, and we were all drunk or high, so we weren't exactly firing on all cylinders. We knew we couldn't take him to the hospital, because then we would get in trouble too—suspended, expelled. We couldn't risk our entire futures—and what was the point, really, when he was already dead?"

I stared blindly at her. I could picture it. A dark, cold, starless night. I remembered the chill in the air that evening, and how I hadn't slept really, because I had been so anxious and excited to see Jake again. And while I was stirring listlessly in my bed at my parents' house in Hillsborough, a couple hundred miles north at some place called the Ledge, Jake was taking his last breath, dying alone and afraid, surrounded by his so-called friends who were too selfish and stupid to help him.

"Thank god for Alistair," Margot said. "Without him, I don't know what we would have done. But Alistair, he always has a plan. He always takes charge. He was brilliant really."

"Alistair?" I asked.

"Yes, it was all his idea—to make it look like a suicide," Margot said. "He and one of the other senior boys tossed Jake over the Ledge into the ravine. Alistair forged this note and it was almost too perfect when the school authorities searched Jake's room later and found the exam he had stolen as his last initiation task. The story basically wrote itself—a scholarship student who looks like this golden boy from the outside is secretly desperately insecure. He doesn't feel he measures up. He cheats to get ahead, and then someone finds out and threatens to turn him in. He can't take it. So he kills himself. Everyone loves a good pathetic tragedy. They ate it up—barely questioned it."

I remembered hearing about the stolen exam. I *had* questioned it. Jake had always been a straight-A student. Confident and smart. So unlike the portrait of the person conjured up in that suicide letter. I had known something was off, something wasn't right. But then my mother had told me to stop asking questions, to stop picking things apart so that everyone could start to heal.

"It wasn't until later—when the autopsy report came out—that we discovered Jake didn't die of an overdose," Margot said. "He drowned. Turns out, he was still breathing when we threw him in."

They had killed Jake and then they had turned him into something he wasn't.

"But if Jake had Percocet in his system when he died, wouldn't that have shown up on the autopsy?" I asked.

"It did," Margot said. "They found evidence of alcohol, acetaminophen and oxycodone in Jake's system when they ran the tox screen. They're listed in the autopsy. But that's not unusual for suicide cases. I'm sure Jake's family was made aware of the results, but I can understand why they might not have shared that particular detail with many people."

I exhaled the breath that I had been holding. "Why did you tell me all of this?" I asked Margot.

Margot shrugged. "Because I knew it would kill you to know," she said. "And I'm really going to enjoy watching you rip your marriage apart over this."

"My marriage?"

Margot took a sip of wine and gave me a cruel smile. "Just imagine it. Every time you look at your husband—for every day of the rest of your life—every time you kiss him, or pour him a glass of wine, or laugh at one of his jokes, or make love to him, you'll know he's the person who's responsible for Jake's death. If it weren't for Alistair, Jake would still be here. In fact, if it weren't for Alistair, who knows? You and Jake would probably be married right now, and settled in the suburbs with a house full of little brats. It's kind of funny if you think about it, you ending up with the guy who stole Jake's life."

"You're going to pay for what you've done," I said. "All of you— all of you are going to pay."

There had to be consequences. I would make sure of it.

"What *we* did?" Margot asked. "Don't you mean, what *Alistair* did?"

"You were all there," I said. "You could have done something. You could have stopped him. You're just as guilty."

Margot looked at me like she almost felt sorry for me. She wiped the corners of her mouth with a napkin in a precise gesture so that it didn't smear her lipstick. "Oh, honey, don't be so clueless," she said. "What evidence do you have to bring any sort of case?" She gestured at the photographs on the table. "A couple of paltry pictures that put us at the place of Jake's death on the night he killed himself? Those don't *prove* anything. Short of a confession, which none of us are going to give you, you don't have a leg to stand on here. We're not seventeen-year-old kids, scared of getting expelled for being out late and doing drugs on a school night. Like it or not, this all ended a long time ago."

I reached for the photographs and tucked them into my purse. She was wrong. She had to be wrong. They couldn't just kill Jake and completely rewrite his story and then walk away with no consequences. This was murder we were talking about. Murder.

I slung my purse determinedly over my shoulder and stood.

"We'll see about that," I said, and walked out as fast as my shaky legs could carry me, nearly knocking over the waiter and our entrees in the process.

thirty-one
CHARLIE CALLOWAY

2017

It had been three days since Drew had been expelled. I couldn't stand being in my room anymore—not with Drew's bare mattress and her empty closet and the naked hook on the door where she used to hang her bath towel. I also avoided the dining hall, where I would have to see Stevie and her judgmental glare, or Dalton and Crosby, who looked nearly as glum as I felt. So, I went to class and then the library until it closed and I ate cereal and whatever sustenance my mini fridge could provide and avoided everything else altogether.

I had just come back from the library that evening and unlocked my door. When I flipped on the switch, I jumped.

Because Drew's mattress wasn't empty anymore. There was someone sleeping there.

"What the fuck?" I said, putting my hand on my chest. I could feel my heart pounding in my rib cage.

Greyson threw up a hand to shield his eyes from the light and blinked at me. "Hello to you too," he said.

I came in and closed the door quickly behind me. "Jeez, you scared me," I said, dropping my bag on my bed. "What are you do-ing here?"

"I came to see you," Greyson said, sitting up. "I was worried after I got your text, and you haven't really been responding to my calls."

"No, I mean, what are you doing here in my room?" I asked. "Like, how'd you get in?"

"I was asking around for you on the quad and I met this girl— Hayley? Harmony?"

"Harper?" I asked.

"Yeah, that's it. I told her I was a friend from home and that I wanted to surprise you and so she snuck me into the dormitory hall and showed me which room was yours."

Hmm. That was oddly nice of her. I couldn't help but think she had some hidden, evil agenda, though what that could possibly be, I didn't know. Maybe I was just being paranoid.

"Then I just jimmied the lock," Greyson said. "What? Like it's supposed to be hard?"

"Okay, MacGyver," I said.

"If you don't want me here, I can leave," Greyson said.

"I didn't say that," I said. Because it was nice that he was there, and I really didn't want him to go. "Sorry about not returning your calls. I've just . . . been in a mood. I haven't really felt like talking to people."

"I understand," Greyson said.

"Are you hungry?" I asked.

"I'm a guy," Greyson said. "We're always hungry."

I went over to my mini fridge and pulled out bagels, a jar of pizza sauce, and a bag of mozzarella cheese.

"Tonight, we feast," I said.

Greyson and I sat on the floor of my dorm room, the spoils of our dinner spread out around us—plates smeared with pizza sauce, a half-empty bag of pretzels, four empty soda cans, and an empty carton of cookie dough ice cream.

"How're Claire and the boys?" I asked, leaning back against my bed. I was so full I felt like I might throw up.

"They're . . . good," Greyson said.

"What's with the pause?" I asked.

"I didn't pause," he said.

"You did," I said. "Come on. You can tell me. I just made you listen to everything that's going wrong in my life. The least I can do is return the favor."

Greyson sighed. "It's just . . . okay, so I haven't really talked about it with anyone," he said. "My mom's been sick."

"Like the flu?" I asked.

"No," Greyson said. "Like sick sick. Cancer. She got the diagnosis a few years ago. And she's in remission now, but it's just been really tough on her and the boys."

"Is that why you moved home?" I asked. "To help out?"

"Yeah," he said.

"Well, I feel like an asshole, then," I said. I cringed when I thought about the comments I had made about Greyson's being a man-child, freeloading off Claire by living at home.

Greyson laughed. "No, you're not."

It made sense then, the strange comment Claire had made to me when we were in her kitchen, how it was good for Greyson to get out of the house, have some fun.

There was a knock at my door.

"Shit," I said. "That's probably Ms. Stanfeld. It's almost curfew."

I stood and picked up Greyson's gym bag and handed it to him.

"Get in Drew's closet—quick," I said.

He scurried to hide and I opened the door.

But it wasn't Ms. Stanfeld. It was Dalton.

"Hey, Charlie," he said.

"Um, hi," I said. "What are you doing here?"

"I just came by to see if you were okay," he said, but something about him seemed off somehow—the way he buried his hands in his front pockets, the way he squared his shoulders. He seemed tense. "You missed dinner."

"Yeah," I said, "I just didn't really feel like being around a bunch of people right now."

As I talked, Dalton's gaze slid behind me, to the plates and food scattered across my floor. And then to something else. I turned and saw Greyson standing there.

"So it's true," Dalton said. His voice was suddenly steely, his eyes guarded as he appraised Greyson.

"What's true?" I asked.

"Harper mentioned she ran into some guy who was looking for you, asking to be let into your room."

Of course she did.

"This is my friend Greyson," I said, taking a step back and opening my door wider. "From back home. He's an old family friend."

Yes, that was good, knock him over the head with the word "friend."

Greyson nodded at Dalton, but he looked different too, taller somehow. Tougher.

"Hi," Greyson said.

"Well, I'll leave you two to your little party then," Dalton said. "Or whatever it was that you were doing."

"Dalton," I said, because I didn't want him to think what he was obviously thinking. "It's not like that. We were just—"

"Cool," Dalton said, cutting me off. "It's fine."

He turned and started off down the hallway, and I was about to follow him, to explain, but I saw Ms. Stanfeld two doors down, making the rounds. So I let him go.

The next afternoon, I loitered in the corridor outside the dining hall after lunch. I was waiting for Dalton; I wanted to explain about

Greyson and the other night. I could tell he had gotten the wrong idea about the whole thing. He obviously thought Greyson was more than a friend. I had to set him straight.

"Charlie."

I heard someone call my name and I turned around. It was Stevie; she had her backpack slung over her shoulder and an armful of books.

"I haven't really seen you around the past couple of days," she said guardedly. Some of the ice had thawed in her voice since the last time we had spoken.

"Yeah," I said. "I've been busy." *Busy avoiding you and everyone else.*

Stevie shrugged. "Well, I was just going to grab a bite to eat. Yael's in there already. You should join us."

It was a peace offering and it softened me a little. Drew had been the glue that held our group together, but just because she wasn't here anymore didn't mean that I should just let my relationship with Stevie and Yael dissolve. Did it?

"Thanks," I said. "I, um, already ate, but maybe another time?"

"Sure," Stevie said. "Hey, if you're not doing anything tonight, maybe you could come by the dining hall later? The student council is working on the Trustee Benefit Gala, and we could use an extra pair of hands."

"The Trustee Benefit Gala?" I asked. "I thought that wasn't until December."

Knollwood held the Trustee Benefit Gala at the end of the fall semester every year in the banquet hall across campus. It was a fancy black-tie dinner at five hundred dollars a plate that filled the scholarship fund for the upcoming year. My father always bought tickets for me and my friends so we could sit together, and he'd give us each a grand to bid on things in the silent auction. Last year, Drew and I had pooled our funds and gotten a high-end espresso machine for our dorm room. Stevie had bought a private lesson with the concertmaster of the New York Philharmonic; Yael had gotten a pair of Tiffany diamond stud earrings.

"Yeah, but there's a lot of planning to do," Stevie said. "I could really use your help."

Just then, the door to the dining hall opened, and I saw Dalton come out with some of his friends.

"Okay, maybe," I said quickly to Stevie, even though organizing sanctioned school events was totally not my thing. "I gotta go, but I'll catch up with you later, okay?"

I didn't wait for her to respond. I was already halfway down the corridor, running after Dalton.

"Dalton, wait up," I called. For a moment, I thought maybe he wouldn't stop, but he did. He turned around reluctantly, and I could tell by the way his shoulders slumped forward and he kept his hands in his pockets that he was already annoyed with me.

"Yes?" he asked, an indifferent glaze in his eyes.

"Can we talk, please?" I asked. "It will just take a moment."

I could feel his friends looking at me. Marcus Lansbury and Zachery Fitzpatrick and Leo.

"Ooooh, trouble in paradise," Zachery singsonged.

"Come on, guys, let's give them some space," Leo said, tugging on Zachery's arm.

"No, no, it's fine," Dalton said. "You guys can stay."

I sighed. Did we really have to do this with an audience?

"What's up, Calloway?" Dalton asked. His voice was cold and empty.

"I wanted to explain," I said.

"Explain what?"

"Greyson," I said. I looked at Leo and his friends standing there and then looked away. *Just pretend they're not there,* I told myself.

"Who?" Dalton asked.

It took all that was in me not to roll my eyes. Was Dalton really doing this? I was trying to explain, to set things right. Why wouldn't he let me?

"Can you just hear me out, please?" I asked. "It wasn't what it looked like, the other night. Greyson is an old family friend—"

Dalton put his hands in his pockets and laughed. "Look, Calloway," he said. "I don't give two fucks what you do with your friends."

"Okay," I said, taken aback. "Okay, fine."

Dalton shrugged. "I'm just tired of playing," he said. "That's all."

"What do you mean, you're tired of playing?" I asked.

"Nothing, okay?" Dalton said after a moment, as if he had thought better of what he'd just said. "I didn't mean anything."

I looked at Leo. Panic flickered in his eyes as the cold, nauseating realization hit me. Dalton had been *playing*. The whole time, when I thought he liked me, he had just been playing a stupid game.

"You put me on your fucking board game?" I asked Leo.

Me. Leo had put *me* on his sick Board of Conquests. He had put me on there knowing that I would become some target for his friends to mess with.

Suddenly, I remembered that evening in my room when Leo had asked me about Dalton. He had warned me about getting involved with him. At the time, I had taken it as genuine concern for my well-being, but now, I saw what it really was. Leo hadn't been looking out for me—he had been looking out for himself. He knew that Dalton was just with me so that he could check off a box on his board, and Leo didn't want him to win.

"Charlie—" Leo said.

"What base was I?" I asked.

"I didn't—"

"What base was I?" I shouted.

I could feel people staring. I didn't care.

"Fourth," Zachery said. He had a cruel smile on his face, like he was delivering the punch line to a dirty joke. "You were fourth base."

I looked at Leo. His jaw was set in a hard line, like he was waging some sort of battle inside himself, and he wasn't sure yet which side should win.

I didn't say anything. I pushed open the French doors to the patio, and I ran.

I didn't go back to my room. Instead, I got in my car and drove down to the Ledge.

I sat by myself on the edge as daylight faded around me and looked down into the black waters of the ravine running a hundred feet below. I took out my phone and dialed Drew, but it rang and rang and she didn't answer. I knew that her parents had probably taken away her phone privileges, but I was desperate. I needed to talk to her. When I got her voice mail for the third time in a row, I hung up and stared down at the ravine.

I hadn't meant to do it, I hadn't meant to let them in, but somehow I had. Dalton and Leo and Drew and Stevie and Grandma Fairchild and Uncle Hank and my mother, all over again. I had let them in—I had made the mistake of caring, of trusting, and now, in one way or another, they had all abandoned me, screwed me over.

For a moment, I closed my eyes and pictured the bottom of the ravine and wondered what it would be like to just let go of it all, to jump.

thirty-two
ALISTAIR CALLOWAY

JULY 2007

My eyes traced my wife's profile in the photograph. That was her. Grace. Sitting at a booth in a greasy diner off the interstate between Hillsborough and Hartford. Hal's Diner. I had never heard of it, never been there. It wasn't the type of place I would ever take Grace and the girls, wasn't the type of place locals patronized. It was a dive diner frequented by truckers looking for a warm meal at two in the morning or drunks trying to sober up after the bars closed down. And apparently, a place frequented by adulterous housewives looking to have secret rendezvous with their lovers.

"What's his name?" I asked.

The man across from Grace in the booth was average-looking. The photo had been taken from across the parking lot with a telephoto lens, so I could see the man my wife was fucking in exquisite detail. He was in his early thirties, and he wore a cheap-looking department store suit that was too long in the sleeves. His hair was starting to thin at the temples. If I had seen him on the street, he wouldn't have inspired a second look. He was exactly the type of man I wouldn't have hesitated to leave my wife alone with. But here he was, in a booth in a dark diner off the interstate with my wife, holding her hand.

"Peter Hindsberg," Mr. Lynch said.

"Peter Hindsberg," I repeated, racking my mind for any recollection his name might stir, and finding none. I had never heard of him.

For weeks now, Grace had been acting odd. Cold. Withdrawn. Unaffectionate. One night after dinner as she was washing the dishes in the sink, I came up behind her and put my hands in her back pockets, kissed her neck, and she flinched. She actually flinched. She turned her neck, drew away, like my touch had offended her.

"Not now, Alistair," she had said. "I'm not in the mood."

She was never in the mood anymore. We hadn't made love in weeks. And she was spending all of her time at the lake house with the girls—she never brought them to the city anymore. She was just out there, every night, alone.

I thumbed through the rest of the photographs on my desk. Pictures of Grace at the lake house with the girls; pictures of Grace and the girls in town; pictures of Grace and the girls at Grace's parents' house. And then Grace, in a sleazy diner in a dark booth with him.

"Do you have any pictures of . . ." I trailed off, not knowing how to ask for pictures of my wife in bed with another man. "Where are the rest of the pictures?" I asked instead.

"I only caught them together once," Mr. Lynch said. "They were at the diner for an hour. They left separately. Grace went home alone. He never came to the house, at least not during the time that I was tailing her."

At least Grace had the decency to keep her transgressions out of our home, away from our girls. Well, at least as far as we knew.

Mr. Lynch set a thin folder in front of me. "I pulled Grace's phone records," he said. "This is a log of her calls to him."

I took out the piece of paper and skimmed the entries. The first call was from Grace to Peter's private cell phone a couple of weeks ago. After that, they traded calls several times a week. Some of the calls were just a few minutes long; some were as long as an hour.

Most of the calls were made in the evening. I pictured Grace sitting on our bed at night, a glass of white wine on the nightstand next to her. Her hair wet from the shower, her bare, freshly shaved legs on the sheets. Her phone cradled to her ear as she spoke in low, sultry whispers to *him,* so as not to wake our girls, who were fast asleep down the hall.

"After their meeting at the diner, nothing," Mr. Lynch said. "The calls stopped."

I picked up the pictures, flipped to the next one in the deck. Grace was visibly upset in this one. She was crying.

"What do we know about him?" I asked. "This Peter Hindsberg?"

"He's an insurance fraud investigator at Hartco Insurance," Mr. Lynch said. "He was the one assigned to that workers' comp claim one of your landscapers filed a few months back at the lake house. Looks like he came out to the house to meet with Grace. Only, they didn't cut ties when the claim was settled.

"I did some digging, and it turns out Grace and Peter went to high school together. He was a couple years younger than her but they knew each other."

"I've never heard of him," I said. "Grace has never mentioned him."

Mr. Lynch shrugged. "You run into an old acquaintance you knew back when you were kids, you strike up a conversation. There's a flicker of attraction. One thing leads to another. It's more common than you might think. But the good news is, whatever was going on between them appears to be over. I haven't seen any signs of contact between Grace and Peter since they met at the diner. Turns out, Peter's also married. His wife just had their first baby. I'm guessing his conscience caught up with him."

"You're sure it's over?" I asked.

"Looks that way," Mr. Lynch said. "But I can keep an eye on things, if you want, Mr. Calloway."

"No," I said. "No, I'll handle it. Thanks, Sean."

I reached for my intercom and held down the button to buzz Rosie. She appeared at my door a second later.

"Yes, Mr. Calloway?" she asked.

"Take care of Sean here, will you?" I asked.

"Right away," Rosie said.

I stood to shake Mr. Lynch's hand. When they were both gone, I sank back into the seat behind my desk. I looked at the photographs and rubbed my chin.

Grace. What to do about Grace? I wanted to hurt her the way she had hurt me. And I wanted her to find out that I knew in the same way I had found out about her affair. It would be cold. Impersonal.

I tore out a piece of paper from a yellow legal pad on my desk. In block capital letters I wrote, *I KNOW*. I folded it and put it into an envelope. Then I picked up the stack of photographs. I contemplated just putting the one from the diner in there. The picture of Grace and Peter Hindsberg holding hands. But then my eye caught on another photograph on my desk. It was a picture of my oldest daughter, Charlotte, playing in the backyard at Grace's parents' house. It wasn't just me that Grace had betrayed. It was our family. I turned the picture of Charlotte over and on the back, I wrote, *STOP*. Then I slid the photographs into the envelope and sealed it. I imagined her getting the envelope with no return address in the mail in a few days. Opening it. The sickening trickle down her spine as she saw the photographs and the note and realized that I knew. I knew everything.

thirty-three
CHARLIE CALLOWAY

2017

I could feel Dalton's steady gaze on me in class, but I steadfastly ignored him, looking everywhere but in his direction.

I hadn't spoken to Dalton since the incident outside the dining hall three days ago, but he had tried, on several occasions, to speak with me—notes in my mailbox (*Charlie, I'm so sorry, can we talk?*), a bouquet of roses delivered to my desk in homeroom. His favorite trick was trying to corner me after class in the hallway, so I had gotten in the habit of getting excused from class a few minutes early every day so that I could make a quick getaway.

Greyson was still around. He had gotten a hotel room in Falls Church and would come by campus in the evening to see me. I had told him everything—from what I knew about my father and Jake's death and my mother's disappearance, to what had happened with Dalton, and Greyson had insisted on staying, to make sure I was all right and to help me look into my mother's case.

Greyson spent most of his day at the library in Falls Church doing research, so I was surprised when I returned to my room after my afternoon classes and found him there, sprawled out on Drew's bed with some files.

"I found this today," Greyson said, climbing off the bed and handing me a small stack of papers that had been stapled together. "It's a copy of Jake's autopsy report."

"How'd you get that?" I asked, laying my bag on my desk and taking the report from him.

Greyson shrugged. "Public record."

I skimmed the documents. The pathologist's description of Jake's body was difficult to read. *Blanching and bloating of the epidermis . . . Water found in stomach . . . Aspirations of fluid in the air passages . . . Pink foam in mouth.* The estimated time of death was listed as between eight P.M. and midnight on December 21, 1990. Under "Cause of Death," he had listed: *Pulmonary edema.*

"Pulmonary edema?" I asked, looking up at Greyson.

"It means fluid in the lungs," Greyson said. "Drowning."

"So Margot was telling the truth," I said.

"Looks like it," Greyson said, pointing to a place on the next page. "And here, it states that there were no abrasions or bruising on Jake's body consistent with a struggle—nothing to suggest that he was bound or forced into the water."

"So, suicide," I said.

"Yep," Greyson said. "Couple that with the note my mom told us they found in Jake's room and Jake's death seems pretty cut-and-dry."

My eyes scanned the report, searching for something, anything, that would point in another direction. "What about this? The tox screen results. Jake tested positive for alcohol, acetaminophen, and oxycodone," I said.

Greyson nodded. "Relatively low levels according to my research, but yes, quite the illicit cocktail. According to the report, though, drowning was the official cause of death."

"So Jake was drinking the night he died?" I asked.

"It appears so," Greyson said.

"And taking drugs," I said.

I blew out my breath and thought. Oxycodone and acetaminophen. Percocet? Students passed Percs around campus like candy. I'd never had a prescription, but even I had popped a few pills at a party once when Sheila Andrews had brought her leftover stash from her wisdom teeth extraction. It was what most kids considered a safe high—much less dangerous than taking heroin or other illegal narcotics.

"Maybe there's something else here," I said. "Something that was overlooked."

"Like what?"

"I don't know," I said. Maybe I was crazy. Maybe I was grasping at straws, looking for connections that didn't exist. But there was something linking my mother's disappearance and Jake and my father, and my gut told me it had to do with Jake's death.

"There's, uh, one other interesting thing that I came across today," Greyson said. He scratched the back of his neck, like he was nervous to tell me.

"What?" I asked.

He went over to his bed and grabbed another piece of paper. When he handed it to me, I saw that it was a photocopy of an old newspaper clipping. It was an engagement notice. My father's engagement notice. Only, it wasn't to my mother. There was my father in the photograph, and next to him in the portrait was another face I recognized.

"My father was engaged to Margot?" I asked.

"Apparently," Greyson said, shrugging. "I'm guessing he never mentioned that?"

"No," I said. But then again, there'd been a lot he and my family had kept from me.

Suddenly, there was a knock at the door.

"I know, I know," Greyson said, holding up his hands. "Into the closet I go."

I smiled at him. "Thank you," I said.

When Greyson was safely hidden in Drew's closet, I opened my door.

It was Leo. He was holding a small box and some sort of playing board was tucked under his other arm.

I almost shut the door in his face, but he reached out and held it open before I could stop him.

"What do you want?" I asked.

I hadn't spoken to Leo since the incident outside the dining hall, and I really didn't care to ever speak to him again. His betrayal stung even more than Dalton's.

"I'm sorry," Leo said. "Let's start there."

I had never heard Leo apologize for anything before, and it sort of caught me off guard.

"I only put you in the game because I knew you were too good for any of the guys here, and you'd never go for them," Leo said. "When you started to go for Dalton, I tried to warn you about him. I didn't see things playing out this way, or I would have never done it in the first place."

"I thought you had my back," I said.

"Listen, Charlie, I would never let anyone hurt you," Leo said. "The only reason I didn't step in again was because Dalton convinced me he actually liked you and him being with you wasn't about the game at all. He's still really into you. He only brought up the game the other day because he was upset."

"That's great," I said. "But I don't really believe anything either of you have to say anymore."

"Just hear him out," Leo said. "Hear him out, and then you can decide if you want to believe him or not. I'm supposed to give you this first."

He handed me a board.

I took it and unfolded it. It had a bunch of blank boxes on it.

"It's a puzzle," Leo said. "You're supposed to put all the letters together and figure out what it says."

"What letters?" I asked.

"Here," Leo said, handing me the box. I opened it. There was a cupcake from the gourmet cupcake shop in Falls Church. On the top of the cupcake was a little tile with a letter on it: "Y."

"Just one letter?" I asked.

"No, there'll be other letters," he said.

"I think I've had enough of your little games to last me a life-time," I said.

"Trust me," Leo said. "You'll like this game. Listen, I've got to get to practice, but we'll talk later, okay?"

"Fine," I said.

When he left, I set the playing board and the tile down on my desk.

"You're not really doing this, are you?" Greyson asked. He had come out of the closet, and he had his arms crossed over his chest, looking all disappointed.

"Doing what?" I asked.

"That thing some girls do, where the guy is horrible and then makes some gesture, and the girl forgets how horrible the guy is, just in time for the guy to do something else horrible."

"No," I said. "I'm not doing that."

"Because this wasn't some stupid fight, Charlie," Greyson said. "This guy—he completely used you. And your cousin is an asshole for letting him."

"I know," I said, cutting him off. "I know, okay? I was there. A stupid cupcake isn't going to give me amnesia."

"Okay," Greyson said.

There was another knock at the door.

"Jesus," Greyson said.

"Can you just get in the closet?" I asked.

Greyson sighed and rolled his eyes but did as I said. It was Crosby at the door with another cupcake and another tile. Over the next half hour, half the soccer team came to the door with a boxed cupcake and tile, and I had solved the puzzle. It said, *I'm an asshole. I'm sorry.*

"Wow," Greyson said, looking at the solved puzzle on my desk. "Preppy really goes all out."

There was another knock on my door and I opened it reluctantly. Dalton was standing there. I would have shut the door in his face, but he looked all humbled and apologetic, so un-Dalton-like.

"Hi, Charlie," he said. "Can I come in?"

"I'm with someone," I said, opening the door enough that he could see that Greyson was there.

"Hi," Dalton said, reaching out his hand to greet Greyson. "I don't think we were properly introduced last time. I'm Dalton. It's really good to meet you."

Greyson just stood where he was, his arms crossed over his chest. "Yeah, I can't really say the same," he said. "Charlie's told me all about you, and it wasn't really a ringing endorsement, if you catch my drift."

Dalton dropped his hand to his side, clearly caught off guard by Greyson's frank comments.

"You have three seconds to get the hell out of here before I reconfigure your face with my fist," Greyson said. "And you can take your smarmy apologies with you."

"I didn't come here to stir anything up," Dalton said, raising his hands at his sides as if he were surrendering. "Whether you believe my apology to be genuine or not, it is. And really, it's not up to you. This is between me and Charlie."

Greyson stepped forward, putting himself between me and the doorway.

"Greyson, it's okay," I said.

I tugged on the back of his shirt but that did little to get his attention.

"Greyson," I said again. "I can talk to him. It's okay."

"You don't have to," Greyson said. "You don't owe him anything."

"I know," I said.

"Okay," Greyson said. "But I'll be right out here. Like literally right out here. And this door stays open."

Dalton took a step back so Greyson could go out into the hallway. I motioned Dalton into my room and shut the door most of the way, leaving about an inch of open space between the door and the frame.

"Charlie, I'm sorry about what I said," Dalton said, taking a step away from the door and lowering his voice so that Greyson couldn't hear us. "Being with you was never about that stupid game for me— not for one moment. I was into you before Leo ever put your name on that board. It's just taken me a long time to get up the nerve to do anything about it, because, well, you don't exactly make things easy."

He smiled and I bit my lip.

"I'm sorry about the way I treated you the other day," Dalton said. "I didn't mean any of the things I said. That wasn't me."

"So why did you say that, if you didn't mean it?" I asked, crossing my arms.

"Because I was upset," Dalton said. "It's obvious I like you. Everybody knows it. But you're still so . . . *guarded* with me. And at first I just thought that was how you were—that maybe you had trouble opening up or something. But then I saw you in your room with another guy, and I just felt like—like an idiot. Like maybe the reason you were being distant wasn't because you had trouble opening up, but because you didn't like me as much as I liked you."

"I did like you," I said.

And I had been distant, cold even, at times. I knew that.

He shoved his hands into his pockets. "I don't know—maybe it was stupid. But that's how I felt. And I went from hurt to angry to that person who said those things. And I'm sorry."

Part of me felt like I should apologize too, for treating him the way I had. But a larger part, the more stubborn part, felt that apologizing would mean that I was apologizing for what he had done—that the way I had treated him had caused him to treat me the way he had, and that wasn't true. Was it?

"I didn't come here expecting anything," Dalton went on. "I just came over because I wanted you to know how sorry I am about what happened."

"Well, thanks, I guess," I said.

He stood in front of me, his shoulders all slumped and his eyes all remorseful. He looked genuinely sorry. And I mean, this was Dalton. This was the guy who had put his arm around the back of my chair in the dining hall. The guy who had defended me against his friends. The guy who had held me as if I were fragile and might break when he kissed me. The guy who looked at me like—like no one had ever looked at me. Before the other night, he had always treated me with the utmost care and respect.

"Well, I'll go now," Dalton said. "Thank you for hearing me out."

"Sure," I said.

When he left, Greyson came back in and closed the door. "Glad that's over," he said.

"Yeah," I said.

"It is over, isn't it?" he asked.

I didn't answer him.

"Charlie?"

"It's just—what if he really is sorry?" I asked. "I know that sounds stupid, but what if he got upset the other day and just made a mistake? What if it was never about the game, and he just said that to hurt me in the moment? If I'm being honest, I haven't always been very nice to him, either."

"You're right," Greyson said. "You are sounding really stupid right now."

I glared at him. What right did he have to talk to me like that? And really, what did he know about Dalton?

What if Dalton really did care about me, and we were good together, and I let him go? What if I had something good here, and I was letting it slip through my fingers because my pride was hurt?

"Maybe this was a bad idea, you coming here," I said. "Maybe you're confused about what we're doing here."

"And just what is it that you think I'm confused about exactly?" Greyson asked.

"Me," I said. "This. Us. I don't—I don't have feelings for you," I said.

Greyson scoffed. He looked as if I had slapped him. "Charlie—I don't—" He stopped. "I came here because you're my friend. And because you seemed like you really needed someone. That's all. But you're right. Maybe it wasn't a good idea."

He picked up his bag and started throwing his things into it.

"You're leaving?" I asked.

He didn't answer. He zipped up his bag and set the files he had brought over on the edge of my desk.

"Greyson?"

"I hope you find what you're looking for, Charlie," he said. "I really do."

thirty-four
GRACE CALLOWAY

AUGUST 1, 2007

The letter, if you could really call it that, had only two words on it. In thickly drawn, all-capital letters, it read: *I KNOW.*

Inside the envelope with no return address were the photographs. Pictures of me and Peter at Hal's Diner off the interstate, a place I'd carefully chosen because I knew no one would see us there. Only, I was wrong. Someone had seen us. Or rather, someone had been following us. And not only had they caught us together, but they knew. They knew about the case that I was trying to build against them. They knew that I had those pictures that placed them with Jake on the night of his death.

After my conversation with Margot, I realized I didn't have enough concrete evidence to turn to the police and start making accusations. So, I'd called Peter and enlisted his help. I'd reconnected with Peter at the beginning of the summer when he'd come out to the house to take some photographs for a workers' comp claim he was investigating that involved one of our landscapers. It was a pleasant surprise to see him—I hadn't seen Peter since high school. We'd been on the swim team together. He'd been a shy but inquisitive kid, the kind who observed more than he ever let on, so it didn't surprise me that he'd chosen a career that involved solving puzzles for a living. We'd spoken about his line of work. He'd told me he had studied criminal justice in college and had his private

investigator license, that he was planning to start his own investigation firm and was beginning to take on his own cases. When I
realized I couldn't turn to Alistair for answers, Peter was the first
person I called.

But Margot must have told someone about the photographs I'd
shown her. I wondered which one of them was following me, or if
it was more than one. Threats weren't really Margot's thing. She'd
been so forthcoming, so fearless, at the restaurant. But I knew
some of the others were capable of it—thinly veiled threats aimed
not just at me, but at my children.

Because the pictures weren't just of me and Peter. They were of
Charlotte and Seraphina. And on the very last one, a close-up of
Charlotte, there was a word written on the back: *STOP*.

When I got that letter, I called my mother to come over to watch
the girls while I went out. I told her I was going to the gym. I
dressed in workout shorts and tennis shoes, an empty duffel bag
thrown over my shoulder. I went to the bank instead. I emptied out
our safety-deposit boxes. Alistair had cash stowed away in a dozen
different safety-deposit boxes at half a dozen banks. He called it
our rainy-day fund. In case of an emergency, he said. But now, this
would be my rainy-day fund. Mine, and Seraphina and Charlotte's.
We would get out of there, and we wouldn't look back.

By the time I returned to the house, it was early evening. My
mother's car wasn't in the driveway, but Alistair's was.

"Hello?" I called when I opened the front door.

"There you are," he said.

I turned to see Alistair standing in the living room, a glass of
scotch in his hand.

My heart skipped a nervous beat in my chest when I saw him. I
readjusted the strap of my gym bag on my shoulder. It was heavy
now, full of money, and the strap cut into my skin.

"I didn't know you'd be here," I said, trying to keep my voice level, calm, as I closed the door behind me. He usually came to the lake house on weekends; it was only Wednesday. I tried to give him a smile but my face felt stiff. "Where are the girls?" I asked.

"I sent them home with your mother for a little sleepover," he said. "I told Alice we needed some time together, since I've been working so much. She didn't seem to mind."

Something hard dropped into the pit of my stomach. I'd have to spend the entire night in this house alone with Alistair?

"That was nice of her," I said, trying not to sound disappointed. "I don't have anything ready for dinner, but maybe we can go out? I just need to shower."

I headed for the stairs up to our bedroom, a quick escape, but no sooner was my foot on the first step than he stopped me.

"Grace."

I paused, my foot frozen on the step.

"Come here," he said.

He knows about the money.

I didn't know how he could possibly know, but he did. I could hear it in his voice.

I half turned to face him, my foot still on the step.

He doesn't know, I told myself. *Just be calm. Make an excuse. Get upstairs. And hide it.*

"Yes?" I asked, trying to keep my voice steady.

"Come. Here," he repeated. "I'm not going to ask again."

I readjusted the strap of my gym bag on my shoulder and walked over to him, trying to hold his steady gaze.

He doesn't know. He doesn't know. He can't know. How could he know?

I stopped in front of him, so close he could reach out and grab the duffel if he wanted to. I placed a protective hand on top of it.

"Do you really think we're not going to talk about what you've done?" he asked. "That we're just going to pretend like nothing happened?"

I could smell the alcohol on his breath. I saw the darkness in his eyes—the way the light went out of them. The hairs on the back of my neck stood up.

The Alistair I knew was softhearted and sweet-tempered. True, we had grown aloof and distant from one another in recent years, but he was a kind and gentle father to our daughters—the man who kissed the skinned palm of Charlotte's hand when she fell off her bicycle, the man who sang "Splish Splash" to Seraphina at tub time, to her infinite delight and amusement. But I knew others saw a different side of him. He was a wolf in the boardroom; he had teeth, a formidable bite that outranked his bark. I felt it in the way others reacted when he came into a room—the stiffening in their shoulders, the slight intake of breath before they spoke, the subservient way they nodded their heads as he talked—as if they were steeling themselves for the onslaught. Now, for the first time in our marriage, I saw Alistair the way others must have seen him. And it terrified me.

"I don't know what you're talking about," I said, but my voice sounded small and mousy, weak. Even I didn't trust what it said.

For a moment, his face was perfectly still, and then, in a flash, it became a twisted mask of pain.

He threw his glass of scotch against the wall behind me. There was a pop as the glass broke, and then a thousand tiny pieces shattered around us. I flinched.

"Alistair—" I said, in shock.

He grabbed the hair at the nape of my neck and yanked my head back.

I screamed as the white-hot electric pain tore through my scalp and I dropped the bag.

"Peter Hindsberg," he said.

He knew. He knew about the private investigator. He knew about the money. He knew everything. But how?

"Show me every place you defiled our marriage," Alistair said. "Was it here, in this room?"

He tugged on my hair and turned my head toward the dining room.

"Or maybe there, on that table?" he asked.

"You're hurting me," I said. Tears stung my eyes.

And I scrambled to make sense of it. Peter? He thought that Peter and I had—?

He tugged me a few paces to our right and pushed my face down hard into the couch cushions. My nose flattened against the rough gingham fabric. I couldn't breathe.

"Or maybe here, on this couch?" he asked.

Then he ripped me up from the couch and turned me around to face him, his hands on my shoulders. I gasped for breath and clambered back away from him, out of his grasp.

"I didn't," I coughed, my throat raw. "I didn't. I didn't. I swear I didn't."

I lost my balance and I fell. My shoulder hit against the side of a bookcase and sang with pain. I crumpled onto the floor, sobbing. My vision blurred. I clamped my hand to my injured shoulder. When I drew it back, I saw blood.

When I looked over at Alistair, he was crouching, his hands to his temples.

"Why did you do this?" he asked, again and again, under his breath. "Why?"

And I didn't know who he was talking to—me or himself.

When he looked up at me through his hands, I saw that he was crying.

When I woke in the morning in our bed, there was a dull ache in my shoulder. I opened my eyes and looked down at the bandages

Claire had given me last night in her kitchen, her boys fast asleep upstairs.

"I fell," I had told her over and over again. "I fell."

But I knew she knew.

She had driven me home after, had insisted she stay the night on the downstairs sofa, even though Alistair's car was gone from the driveway and there wasn't a trace of him in the house.

My head was still groggy with painkillers. It was difficult to make out a coherent thought.

Someone rattled the door handle to my room. I had locked it the night before—a small part of me was afraid that he would try to return in the night. I cowered back in my bed, pulling the covers more tightly over me.

Go away, I wanted to say, but the words got caught in my throat.

"Mommy?" a voice called out.

It was Charlotte. Charlotte. Charlotte. Charlotte. Poor, precious Charlotte. I had to get up. I had to go to her. But I couldn't bring myself to move.

thirty-five
CHARLIE CALLOWAY

2017

Hanging out with Dalton again was easier than I thought it'd be. At the very least, it felt good to know I had someone who was there for me, especially when so many people had bailed. Things with Stevie and Yael were tense, and Drew was gone, and I wasn't talking to Greyson. So I fell in with Dalton and Leo and their friends again. I sat at their table for lunch and dinner. We hung out together on the weekends. And Dalton and I spent most of our evenings together in the library or in one of our rooms until curfew studying.

"You know, I really don't like the idea of not seeing you for a whole week," Dalton said as he walked me back to my room one evening. He had his arm around me and pulled me close. It was November, and a light snow dusted campus. "You could come home with me for Thanksgiving break, you know," he said. "Meet the whole Dalton clan. And my mom's always asking about you. I'm sure she'd love to spend more time with you."

"Your mom?" I asked.

"Yeah," Dalton said, kissing my hair. "Guess she's a big fan of yours. Not that I can blame her."

"I don't think my father would like that very much," I said.

"Why not?"

"Just because he'd miss me," I lied. "I haven't seen him since that dinner we had in the city."

I had never mentioned my father's phone call to Dalton, how my father had warned me to stay away from Margot, to stay away from him. My father had sounded so angry over the phone, so commanding. But why? Margot had been engaged to my father at one point, and obviously something had happened to end their relationship. But surely a bad breakup over two decades ago wouldn't cause my father to act as dramatically as he had. My father's demand that I stay away from Margot had to be related to something else. Maybe Margot knew something my father didn't want me to know. Margot had been at school with my father and Jake. She had been an A. She had known my mother, somehow. It suddenly occurred to me that if anyone knew how all the pieces of the puzzle fit together, it was Margot. And maybe, just maybe, she would be willing to tell me.

"Okay," I said.

"Okay?"

"Okay to Thanksgiving," I said. "I'll come home with you."

"Really?" he asked.

"Really," I said.

He didn't ask what had changed my mind and I didn't tell him. Instead, he leaned down and kissed me, and I kissed him back.

The Daltons had an oceanfront mansion in Southampton on three acres of land. The family gathering was small for the holidays, because Dalton was an only child, and half of Dalton's family was British and didn't celebrate Thanksgiving. So, it would be just Dalton, his parents, and Margot's sister Regina, her husband, and their three kids, the oldest of whom was ten. Dalton's father wasn't coming in from the city until Thursday for Thanksgiving dinner.

I had told my father I was spending Thanksgiving with Drew and her family, and he was disinterested enough in my life not to follow up or ask for anything pertaining to proof.

Dalton's little cousins were obsessed with him and spent most of their time following him around, begging for wrestling matches or for him to play games with them. So we spent most of our time entertaining them, while I searched for a moment to get Margot alone and ask her my questions.

"How about a game of Hide and Seek?" Dalton proposed one evening after dinner. His cousins squealed with delight and immediately started to argue over who would have to hide first.

"I'll do it," I said, raising my hand and standing from the couch. "I'll go first." I could feel a headache coming on, and I really couldn't take any more of their squabbling. Besides, a few minutes of peace and quiet by myself sounded all too tempting. If I could find a really good hiding spot, curl up, and fall asleep for a half hour, that would be heaven. "But close your eyes," I instructed the cousins. "Close your eyes and count down from one hundred."

They put their hands over their eyes and started counting loudly. "One hundred, ninety-nine, ninety-eight . . ."

I pointed at Dalton. "You too. Close those eyes, mister."

He smiled at me and made a big show of putting his hands over his eyes, and I turned and darted out of the living room.

The house was huge, with eight bedrooms and four and a half baths. There were a million different places to hide. I darted through the kitchen, where the adults were standing around the marble island, glasses of red wine in hand.

"We're playing Hide and Seek," I whispered, putting my finger over my lips. "You never saw me."

Margot laughed and put a finger over her lips. "Saw who?" she whispered.

I ran into the den next. I opened a door I thought was a closet but found a set of stairs instead. Perfect. The basement. I turned on the flashlight on my phone and started down the stairs, shutting the door quietly behind me.

It was pitch-black and cluttered with old furniture, covered in sheets, and piles and piles of boxes. It smelled slightly of mildew. I was working my way through the labyrinth when I hit my shin on something hard.

"Ouch," I muttered into the darkness.

I turned the flashlight of my phone on the sharp, boxy edge I had walked into. The light revealed a pair of dusty old suitcases.

At that moment, the overhead light to the basement flickered on. I heard Dalton at the head of the stairs. I should have turned the light on my phone off and ducked down for cover, but I couldn't move. Something about the suitcases had caught my eye. It was the print—a faded brown paisley. My mother had had a pair just like them once.

"You down here, Charlie?" Dalton called.

I could hear his footsteps coming down the staircase, but I couldn't see him. My view of the stairs was blocked by a refrigerator-sized box. I reached out and ran my finger along the label on the face of the luggage—Burberry.

I dropped my phone and took a step back. Yes, these suitcases were just like the ones my mother had owned, the ones that she had taken with her when she left.

I felt like I was falling, falling, falling, as my heart hammered away in my chest and my breath grew shallow and my head rushed to make sense of it all.

It was just a coincidence, I told myself. Hundreds of people had the same luggage as my mother. It was just a coincidence that Margot had the same old set of luggage in her basement. These weren't *those* suitcases. They didn't belong to my mother.

Only . . . only, what if they did? I remembered my mother's luggage had a rip in the inner lining. If I opened the suitcase up, and there was the same rip . . .

I reached toward the suitcases again, but something hard pinned my arms to my sides. It was Dalton. He had found me, and he had me in a viselike grip, his arms around me like a steel cage.

"Got you," he said.

thirty-six
ALISTAIR CALLOWAY

AUGUST 4, 2007

Charlotte, still in her bathing suit and boat shoes, rolled around the living room floor with her sister. They were playing some sort of game that only they understood. Seraphina grabbed Charlotte by the ankles and Charlotte retaliated by blowing a raspberry onto her sister's cheek. Seraphina erupted into shrieks of laughter.

"Why don't you two go up to your room and play?" I asked as I threaded my way around them and sat on the couch with my brief-case.

"Fiine," Charlotte said, nailing the type of exasperation that a teen would be proud of, even though she was only seven. Seraphina mimicked her.

"Fiine."

As the girls laughed and stumbled up the stairs, I heard Grace come in from the back patio.

"I'm going to take a shower," Grace said. "Want to put burgers on the grill in an hour?"

I looked up from the reports in my lap. "Sure," I said. "Sounds good."

I squinted down at the small type on the page and the words blurred slightly around the edges. I glanced around me, hunting for the spare pair of reading glasses that I kept at the lake house. They weren't on the coffee table. I got up and went into my study across the hall, searched the desk, pulled out the drawers, but the search came up empty. Then I remembered. I'd left them upstairs in the bedroom the other weekend. I'd been reading before bed, and I'd set them on the nightstand.

Upstairs, Grace had closed the door to the bedroom, so I knocked lightly and then tried the handle. It wasn't locked, so I went in. I heard the bath running. As I walked over to the nightstand, I saw the bathroom door was ajar. I could see through to the mirror behind the vanity, and in the mirror, I caught my wife's reflection. She was naked, standing outside the shower, her hand under the faucet, testing the temperature of the water. I felt my stomach clench at the sight of her.

The morning after our fight, I'd sent flowers, a bouquet of purple hyacinths and tulips. I called her that evening from the office. I was working late, a carton of Chinese takeout growing cold next to my keyboard. Really, I couldn't bear to go home to our empty apartment, to the bed where I slept alone and the quiet rooms where Charlotte and Seraphina's things were pristinely tucked into cubbies and drawers, untouched. I didn't want to be alone with my thoughts, with the knowledge of what I had done, what Grace had done, of what we had done to each other.

I picked up the phone and called the lake house. Grace answered after several rings, slightly breathless, as if she had run to catch the phone before the call dropped. I pictured her on the cordless in the upstairs hall, ushering the girls through their bedtime routine. I could almost hear them giggling in the bathroom behind her, the water running in the sink as they brushed their teeth. Grace would be wearing that old pale pink silk robe I'd gotten her for Mother's Day several years ago, the one that was fraying in the sleeves.

"Hello?" she said again into the phone.

"Grace," I said. "It's me."

She was quiet. I could see her in my mind's eye. She was biting her lip, the phone to her chin, as she debated whether or not to hang up.

"Did you get the flowers?" I asked.

"Yes," she said. She sighed. "I was going to throw them out but the girls saw them first. You know how they feel about the color purple."

I smiled.

"Sera called them princess flowers," Grace went on, her voice dry and sad. "We spent the afternoon making flower crowns."

My chest ached. I opened my mouth to say something, then closed it.

"Grace, the person who did those things," I said after awhile, "it wasn't me. You know that."

I could hear her breathing. "Alistair," she said, "what happened the other night—"

"Won't ever happen again," I said. "You have my word."

She didn't say anything.

"You and—" I couldn't bring myself to say his name. "That's over?"

Grace paused. "Yes," she said. "It's over."

"Okay, then," I said after a moment, as if we were business partners negotiating a deal, and we'd both given up something that we hadn't wanted to part with.

Last night, when I got in from the city, the house was dark. The girls were asleep and upstairs, Grace sat on our bed in her robe, watching television. She got up when she saw me come into our room. Neither of us spoke. I walked over to where she stood and got down on my knees in front of her. I wrapped my arms around her waist and said into the silk knot of her robe, "I'm trying. I want to try."

Grace didn't say anything. She just reached down and rested her hand in my hair, her fingers grazing my temple.

I slept in the guest bedroom down the hall. I set my alarm for five thirty that morning so I could wake up before the girls and slip into bed with Grace, all to preserve the girls' cherished Saturday morning ritual of bursting into our room at dawn and waking us to make them breakfast by jumping on the bed. I could feel the weight of Grace's body beside me as I lay there and we waited, both pretending to be asleep. After a while, I opened my eyes and watched her—her dark hair cascading over the pillow, her lashes still against her cheeks, her lips slightly parted. I almost reached out to touch her, but then I heard the door creak open, and Seraphina's giggles, and Charlotte shushing her. I felt the bed move as their little bodies climbed onto the mattress.

I don't think Grace heard me now as I came into the bathroom because when she glanced in the mirror, she seemed startled to find me there behind her.

I stared unabashedly at my wife's naked body. The swell of her breasts. The curve of the small of her back. Her normally translucent skin had darkened, ripened in the sun. How many times had we made love in that bathroom—in the shower, on the vanity, on the tiled floor? The steam curling the ends of Grace's hair, the sound of the water thrumming against the granite, muffling her moans? I came up behind her and put my arms around her, cupping her breasts in my hands, pulling her taut against my body, so she could feel the thickness of my want.

I felt her stiffen in my arms.

"Don't," she said.

I reached up to stroke her neck. I only wanted to make her feel good, to remember how good it was when we were together. We had agreed to try, hadn't we? My finger slid over the ridge of something and my hand stilled. In our reflection in the mirror I saw it—the bandage on her left shoulder. I hadn't seen it at first under the harsh fluorescent lights of the bathroom, and Grace had kept her shoulders covered all day. But there it was—the irrefutable proof that our fight earlier that week had happened. The marks that I had left.

It was an accident. She fell. And I had been there, yes, but it wasn't my fault. Of course I had been upset. Of course I had said terrible things and maybe handled her a little roughly. But she had lied. She had betrayed me, betrayed our family.

Peter Hindsberg. Peter fucking Hindsberg. Why him? Who the fuck was he? An insurance investigator in Hillsborough? What about him was worth forsaking the life Grace and I had built together?

"Alistair," she said.

I reached down and pulled the knob of the shower to turn off the faucet. Steam peeled off the granite. I could feel the heat coming off the water.

"Get in," I said.

I saw the fear in Grace's eyes, but it only fueled my anger. I leaned down and kissed her, cutting off her protests. I watched her close her eyes and go somewhere else in her mind, far away from me. Somewhere I couldn't follow.

Afterward, I sat under the hot water of the shower for a few minutes by myself. When I got out, the bathroom mirror was coated with steam. I wrapped a towel around my waist and shaved. When I came out of the bathroom, Grace was dressed in jeans and a loose T-shirt. That's when I noticed that my suitcase was open on the bed, and Grace was by the dresser, the drawer out; she was tossing my collared shirts into it.

"I want you to leave," Grace said. "You're never going to do anything like that to me, ever again."

"So he can touch you, but I can't?" I asked.

Grace didn't say anything.

"I thought we said we were going to try," I said.

"*You* said we were going to try," Grace countered, her eyes hard and cold when she looked at me.

"What's that supposed to mean?"

But she looked away and didn't answer me.

"Just go," she said.

"Damn it, Grace," I said, coming around to the other side of the bed where she was. She took a step away from me, as if my impending touch repulsed her. I grabbed her by the wrist, pulled her toward me so that she was in my arms.

"Look at me," I said.

"Get your hands off me," Grace snapped.

"Mommy?"

We both looked over and saw that our bedroom door was slightly open, and there was Charlotte, her hand on the handle, staring at us.

Grace turned away from her so she couldn't see her face.

"Why is Mommy crying?" Charlotte asked.

Damn it. Was this really happening?

I let go of my wife and went over to the door and picked up my older daughter.

"What do you say we get an Eskimo Pie?" I asked, putting on a smile.

"Okay," Charlotte said.

I carried Charlotte downstairs to the kitchen and dug two Eskimo Pies out of the freezer. Then I took her out to the back patio and we sat on the steps, looking out at the lake. Not an hour ago we had all been out there on the water, having the best time. When had everything gone to shit?

"Won't she be mad we're eating these?" Charlotte asked, licking a piece of melted chocolate off her finger.

I sighed. I didn't know how to be there right now. I was too angry—too furious at Grace—and if I stayed, I knew I would do something that I would regret.

"Charlotte, I need you to be a big girl and look after your mother while I'm away," I said. "Do you think you can do that?"

"You're going back already?" she asked.

"I have an early meeting in the morning," I lied.

"Don't go," Charlotte begged. "You promised you'd take me out on the boat again tomorrow."

"Next weekend, okay?" I said.

"Can I come with you?" she asked.

Christ, how bad was it there that Charlotte didn't want to stay? When I was a kid, I would have killed for a place like that to go to in the summer. But maybe Grace was too preoccupied with licking her wounds from her failed affair to pay attention to our kids.

Part of me wanted to take Charlotte with me. To just pack a bag for her and Seraphina and put them in the car and get out of there. But I knew Grace would cause a scene if I tried to do that. She'd run out crying and screaming and she'd scare the shit out of our kids, and then I'd have to pay for therapy for both of them for the rest of their fucking lives so they could erase that image of their pathetic mother.

"I need you to stay here and look after your mother," I told Charlotte again. "Can you do that for me?"

Charlotte nodded, and I patted her head and stood. I went inside to finish packing. Grace wasn't in our room when I returned. I don't know where she went, but I didn't bother looking for her to say goodbye. I went straight to my car, threw my bag in the trunk, and peeled out of there.

Peter Hindsberg. Peter fucking Hindsberg. As I drove, I couldn't get those photographs out of my head, and I couldn't stop making my own mental pictures of the two of them together.

Halfway to the city, I stopped my car. I thrummed my fingers against the steering wheel. I turned the car around.

part four

thirty-seven
CHARLIE CALLOWAY

2017

I couldn't sleep. Instead, I stared up at the ceiling of my bedroom in the dark and listened to the strange middle-of-the-night noises of Dalton's home. On the floor above me, I heard a toilet flush, the sound of water rushing through pipes in the walls. I heard footsteps, the creak of floorboards, the shutting of a door. And I waited. I waited for silence, for the stillness that would tell me everyone was sound asleep and I could finally make my move.

All through dinner, I hadn't been able to look at Margot. We had been seated next to one another, and once, when I went to pass the dish of green beans, my hand grazed her fingers, and I almost dropped the dish. I felt the hairs on the back of my neck rise up. I excused myself to go to the bathroom, and in the safety of the washroom on the main floor, I sat on the marble vanity and texted Greyson.

I hadn't spoken to Greyson since his very dramatic exit from my dorm room a few weeks back, and I didn't really want to talk to him now, but I didn't have a choice. Greyson was the only one who knew what was going on, the only person who wouldn't need a very detailed play-by-play to be brought up to speed. And I needed to talk to someone. I needed to know I wasn't crazy.

I think I might have found my mother's suitcases, I texted. **The ones she left with.**

I knew I wasn't imagining things or misremembering. I recalled those suitcases vividly—a pair of Burberry cloth suitcases in a paisley print, the luggage my mother used to pack for weekend trips to the city, the ones that disappeared with her. They were mentioned in the PI's reports.

Though, if they didn't belong to her, this would not be the first time I had thought I'd spotted my mother's luggage and been mistaken. Once when I was nine, I had seen those suitcases while going through security at JFK, and I had run after the woman carrying them, sure that she was my mother, until she turned around and revealed herself to be a middle-aged Polish lady (she had stared down at me with sunken eyes, asking in her thick accent, "What, child? What?" as I looked dumbly up at her). Maybe that's all this was, too: an unlucky coincidence.

I used to imagine my mother with those suitcases, traipsing through foreign airports, on her way to somewhere warm and exotic. But what if all this time, they had been sitting in a dark basement in Southampton? Margot's basement. But how would they have gotten there? And if they were there in Margot's basement, where was my mother?

My phone vibrated in my hand, and I looked down to see Greyson's name on the screen. He was calling me. I cupped my hand over my mouth and answered my phone in a whisper.

"Hello?"

"Charlie, what's going on?" Greyson asked. "Where are you?" He sounded slightly out of breath.

"Don't be pissed," I said. "But I'm at Dalton's family's place in Southampton."

I heard Greyson mutter an expletive under his breath. "What's the address?"

"You're not coming down here right now," I said, much louder than I meant to. My voice echoed in the tiled room. Crap. I lowered my voice again. The Daltons were right down the hall. I couldn't risk their overhearing. "I'm fine," I said. "I mean, they might not actually be her suitcases. People have the same luggage. But it's the same print and brand and it just spooked me."

"Where'd you find them?" Greyson asked.

"In the basement," I said. "Next to these boxes and old furniture covered in sheets. Like I said, it could be nothing."

"Get the hell out of there," Greyson said. "Charlie, just leave. Right now. Grab your stuff and go. I'll drive down and get you."

"I'm not leaving," I said. "I haven't gotten to see what's in them yet. My mother's suitcases had this tear in the lining. I need to open these up and see if—"

"Charlie, are you crazy?" He sounded angry. "If those are your mother's suitcases, then that means . . ."

Greyson stopped and I felt the weight of the invisible ellipses, the things he wouldn't say. That my mother hadn't taken off of her own accord. That she hadn't left us. That she was dead, just like they all believed. That she wasn't coming back.

"We don't know what it means," I said. "It could mean anything."

"Charlie, listen to me," Greyson said. "Your father and Margot were engaged. They were in the A's together; they go way back. Don't you think it's possible that if your mother's suitcases are in Margot's basement, that maybe she helped him . . ."

"Helped him what?"

"Get rid of the evidence?"

"Maybe Margot helped my mother leave," I said stupidly.

"If your mother left, why would she leave her suitcases in Margot's basement?"

"I don't even know if they're hers yet," I said.

"Charlie, don't—"

I hung up. Greyson called back right away and kept calling back, so I put the "Do Not Disturb" function on for his contact on my phone and went back to the dinner table.

I didn't have a choice. I had to get back in that basement unnoticed, open those suitcases up, and see if they had that telltale rip in the lining. I had to know if they were really my mother's.

I had started this whole thing alone and I would finish it alone. Because if I had learned anything over the past several months, it was that I could only rely on myself.

Now, as quietly as I could, I lifted back the bedcovers and shifted my weight onto the floor. The floorboards moaned slightly under me. Why did Dalton have to have an old house that creaked and groaned like an elderly person with every movement?

It was a cold evening and the floorboards were like ice under my bare feet, so I crept over to the dresser and put on socks and a hoodie over my pajamas. Then I tiptoed to the door and slowly opened it, holding my breath when the hinges shrieked in protest.

Making my way down to the basement was a slow and arduous process, as I had to stop every time I made a noise and listen for any sounds elsewhere in the house that might alert me that someone had heard me or woken up. I guess the one good thing about the house being so loud was that, just as anyone could hear me making my way down the old staircase to the ground floor, I could hear anyone making their way down the old staircase after me.

The house was dark, and I made my way forward blindly, relying on my memory of the general layout and my groping hands to guide me. When I reached the ground floor, I kept one hand on the wall, sliding along it as I made a right through the hallway into the den, which housed the door to the basement. Just as my hand grasped the doorknob, the front doorbell rang.

The Daltons had one of those annoying grandiose doorbells that went on forever and echoed throughout the whole house. I froze where I was in the dark. I knew I couldn't risk running back up to my room right now—not when Margot would no doubt be making her way down those very stairs to answer the door. I got on my hands and knees and crawled behind a couch to hide.

The doorbell rang again, followed by several loud, thunderous knocks, as if someone were pounding on the front door with their fists.

Who would be visiting at this hour and making such a commotion? It was nearly two in the morning.

I heard footsteps coming down the stairs and **then** caught the flicker of a light being turned on in the back hall. Margot rounded the hall into the den, and I held my breath as she passed me on the floor, praying she wouldn't see me there behind the couch. She had on a cream terry-cloth robe, her hair loose around her shoulders. She passed into the sitting room and when she turned into the foyer, I lost sight of her. I heard her pull the front door open.

"I don't know what the hell kind of stunt you're trying to pull here."

It was a man who was yelling. I heard the voice echo through the walls, a deep, rumbling bellow.

Next came Margot's voice, some reply that was too muted for me to hear. I got up and padded into the sitting room, closer to the foyer, so I could make out what they were saying to each other.

"—not trying to pull anything. I didn't know she didn't tell you. But, really, if you could take a moment to calm down," Margot said.

Was it Dalton's father at the door? He was supposed to arrive sometime today. But what could he have to be so pissed about?

"Where the hell is she? I want to see her this instant, Margot, I swear to god."

My heart stopped. It wasn't Dalton's father—it was mine.

I heard his heavy footsteps plodding into the foyer and up the front grand staircase and I froze. What was my father doing here? How did he know where I was?

"Charlotte?" he yelled. "Charlotte!"

I walked numbly into the foyer and was about to call out to my father, who had just reached the second-floor landing, when I saw Dalton standing there in his pajamas, hair all mussed from sleeping.

"What's going on?" Dalton asked, rubbing the sleep from his eyes.

"You!" my father yelled, coming at Dalton with his finger shaking and his face darkening three different shades of red.

"Alistair!" Margot shouted, bolting up the stairs.

"I've heard all about the stunt you tried to pull," my father said, stopping just short of Dalton, but still pointing at him and shaking. "You're going to stay the hell away from my daughter. You won't text her, or call her, or come near her. And if you so much as touch a hair on her head, I'll rip your fucking arm off."

"Dad," I said. "Stop."

At the sound of my voice, my father halted and he turned on the landing and looked down at me at the base of the stairs. For a second, his anger seemed to drain from his face, and he looked relieved.

But then, just as quickly, the anger was back. Possibly even amplified.

"Charlotte, get your things," he said. "We're leaving."

"It doesn't have to be this way, Alistair," Margot said.

"I'll be in the car," my father said, ignoring her. "You have five minutes, Charlotte, and then I'm coming back in here, and nobody is going to like the things I'll do."

"Fine," I said.

My father turned and barreled past Margot and me down the stairs. A second later I heard the front door slam shut behind me.

"What just happened?" Dalton asked.

"I may not have been one hundred percent upfront with my dad about where I was spending Thanksgiving," I said.

"You better get your things," Margot said rather icily. "Best not to keep your father waiting. Royce, if I could see you for a moment downstairs?"

"I didn't do anything," Dalton said.

I mouthed *I'm sorry* to Dalton behind Margot's back and then walked to my room to get dressed. I pulled on the same jeans and sweater I had worn the day before because they were still lying on the floor where I had discarded them yesterday. I went about hastily packing, throwing all of my things into my suitcase as quickly as I could.

I didn't get to say goodbye to Dalton. Neither he nor Margot was anywhere in sight when I dragged my suitcase downstairs. But I didn't have time to go looking for them, so I took my things and left.

My father's car was idling in the front drive. He got out to put my suitcase in the trunk and then held the front passenger door open for me. He slammed it behind me when I got in.

We drove in silence for the first several minutes. I opened my phone and saw that I had fifty missed calls from Greyson and dozens of text messages. I had forgotten to take him off of "Do Not Disturb" mode. I opened the text messages. The earliest ones were a frenzy of panic.

GREYSON: [8:05 p.m.] Charlie, where r u?
GREYSON: [8:12 p.m.] R u ok?
GREYSON: [8:56 p.m.] Seriously, answer my calls plz
GREYSON: [9:30 p.m.] Pick up
GREYSON: [10:03 p.m.] I'm really worried

The ones in the middle became vaguely threatening.

GREYSON: [10:03 p.m.] I'm going to call your dad if you don't answer so I can get dickweed's address

And the later ones became just plain stupid.

GREYSON: [11:45 p.m.] I didn't have your dad's number so I went down to
    his place in the city
GREYSON: [11:47 p.m.] He's really mad. He's coming to get you
GREYSON: [11:48 p.m.] I told him about Dalton and the board of conquests
GREYSON: [11:48 p.m.] I'm sry. Don't hate me.

Ugh, Greyson had gone to my dad? He had told him about Dalton? What an idiot.

"Don't ever lie to me, Charlotte," my father said, finally breaking the silence between us. "Don't ever lie to me again."

"That's funny," I said. "I thought lying was a Calloway family trait."

"What is that supposed to mean?"

"Jake Griffin," I said. "You told me you barely knew him."

My father stopped the car. He pulled over onto the side of the road and put the car into park.

"Is that why you didn't want me around Margot?" I asked. "Because I was asking questions about Jake, and you were scared she would give me answers? You didn't want me to know the truth?"

"What exactly did Margot tell you?"

"She told me everything," I lied.

"It was an accident," my father said. "We all thought he was dead. He wasn't breathing."

I turned my head and stared out the glass at the snow dusting the road and the countryside. I couldn't risk my father's seeing the shock that I felt registering on my face. What was an accident exactly?

"Everyone was looking to me, to tell them what to do, to fix it. We were scared. We were just kids," my father said. "And then Margot, Margot came up with this idea. To make it look like Jake had— had killed himself. To throw his body over the Ledge and just make it look like a suicide. To forge a note about the exam he had stolen and leave it in his dorm room."

"So you did it?" I asked. "You threw him into the water?"

"Is that what she told you?" my father asked. He looked at me and then away.

I didn't say anything.

"He was too heavy for Margot to lift him by herself," my father said. "She needed someone to help her. She kept saying it was the right thing, that it was the only way to save ourselves, that he was dead anyway, and so why did we have to throw our futures away with him?

"I told her I would take him. I'd drive him to the hospital in Falls Church, and I'd leave his body where somebody would find him right away. But she said that was too risky. That there'd be too many questions. That it could lead back to us. She said we needed to make it so that nobody would come looking for us, for answers. And so Matthew York, he helped her do it. It wasn't until later that we found out that he wasn't dead when we threw him in."

It took me a moment to realize what my father was saying. He and his friends had *killed* Jake Griffin.

"I was weak," my father said, finally looking at me. "In the worst possible way, I was weak. I was too weak to help Margot do it, and I was too weak to try and stop her."

I don't know what made me do it, but I reached over and covered my father's hand with my own.

"I'm sorry," I said.

"I've never told anyone that before," he said.

"Not even Mom?" I asked.

My father looked like I had sucker-punched him. I felt him pull away from me, and I drew back my hand. "Your mother?" he asked.

Now was the time. I could bring up the case file, the photographs, the suitcases. I could ask him for the truth.

"Did she know about Jake?" I asked instead. "Did she know what really happened to him?"

There was a long pause.

"Yes," my father said finally. "But I wasn't the one to tell her. She found out that last summer that she was with us. She came across some old photographs while developing film. She interrogated Margot about it, and Margot told her everything."

That was why my father was so adamant that I stay away from Margot—because she had told my mother the truth about Jake, and he hadn't wanted her to tell me, too.

"Your mother hired an investigator," my father said. "She was trying to find evidence, build a case. I didn't know until after she was gone. I thought . . . I thought she was having an affair. When she disappeared, I went to his house to confront him. I thought maybe, maybe they had run off together. That's when he told me the true nature of their relationship. When my PI discovered the bank tapes—the money missing from the safety-deposit boxes—I knew she'd run off, and why. She'd discovered what I'd done, what I was. She couldn't stand to be with me anymore. And she wanted to hurt me, in the most irrevocable way she could."

I sat there for a moment, in stunned silence. But she hadn't just left *him*. She had left me, too. And Seraphina. And Claire. And Grandma and Grandpa Fairchild, and Uncle Hank. Why would she leave all of us behind, without a word, without a thought, without a backward glance?

"Claire said—" I started. I took a deep breath. I didn't know exactly how to say this. "Claire told me you and Mom got in a fight the week before she left. That Mom got hurt."

Out of the corner of my eye, I saw my father clench his fists.

"We were arguing and your mother fell," my father said. "I didn't touch her. I would never . . . I would never hurt her."

Is that true? I couldn't help but ask myself. Could my mother have been scared of my father? Could that fear have kept her silent and hidden all these years? I couldn't help but think of my mother's last words to my father: *Get your hands off me.*

We sat in silence for a while, and then my father asked, "What made you ask about your mother?"

I contemplated telling him everything—about the photographs Uncle Hank had found underneath the floorboards at the lake house, about the case file I had stolen from Peter Hindsberg's office. Maybe everything my father said was true. In many ways, it all added up—everything clicked neatly into place. Maybe my mother really had left us, just as I'd believed all these years.

But I couldn't get those suitcases I'd seen in Margot's basement out of my mind. Maybe it was just a stupid coincidence. Maybe I was being crazy.

"No reason," I said. "It's just . . . the holidays. I always think about her more this time of year, I guess. Thanksgiving was her favorite."

I paused.

"Do you ever . . . do you ever think about her?" I asked. It was the first time I had asked my father this since I was a little girl.

At first, he didn't answer. He put the car into gear and pulled back onto the road. But after a while, he nodded, almost imperceptibly, and I knew he had heard me.

"I never stopped," he said.

thirty-eight
CHARLIE CALLOWAY

2017

My third and final ticket for the A's was waiting in my mailbox when I returned to school. This time, the ticket was in a small white envelope. I opened it in the entrance to Rosewood Hall.

Item #3: Publish these pictures in the next edition of the *Knollwood Chronicle*

I turned the envelope upside down in my palm and slid out the photographs, but I knew what they were even before I saw them. They were the pictures Leo had taken of me with Mr. Andrews. I looked undistinguishable enough—clearly a student in the Knollwood Prep uniform, but the back of my head was to the camera. Mr. Andrews was clear and recognizable, though, and so was our inappropriate embrace.

What had Mr. Andrews done to incur the wrath of the A's? I knew it was pointless of me to actually ask. The A's were determined to take him down, and they were going to use me to do it.

I slid the photographs back into the envelope and tucked it into my trig textbook. The ticket to get the photographs had seemed like some stupid dare at the time. Something to test how far I was willing to go to prove to the A's that I belonged, that I deserved to be one of them. But this, this seemed cruel. To destroy a man's reputation. And if what was in the pictures was real, maybe Mr. Andrews would have deserved it. But what the pictures didn't show was how I was the one to kiss him, and he was the one to pull away. The pictures were a lie.

I hugged the textbook to my chest as I set off across campus to class. I couldn't see it, but I could feel it there, the envelope tucked into the pages—holding the third and final ticket, the very last test that stood between me and becoming an A.

Leo leaned over my shoulder and plucked Plath's *Ariel* out of my fingers. I grabbed for it, but he held it out of my reach and leaned back into the pillows stacked on my dorm room bed. He dramatically read aloud the last line of the poem and then laughed.

"God, I hate this poem," Leo said. "I know Plath is supposed to be deep, but every time I read this, all I can take away from it is that Plath was fucking her dad."

He tossed *Ariel* next to me on the bed and picked up his Xbox controller. I held the closed book in my hands, ran my fingers across the edge of the pages.

Since that conversation I'd had with my father during Thanksgiving break, I couldn't stop thinking about what he and the A's had done to Jake Griffin. Sure, they had thought he was dead at the time they tossed him over the Ledge. They hadn't meant to hurt him. But then again, the A's weren't completely blameless. They had cared more about themselves—their futures, their own reputations—than they had cared about the well-being of their friend. Because if they had really put Jake first that night, they would have done everything they could to get him help. And at the very least, they could have been honest about what happened and not put Jake's family and friends through the torment of thinking he had killed himself. Maybe the A's weren't murderers, but they were selfish, self-centered, and cruel.

If I was being honest with myself—painfully honest—I had to wonder, if I had been in my father's shoes that night at the Ledge with Jake, would I have done anything differently? Because I had been in his shoes already, in a manner of speaking, and I had solidly played everything in my own self-interest. When Auden was framed for a prank he didn't commit, I let him take the fall and deal with the punishment. Unmasking the A's didn't even cross my mind. But I could have done that, and it might have changed things.

I guess I hadn't played everything just in my own self-interest. I had been loyal to the A's. In a way, my father and his friends had done something similar. They had sacrificed Jake to save one another. It hadn't been an easy choice, and it hadn't been completely selfish. Maybe there was something noble in that type of loyalty.

"Say I did something bad," I said. "Like really, really bad."

"What type of bad?" Leo asked, eyes still trained on the TV screen, pursing his lips like he always did when he was concentrating really hard. "Like lie-to-your-dad-about-spending-Thanksgiving-with-your-boyfriend bad?"

"Ha ha," I said. Leo was still giving me a hard time about that. He was a little pissed I had lied to him about where I was over Thanksgiving break, though he didn't really have the moral high ground when it came to our being honest with each other.

"Say I killed someone," I said. "By accident."

"How?" Leo asked.

"I don't know . . . specifics aren't important," I said.

"Specifics are important," Leo said. "Are we talking, like, you accidentally hit someone with your car? Or is this a crime of passion? Like you got in a fight with Dalton and stabbed him to death with the heel of your Louis Vuitton?"

I sighed. "You choose."

"I choose death by Louis Vuitton," Leo said. "And your secret is safe with me."

"But I mean like, seriously," I said. "This is hypothetical, obviously, but if it weren't, all joking aside, if you knew I killed someone, you wouldn't go to the police?"

"If you *accidentally* killed someone?" Leo asked. "I don't know. No, I guess not."

"Why not? Shouldn't I be held accountable?"

"Family is family," Leo said, shrugging.

"So the fact that we're blood gives me a Get Out of Jail Free card? You wouldn't feel morally compromised?"

"Listen, loyalty to the people you love, to your family, is a moral code. If you don't have loyalty, what do you have?"

"Family loyalty," I said. "That's funny, coming from you."

I still wasn't completely over what Leo had done to me, and I liked to give him a hard time about it.

"You can't forgive Dalton and not me," Leo said. "That's not fair."

"Fine," I said.

I still wasn't sure where that left me.

"You're still going to help me with the donations for the Trustee Benefit Gala tomorrow, right?" Leo asked.

"What do you mean 'still'?" I asked. "I don't remember volunteering in the first place."

"I'm making everyone help, and you're no exception," Leo said. He was president of the junior class and since the student council was in charge of organizing the event, he had to help out. "Besides, I've been so busy lately, I've barely had time to do anything for it, and the gala's on Saturday."

I looked pointedly from him to the TV screen, where his attention was still fully absorbed in his game. "Yeah, you look really busy," I said.

"What'd you get for your final ticket?" Leo asked, ignoring my comment.

"I have to publish the pictures you took of Mr. Andrews groping me in the *Chronicle*," I said.

"That's not so bad," Leo said.

I suppose he meant execution-wise.

"I guess," I said. "Do you have any idea what Mr. Andrews did to get on the A's bad side?"

"It's more like what he didn't do," Leo said. "Or, should I say, *who* he didn't do."

"What are you talking about?"

"I guess Ren had a thing for him, and he didn't reciprocate. It must have really pissed her off."

"So we're framing Mr. Andrews for hooking up with a student because he didn't hook up with a student?"

"Something like that," Leo said.

I couldn't help but think of the dean of arts from last year, and how the A's had driven him off campus by exposing his very explicit emails with a minor to the whole school. Had that been a setup too? At the time, I had viewed the A's as some sort of dark-knight vigilantes, but now . . .

"But doesn't that seem messed up to you?" I asked.

Leo shrugged. "It's not that far off from what we've done so far, is it?"

"Yes, it is," I said.

"How?" Leo asked, putting down his controller. "Remember when the A's framed Auden for messing with Mr. Franklin's photograph? You were all pissed at first because they had left you out of it. We basically got him expelled."

"Yeah, I guess that's true," I said.

"We've lied, cheated, stolen, vandalized, et cetera," Leo said. "How is this any different?"

"I don't know," I said. "This just feels different to me."

But maybe Leo was right and it wasn't different. Maybe, somehow, *I* was different.

"Do you ever think about not doing what they want?" I asked. "Like, just quitting the Game and walking away? Not being an A?"

"Not really," Leo said. "I mean, especially at this point. We've put up with a lot of shit, but we're almost through it. Soon it'll be our turn."

Our turn. Our turn to do what had been done to us to a fresh group of initiates. Our turn to concoct and carry out our own revenge schemes and wage war against Headmaster Collins and the other faculty.

"Besides," Leo said, "trying to quit hasn't worked out so well for others in the past, in case you hadn't noticed. Remember Auden?"

"But what if there weren't consequences?" I asked.

"There will be consequences," Leo said. "You know what they have against us. Do you really want everyone to see those pictures? I mean, forget about what everyone at school will think. What if those pictures got leaked to our parents?"

I was silent. It wasn't just my fate that I was deciding; it was Leo's too.

"Tell me you're not planning on doing something stupid," Leo said.

I just looked at him.

"Charlie?"

This was Leo—Leo—I would be hurting. Sure, Leo hadn't been the most loyal person to me lately, but was I any better if I turned around and did the same to him? *Loyalty to the people you love, to your family, is a moral code. If you don't have loyalty, what do you have?*

"Of course not," I said. "Don't be so dramatic. I was just speaking hypothetically."

"Okay, good," Leo said, picking his controller back up and returning his attention to his game.

I couldn't help but think that what Ren had said that first night at the Ledge was true—secrets bound us to one another. Not just me and Leo and the current A's, but all the A's. Now we were all inextricably linked. Either we were all going to get away with everything together, or we were all going to have to go down together in some respect—a collective crash and burn—because we were all guilty, in one way or another, of something.

But then, who wasn't?

Somehow, despite my best efforts not to be helpful, I found myself in the dining hall on Wednesday afternoon sitting at a table with Dalton, Crosby, and Leo, cataloging donations for the Trustee Benefit Gala's silent auction.

"Here's another vacation home," Crosby said, handing me a one-page printout description and accompanying photographs of someone's ski lodge in Jackson Hole.

Apparently, everyone's favorite thing to donate to the silent auction was a weeklong getaway to their vacation home (or luxury condo at Lake Tahoe, or chateau in the south of France, or Tuscan villa, or winery in Napa). It required the least amount of effort while simultaneously allowing people to flaunt just how rich they were, and all in the name of charity. It was the ultimate #humble-brag.

"'Rustic lodge allows you to commune with nature,'" I read from the printout. "What exactly do you think screamed 'rustic' to this guy?" I asked. "Was it the fourteen-person jetted marble-slab Jacuzzi? Or the in-home personal theater in the basement?"

I angled the paper with the pictures so Crosby could see.

"People think that just because they're in the middle of bum-fuck nowhere, they're automatically camping or something," Crosby said.

"Once, we got stuck in Atlanta in a layover and had to stay at a

Hilton by the airport," Dalton said. "My mother actually used the words 'roughing it.'"

Dalton laughed and put his arm around the back of my chair. I felt his fingertips graze my shoulder, and I tried not to stiffen at his touch. The truth was, I'd felt odd being around Dalton ever since I had spotted those suitcases in his basement. And the hardest part was, I couldn't exactly tell him what was up with me, because either I was being completely insane and the suitcases were just coincidentally the same type that my mother had owned, or they were actually her suitcases and Margot was weirdly tied up in her disappearance. I knew I had to get back in that basement and open them up, but I had no idea how I was going to do that.

Part of me had been trying really hard not to think about those suitcases. Because if they did belong to my mother, what did that mean? I had never really allowed myself to believe that my mother hadn't left us of her own free will. The alternative was just too horrible to imagine—that my father might have played some part in her disappearance, that he might have hurt her in some way. But if my mother hadn't left us, then that meant that I had been wrong about a lot of things. All of this remoteness I carried around inside me was unfounded and misdirected. These walls I put up, the coldness and distance I cultivated like a shield—they were unnecessary. Because I hadn't been betrayed and abandoned; I had been wanted and loved.

That thought disarmed me.

"How do we determine the minimum starting bid for each of these?" Crosby asked.

"I'll need to see what we made on ticket sales first," Leo said. "Then we'll know how much to gouge people at the auction to meet our goal. Charlie, can you get the cash box from Stevie and see if she has a final number yet?"

"You're very bossy lately," I said. "I think all this political power you wield is going to your head."

"Yeah, don't be such a tyrant, Calloway," Dalton said. "At least say 'please.'"

"Has a class president ever been impeached before?" I asked.

"There's no precedent for that, I'm afraid," Dalton said.

"We could stage a coup," I said. "I have a free period after trig tomorrow."

Leo sighed. "Pretty please with a cherry on top, will you go ask Stevie what we made on ticket sales and bring me the cash box?"

"Well, since you asked so nicely," I said, standing.

I meandered across the dining hall to where Stevie and Yael were sitting with the cash box. I hadn't talked to Yael since Drew was expelled, and I hadn't spoken to Stevie since she had made that peace offering outside the dining hall a few weeks back. I still felt a little bad about brushing her off, but I hadn't meant to. It was more bad timing than anything.

I knew that I had kind of been an ass, and that Drew was the common factor that linked us, the glue that held our friendship together, but still. Stevie and Yael were my friends (weren't they?), and I missed them.

"Hey there," I said, a little too cheerfully. I knew I sounded fake, but I couldn't help it. I didn't have much practice playing nice and trying to ingratiate myself with others. I had never cared to before.

Yael stopped midsentence. The smile slid off her face when she saw that it was me. Stevie looked at me briefly and then back at the calculator in her hand. There were stacks of checks on the table in front of her.

"Leo needs the cash box and the final ticket sale count," I said.

"It'll be a minute," Stevie said, still not looking at me.

"Okay," I said, sinking into the chair next to her as she punched another number into her calculator and the number on the screen grew. "Do you need any help?"

"That wasn't an invitation," Yael said, glaring at me.

I hadn't exactly expected a warm welcome, but this was down-right cold. I mean, I was at least trying here.

"What exactly is your problem?" I asked.

Yael sighed. "You can drop the act, Charlie," she said. "We know it was you."

"You know what was me?"

"Really? That's how you're going to play this?"

"Yael, I'm not playing anything. I honestly have no idea what you're talking about."

"The damn fish we found in our room," Yael said, her voice rising. Stevie leaned forward and shushed her, and Yael lowered her voice to a fervent whisper. "I'm talking about the damn fish."

"The fish?" I asked.

This whole time, I'd thought they were mad at me because they thought I was the one who asked Drew to steal the exam. I'd also considered they were mad at me because I'd been spending so much time with Dalton and the boys, like I had forgotten about them or something. But they weren't talking to me because of something to do with a fish?

"You know, you walk around all high and mighty with your secret little friends in your secret little group with your secret little secrets," Yael said. "And you think everybody doesn't know."

"Yael—" Stevie started, but Yael cut her off.

"No, I'm not scared of her and her precious friends," Yael said. She turned back to me, a fire in her eyes. "I overheard Darcy and Ren in the restroom a while back, talking about how they made you and Leo take the term 'kissing cousins' to a whole new level. That's a strange kind of friendship, making you stick your tongue down your cousin's throat before they deigned to hang out with you. They seemed to have a good laugh about it."

My cheeks flamed red. "I don't know what you're talking about," I said.

"Just know this," Yael said. "If you start coming after us, we'll come after you. We know things, too."

"Yael," Stevie said. "Stop."

Yael looked at Stevie and took a deep breath. Then she glared back at me.

"You know what?" Yael said. "I'm not going to stoop to your level. Keep your self-involved games and your power plays and your manipulative backstabbing bitch fests. Just keep them the hell away from me."

I looked at Stevie to see if she agreed with her in all of this. She was breathing heavily, staring straight ahead at the table, refusing to meet my eye. After a moment, she sighed and began to gather the stacks of checks and pile them into the cash box.

"Here," Stevie said. She jotted a number down on a Post-it note, threw the calculator into the box, and shut it tight. She stuck the Post-it note on top. "Here's the revenue from ticket sales," she said, pushing the cash box toward me across the table.

"Stevie?" I said.

She looked at me then, and I almost wished she hadn't, because I could see it in her eyes, how deeply I had disappointed her.

"Let's just go," Stevie said to Yael, pushing back her chair.

Yael leaned across the table toward me and said so low so that only Stevie and I could hear her: "You'll make a perfect A, Charlie. All you care about is yourself."

When they were gone, I marched angrily across the dining hall to the boys' table. I slammed the cash box down on the tabletop, and Dalton stopped midconversation and looked up at me.

"We need to talk," I said.

"What's wrong, babe?" Dalton asked.

"I want to know about the fish," I said, lowering my voice. It was just Dalton and Crosby at the table. Leo was across the room talking to Mr. Davis, the junior class adviser. But still, I didn't want to risk anybody's overhearing.

"What fish?" Dalton asked.

"Dude," Crosby chuckled, and nudged Dalton's shoulder. "You remember. The fish in Little Miss Priss's room? That was sick."

Dalton started to laugh. "Oh yeah, almost forgot about that."

"I don't get it," I said. "Why would you put a fish in Stevie and Yael's room?"

"To get that little bitch back after what she did to Drew at the disciplinary hearing," Crosby said. "You don't recommend expelling an A and just get off scot-free.

"Yo, check it out," Crosby went on, reaching into his pocket and pulling out his phone. He opened his photo album and scrolled through his pictures, and then held out the screen for me to see. "Fucking hi-lar-ious."

It wasn't a fish, it was *the* fish—the one Leo and I had stolen from the Poseidon Fountain and hidden in the old prop room. It was lying in Stevie's bed, half covered in a sheet, and written in what looked like blood were the words *Snitching bitches will sleep with the fishes.*

"Is that blood?" I asked.

"Yep," Dalton said. "Look in its mouth."

I glanced at the gaping mouth of the fish, which had been stuffed with what looked like—

"Do not tell me those are used tampons," I said.

"That smell was rank," Crosby said, still laughing.

My stomach twisted. "Why would you do something like that?" I asked.

"Haven't you ever seen *The Godfather*?" Crosby asked, looking incredulous. "It's a classic."

"Relax," Dalton said, reaching out and grabbing my hand be-cause he could tell that I was upset. "It was just a joke. You have to admit, Stevie is kind of tightly wound. We were just having some fun."

"Stevie can be . . . *neurotic* at times," I said. "But she's my friend." *And she didn't deserve that.*

"Your friend?" Dalton said. "When's the last time you two even hung out?"

His question was like a slap in the face. I didn't have a retort, because he was right. I hadn't hung out with Stevie since Drew was expelled, and even before that, we hadn't spent that much time together since Dalton and I became a thing and I had become involved in the A's.

"Sometimes you outgrow people," Dalton said. "And usually for a reason."

"What is that supposed to mean?" I asked, drawing back.

"Come on, Charlie," Dalton said. "Stevie Sorantos? Do I really have to spell it out?"

I crossed my arms over my chest. "Yeah, I guess you do."

Dalton sighed and turned back toward the table. I saw him roll his eyes at Crosby. "Don't be so dramatic, Charlie," Dalton said. "The whole thing was a joke."

"Well, I'm not laughing," I said. I grabbed my bag from the table and slung it over my shoulder before I marched away.

"Where's she going?" I heard Leo ask as he returned to the table.

"To find her sense of humor," Crosby said.

In the library later that evening, I sat at one of the study tables with Finn, a score of old newspapers and yearbooks spread out around us. We were doing research to write our article on the story be-hind Knollwood's ghost, which was due that Friday. It would go into this year's last edition of the *Chronicle,* but to tell the truth, I was having a hard time concentrating. I was still reeling from my fight with Dalton and my altercation with Stevie and Yael, and the very last thing I wanted to be doing was writing a false article on the death of a boy that my father was involved in. Somehow, on top of everything else, I had to juggle keeping the story I knew out of the story I was telling. I couldn't slip up and put in some detail that wasn't in the newspaper accounts or the yearbook and open a whole other can of worms.

"Why are all ghost stories morality tales?" Finn asked, flipping through an old yearbook.

"What do you mean?" I asked.

"Jake—he seemed like this Knollwood golden boy," Finn said. "Star of the tennis team, on the student council, popular, good-looking, successful, et cetera. Seems like he had it all, and then one day he cheats and falls from grace and becomes ever after this paradigm of failure that hangs over campus. It's like he's this specter of doom warning you what will happen if you stray outside the lines. Hence, morality tale."

"I hadn't thought of it like that," I said. My phone vibrated in my purse and I pulled it out. I had two missed calls from Dalton and one text message (Where r u?), and a slew of texts from Greyson.

GREYSON: I'm sry I screwed things up for you. I just want to know that you're ok. Plz text back.

I typed out a quick response. I was still pissed at him for what he had pulled with my father at Thanksgiving.

ME: I'm fine. Plz leave me alone.

I threw my phone back in my purse.

"Well, I must have done something right today," Finn said.

"Why do you say that?" I asked.

"Because the epitome of masculine beauty has made an appearance, and, if I'm not mistaken, he's headed this way."

I turned my head and saw Dalton near the entrance, by the librarian's desk. I whipped my head back around and picked up the book closest to me and buried my head in it, trying to shield myself from view. "Why do you think he's headed this way?" I asked.

Finn rolled his eyes. "Because you're here, and if you hadn't noticed, Dalton kind of follows you around."

"Do you think he saw me?" I asked, slouching down in my seat.

Finn's face split into an ear-to-ear grin, which gave me my answer.

"There's something about the way he walks that just gets me," he said, leaning his chin onto the palm of his hand and staring unabashedly at what I was sure was the approaching figure of my boyfriend behind me. "It's like the world is his runway. Do you think he's had professional training?"

"We're kind of in a fight," I said. "A big one."

Finn sighed. "The best part of my day is watching him in our Ethics and Morality seminar. He makes utilitarianism sound sexy."

"Do you think I have enough time to make a stealthy exit?" I asked, starting to gather my things.

"No, but do you think you could introduce me?" Finn asked.

"Finn," I said.

Finn shushed me and glanced down at his laptop screen, his ears growing noticeably red even in the dim library light. "Be nice," Finn chastised me in a whisper. "He's here."

I turned my head, and there was Dalton. He set a white to-go cup down on the table in front of me and gave me a hopeful smile.

"I brought you a coffee," Dalton said. "Bone-dry cappuccino with skim milk from the coffee cart outside the dining hall. Your favorite."

"Flowers would probably have been safer," Finn said. "Caffeine is just going to give her more energy to devote to being pissed at you."

Dalton chuckled. "You're probably right. Didn't think of that." He held out his hand to Finn. "I don't think we've met. I'm Dalton."

Finn eagerly took his hand. "Finn," he said. "We actually have Ethics and Morality together."

"That class is the worst," Dalton said.

"Totally," Finn said. "Terrible. I hate it."

I glared at Finn and mouthed, *Traitor*, at him.

"I was hoping to maybe get a word with Charlie, if you don't mind," Dalton said.

"Actually, Finn and I are in the middle of—" I started.

"—saying goodbye," Finn cut me off. "I'm going to go finish up the draft of our article. It was a pleasure to see—I mean meet—you, Dalton," Finn said.

"Likewise," Dalton said.

I glowered at Finn as he gathered up his things and left. Dalton sat down in the seat next to me and turned his chair so that he was fully facing me.

"I know I'm probably supposed to already know this," Dalton said. "But humor me anyway. Can you please explain to me why you're so upset?"

"Because of the fish," I said.

"Yes, but what about the fish exactly?"

"One, you were really gross and mean to my friend," I said, and I held up a hand before he could say anything. "And, yes, despite what you may think, Stevie is my friend—or *was* my friend, before your little fish prank.

"And two, you used Leo and me to steal that fish. We did all the grunt work, and little did we know that that was going to be used to harass someone I care about. And that seems to be a pattern—

the initiates taking all the risk and doing all the work and being kept completely in the dark on what it's all for, and having to deal with the consequences if there's fallout."

Dalton nodded, like he was really listening and considering what I had to say, which disarmed me a little, because I was ready to knock his head off, or go verbal blow for verbal blow.

"Listen," he said after a minute. "About the fish—if I had known you weren't on the outs with Stevie, I wouldn't have done that. And about the second thing—I know it's frustrating right now, because it feels like you're being left out of something. I felt exactly the same way when I was in your shoes, and I may have forgotten what that's like a bit being on the other side of things. But trust me, once you get in, you're all in. This—right now—is the hard part, and you're almost through it. And once you get through it, all of this will feel worth it."

"Will it?" I asked. "Because right now, it seems like I'm doing a lot of grunt work for people's elaborate pranks and revenge schemes, so that next year I can make someone else do the grunt work for my own elaborate pranks and revenge schemes, and that just isn't looking worth it to me."

"I know it seems like we dick around a lot, and pull pranks and stuff," Dalton said. "And yeah, we do that stuff. But that's not what the A's are really about."

"It's not?"

"No," Dalton said. "It's about . . . belonging to people who know you better than anybody. People who know your worst parts and stick by you.

"I know Crosby and I seem really close now, and we are, but that never would have happened if not for the A's and all the shit we went through during initiation," Dalton said. "Now, Crosby, he's like my brother. He's family."

I thought about my father and his friends. How he'd always talked about his time at Knollwood as if it were some kind of mythical paradise, and the friends he had made there, and the good times and memories they shared. And it was true that many of the people who remained in my father's life from high school were probably A's.

Dalton reached out and took my hand and gave it a little squeeze. "Charlie, the A's isn't about the two years we're together at Knollwood. When you're in the A's—it's for life. I hope—I really want—for you to be a part of that with me."

I bit my lip. I knew that he was right. Being in the A's meant a lifetime of exclusivity. It meant power. It was a rare, special kind of bond. There was a reason why I had wanted so badly to be a part of it.

But another part of me knew that the things Yael and Stevie had said about the A's were also true. The A's were self-entitled rich kids playing god. They took their pleasures at the expense of others with little compassion, empathy, or shame. At their best, the A's were brazen and self-empowered and "carpe diem"; they saw what they wanted, and they took it without apology. At their worst, they were selfish and conceited and cruel.

I knew I had to choose: in or out. I couldn't have it both ways. But at the moment, I felt too inwardly divided to choose.

So, I didn't say anything. I just gave Dalton's hand a little squeeze back and prayed he couldn't feel my indecision in the gesture.

thirty-nine
CHARLIE CALLOWAY

2017

I'd become one of those people I used to make snarky comments about straight to their faces—the people who show up hours before an event is supposed to start and help hang streamers from the ceiling. It was all Leo's fault. He'd harassed me and Dalton into helping set up the silent auction for the Trustee Benefit Gala in the banquet hall on Saturday morning.

"Thanks for coming," Leo said, handing Dalton and me a clipboard that contained all the bidding forms for the silent auction.

"I hate you," I said.

"It's not that early," Leo said.

"Anything before noon on Saturday is early," I said.

Leo handed me his latte. "Here, for sustenance," he said.

I took a sip, but I was still feeling surly, and I doubted the caffeine would help. It wasn't really the getting-up-early thing that had me in a bad mood. It was that the last edition of the *Knollwood Chronicle* went to the printers tonight, and either I had to get the pictures of me and Mr. Andrews in there, or I had to prepare myself for the fallout of failing my last ticket. Not only would I not be an A, but Leo and I would have to brace ourselves for our public humiliation if the A's released our pictures in retribution. Which, let's be honest, they most likely would.

It wasn't even the execution of getting the pictures in the paper that bothered me. I had already figured that part out. Part of Finn's grunt work as a freshman was that he had to deliver the flash drive with the final version of the *Knollwood Chronicle* from the newsroom to the printer by midnight the night it was due. Which meant that all I had to do was intercept Finn tonight between the newsroom and the printer, and switch out the real flash drive with an identical flash drive preloaded with my own story and scandalous photographs. My story would not only be front-page news, it would be the only news in the *Knollwood Chronicle* this week. That was, if I decided I wanted to go through with it.

"Now, these are the bidding forms. The printouts with the descriptions and pictures of the auction items are on the tables over there," Leo said, pointing. "You guys will just need to lay everything out. There's also some decorations, tablecloths, et cetera, over there by Stevie, so feel free to grab some. Make everything look presentable."

"Got it," Dalton said, way too cheerfully, beside me.

"Thanks again," Leo said before darting off to greet another set of volunteers.

"So, uh, is your dad coming tonight?" Dalton asked as we set the auction forms down on the table and started to sort through things.

"Yeah, he comes every year," I said. "Why?"

"Is he, uh, over what happened?" Dalton asked, looking uncomfortable and scratching the back of his neck.

"What do you mean?" I asked.

"You know, when he wanted to punch my face in at Thanksgiving because of the whole Board of Conquests thing?"

"Oh," I said. That hadn't really crossed my mind lately with everything else that was going on. "We never really talked about it."

"You never talked about it?"

"Talking isn't really our thing," I said. "I mean, I'm sure you're still not his favorite person, but he's not going to, like, assault you tonight or anything if that's what you're worried about."

"I guess that's something," Dalton said. "But I'd really like for your dad not to hate me. Usually I do a lot better with parents."

I was about to make some retort that maybe next time he might want to abstain from playing a piggish game of sex bingo with his friends, but when I looked up from the table, I saw Margot standing behind him. She was impeccably dressed in a Canada Goose parka and winter boots.

"Charlie," she said in greeting, rather icily.

Well, *she* was obviously still upset over the whole Thanksgiving fiasco. I gave her a little nod of acknowledgment in response.

"Mom, what are you doing here so early?" Dalton asked, turning and giving her a kiss on the cheek as she embraced him.

"They won't let me check into the hotel in Falls Church until three," Margot said. "So I thought I'd surprise you and take you out for brunch."

"Oh," Dalton said. "Well, I kind of promised Leo I'd help set up the silent auction. Maybe I could meet you somewhere in like an hour?"

Margot frowned and tilted her wrist to check the time. The white pearl watch face with small, circle-cut yellow diamonds around the bezel caught my eye. It was the same watch I'd admired the first time I'd met Margot, in the city. I'd always **liked** yellow diamonds, partly because you didn't come across them very often. My mother had had a canary diamond engagement ring. She'd take it off when she was gardening or washing the dishes and string it on a thin gold chain she wore around her neck, so that it hung over her heart. Sometimes when I'd sit on her lap as a little girl, she'd wiggle the ring off her finger and let me hold it, and I'd try threading it on my too-slender fingers. I used to marvel at the large emerald-cut diamond, which was such an unusual color. The color of daffodils and summer squash. The diamonds on Margot's watch were exactly the same shade.

But the unusual color of the diamonds on Margot's watch was not the only thing that caught my eye. This close, I could see Margot's watch was a ladies' Oyster Perpetual Caliber 2235 model. I knew because I'd considered that same model when shopping for my own wristwatch last year for my sixteenth birthday. I'd eventually decided against it and chosen a vintage Rolex Bubbleback from circa 1933. The Oyster Perpetual model that Margot wore on her wrist was new. Rolex didn't start manufacturing it until the late 1990s. And yet, in the city, when I'd asked Margot where she'd gotten it, she'd claimed it was an heirloom.

"That'll be too late," Margot said. "Most places stop serving brunch at two. And I'm craving a mimosa."

"It's fine," I told Dalton, trying to keep my voice level. "Go have brunch with your mom. I can handle setting up."

"Are you sure?" Dalton asked. "I feel kinda bad."

"It's a one-person job anyway and Leo roped me into it a while ago," I said. "There's no reason we should both have to suffer through it."

"Okay, if you're sure?" Dalton asked.

"I'm sure," I said.

He leaned in and gave me a peck on the forehead and I tried not to flinch at his touch. "You're the best," he said. "I'll see you tonight?"

"I'll be here," I said, and I gave him a weak smile.

When they were both gone, I glanced around the room to make sure that no one was looking in my general direction and then sank behind the table.

What. The. Hell?

The suitcases in the basement were one thing. But the watch with the same unusual-color diamonds as my mother's engagement ring? And Margot's watch was not an heirloom, it was maybe a decade old at most. My mother's ring, on the other hand, was an heirloom. It had belonged to my great-grandmother.

I could feel my heart hammering in my chest. I couldn't breathe.

I remembered the engagement notice Greyson had found in an old issue of the *Times*. Had my mother's engagement ring once belonged to Margot? My stomach twisted. I felt like I was going to be sick.

Keep it together, Calloway, I told myself. *You have to keep your shit together.*

Now, more than ever, I couldn't fall apart.

I stood up straight and took a deep breath. I shook my head to clear it. I could do this. I could do this. But I couldn't do it alone.

I took out my phone and scrolled through my contacts. When I found the one I was looking for, I pressed the little phone icon next to the name. I put the phone to my ear and listened to the ringing on the other end, and then that familiar voice answered.

"Hey," I said. "I need your help."

My father picked me up at my dorm room at seven o'clock and we walked together, arm in arm, across campus. He wore a crisp black suit and silk tie under his winter coat, and I wore a midnight-blue A-line evening gown with a beaded bodice that my father had brought with him from the city. His assistant Rosie had picked it out for me. I also wore my mother's old necklace, the one with the cheap crab pendant. Jake had given it to her, I was sure. According to the "In Memoriam" page in my dad's old yearbook, Jake had been born in early July. He was a Cancer; the crab was his zodiac sign. My mother had held on to that necklace all of those years; Jake must have meant a great deal to her. I wore the necklace now as a kind of amulet. I wondered if my father recognized the necklace, but if he did, he said nothing.

The lights from the banquet hall spilled onto the front lawn, and as we made our way up the stone steps, we stopped here and there to greet my father's friends. It was the one event at Knollwood where the parents and alumni outnumbered the students.

"Alistair, old man," Matthew York said, grabbing my father's arm. He was with his daughter Meryl. I didn't really talk to Meryl, even though she was an A initiate, like me. She was quiet and kept to herself. She had a long, stern-looking face, and so I'd always assumed she was a little bit mean.

"Haven't seen you at the club lately," Matthew York said to my father. "What've you been doing with yourself?"

My father stopped to answer him and I gave his hand a little squeeze and mouthed that I would meet him inside. He nodded at me.

"Teddy around?" I heard Matthew York ask my father.

"Yes, Grier's here, too," my father answered. "My niece just applied for next year."

I checked my coat at the front door. Inside, the room was crowded with tables set for a grand three-course meal, women in evening gowns, and men in suits. In the middle of the room was the dance floor, and Headmaster Collins was in the center of it, finishing his welcome speech to the parents and alumni. The Trustee Benefit Gala always began with that speech, followed by cocktails and the silent auction, and ended with dinner and dancing. I spotted Uncle Teddy and Aunt Grier at the edge of the crowd and I walked over to them.

"You clean up nice," Uncle Teddy said.

"Charlotte, it's good to see you," Aunt Grier said, and she gave me a curt smile. I gave her a perfunctory smile back. I'd always felt a certain distance between me and my aunt that I could never quite bridge. She was never cold, exactly—after all, she and Uncle Teddy had taken me into their home at one point, raised me and Seraphina alongside my cousins for two years. After hearing her interview in the PI's files, I understood why it always felt like she was holding me at arm's length. It probably didn't help that I looked just like my mother, either.

Aunt Grier's clutch buzzed and she handed Uncle Teddy her glass of champagne.

"It's the sitter," Aunt Grier said, glancing at the screen. "I'm going to take this outside. I'll be right back."

When she was gone, Uncle Teddy took a sip of champagne from her glass and asked me, "Did you finish going through the files I sent?"

It took me a moment to understand what he was referring to, and then I remembered: the PI's case files on my mother.

"Yes," I said. "Thanks for sending those."

"Did you find the answers you were looking for?" he asked.

"Yes and no," I said. "I got some answers, but somehow more questions, too."

Uncle Teddy nodded.

"My uncle Hank said the two of you had an interesting conversation, though," I said.

"Did he?"

"Apparently, you threatened him and made him hand over the photographs he found at the lake house?"

"I tried asking nicely first," Uncle Teddy said, taking another sip of Aunt Grier's champagne. "But Hank has always been a bit . . . gruff. When he refused, I might have gotten a little . . . *colorful* in my response."

"Why would you do that?"

Uncle Teddy sighed. "If you listened to those interviews, you already know."

"You and my mother used to date," I said.

"It was more than that. She was the first girl I ever loved," Uncle

Teddy said. "Listen," he said after a moment, "I want you to know, that whatever was said in those interviews, whatever some people might think, Grace never cared about the money. If anything, she loved your father despite his money, despite who his family was."

"You really think she loved him?" I asked. I used to be so sure of the deep affection my parents had for one another, so sure of their tight bond. But after everything I'd learned over the past couple months, I'd started to doubt it.

"Yes, I do," Uncle Teddy said. "As much as it pains me to admit it."

"You don't think she ran off, do you?" I asked.

Uncle Teddy shook his head. "No, I don't. But I've never had any solid evidence to the contrary. And when you mentioned those photographs, well, I had to see them."

"What did you make of them?" I asked.

"Not much," Uncle Teddy said. "They looked like some sort of blackmail, maybe, but I couldn't make heads or tails of it, to be honest with you."

"I couldn't either," I lied. If Uncle Teddy didn't know, then he hadn't spoken to my father about the photographs, or, if he had, my father hadn't told him the truth. I wasn't sure why I was protecting my father when I still wasn't sure I believed his story, but for some reason, I was.

"Apparently, Clementine convinced the sitter she's allowed to have processed sugar," Aunt Grier said, returning clearly agitated. "She ate half a bag of your secret stash of marshmallows and is now running around the house like a crazy person and refuses to go to bed."

"Come on," Uncle Teddy said, putting his hand at the small of Aunt Grier's back. "Let's go look at overpriced vacation rentals. That will calm you down."

He gave me a wink as he steered my aunt in the direction of the silent auction tables across the room.

Someone put their arms around me from behind and I stiffened. Then I heard Dalton's voice in my ear as he tugged me close.

"You look ravishing," he said.

I wanted to remind him that the word "ravish" came from the Latin word *rapere*, which meant "to violently seize or take away by force." I knew that meaning of the word was archaic now, but I still found it a little offensive that women were supposed to take it as compliment when men were basically saying, *You look so good I want to carry you off by force and have my way with you*. But I bit my tongue.

"You know, when we were setting up earlier, I noticed there are a lot of dark corners and empty hallways in this building," he whispered. His hands circled my waist. "I could show you."

"Is your mother here?" I asked.

His hands stilled. "My mom?" he asked, sounding disappointed.

"Yes," I said. "When I was putting together the silent auction this morning, I saw something she might really like. I wanted to show her."

"Can't you do that later?"

I pivoted out of his arms and gave him a quick, pacifying peck on the tip of his nose. "I'll come find you after," I lied.

I found Margot making the rounds at the silent auction tables.

"Looking for anything in particular?" I asked.

Margot straightened and gave me a smile. She was wearing a classic off-the-shoulder gown in black. She looked polished and stunning.

"The vacation homes are always my favorite part," Margot said. She took a sip from her champagne glass. "Oliver—Royce's father— and I are thinking of investing in a place in Napa. I was seeing if there were any places I might stay while I looked."

"If travel is your thing, I have something that might interest you," I said.

She followed me to the end of the table, and I pointed to the item card I had staged there that morning. I studied her face as she read to gauge her reaction.

Vintage Burberry Cloth Luggage Set in Paisley Print, $500

Wouldn't you just kill for a striking set of luggage that will make you the envy of every girl in town? This vintage Burberry cloth luggage set in paisley print is perfect for a quick getaway. Get noticed with this elegant and graceful style.

Luggage set is in nearly mint condition with only a slight tear in the inner lining. Don't let this steal pass you by.

Margot was silent for a moment. Then she gave me a knowing smile.

"You're a clever girl, Charlie," Margot said, taking another sip of her champagne. "And you have a certain fortitude that I admire. You must get that from Grace."

"Don't," I said, my voice bare and cold. "Don't talk about my mother as if you were her friend."

I was sure now that the blond woman I had seen down by the lake that night ten years ago with my mother wasn't Claire. It was Margot. And the embrace I'd thought I'd understood at the time had been something else entirely. Not an embrace, but a struggle.

"You killed her," I said. "I saw you that night down by the lake. And before my mother, there was Jake. You killed him, too."

Margot sighed and took a sip of her champagne. "That's too strong a word for what happened with Jake," she said. "We were kids. I was seventeen. Jake took those pills of his own volition; no one forced him. And if we hadn't done what we did, he probably would have died anyway. That's the ugly truth of it. He wouldn't have made it to the hospital. We didn't know what we were doing, but in the end, it was good that we didn't, because we probably wouldn't have had the guts to do it. We gave him a swift and pain-less end. It was merciful, what we did."

"I would hardly call that merciful," I said.

"He was unconscious," Margot said. "He didn't feel anything."

"You can't know that for sure," I said.

"I do," Margot said. "I stood at the Ledge and I held him. His body was so still and cold and lifeless that we thought he was dead. And when he went into the water, he just—sank. He was there one moment, and gone the next."

"So you admit that you were the one to throw him in?" I asked.

"Your father was supposed to be the one to do it," Margot said. "But he was too weak to stomach it."

"So first there was Jake," I said. "And then my mother found out the truth. And you couldn't have that."

"I told her what happened that night, because she wanted to know," Margot said. "And that was supposed to be the end of it. But then she hired an investigator. He showed up one day asking questions."

Margot shook her head at the memory, as if it still grated on her nerves.

"Where is she?" I asked. "Where did you put her?"

Margot looked at me and gave me a sad little smile. "I want to be very clear, Charlie, so that you understand me," she said. "I've worked very hard to get to where I am. And I won't ever let anyone take that away from me. Not Jake. Not your mother. And not you.

"You're smart, Charlie, so really think this through," she said. She held up a finger.

"First, there's Jake," she said. "You can't make a case about Grace without talking about what happened to Jake. And there are wit-nesses for that night—people who will say it was your father who did it and who blackmailed us into staying quiet. I could never lift Jake by myself; I couldn't have acted alone. But your father could have, and we'll all say he did, because why should we all take the blame when it can so conveniently be shouldered by one?"

She held up another finger.

"And then there's Grace," she said. "I suppose you think you have evidence. But all you really have is a pair of suitcases that could have easily been planted in my basement by you or Alistair— both of whom have very conveniently been up to my house recently. If I'm not mistaken, you've touched those suitcases. Your DNA is probably all over that basement."

Margot clucked her tongue.

I couldn't believe the lies she was spinning, how easily she manipulated the facts until the story played in her favor. In the end, that's what it would all come down to: the best story. It didn't matter what the truth was; all that mattered was what people would believe. And what if they believed her?

"It's amazing to me how much credit men always get," Margot said. "Even for things they have no part in. I never lifted a finger to point people in Alistair's direction, and yet look how viciously they went after him. You wouldn't want to see the damage I could do to your father if I actually tried."

"One day," I said, "all of your lies are going to catch up to you."

Margot shook her head. "That's what you still don't understand, Charlie. That's the thing about the truth: nobody wants to tell it. Not even you. Nobody tells the whole truth and comes away unscathed."

I opened my mouth to say something, to level at her some threat, but nothing came out. Because as much as I didn't want to believe what she was saying, I knew that she was right.

It was just like what Ren had told me that night that I became an initiate of the A's: secrets bound us to one another. It was a bond that could make us, just as surely as it was a bond that could destroy us all.

forty
GRACE CALLOWAY

AUGUST 4, 2007
9:25 P.M.

I finished my sprint across the lake, my breaths racking my body, my heart exploding in my chest. I turned over onto my back in the water, taking a deep breath through my nose and exhaling slowly, puffing out my cheeks, to steady my breathing. That sweet sense of exhaustion settled over me, my muscles tingly and weak—so weak I could barely hold myself up. I let the water buoy me, my ears slipping below the waterline so I could hear the hum and echo of the lake.

My mind drifted, as languid now as the muscles I had worked past their breaking point. I thought about the photographs of me and Peter and the girls that I'd hidden underneath the floorboards of my bedroom, and the five hundred thousand dollars in cash I'd packed in my suitcase, along with the forged passports that Peter had secured for me and the girls.

Tonight, I'd take the girls and we'd drive down to Teterboro, where I'd arranged to charter a private jet to Mexico City. I had used my new identity when making the arrangements and had paid extra for a pilot who would be discreet. From there, the girls and I would fly on to Léon, where we'd board a bus to take us the remaining hour and a half southeast to San Miguel de Allende, a Spanish colonial town in central Mexico nestled in the Bajío mountains—the last place anyone would think to look for us. We'd stay in a hotel until I could find a small house on the outskirts of the city to rent.

I hadn't told anyone where we were going or what I knew about Jake's death—not Hank or my mother or Claire. I didn't want to put them in the same sort of danger I'd landed myself and the girls in. Once we made it to San Miguel, I would find a way to send them word that we were safe.

I'd already packed my suitcases and loaded them into my SUV. In half an hour, I would wake the girls and pack their things. We'd touch down in Mexico before Alistair woke up tomorrow, before anyone would notice that we were gone or think to look for us.

I was still trying to figure out the best way to handle Charlotte. Seraphina would go easily, too groggy with sleep to ask questions. She'd doze in her car seat on the drive down, and I'd carry her from the car to the plane, her warm body clinging to mine. But Charlotte would be alert and inquisitive as soon as I woke her, and I knew she wouldn't go anywhere without Alistair. I knew how stubbornly she loved her father, how blindly, how resolutely.

Every Friday evening, she'd insist on staying up late to wait for Alistair to drive in from the city. We'd sit on the couch in the front living room watching Nick at Nite, the girls growing bleary eyed and yawning. But as soon as Alistair's headlights turned down the drive and reflected off the television screen, Charlotte would snap awake and shake her sister, and they'd race out onto the front step in their nightgowns and bare feet to greet him.

But last night, much to their disappointment, I'd sent the girls to bed at their normal bedtime. Seraphina sulked but Charlotte raged.

"You can't tell somebody when to go to sleep," Charlotte said. "That's like telling someone when to breathe. You can't actually make me."

It was such an articulate argument for a seven-year-old. How had enforcing bedtime become a larger discussion on Charlotte's autonomy over her own body? She was surely Alistair's child, through and through.

"Bed," I said, too exhausted to get into it. "Now."

"I'll go to my room but I won't go to sleep," Charlotte said as she marched off upstairs.

"Brush your teeth first," I called after her.

She was determined to keep herself awake until Alistair came home. When I went up to check on her an hour later, I found the stubborn girl had fallen asleep propped up against her pillows, sitting upright in her bed.

When Alistair had arrived, he'd woken the girls anyway, against my protests. The three of them rushed outside to catch fireflies, Alistair calling over his shoulder for me to bring mason jars from the pantry. When I came out, I saw them, barefoot in the front yard, hands outstretched toward the sky.

How could I reconcile that Alistair—the one who wandered around barefoot in the yard with our daughters catching fireflies, with the man who had done those terrible things to me this evening? I could still feel his hands on me as he pressed me up against the shower wall, one hand on my neck as he thrust his body against mine, the water in my mouth, so I could barely breathe.

I gagged and choked.

It took me a moment to realize what was happening, that there was actually something, someone, holding me down, their hands on my shoulders, twisting around my neck, pushing me below the water. I coughed, trying to get my bearings, my heart hammering in my chest. I felt a hot wave of adrenaline course through me as I clawed at their fingers, trying to loosen their grip, but they only applied more pressure, pushing me farther down.

It was shallow enough that I could stand. My toe stubbed the rocky bottom of the lake and I stood, pressing myself upward, out of the water. The top of my head met the underside of their jaw, and I heard the hard clacking of teeth. Their grasp on me slipped slightly, and I thrust out and hit at them blindly, as I gulped in air and tried to blink the water out of my eyes. I felt my fist knock into flesh, breaking their grip on me. They groaned.

My eyes cleared then and in the dim moonlight I saw the familiar curves of her face, the blond tint of her hair. Margot.

She lurched toward me, grabbing on to my shoulders, trying to force me back beneath the water, and I grabbed on to her, one hand clawing at her shoulder, the other pulling at her hair. I brought my knee up, hard, into her stomach, and I heard the breath go out of her as she released me. I turned and ran toward the shore, back toward the house, but the water muted my strides, pulling at me, slowing me down.

My chest was heaving and my legs shook as I ran, all my energy sapped from my sprints and that initial surge of adrenaline. I could hear her close behind me in the water, closing the gap between us. I wasn't fast enough. She thrust herself forward, onto my back, and I screamed—a shrill, bloodcurdling call into the night.

Margot grabbed and tore at me, one hand in my face. I bit down on her fingers, drawing blood, and she slipped off of me. I swung around to face her, and our arms locked around each other. We grappled with one another, each trying to push the other down.

I gasped for breath. My legs felt leaden. Margot grunted and shoved me backward and I fell. I felt the weight of her body slam on top of me and I took an involuntary breath, lake water flooding into my mouth. Margot's hands encircled my neck and she squeezed, tighter and tighter, her thumbs cutting off my trachea. My jugulars beat against her palms like rabid drums. She pushed my face underneath the water and it was in my eyes, my mouth. I struggled against her with all that was in me, with my shaking, weakened arms, but I couldn't get up.

I thought about my girls, all alone in the house, asleep upstairs.

What would happen to them? I tried to think of some way to protect them, the way my whole life I had tried to protect them, to shelter them from the sadness and the evil in the world, from all the injustice and the cruelty. Now I saw how futile that was, how misguided. I shouldn't have kept the darkness from them; I should have taught them how to survive it, how to shine through it. I should have taken them outside on a moonless night and pointed up at the stars, at those pocks of light in the darkness, how they lit up even then.

I took another involuntary breath and felt the water claw its way down my throat, into my lungs. She held me there, until my body went still and limp, the beat of my pulse flickering out.

forty-one
CHARLIE CALLOWAY

2017

It was the busiest I'd seen the dining hall on a Sunday morning all semester. Most of the alumni whose children attended Knollwood were crowding the pancake bar or sitting along the long oak tables with their kids, eating breakfast. I grabbed a bowl of cereal and a glass of orange juice and sat down at an empty table. I checked my watch. My father had said he'd meet me for breakfast at eight thirty this morning before heading back to the city. It was nearing eight forty-five.

"Are you feeling better?"

I looked up to see my father standing there, two mugs of coffee in hand.

I'd left the gala early, telling only my father that I was leaving, and I'd made an excuse about a disabling migraine.

"I came by to check on you afterward," he said as he sat down across from me. He slid one of the coffee mugs across the table toward me. "I knocked on your door but you didn't answer. Your light was off."

"Sorry, I was out cold," I lied.

In truth, I didn't answer because I hadn't been there. I'd gone back to my room only briefly to change, make some last-minute alterations to my article for the *Knollwood Chronicle,* and load that and my pictures onto the flash drive I'd purchased the other day at the school gift shop. Then I'd snuck across campus to intercept Finn and switch out his flash drive with mine. I didn't get back to my dorm room until nearly one in the morning.

Afterward, I hadn't been able to sleep. It kept running through my mind, the magnitude of what I'd done. I couldn't take back what I'd written or those pictures. They would be out there in print, for the whole school—the whole world—to see. Forever. I'd tossed and turned and only just drifted off to sleep when my alarm went off, and then I'd had to drag myself out of bed to go meet my father for breakfast before he headed back to the city.

"How long has this been going on?" my father asked, forcing me out of my reverie.

"What?"

"Your migraines," he said. He had that worried crease between his brows.

"Oh," I said. "Not long. It's nothing, really."

"You don't look well," he said. "Maybe you should come back with me to the city. I can get you in to see Dr. Carmichael first thing tomorrow morning."

"I have finals next week," I said. "I can't miss them."

"Your health is more important," my father said. "I'll have Dr. Carmichael write you a note. You can take your finals when you're feeling better."

I forced my eyes up from my cereal bowl to my father's face. He looked so concerned, so protective, so *fatherly*. It pained me to look him in the eyes after what I'd done, how I'd betrayed him. And for him to act so kindly toward me, precisely because he didn't know yet. But he would understand, wouldn't he? In the end, he'd forgive me. Right?

I should tell him the truth, I thought. I knew that I should tell him, because he would find out soon enough. I opened my mouth, but before I could say anything, Dalton materialized behind him, breakfast tray in hand.

"Where'd you disappear to last night?" Dalton asked.

He rounded the table and sat down next to me. To my discomfort, I saw Margot was right behind him. She sat down across the table from me, next to my father.

"Alistair," she greeted my father with a smile, and he acknowledged her with a curt nod.

"Migraine," I said.

Dalton rubbed my back. "You doing okay now?" he asked.

"I'm fine, thanks," I said.

"Maybe Mom could take a look at you and prescribe something?" Dalton asked, looking at Margot.

"That's very generous," my father said quickly. "But I'd prefer if Charlotte saw our family doctor."

"That's probably best," Margot said. "So, Alistair, how'd you fare at the auction?"

As their conversation turned from me to vacation home rentals, I noticed a sophomore girl at the next table over gawking at me. She looked away quickly when I met her eyes. And then I saw it—spread out on the table in front of her was that day's issue of the *Knollwood Chronicle*.

I glanced around the dining hall, and I saw it wasn't just her—most people were starting to stare. I felt it gathering around us like a storm about to break. The collective gasps, the gawking silences. That old familiar weight of being held up for speculation. As I scanned the room, my eyes locked with Leo, who was standing in the entrance to the dining hall. His face was white as a sheet. My cool, confident cousin looked terrified.

Just then, I saw something out of the corner of my eye, and I turned just in time to see Ren Montgomery barreling toward me. She tackled me, pushing me off my chair and onto the table. My glass of orange juice went flying, its pulpy contents landing in Margot's lap; my elbow landed hard in my bowl of cereal; my tailbone sang with pain as it met the hard wood of the table behind me.

"What the hell, Ren?" Dalton said, yanking her off of me and then putting himself between us. "What's your problem?"

"What's my problem?" Ren spat. "Why don't you ask your backstabbing bitch of a girlfriend who just fucking outed us to the entire fucking world."

"What are you talking about?" Dalton asked, looking from me, still splayed out on my back on the table, to Ren, and then back at me.

"I'm talking about all of our dirty little secrets that Charlie just made front-page news," Ren said. She was hysterical. She turned around and plucked the issue of the *Knollwood Chronicle* from the sophomore sitting at the table next to us and shoved the paper into Dalton's chest. "Extra, extra. Read all about it!"

I sat up and pulled my elbow out of my cereal bowl. The sleeve of my sweater was drenched.

"You're done," Ren said, pointing her finger at me. "You're over."

As I sat there, holding my throbbing, milk-soaked elbow—a disheveled mess on display for the whole school to see—I knew that she was right. Because the gun I'd loaded for the A's at the beginning of the year, I'd just pulled the trigger.

"What's this?" my father asked, taking the paper from Dalton.

"The truth," I said. I looked at Margot, her stare hardening as her suspicion of what I'd done crystallized on her face. "All of it."

My father looked down at the paper in his hands, and he started to read.

It was the story I'd written, and the photographs. I'd published them after all. Not the ones of Mr. Andrews, as I'd originally planned, but the ones of the A's at the Ledge the night that Jake died.

I'd decided, finally, what type of person I wanted to be.

HAUNTING TRUTHS
By Charlie Calloway

Since I started at Knollwood Augustus Prep, I knew that the
school was haunted. There were whisperings of a ghost, a
boy who had died years ago, so long ago that his name and
the circumstances of his death had long been forgotten. Still,
the story of the ghost was as much a part of the school as the
old library, or Headmaster Collins, or Knollwood's tradition
of graduating some of the best and brightest students in the
country. Everyone knows that a sighting of the ghost is a
harbinger of bad luck, and everyone or their friend has a story
of seeing the ghost before being on the receiving end of a bad
breakup, or a failing exam grade, or a rejection letter from a
dream school.

Lately, I've been doing a lot of thinking about ghosts—about
the things that haunt us, and the stories we tell—because
surely, these say something important about us. What are the
things that won't let go of us, or that we won't let go of? And
why tell these stories, over and over and over again? It seems
like there's something beyond the story itself we're trying to
communicate, something just beneath the surface, something
important that must be understood.

It turns out there really was a boy who died at Knollwood.
His name was Jake Griffin and he drowned in Spalding River
on December 21, 1990. Jake Griffin was a scholarship student,
an outsider, and the story goes that he cheated on an exam and,
fearing expulsion, went up to the Ledge and jumped.

I understand why this story was told and why it was so easy
to believe and why it is told still. Jake Griffin was a boy from
a working-class family who had infiltrated the hallowed halls

of Knollwood Augustus Prep, and he couldn't hack it. Through
his suicide, everyone was absolved of his failure and his death.
There's something in the retelling of this story, even when it is
stripped to its barest details—a dead boy, a ghost, a haunting,
a harbinger of bad luck—that we're drawn to, that we can't let
go of. The specter of failure haunts all of us. It is terrifying that
maybe we're not good enough after all, maybe we never will be,
maybe people see right through us. What's more horrifying than
that we ourselves are ghosts, a mere shadow of what we pretend
or want to be?

There's more to Jake's story than what we're told. In fact,
Jake didn't get caught cheating on an exam. He wasn't driven to
the Ledge that night by the depths of despair. He didn't jump.
Ironically, what brought Jake to the Ledge that night was victory,
not defeat. After several months of completing numerous
trials, Jake had finally won his way into the most elite group on
campus—the A's. And it was in the throes of this celebration
that Jake overdosed on Percocet, stopped breathing, and died.
Or, at least, his friends who were with him that night thought
Jake had died. They didn't call for help or medical assistance. In
their haste to protect their own reputations and futures, they
tossed Jake's body over the Ledge. It was only later, when the
autopsy report was released, that they learned that Jake had
been unconscious at the time, and they had left him to drown in
the cold river below. In the wake of this discovery, no one came
forward. Instead, they told lies that came to be taken as truths,
to protect themselves.

I understand why we don't tell this story. It is an ugly story,
and it is difficult to look at head-on. We immediately want to
look away, close up our ears. That some of Knollwood Augustus
Prep's most distinguished students—now our golden alumni—
cruelly left a young man to die is not a story we like to tell

or hear. It doesn't reflect well on us, may even lead us to ask ourselves uncomfortable questions about who we are and what we're doing here, the values we're really perpetuating.

I've been asking myself that question a lot this past year— who am I? And who do I want to be? And I've come to realize that I can't really answer that question unless I'm willing to be honest about a lot of things. So, here goes. The truth. The whole truth and nothing but the truth, with its many ugly faces.

I'm an A. Or, at least, I'm an initiate of the A's. My last "trial" to get into the A's was supposed to be publishing pictures in this issue of the *Knollwood Chronicle* that made it look like a faculty member was hooking up with a student. The pictures were a lie meant to punish and humiliate a teacher for turning down the advances of another A, as twisted as that sounds. And since I'm not going to publish them, I suppose I'm not an A anymore. And I'm okay with that, even though for the majority of this year I thought all I really wanted was to be in that illicit group. I, like most of you at this school, have often looked at the A's as if they were gods. It's only recently that I've come to realize that what I mistook for courage was really gross ego, and what I mistook for power was really coercion and the worst kind of bullying.

I've done a lot of things this past year that I'm not proud of, and many of those things were done in pursuit of becoming an A. I made out with my cousin in the back of Ren Montgomery's Audi and let her take photographs of us to use as blackmail in the event that I slipped up; I stole the diamond collar from Headmaster Collins's pit bull (and I have the scar to prove it); I sat silently by as Auden Stein got suspended for something he didn't do, even though I might have saved him if I'd only spoken up with the truth.

But I'm tired of the silence. I'm tired of hiding the parts of myself that I don't want other people to see. I'm tired of the lies and the half-truths and the destruction that they wreak. I know in telling these things I will hurt people—including those who deserve it and those who don't, people I love and people I hate. I myself won't come out of this unharmed. Someone once told me that no one tells the truth and walks away unscathed, and it turns out, they were right.

My father, Alistair Calloway, was at the Ledge the night that Jake died. He couldn't bring himself to dispose of Jake's body, so Margot Dalton (then Whittaker) and Matthew York did. They all kept quiet when they discovered the hand they'd had in Jake's death. Ten years ago, my mother found out the truth about what happened to Jake, who had been her high school sweetheart. And when she tried to come forward with that truth, Margot silenced her. I saw Margot with my mother down by the lake the night she disappeared. Last week, I discovered my mother's suitcases in the basement of Margot's Southampton house and today I realized my mother's canary diamond from her engagement ring might be the very same yellow diamonds surrounding the bezel of Margot's watch.

There's the whole ugly, haunting truth. Today, we all must finally step out of the shadows and let the light illuminate our hard edges and the sins we've committed in the dark.

Below the article, I'd put the photographs of Jake Griffin and the A's, and I'd listed the name of every A I knew.

When my father finished reading, he looked up. For one long, silent moment, he looked at me and I tried to read even a trace of emotion on his face, but there was none. Then, he looked at Margot.

Dalton was looking at Margot, too. He opened his mouth to say something, then closed it again. I looked around and realized that at some point, a mass of people had congregated in the din-

ing hall. There was my photography teacher, Mr. Andrews, by the
coffee cart. My uncle Teddy and aunt Grier were three tables over.
I noticed Stevie and Yael near the entrance, gaping. It seemed like
everyone in the dining hall was staring at Margot.

Margot pushed back her chair and stood.

"I don't know what scene you and your daughter are trying to
orchestrate here, Alistair," she said. Her voice shook and betrayed
her. "But I don't want any part of it."

My father reached out and grabbed Margot's wrist. She flinched.
His eyes caught on the yellow diamond bezel of her watch.

"Charlie," my father said, his voice quiet, but calm and steady,
"call the police."

Margot tore her hand out of my father's grasp. "Let go of me."

She clasped her freed wrist in her other hand like she was injured. She looked at Dalton, and then at me, and then her gaze
flitted to the audience that had amassed around us. There were a
hundred silent witnesses as Margot fled, powerless and cowering,
toward the door.

Half an hour later, I found myself alone in the headmaster's office,
waiting for Headmaster Collins to arrive. My father was in the
hallway, speaking with the police and a very agitated Old Man
Riley.

My phone buzzed in my pocket. It had been going off for the
past half hour, since the drama in the dining hall had exploded,
but with everything going on, I hadn't had a moment to look at it.
I pulled it out now and unlocked the screen.

Word about my article had traveled fast. I had a dozen missed
calls. Three from my sister in Reading. One from Greyson. Six from
Drew. I guess her parents must have let up on some of their phone
restrictions.

I opened my messages and saw several texts from a group chat.

DREW: So I leave and I miss all the fun apparently?

YAEL: Your girl Charlie just dropped a bomb on those A-holes

STEVIE: Charlie where r u? R u ok? I can't believe that about your mom!

DREW: Yeah, like what the fuck is going on?!

YAEL: R they going to arrest that psycho bitch?

STEVIE: C, answer your phone plz

DREW: Call me later you guys! I need deets. The parental unit finally gave me back my phone.

YAEL: C, u did good, girl. We're here if you need us.

Well, at least some people didn't hate me.

The door opened and Headmaster Collins came in looking all stern and serious.

"It's a circus out there," he said, closing the door behind him.

I put my phone back in my pocket and sat up straight. Headmaster Collins took a seat behind his big oak desk. I could tell he hadn't been prepared to be called in this early on his day off, because he was unshaven and his hair was only half combed. The top button in his collared shirt had been buttoned in the wrong hole, but I didn't have the heart to tell him.

"I won't pretend it wasn't brave, what you did," Headmaster Collins said. "You acted with valor and integrity. It's heartening to see that at least some of the values we've tried to instill in you in this institution have taken root."

Headmaster Collins folded his hands on his desk and looked at me solemnly, and I knew I wasn't going to get off that easily, with just a pat on the back and a "job well done."

"That being said, doing the right thing doesn't exonerate all of the wrongs that were committed," he said. "Theft. Vandalism. Cheating. Lying. I can't turn a blind eye to the serious misconduct that went on."

"Am I expelled?" I asked.

Headmaster Collins sighed. "Every member of the A's is going to face expulsion," he said. "However, in light of your coming forward, I'm willing to make an exception in your case. There's only one week left in the semester. I'll let you sit for your exams and finish out this semester. If you withdraw enrollment for the spring, I won't put an expulsion on your academic record. You can start again somewhere new. I'm sure, with a sizable donation, another institution can be persuaded to take you on midyear."

I'd known expulsion was a possibility when I'd written the article. But still, the reality of it hit me hard. No more Knollwood. This place had been my home for the last two and a half years and now, it was being taken from me. Still, I knew things could be worse.

"Thank you," I said.

There was a knock at the door.

"That would be your father," Headmaster Collins said. "I know he would like to have a word with you before you give a statement to the police. So, I'll give you two a moment."

When he left, my father came in and sat in the seat next to me.

We were both silent. My feelings toward my father were complicated. Part of me felt guilty for outing his secrets so publicly in the Knollwood Chronicle. Especially since I knew now that he hadn't actively participated in my mother's murder. The things he'd told me were mostly true. But still, my father wasn't blameless. He had treated Jake cruelly, and I couldn't help but wonder if the things Claire claimed about my father were true—that he had been cold toward my mother, that he had physically hurt her. Those last words I'd heard my mother utter to my father still haunted me: Get your hands off me.

"Do you think they'll have enough to pursue a case against Margot?" I asked after a while.

"Well, they'll have your eyewitness report of what you saw that night by the lake," my father said. "And some circumstantial physical evidence with the watch and the suitcases. That's something. The bad news is, by the time they get a search warrant and go to the Southampton house, Margot will have had the opportunity to destroy that evidence."

"She can't," I said, "because she doesn't have it anymore. Well, at least, she doesn't have all of it."

"What?" my father asked.

"I called Greyson yesterday," I explained. "He drove up yesterday afternoon and got the suitcases. He's gotten very good at breaking and entering."

Shock registered on my father's face. Then, he laughed. It caught me off guard and I chanced a look at him. He rubbed his chin and was serious again.

"I wish that you'd confided in me," he said. "I wish you'd come to me about all this. And when I think why you didn't," he said, "it occurs to me that the reason you didn't was because you didn't trust me."

I stared down at my hands. I couldn't bring myself to look at him. Because he was right. I had doubted him. I had chosen not to trust him. In my darkest moments, I had thought he might be exactly the person that the tabloids made him out to be.

"But the truth is—I deserve that," my father said. "For years, I held myself blameless. I told myself Grace had chosen to leave, and I was angry with her—so angry with her. But now I see I was partly responsible. It was my actions as a selfish, spineless teenage boy that killed Jake; my inability years later to be truthful with your mother when she asked me about Jake's death; and my crass assumptions and callousness toward her that last summer that led her not to confide in me. Without those things, Grace would still be here. I don't know if I can ever really forgive myself for that, so I don't know how I can ask you to."

I looked up at him. I didn't know what to say.

"My whole life, I've tried to protect you," he went on. "Maybe that's difficult for you to see. I know I didn't handle everything in the right way. When your mother . . . disappeared, I was broken. Utterly broken and angry. I felt like this raw shell of who I used to be. There was a time when I didn't feel capable, or worthy, of being your father. And that was why I sent you and your sister away to stay with your uncle. I tried to stay away from you. I thought you were better off without me."

"I thought it was because you were angry with me," I said. "Over what I'd said to Uncle Hank. And that story that came out afterward."

My father shook his head. "I wasn't angry with you, Charlotte," he said. "I was angry with myself.

"When I think about the way I behaved that last summer with your mother," my father said, his voice breaking slightly. "The things I did, the things I said to her, which turned out to be the last words I'd ever speak to her . . ."

I felt something warm slide down my cheek, and I realized I was crying.

"And then when everything came out today," he said. "What you wrote about Margot, about Jake and the part I played that night . . ."

He trailed off and was silent. He just looked at me, his face, for a moment, unreadable. I noticed the crow's-feet that peeked out at the edges of his eyes, deeper than I remembered them. The roots of his hair near his temples were tinted gray. For the first time in my life, I realized my father looked old. Tired.

"There isn't a day that goes by that I don't think about that day and wish that I had done things differently," he said. "I've wished for a long time that I could be a different type of person, but time and again, I've fallen short, lost my way. Today, thanks to you, I finally got to prove to myself that I can be different.

"I gave the officers out there a statement about what happened that night, with Jake," he said. "I took the responsibility I should have taken a long time ago."

"What does that mean?" I asked. Would my father be prosecuted? Would he go to jail? "What will happen now?"

"I don't know," my father said.

I wanted to forgive my father, I did. I just wasn't completely ready to. But I knew that one day, I might be. So, I reached out and held my father's hand.

It took them a few days of digging up the yard at the Daltons' Southampton house before they found what remained of my mother in Margot's kitchen garden. In the end, they found only bits of her, pieces of bone. I don't know what exactly I expected them to find of her after all this time—something discernibly her, something to hold on to, something I recognized? When they showed me the bone fragments, worn smooth and pale white by the ravages of time, I held them in the soft palm of my hand, and I felt nothing but their coldness. Here she was—I held her in my hand, all of the parts of her that remained, and I didn't recognize her at all.

I suppose, in some ways, that was only fitting. My mother had loomed large in my life. She was such an inextricable part of who I was, of who I would become. And yet, I had played only a small part in hers. Before I even existed, she had been many different things to many different people. If my investigation into my mother's past had taught me anything, it was that no one can really understand the whole of a person. In many ways, my mother, my father—the people I was closest to, the people who meant the most to me—were strangers. Beautiful strangers.

We laid my mother to rest in the spring in the Calloway family plot in Greenwich. My father bought her a rose-colored tombstone on which they had engraved:

GRACE ELIZABETH CALLOWAY

1974–2007

Beloved Wife and Mother

What lies behind us and what lies
before us are tiny matters
compared with what lies within us.

epilogue
CHARLIE CALLOWAY

SEPTEMBER 2020

"There's a spot," I say, pointing to a section of empty curb three houses down from my grandparents' house. Their driveway is already full—I see my uncle Lonnie and aunt Caroline's minivan and my uncle Hank's rusted truck. We're the last ones here because we stopped at the train station to pick up Seraphina after driving up from the city. She's in her final year at Reynolds.

"Got it," Greyson says as he pulls into it and puts the car in park.

We unload our trays of food—I picked up a tray of cookies at the store, Greyson made his famous pulled pork, and Seraphina brought a box of cupcakes with her from Reading.

We don't knock; we just go straight in. As usual, my grandparents' house is full of people and noise. We call out a communal hello as we come through the door. I spot my grandma and give her a hug.

"I brought Grandpa's favorite cookies," I say, handing her the plastic tray.

"You spoil him," Grandma says, taking the cookies and retreating to the kitchen.

"There you guys are," Claire calls out as she enters the living room, beer in hand.

Greyson leans down to give her a kiss on the cheek. "Hey, Mom," he says.

"How's NYU?" Claire asks me.

"It's great," I say.

"Meet any cute boys?" Claire teases.

Greyson puts his arm around me and pulls me close as I laugh. "Hey now, none of that," he says, planting a kiss in my hair.

After my article about the A's came out at Knollwood, I spent the remainder of my junior year at Reynolds with my sister, and when I graduated the following year, I decided to take some time off to do Outward Bound. While my friends were starting college (Drew at Wellesley, Stevie at Berkeley, and Yael at Columbia), I was backpacking across the border lakes region of Minnesota and Canada and kayaking Lake Superior. It wasn't something I had ever imagined myself doing, but it taught me to harness a strength I had only just begun to realize I had. When I came back, I turned down the Wharton School at UPenn and enrolled in the documentary film program at NYU. Again, not a path I could have imagined for myself only a year before, but the right one. With everything that had happened with my mother, I realized how important the stories that we tell about one another are. The stories we tell can change the way we see one another, can even change the way we see the world. I wanted to tell those stories; I needed to tell them.

I started classes a few weeks ago. I'm renting an apartment in Greenwich Village with Greyson.

After my father's testimony regarding Jake's death, he and the other A's who had been there that night were convicted of negligent homicide in a suit brought against them by the state. Afterward, Jake's family brought a civil case against them, which was settled out of court for an undisclosed amount. My father served one year at the state penitentiary and is currently serving his probation. He was forced to step down as president of the Calloway Group, but I know he's been in negotiations with Uncle Teddy and my grandfather about coming back in some way, serving as a consultant, perhaps, though I doubt they'll let him have a seat on the board. Seraphina and I made a few trips up to the state penitentiary to see him while he was there. We talk occasionally, but building a new relationship with my father on the foundation of all that has happened in the last two years, all that I now know, is going to be a long and slow process. I'm still not sure what it will look like in the end.

Margot's case regarding my mother's murder garnered a lot of media attention. Seraphina and I both had to endure the reporters and the tabloids on campus until the verdict came out. In the end, Margot was convicted of first-degree murder and was sentenced to life in prison without the possibility of parole.

I grab a plate of food from the kitchen and make my way into the den to watch the game. I spot Uncle Hank on the couch, sitting next to my cousin Patrick, and I give him a little wave. Uncle Hank nods back at me.

As dusk falls, my grandma brings out the frosted cake for my mother. She would be turning forty-six this year. We all gather around the table in the kitchen and sing. Then I lean forward and blow out the candles.

Later, as Greyson and I head back toward the city after dropping my sister off at the train station, we take the long way out of town, out toward Langely Lake. From the road, I look out at the house my father built for my mother, all those years ago. It sits empty, its doors locked, the windows boarded, looking blindly and forlornly out at the water. My father put it on the market over a year ago, but so far, there haven't been any buyers. He's stopped paying to keep up the grounds. Creeping Jenny fills the yard, wool grass grows knee-high, even a handful of dogwood saplings appear here and there. The stone on the house has started to weather, and I can imagine it one day, many years from now, swallowed up by vines and weeds, reclaimed by the woods.

acknowledgments

First, thank you, reader, for giving your time to All These Beautiful Strangers. That is an invaluable gift, and I am full of gratitude.

Thank you to my wonderful editor, Carrie Feron, who shepherded this book to completion. Thank you for your patience, your guidance, and for always seeming to know exactly what the book needed. I am indebted to you and my whole team at William Morrow/HarperCollins, who showed the book such care, especially Danielle Bartlett, Katherine Turro, Jennifer Hart, Kelly Rudolph, and Julie Paulauski.

To my agent Suzanne Gluck and the whole WME family—especially Laura Bonner, Matilda Forbes Watson, and Sylvie Rabineau—thank you. You are all rock stars.

To Anthea Townsend, Naomi Colthurst, Sophia Smith, and the team at Penguin Random House Children's UK—working with you has been a dream.

Thank you Brendan Kenney, Bruna Papandrea, Steve Hutensky, and everyone at Made Up Stories for your early enthusiasm and support for the book and for helping it to find its place in the world. Many thanks to Aja Pollock for your fine eye for detail and stellar copyediting and to D.P. Lyle for your medical expertise.

To Tiff, Katy, Lauren, Devonie, Meggie, and Amy—thank you for your friendships, for your excitement through all the highs and for your encouragement through the occasional lows; you've made this whole journey so much more fun.

Thank you, Trevor, for so many things—for your insightful notes and your ingenious plot solutions when I was in a rut, for putting together my author website and for freely lending me your time and talents for my author photos. So much of you is in this. Thank you. Living each day alongside you is a gift.

Mark, thank you for your provocative and outlandish story ideas, none of which made it into this book, but, maybe the next one. To Mom and Dad, who never, not once, voiced any doubts about me becoming a writer, even when I had doubts myself. Thank you for your unwavering love and support and for being the best parents a person could ask for.

And last, but certainly not least—Annie, thank you for continually asking, "What happens next?" and for your very vocal impatience for receiving the next chapter (and the next, and the next). You were the first reader of All These Beautiful Strangers— and for a long time, the only reader—and you believed in it from the beginning. Thank you. Without you, this book would not exist.